HARRY OF MONMOUTH

HARRY OF

MONMOUTH

A. M. MAUGHAN

WILLIAM SLOANE ASSOCIATES

NEW YORK

1956

TO

MY MOTHER

*"My true intent was all for
your delight."*

CONTENTS

THE BOY

"God save the King. Will no man say 'Amen'?"

The honor of Monmouth had many years lain in the hands of Lancaster. The castle was fair and sternly built, set above the Monnow, its first stones raised there by the Normans, and sacked by Simon de Montfort ninety years ago. Now did John of Gaunt hold it; the June day and the fourteenth century creeping toward twilight.

He walked in the stone solar room of the keep, above the guardhouse: that proud man, whom men spoke of as John of Gaunt but who bore many mightier titles—Duke of Lancaster; Earl of Derby, Lincoln and Leicester; Lord of Beaufort, Nogent, Bergerac and Roche-sur-Yon; Seneschal of England and Constable of Chester. With him were his son, Henry of Derby, and his daughter-in-law, Mary de Bohun. The royal blood flowed here, for Gaunt was uncle to the King, and Derby, his son, the King's full cousin.

When it was near dusk, the nurse brought Gaunt's eldest grandson to bid him good night. The boy was only six, of thick dark hair and hazel eyes. Gaunt looked upon him, marking him keenly, for, by God's grace and in the fullness of time, he would one day bear the weight of those same titles that burdened his grandfather's shoulders.

The boy came first to him and bowed. "Good night, my lord grandfather."

Gaunt answered him, "Good night, Henry."

To Derby the boy said, "Good night, my lord father."

"Good night, Harry."

"Good night, my lady mother."

"Good night, my Hal."

As she answered him, Mary put her arm about his waist and

drew him to her. When they were thus together, there was no mis-
taking their kinship of mother and son. Gaunt saw his daughter-
in-law, beautiful beyond any of the fairest of the realm, dark
eyed as were all the de Bohuns, and with her dark hair bound up
beneath her jeweled chaplet. He looked upon her with a grim
tenderness.

The boy's father, Lord Henry of Derby, swung his son joyously
off his feet. He was twenty-seven, not tall but fine built, his hair
the red-gold of the Plantagenets, though his moustache was darker.
He tossed his son from arm to arm with a fair ease.

"What now, my crusader?" he said. "How goes the battle? How
many Saracen knights slain?"

The boy answered eagerly, "Fifteen. They were all about the
bailey garden. They had turbans with spikes in them."

"And crescents on their banners," Derby said. "And curved
swords for Christian necks. There goes one now behind the tapet.
Get you to cover."

They rolled under the oaken table together with much noise
and laughter. Mary gave her father-in-law a quiet smile. She rose,
not easily, for she was seven months pregnant, and went on her
knees by the table. "For shame," she said. "All this excitement before bedtime."

"In sooth, Henry," Gaunt said to Derby, "that boy comes to ruin.
You ought well to beat him more often."

"It is because we lost our first-born, my lord," Mary said. "Lay it
all to that."

"Indeed, your lady has no cause to fret herself whatever," the
nurse said. She was named Joan Waring, a full-breasted young
Welshwoman, pleasant-faced. She much loved her charge, for he
had ailed in babyhood, the physicians despairing of him. "Four of
them you have now; and I do not doubt the Good Lord expressly
intended this one for Duke of Lancaster. The one you lost was a
fine little lad, look you; but I think you do not have a worse one
here."

Gaunt gave them no words. He knew well of the fight to raise sons for Lancaster. He himself had thrice gone to a marriage bed, yet Henry of Derby was his one son born out of bastardy. When Joan Waring and the boy had gone, Derby spoke of him.

"Sir," he said, "does the boy not please you?"

"He pleases me well," Gaunt said. "Yet he has too great an energy. You will have to bridle it."

"Bridle it?" Derby said. "In faith, sir, the kingdom languishes for a spark of Lancaster energy." He spoke now with a darkening face. "It stifles me," he said, "the whole perfumed breath of Richard's court. Oh, my toes are itching to be gadding again."

He had many times gone from them, to the courts of Europe, to Bohemia and to the Holy Land.

Gaunt said, "You ought well to stay awhile. Would you have your sons grow up not knowing you?"

"Yes, stay, my love," Mary said. She was still on her knees by the table, but Derby set his arms about her and raised her. "Stay with me this time, and I'll have another girl for you. Then will she look like you, as Blanche does, and not be a brown-haired de Bohun, as are the boys."

"Oh, my sweet," Derby said. "Lay it all at Cousin Richard's door. I would not have gone from you these months and years, spending my youth against the Turk, if England had offered me but one small way of spending it."

"Peace, Henry," Gaunt said sharply. "He is the King."

"Good my father," Derby said. "I know it."

When, after their meal, they sat together, messengers from London rode over the Monnow bridge and brought their flagging horses to the inner court. They brought sad news, for the Queen had died that day at Sheen. Derby, who first heard it, went back to his father and his wife, taking Mary's hand as he told them. They heard him, much shocked.

"Dead?" Gaunt said. "It is not possible. She was well—in health —when I left the city two days back."

"It was the plague, my father," Derby said. "She lived but three hours."

"I must go to him," Gaunt said. "He will be out of his wits."

"We shall both go to him, sir," Derby said. "They are saddling the horses now. We can ride by torchlight." He raised his wife's face and kissed her. "Guard yourself, sweet," he said. "You are well used to these partings, and this will be a short one."

"You will be back?" she said. "Before my lying-in?"

"Yes," he said. "I vow it."

When they had gone, Mary stood at the casement to watch them ride out. The night was still, and the flickering cressets struck jewellike against the trappings of the horses and the burnished spurs. She watched them from her sight; then went up the stone stairway to her sons' bedchamber.

She had wed Henry of Derby when he had been fourteen and she no more than ten. She had been a grave child, most fair, but a lover of books and music and the things of the spirit. Almost had she taken upon her the habit of a nun, for she had been schooled in the Convent of the Poor Clares. At ten she had seemed, in truth, to many to have drifted already from the world. Yet great Gaunt had much desired her for his son; not indeed because a grave, dark-eyed child had the power to stir him (though she had done so), but because she was the heiress of the de Bohuns.

He had brought her to Arundel Castle where, walking on a May morning, she had first glimpsed Henry of Derby's red-gold head. It was as if the sight of him won her back to the world. Their attendants marked that the two children looked upon each other with a boy's and girl's pleasure, as if they, by some magic, began to guess at love.

They had married in the Chapel of the Savoy with much pomp, since the boy bridegroom was cousin to the King. Richard was of an age with Henry of Derby. He himself had married later to a princess of Bohemia—Anne, his Queen, who this night lay cold under the stars at Sheen Palace. Men jested that whatever befell to the young lord of Derby befell likewise to his cousin the King. Both had married learned and fair wives, but whereas the Queen had ever been childless, Mary had borne a great family.

She was now twenty-three and the child she carried was her seventh. Her first-born had died, but after had come four other boys, Hal, Tom, John, and little Humphrey. Then had there been a girl, the baby Blanche, as flaxen-haired as the fair grandmother after whom she was named.

The boys slept all together in a wide stone chamber above the gatehouse. Their beds were set one against each wall, smaller than a grown man's bed, but carved in oak and with their great testers woven in blue and white, the livery of Lancaster. The nurses had set a rushlight burning on the mantelshelf, where its faint flame hung upon the colors of the tapestries. Mary saw all her sons' brown heads still upon their pillows: three-year-old Humphrey, asleep on his stomach; John, named after Gaunt, who was four; sturdy Tom, who was five; and six-year-old Harry. They were all unruly boys and much spirited. Mary saw them quiet now, when they seldom were.

All save Harry slept. When he sat up, Mary went to him. "I heard the horses," he said. "Was it Father who rode out?"

"He rode with your lord grandfather," she said. "They journey to the King. The Queen, our lady, has died this noon."

He said in a low voice, "I know not how he can bear it."

"He bears more than that," Mary said. "He is the King. . . ."

When he looked upon her doubtfully, she spoke again. "It is a harsh task," she said. "You'll understand better when you are grown."

"Who will be the King," he said, "when I am grown?"

"Richard is young," Mary said. "He may well marry again."

"My lord grandfather thinks he will never have a son."

"Well, then, it will doubtless be your cousin Edmund Mortimer for the bearing of the crown," Mary said. "God will send us a King. But whoever he be, will you not serve him faithfully, bearing him faith and truth?"

He greatly loved his mother. When she bent to kiss him he set his arms about her neck, saying, "I'm glad you never became a nun. I could have borne none else for a mother."

She laughed and put him from her. When she was about to go she spoke again. "Will you not pray that God will rest the Queen?" she said. "And pray that He may send the King ease."

II

Four weeks later Mary rested in the gardens of Leicester. With her was her mother, Joan de Bohun, the Countess of Hereford, a tall, handsome woman, determined of will and of a tongue so forthright that not Gaunt himself would willingly gainsay her. She and Mary sat in carved chairs which the servants had borne for them onto the terrace. Below them among the mulberry trees the three elder boys wrestled like spirited pups. Mary watched them with pleasure, but she was now great with the child. She felt herself wearied this time beyond anything she had known before.

The youngest of the boys, Humphrey, came behind them, seeking to climb down the first great step of the terrace. Mary lifted him and set him beside her. "There, Sir Chick," she said. "Do you want to join with your brothers?"

"Mother," Tom said. "Why can Hal bear our arms on his pony's trappings when he rides and I cannot? I ride as well as he does, and I'm of Lancaster."

"It is because Hal is the eldest," Mary said.

"He gets all things," Tom said. "He is only eleven months older than I am. I wish I were the eldest."

"Nay, now," she said. "You would not if you were."

"It is because he is to be Duke of Lancaster," he said. "I wish I were to be it. Why is it that he can be a Duke and I cannot only because he is older?"

"You would not like it, my Tom," Mary said. "You know how we use Hal because he is the eldest. Remember last time you were all at fault—you three we sent to your beds, but Hal we beat; though you were all equal in blame."

She sent them from her, bidding them go and play in the grass by the outer bailey. "See you do not go near the moat," she said. "Look to Humphrey, Hal."

"You've a noisy, unruly brood, Mary," Lady Hereford said. "Yet I do not think you could well find four bonnier boys. Why is it you are harsh with Hal?"

Mary sighed and said, "Tom gave you answer. He said it is because Hal will be Duke of Lancaster."

"Oh, fie," Lady Hereford said. "That is Gaunt's talk. There are prouder titles, though there be no prouder men."

"Yet it is a great trust," Mary said. "What name has borne more weight in the realm these twenty years?"

Derby came to them along the terrace and took his wife's hand. She looked at him smilingly. After a space, as they talked, she bowed her head suddenly and set her hands to her belly. Derby put an arm about her and spoke her name.

She lifted her head and tried to smile. "Oh, Henry," she said. "Another son, or a daughter, to Lancaster."

Derby raised her and carried her swiftly up the terrace. Young Harry, looking back, saw his mother borne in his father's arms, her pointed shoes slack beneath the hem of her gown and her great sleeves crimson like drops of blood against gray walls.

Later his nurse, Joan Waring, came to him when he was abed, weeping and scarce able to speak. There was another daughter to Lancaster. Yet that strange interlocking of destiny which had ever bound Henry of Derby's fortune with the King's was not to be gainsaid. Lady Derby had followed the Queen, and the weeping midwives and the careful physicians could do no more save stand and watch her go.

III

Up and down the narrow, tapestry-hung room went the boy—up and down, past the window, with its glimpse of the river and the trees, now a dusty shriveled green; past the rich-draped bed and the rosewood table with its sconces. It was to him as if these familiar things mocked him. Among them and in the circle of the Monmouth hills life had seemed to him once a secure and pleasant thing, a knight's tourney, not the battlefield it was in truth.

It had been four years ago that his mother had died. He missed her sorely, for he could remember her best, whereas to Blanche and little Philippa, even to Humphrey, she was now as a name. The King had married again. It was a strange and, many men thought, a godless match, for Richard was now thirty-two and his wife was a six-year-old princess of France. Henry of Derby had taken no second wife, seemingly feeling, as did his son, that there was none Mary de Bohun's like.

Yet now his father was no longer mere Henry of Derby but Duke of Hereford—men dubbing him Harry of Hereford, Lancaster and Derby; as he himself, his father's heir, was Harry of Monmouth. And, since the heir, he himself might even now be Duke of Hereford in succession to his father, for today Derby fought with Thomas Mowbray on Gosford Green. It might well be that this hour his father lay there, his mail pierced and Mowbray's lance in his heart.

The thought seemed to him horrible beyond all others. His father and Mowbray had long hated each other. They had met together nine months ago in fog on Brentford Bridge, each man sending his attendant squire and his page from him that they might be alone. None knew what had passed between them in the chill of the fog, but violence had sprung from it. Derby had ridden away, leaving his gage at Mowbray's feet. Mowbray had seized it up crying, "My body against yours."

Men thought that the King, of a surety, would turn them from their intent, since one was his cousin and the other his most secret confidant. Yet he had not done so. Even it seemed he was not ill pleased. This day on Gosford Green, outside Coventry, some twenty miles away (for his father and their household lodged here at Kenilworth), the lists were up and it was "confidently expected it would be a fight to the death." Many had flocked to Coventry throughout the week end, sleeping in the hedgerows and the ripening September wheat to see the two Dukes—Mowbray being Duke of Norfolk—meet body to body. All men knew that death, riding in the lists, rode in cruel splendor. The people gawking through the rails upon the square of fading green grass would see much to feast their eyes upon—Derby, riding in blue and green, with the antelopes of Lancaster embroidered in gold on his horse's trappings; Mowbray's horse barbed in crimson velvet inlaid with silver mulberry leaves; the golden-haired, golden-bearded young King. It seemed to the boy that he was one with those who watched and could likewise see the Earl Marshal with his trumpeters and heralds in their blue and crimson tabards; and that he could hear the trumpets summoning the Lord Appellant and the Lord Defendant to combat. So would they lower their lances and ride upon each other, that his father might kill Mowbray or Mowbray kill his father.

He set his mind against it. In the London taverns where they were setting their wagers coldly as on a Shrove Tuesday football match, his father was favored. Yet Mowbray was held to be a good jouster, scheming and keen-eyed. Likewise, since the Dukes stood accused by one another of treason, this was to them as trial by combat. His father might live, yet if he were unhorsed or fell behind Mowbray's tally of points, all guilt would be assigned his, and he might well go from the lists to the headsman's axe.

There was a sound of hoof beats in the courtyard below him, and his heart chilled. He went slowly to the open casement, scarce daring to look from it. Below a group of horsemen were dismounting—two of Derby's squires, his grandfather, a page, and his father himself, unhurt, his red-gold head bent above his horse's mane. Almost, in his joy, he called out to them; then it was borne upon him by the silence and Derby's bent head that there was nothing here to betoken victory.

After a space a servant came to the door, bidding him go to his grandfather. Gaunt was alone in his bedchamber, seated before the casement. He bore the gilt collar of SS about his shoulders, wearily, as if it weighed too greatly upon him. Once Chaucer had

spoken of Lancaster as "upright as a bolt," but today the great
Duke was bent as by sudden age.

Gaunt spoke at last, never turning his head. "You know your
father is unhurt, Henry?"

"Yes, my lord."

Gaunt said in a harsh voice, "They did not fight."

"My lord," Henry said, "how could they not?"

"We never doubted they would ride upon each other," Gaunt
said. "The Earl Marshal had thrown down your father's gage.
Your father had even set his spurs to his horse. Then the King
flung his warder out into the lists and so stayed them."

Speaking, he half turned his head so that the light fell across his
face and gray forked beard. It was a stern, aging face, much
marked. Pride had early ravaged it—pride and the lust of ambi-
tion; and something other, a thing more tender. There were lines
of devotion, as of arrogance, that seared it.

After a little he spoke as if he spoke his thoughts. "These twenty
years have I watched them grow to manhood," he said, "my son
and the King my nephew—watched and served the one so that
through him the realm was served, and not my own interests as
my enemies said. And I have known the day would come when
these two might well destroy each other."

Henry could give him no answer. Gaunt looked upon him and
said, "The King has decreed that the matter between your father
and Mowbray is too weighty to be settled by combat. He himself
pronounced punishment. Your father is banished the realm these
ten years."

"Oh, my lord," Henry said. He broke out, "I lost my mother
four years ago. Am I to lose my father too?"

"You may thank God you did not lose him this morning at the
point of the lance and that you are not Mowbray's son. Mowbray goes for life."

"But it is not just," Henry said. He was afraid of his grandfather, as was all England, the King not excepted; nor did one
speak thus of the King to Gaunt, but his grief loosed him from

caution. "What has my father done, save defend his honor? He is loyal—all men know it—as are you, my lord."

Gaunt looked upon him without compassion but with a quiver of grief. He said, "Your father will come back to you, Henry."

"But it is so long. I shall be twenty-one."

Gaunt answered him, "Aye, and what of that?"

"My lord," Henry said. "All those years without sight or sound of him. It will be just as if he were lying beside my mother at Leicester."

"You will be twenty-one," Gaunt said roughly. "And you think you have come to this world's end because of it. I am fifty-eight, Henry. Think you my son will come back to me? These twenty years I have served my liege lord, the King. I have given him my counsel, my sleeping and waking, my right hand in war; aye, and my conscience, God help me; but it has not been enough. He takes my son, and takes him from an old man who'll not see his homecoming." He sighed and drew a hand across his eyes. "Yet is he the King," he said. "He will be served."

IV

Derby had but a month to set all things in order. He rendered his vast estates into the hands of stewards and sought to find homes for his six small children, lacking now both father and mother. The two little girls, Blanche and Philippa, and Humphrey he gave into the care of the boys' tutor, Sir Hugh Waterton at Eton Tregos. The three older boys he would have sent to Pleshy Castle, to their grandmother, Lady Hereford, but Gaunt desired to have Henry by him.

He had the boy brought to him at his castle of Leicester. It was October now, and the chill of the dying earth hung sharp and rancid about the castle walls. Derby had lingered another two days at Kenilworth, there to part from his five younger children before the servants bore them off to Pleshy or Eton Tregos. On the last day of the month he himself rode to Leicester with his baggage borne on two sumpter horses and with few attendants. It was a sad little band, not riding in finery or bright chivalry.

Gaunt awaited him in the great hall. When he knew the horses to be near, he sent the servants to bring Henry down to him. He looked bleakly upon the boy, his own ravaged face wearied and much aged. "Your father is coming to take his leave of you, Henry," he said. "Hearken to me. You are not to weep. Your father bears grief enough this day."

Derby came in to them, as they stood together, and greeted his father. His face was hardened with grief and with a high anger; but when he looked upon his eldest son it softened.

"Come here, Hal," he said. "Let me look on you." He set his hands on Henry's shoulders and drew him forward. After a little he said, "You'll be twenty-one, full-grown to manhood, before I'll look on you again. It may be I'll not know you. And you—how will you take to a father whose head is graying and who talks your English tongue Frenchly for lack of speaking it?"

"You will be little more than forty, Henry," Gaunt said. "All time lies before a man at forty."

"All time," Derby said with bitterness. "Time to make up the lost years? My estates will decay. I'll be helpless while rogues defraud them. My sons will be strangers to me. And what men will they become with neither father nor mother to shape them?"

"I have the King's promise, Henry," Gaunt said. "Should I die before you return, your inheritance will be safe."

"Oh, before heaven, my father," Derby said with forced cheerfulness, "you'll have many years yet." He set his arms about his son. "Your shoulders must bear the hopes of Lancaster, now, Hal. *Adieu.* You'll not forget your father?"

He embraced him again and went from him. Gaunt walked with him to the top of the great stairs, at the bottom of which the horses stood. He saw the fierce anger in his son's face and spoke to soothe it. "I know your thoughts," he said. "For my sake, strive to set them behind you. I would not have you sail from these shores hating the King."

"Afore God," Derby said, "what would you ask of me?"

"Only this," Gaunt said. "The land is poor and much stricken. She can ill bear any added evil, and I know not what evil may come if you and Richard look upon each other with hate."

"For the saints' sake, my father," Derby said, "do not ask me to kiss this rod. I think no man were ever used with a blacker treachery than I at the hands of my King and my cousin."

Gaunt spoke no more of it. He and Derby took their farewell, speaking with tenderness to each other. When his son had ridden from him, across the drawbridge and onto the London road, Gaunt turned his steps back to the castle, the peering servants scattering from his look. Henry sat still in the great hall by the hearth, his head turned from him. Gaunt looked upon him grimly, for his compassion had gone upon his son.

"Aye, boy," he said, "now can you weep."

v

Gaunt had lived wildly in his youth, both lusting and loving. His third wife was Katherine Swynford, who had been his mistress for twenty-five years. She had borne him three strapping sons, grown now with Derby to manhood. Gaunt well loved them, and their bastardy had been much heartbreak to him.

All men still spoke of the Duchess as Dame Katherine. She presided over her household at Leicester, kind to the boy whom Gaunt had rendered into her hands but no rock to lean on. Her sons were otherwise. Henry much loved his three bastard uncles, and most the youngest of them, Thomas Beaufort, Earl of Dorset.

Dorset had but little of the high imaginings and strung nerves of the Plantagenets; the good red commoner's blood of his mother had washed it out. It seemed to the boy—himself Welshly bred among the legends of Arthur and the music of the valleys—that his uncle was as the English oaks, sturdy and abiding and a covert against the tempest. Dorset had married early, but as yet his lady bore him no child. He used Henry tenderly, as he might his own

son, often riding to Leicester that he could fish with him or bring
him out with the gerfalcons into the woods. Henry looked eagerly
to his comings, for he sorely missed his own brothers.

In the last week in January, four months after Derby had
gone to his exile, Dorset rode to Leicester Castle, coming in the
half-dark through the bailey garden to the side door of the solar.
When he entered, he heard the notes of a lute and saw that
Henry played alone in the light of the fire. As Dorset watched,
the tapestries across the far door were swept aside, and Gaunt
came swiftly in, the swinging collar of SS about his neck aglint as
he came.

He struck his grandson's hands from off the lute strings, his face
dark with anger. "By my faith," he said, "I forbade it. Do you
disobey me?"

The boy answered him calmly. "I am very sorry, my lord. I
thought you were still at Kenilworth."

"Do not lie to me, Henry."

"I do not lie to you, my lord." His eyes had lighted on Dorset
in the dim alcove, and Gaunt followed his look, the anger soften-
ing in his face as he recognized his son. He bade Henry go in a
milder voice. When the door had shut on him, he spoke quietly to
Dorset. "You think I am harsh with the boy?"

"In truth, my father," Dorset said, "I know not his fault."

"A small one," Gaunt said. "You know the air he played?"

"A very old air," Dorset said. "One that the soldiers have ever
sung."

"One that the soldiers sang," Gaunt said. "Aye, they sang it—
those that marched under me—when we marched on Najera. In
truth, Tom, I can no longer bear to hear it."

"But, my lord," Dorset said, "there was no greater march in our
history. It ought not to give you sorrow to think of it."

"It is an old man's sorrow," Gaunt said. "There seemed in us
some first spring shoots of greatness then. Now I come near death,
and this black frost lies on the realm."

"My father," Dorset said, and sought for words.

"Nay, it is true," Gaunt said. "See what we have become. Of Edward's sons only I and your uncle of York are left—two broken and aging men. Of all he wrought, of all our steel hewed back in France, only Calais and Guienne remain. The great Empire of the Plantagenets—Normandy, Aquitaine and Anjou all lost to us. The French ravage our coasts, burn Winchelsea and Southampton, flaunt their spread sails in the very Thames. The Scots hold the north in jeopardy. Even those that were once the stay of the realm, the Cheshire archers, turn upon their own countrymen in plunder and rape until their name is a terror. Thus England—while my son, whose energies might have succored us, drags out his youth in banishment."

"Sir," Dorset said, "these words ought well to be spoken in Richard's ears."

"Richard heeds me no longer," Gaunt said. "He heeds his flatterers."

"Oh, my father," Dorset said, "I never spoke treason to you before, but the King repays you very ill."

Gaunt sighed and drew his hand across his brow. "Was not that the curse of Lancaster?" he said. "That those most beloved should deal the deepest wounds."

"Love him?" Dorset said. "Love Richard?"

"I love him well," Gaunt said. "I watched him grow to manhood and bear his kingship upon him like a cloak. I told myself I saw his father in his face, when my heart told me that if there was a spark of my brother, the Black Prince's spirit still in England, it burned in my own son."

He began to speak then of his youth. "You think I boast of my life," he said. "I do not. I am not proud of much of it. The lust of power flamed in me more than in any other man. I fought England longer and with greater might than ever I did France."

"My lord father," Dorset said, "you have propped the whole realm."

"No," Gaunt said. "I would have you know the truth, Tom. It was not always so. Of all men in England was I the most hated.

Men's tongues dripped filth when they spoke of me. It was said I brought my wife and my whore to the same bed. There were many such lies, yet in one thing they spoke true. Could I have purchased a crown, I would have sold the very land to do it."

Dorset did not know how to answer him. Gaunt gave him a quiet, still look and went on. "I sought this crown," he said, "as I sought the crowns of Castile and France, but with a greater fury. I fought England many years, seeking my ends—fought her with lies and intrigue, as I might have fought an enemy in the lists, until she prevailed upon me."

"Sir," Dorset said, "all that you did turned to the realm's service."

Gaunt answered him slowly. "God sent me good punishment," he said. "I grew to love greatly where I had sought to destroy. When I look about me and see the land's sickness and her peril, it rends my heart from me."

While he spoke, one of the pages came in, bearing lighted candles to set upon the table. Dorset saw his father's face suddenly, in their brightness, and felt his heart grow chill. It seemed to him that death sat in his father's ravaged face, enjoined with the pride, the lust and the iron control. It was to him as though he looked upon a dying man.

Eight days later he rode again to Leicester, where his father lay dying. Gaunt knew no man, not even the three sons born in bastardy, who kept vigil by his bed, nor their mother, so long beloved by him. He twice spoke Derby's name; then named the realm, as if his last breath caressed her. He died quietly, about the hour of prime.

VI

A fortnight after Gaunt's death, Henry walked with one of the pages in the Leicester meadows, leading their horses. He kept a record of the days of his father's banishment, and when the page asked him what he carried, he showed it to him.

"I mark off each day as it comes," he said. "See, all these are scored off since October, and this that I've penned about in red and gold is the day my father returns."

The page asked him how many days were still to go. He was some three years older than his young lord, and he spoke in superior fashion.

Henry answered him, "Three thousand four hundred and seventy-five."

"In truth, my lord," the page said, "it sounds a lot."

They returned shortly to the castle, quiet-girt among its trees. This day would Henry leave it, riding back with his grandmother, Lady Hereford, to Pleshy. He had mourned his grandfather; for Gaunt's ravaged splendor was not to be shut out, and there was magic in a name that recalled Crécy. Yet it seemed to him a goodly thing that in a day's space he would be back with his brothers, with the Pleshy woods to ride in and the clear pools for fishing. He felt himself with more joy in the day than he had known since his father's banishment.

While the page brought the horses round to the stable, he walked on alone. His way lay through the gardens, where the yellow crocus splintered in gold about the lawns, and all was sheltered and enclosed in walls of stone. There were timbered galleries here, hung greenly in summer with figs and apricots, and above them, emblazoned on the woodwork, like gems in the blackening oak, were the arms of the Plantagenets, of Lancaster, of Derby and of Chester. When he drew near he saw that soldiers clung to the gallery rail above his head. As he watched, they set their bills against the painted arms of his house and wrenched them from the roof.

"What do you do?" he said. "They are my father's arms."

One answered, "Best go to your grandam, my hinny."

As he spoke, Joan Waring, Henry's nurse, came out of the great doors and called, speaking first Welsh and then English. "Lord Henry," she was shouting. "Look you now, you are to come to your lady grandmother."

When the boy reached her, he saw that she wept. He went past her into the hall, where Lady Hereford stood beside one of the broad oaken tables Gaunt had had hewn from his own forest timbers. With her was Walter Hungerford, Gaunt's steward, a man of graying hair and bent shoulders, careful and honest. His rent books lay upon the table, and he was bowed over them as if he prayed. A stranger stood with him, scanning each sheet as he turned it; splendidly garbed, his sleeves fur lined and his dagger encrusted, hilt and sheath, in jewels.

The boy broke out to his grandmother, "They are tearing down my father's livery."

She spoke with him gently, though her cheeks quivered against her silken barbette. "They are bidden to," she said. "The King has forfeit all that your father thought to inherit."

"But my father cannot live. How can he come back to England with his inheritance gone?"

"Oh, Hal," Lady Hereford said, "he'll not again come back. The King has banished him for life."

Henry had known many black days in his life, but this was to him as the worst. He broke into a storm of weeping. It affrighted Lady Hereford, for she knew him as controlled. She knelt and set her arms about him, her long sleeves as a shroud.

"Oh, my poor Hal," she said. "There's no cause for such tears. You shall see your father again. When you are fifteen, we'll go on our knees to the King and beg leave for you to go to him. You and he will be together and all Europe for your pleasure. You'll go on a crusade with him—two knights for St. George. See Jerusalem and the Holy Places. Sail in the great Genoese ships we envy so. It shall be, I promise you."

The boy said in a choking voice, "I do not think even Jerusalem will matter to him now. He'll want to walk here where it is green and cast again into the Wye."

"Harry, Harry," Lady Hereford said, "there are other rivers. You and he will have many good days afishing."

"But he will want to be here," he said. "How can he wander about Europe till he dies? The King will break his heart."

Richard had sent his especial favorite, Sir William Bagot, on this mission. He stood by Hungerford now, in his peacock finery, bored with all that passed and impatient to be on his way.

He spoke at last, first with Lady Hereford. "My lady," he said, "time presses. Prepare the boy and let us be on our way."

"Afore God, sirs," Lady Hereford said, "did Gaunt serve the King so ill that this is how the King repays him?"

"Lady," Bagot said, yawning, "the King commands it."

"Leave the boy at least this summer in my charge," Lady Hereford said. "He is but eleven, and he is not strong. He has just had the measle-pox."

Henry knew that the words were of him. He lifted his head and looked at her.

"The King has summoned you," she said. "You are to go to him in London."

When she saw him in dread, she spoke again. "Nay, now," she said, "there's naught to fear. You are to pass under his care."

He spoke in panic, not knowing what he feared. "I'll not go."

"Oh, by the Mass," Bagot said. "My lady, I am here to carry out the King's commands, not to argue with boys. He is permitted one servant and whatever baggage he requires. I beg you have it arranged. For the rest, if needs be I'll have him carried out to his horse."

"It shall be done," Lady Hereford said in a cold voice. To the boy she said, "I shall send William Malbon with you, Hal, to serve you. Come, now, would you have the soldiers see you weep?"

Malbon and Joan Waring prepared all things for the journey as swiftly as they might. Joan bore the baggage out to the sumpter horses. She could not check her grief, and when she came upon the soldiers, she fell on the nearest in rage.

"Eh, but it is a wicked thing that you are doing," she said. "I would not wish it done to the foulest, blackest-hearted knave in

the realm. And it is good people and true people that the King
has served so, and his cousin, too."

Her fury cowed them all. "In faith," one said when she had
gone, "I'd not have her to wife."

Presently Lady Hereford brought Henry out into the court, the
archers standing there and staring upon him. He was calm now,
but they could well see that he had fiercely wept. One hoisted
him up into the high, painted saddle of his horse, speaking kindly
to him.

"Up with you, my young lord," he said. "I make no doubt you
ride as your father."

He set his hands to tightening the girths. Henry said in a low
voice, "What will the King do with me?"

"Do with you?" the man answered. "Why, nothing, I'll be
bound, save show you his fair city."

They set their horses' heads toward London, riding late into the
day. Henry was much worn with grief and weariness. After a little
one of the soldiers—he who had spoken with him—took him up before him on his own horse. It seemed to him a goodly thing to be
able to rest in this man's arms, and he nodded into sleep, his head
turned against the other's shirt, stiff and odorous of body sweat,
yet friendly to his nostrils.

VII

They came to London by the evening of the next day. Henry saw
her for the first time—the King's fair city—bounded by fields that
crept as far as Tyburn.

"See yonder," the archer said. "That leads to Westminster
where the King is crowned."

Henry said, "But I thought that he lives there."

"Aye, he dwells there sometimes," the other said. "Yet now he
lodges in the Tower."

Beyond the Strand lay the city itself, filled with gay booths and
swinging signs. Apprentices bawled at the doors of their masters'

shops, flourishing bright wares—jeweled combs and loving cups, rolls of silk and brocade and woven linen, new-baked bread and comfits, jars of cinnamon and spices from the East. Poverty lay upon the land like a cloak, but here it was masked and all seemed to buy, the streets athrob with folk—great ladies, leading men-at-arms and spruce pages; friars, potbellied under their girdled cassocks; black-gowned clerks and hooded scriveners; the men of the watch; the aldermen in scarlet and the livery of their guilds. Henry had never looked on London's like before. It was to him as if the charm of the King's city crept out and curled its fingers about his heart.

From the Strand they came to the Tower. The boy was brought to a bedchamber in the White Tower, rich hung with tapestry and warmed by fire and candlelight. Malbon helped him to gain his bed and then set straight the bed coverings. Henry longed to sleep, but he was still in fear.

Presently a boy came in, wearing a rich blue bedrobe, with him a gentleman-in-waiting, clad in sad livery and faded looking. The boy was very fair, golden in hair and skin, as of the hue of the Plantagenets, and with much autocracy of manner.

He spoke in surprise, saying, "Who is he? What is he doing here in my bed?"

His waiting man answered him, "It is your cousin, my lord."

"Which cousin? There are so many."

"It is Lord Henry of Lancaster," the man said. "He is to share your bed for the present, being under the King's protection, like yourself."

The boy looked back on Henry. After a space he said, "Welcome, cousin. I am Duke Humphrey of Gloucester."

He came into the bed beside Henry, bidding his waiting man with a lordly wave of the hand to put out the candles. After the man had gone—Malbon with him—the two boys lay silent together in the darkened room. The firelight dappled the stone arches in roseate glow and struck in black shadow the ironworked sconces.

After a little Gloucester spoke, "How many years have you?" Henry answered him that he was eleven.

"I am fourteen," Gloucester said. "So I am lord to you in all things." Presently he said, "You are Derby's son, then. And a pauper, since the King has banished him and taken your inheritance. What of your lady mother?"

"She is dead."

"So is mine," Gloucester said. "She died a year ago—eighteen months after my father. That is why the King had me brought here." He spoke in calm fashion. "I hate him," he said. "He murdered my father."

"Murdered him?" Henry whispered.

"In faith, he did not do it himself," Gloucester said. "It was in Calais Castle. Mowbray's men did it." He began to explain all things, whispering into his cousin's ear. "My father was set under arrest as one of the Lords Appellant," he said. "The King ever hated him. He bade Mowbray see he did not come living out of Calais Castle. Mowbray's men barred the door of my father's chamber and held a feather pillow to his face so he could not cry out. He died thus, striving for his breath, Mowbray looking on."

Henry said, "It could not be."

"You do not believe it," Gloucester said. "You're a fool, then. What think you your father accused Mowbray of that night on Brentford Bridge?"

Henry answered haltingly, "I know not."

"I'll warrant you do not," Gloucester said. "But many guess. Why was your father sent to life banishment? Because he named Mowbray a murderer, and by naming him such he named the King."

"But your father was the King's uncle, as my grandfather was. Richard would have not murdered his own uncle."

"Why would he not?" Gloucester said. "All kings wade knee-deep in blood. My mother said they must to keep their thrones."

It was to Henry horrible—so far away from his own romance-fed notions of the sanctity of kingship that he could not find words. In the strange room, thick with creeping terrors, his mind went to distant Pleshy, where he had imagined he would sleep this night with his brothers. On a sudden he longed for his mother's arms about him.

He turned on his side that his cousin might not see him weep. Gloucester's persistent voice whispered to him, "What is it? Do you weep?"

"No," Henry said into his pillow.

"I wept, too, when I came here," Gloucester said in airy comfort. "But you grow well used to it. They have fine banquets, and I like our other cousin, Aumerle; though no one trusts him. The worst is there are so many tutors."

VIII

On the next day when they had come back to their chamber at noon, Henry took up his cousin's jeweled dagger to look upon it. Gloucester was eager to dominate, as his own father had ever been. He straightway jerked it from his hands. "Let be," he said. "It's mine."

He dealt his cousin a thump on the chest, knocking him backward to the ground; but Henry likewise took after his own father and had Derby's readiness to return blow for blow. He gained his feet and fell upon the other. In a moment they were fighting fiercely the length of the room.

Their cousin, Edward of Aumerle, heard them and came in to them. He was son to the Duke of York, a sandy-haired young man, with a fleshy, good-natured face. Gloucester liked him well, for he had an indolent and careless humor and was ever kindly toward him. Henry had not before seen him.

"Peace, good cousins both," Aumerle said in a mild voice, "or one or other of your tutors will tan your hides."

He set them apart and stood looking down upon them with a

careless affability. "Cousin Lancaster," he said, "for I take you to be cousin Lancaster—if you must fight, it were policy to pick an enemy no bigger than yourself."

Henry had no breath and could not answer him. Aumerle smiled and said, "A lion or a leopard would sort well with you in your present mood. The King's lions rest in their tower yonder. Would it please you to see them now with me?"

Henry answered eagerly, "I should like it well." To Gloucester he said, "Do you come too?"

"No," Gloucester said. "I've seen them many times. They only walk about." They spoke to one another without rancor now, their bout of violence done with.

Aumerle was Constable of the Tower, and he passed without challenge into the Lion Tower. There were stairs inside, leading to a gallery, balustraded at one end, and below a pit, divided by an iron grille. A splendid lion lay at one side of the grille, and on the other padded three golden leopards. There had always been three leopards in the Tower since the Emperor had sent three to Henry II in compliment to the arms of the Kings of England. Henry had never seen such before. He watched in delight, hanging over the balustrade.

From the stairs came the sound of voices, and one voice above the others, high-pitched, authoritative, talking at speed. A group of lords and ladies flowed out into the gallery in a shifting wash of color, the women in tall headdresses, their eyebrows plucked clean away, the men bejeweled and loud in their laughter. A young man headed them, most gorgeously dressed in an amber houppelande, stiff-buttoned to the throat with jeweled buttons. All the golden grace of the Plantagenets was his. A golden fringe of beard, fine as silk, crept round a jaw, in youth delicate, but now, in a manner, thickening. Yet no man could mistake him. This was the King. This was Richard of Bordeaux.

Aumerle, careless of his fine hose, went down on his knees in the sawdust of the gallery, Henry doing likewise. When Richard sat in audience, all who approached his throne were bidden to kneel three times. The King much loved ceremony, lapping himself in its warmth as other men might lap themselves in their cloaks. He was not yet thirty-four, but he looked older. He who, as a boy, had been slender as a reed was coarsening now, his body striving after a fleshiness its tautened nerves would not let it achieve. He talked much, his voice high; and his hands, stiffened by their rings, glinted in gesture, never still. It was as if the King were no more at peace than his ceaseless-padding leopards.

"Well, cousin," he said to Aumerle, "who is it with you?"

"Young Harry Lancaster, as I live," a woman's voice said softly. "He has all his mother's looks."

Aumerle answered, "Lord Henry of Lancaster, if it please your grace."

For a space Richard was silent, then he spoke in courtly fashion, "You are right welcome, cousin. What say you, my lords? Will not our cousin of Lancaster add grace to our court?"

"Indeed, my lord," one said jestingly, "if he has valor to match his person, he'll grace it well."

"You should mayhap take him with you on your Irish wars, sire," another said.

Richard answered, "Why so we may do. Rise, cousins."

He stood for a while talking with Aumerle, then went from them. His retinue closed round him—the women and the peacock-hued young men with their jewels and trailing finery. The King's high voice and the empty laughter of his followers ebbed away down the stairs.

The lion below them in the pit opened his great jaws in a vast yawn. "Why," Henry said, in disappointment to Aumerle, "he has no teeth."

"No, boy," a voice said quietly behind them, "the French have drawn them all."

Only the soldiers and two of Richard's lords remained with them in the gallery. None seemed to know who had spoken.

IX

When they came from the Lion Tower, they met with two who had attended the King there. These were Aumerle's younger brother, Richard of Cambridge, and his sister, Elizabeth of York. Henry knew them to be his cousins, though he had not before seen them.

Elizabeth had been she who had recognized him in the Lion Tower. "I knew you straightway," she said. "They tell me all Mary de Bohun's boys took after her, and your father had to wait for a daughter before he had a fair-haired Plantagenet."

Cambridge yawned and said, "How many whelps has Derby?"

He had a smiling but a chill handsomeness. He and Henry looked at each other, liking each other little. Something cold had fallen over the group of four cousins standing on the tree-girt lawn, as when two knights at the beginning of a duel might raise their lances and the shadow of the blades lie along the grass.

Elizabeth answered her brother in a brisk voice, "Six, Richard."

"Six," Cambridge said. "And Derby half his days away on a crusade." He broke into laughter. "I do not doubt there were but two to look like him."

Henry answered him in anger, "I think you would not say that, my lord, if my father were here."

Cambridge had not thought he would reply. He looked upon him, his handsome brows drawn sharply together.

"Maybe Derby did father him," Cambridge said. "He has the Lancaster liking for a quarrel. Look, boy, remember where that liking took your father—into life exile."

He turned and went from them. It seemed to Henry he had never so lacked his father. Elizabeth, seeing his head droop, bent down to him so that her face was on a level with his. "Nay, now, come," she said. "When was Lancaster so downcast? Some day the King will be kind and your father will come back to you."

"Don't raise his hopes," Aumerle said. "Only a miracle will bring Derby's feet back to English soil."

"Well, we can still pray," Elizabeth said. "Ask Our Lady and St. George tonight, Harry, for such a miracle. I shall do likewise."

That night, when he did her bidding, young Gloucester watched him from their bed. "You're praying very hard," he said. "It was the same at vespers."

"I was asking for a miracle," Henry said. "It is that my father may come back to England."

Gloucester raised his head from the pillow, his mouth hanging slack. "In faith," he said, "you are the greenest simpleton that ever came up from the country. Do you not yet know why you are here? As a hostage, in case your father thinks to get up to any tricks. If he sets foot in England again, you'll need all your prayers yourself."

X

In May, Richard set out upon his Irish wars. He embarked from Tower Wharf, by barge, planning to journey royally. He meant to seek his ease during the campaign. Minstrels, embroiderers, body servants, as many as three hundred cooks, swelled the barges moored in line against the Tower stairs, and vast piles of baggage grew about the wharf. Among these Richard's lords sweated their way, laboring for order. Cambridge, as he rounded the steps from St. Thomas's Gate, all but collided with his two boy cousins.

"The devil take you," he said. "Out of my way." To Malbon who stood with them he said, "What do these two here?"

Malbon answered him, "They are to accompany the King's grace to Ireland."

Cambridge lifted his brows and looked on Henry. "Well, cousin Lancaster," he said. "Since it is old Gaunt's coffers which will float the King to Ireland, it's maybe meet you should come with us. But keep out from under my feet." He set Henry from his path with a thrust of his arm as he might a young dog that had vexed him.

Richard stood idly by the Tower stairs, his fair hair bright in the sunshine, his favorites surrounding him. His seven-year-old Queen clung tightly to one of his long sleeves, weeping bitterly, until her ladies bore her off inside St. Thomas's Gate. Her sobs echoed back, mingling with Bagot's laughter as he leant on the King's arm.

As Richard went toward his barge, one of the Tower beggars halted him, the arm he raised against the King's going scabbled with sores to the wrist. Against the golden King in his yellow robes he looked a thing of decay and death, as if the midden crawled beneath the stepping chanticleer. Richard paused to hear him, but not willingly. The man spoke in thin-voiced fashion, bidding the King not to sail for Ireland. Should the King yet go, news would come to him there that would "make his ears tingle."

Richard answered him, desiring to mock but angry likewise, and his voice high-pitched. He pointed at the river, bidding the man prove the divinity of his message by walking on the water.

The two small boys, sitting on their baggage, watched breathlessly. "Oh, do you think he can?" Henry said. Merlin, magician-counsellor to Arthur, had trodden water, and all in Wales knew that the devil had stood on the Towy to build the bridge near Carreg Cennen.

"I'll go hazard with you he does not," Gloucester said.

He spoke true, for the beggar already stood in the river to his knees, the soldiers driving him down step by step with their bills. Richard at length waved them back. After the beggar had scrambled from the water, he assigned him to his sergeant-at-arms, committing him to the Tower until he should return from Ireland.

The King took his seat in his barge. For all he strove to show only contempt, his nerves were plainly stretched taut as bow strings. His hands sought ever for employment, fingering the folds of his gown, his jeweled collar, his beard. Henry whispered to Gloucester, "In truth, I'm sorry for him. He's unhappy."

Gloucester flung a look of hate at Richard's head in the leading barge. "May God long keep him so."

His cousin answered in a small voice, "The whole weal of the land lies upon him. I would not be a King—not for all the gold of Arabia."

"I should like it," Gloucester said. "All men run to do your bidding, and there's no one to gainsay you."

The barges drew now to the center of the river, and the white walls of the Tower, green set in plane tree and birch, fell gently from them. The Tower had marked their world since their homes had been lost to them. The two small boys pressed closer to each other on their velvet cushions, having none but one another for assurance.

"I wonder if they will have us fight in Ireland," Gloucester said. "I heard say the Irish roast all they take." After a little he said, "I feel sick."

Henry likewise felt sick, but he would not admit it. He said hastily, "I think we'll not be long away."

"No," Gloucester said, brightening. "The Irish are barbarians, all men say so. The nobles themselves go barefoot, and you cannot tell the peasants from their pigs. Anyone could have the mastery of them in battle—even us."

"Even us?"

"Pah," Gloucester said. "You know what I mean. The English never win a battle now."

XI

There was no great fighting in Ireland against the rebels. Richard lodged in Dublin Castle, living lavishly and with much pomp. The boys also were lodged there, studying under their tutors, but learning now the arts of war, which, since they were the sons of nobles, they must do. Sometimes they were bidden to ride with the soldiers, squiring one or another of Richard's lords, though in this they saw no battle. Once when they were returned from such a forage, Richard stood by the gatehouse and bade Henry come to him.

"I hear from your tutors you do well," he said. "You are a good boy, Henry. I watched you ride out this morn. You showed no fear."

Richard began to speak musingly. "It is required of us never to show fear," he said. "Yet fear can gnaw the bones of Kings as coldly as the bones of beggars. It is a hard thing, boy, to be a King."

He went on to talk of other things—of the Abbey Church back in Westminster, which he greatly loved and which he had set his master mason, Hugh Hurland, to refurbish. It seemed to the lords, watching him, that he had warmed to Derby's boy.

The next day he sent for Henry again and knighted him. It was much honor for one so young, and Henry received it in delight. He had small ill will for the King, though he dared not speak of it to Gloucester. It seemed to him that if his father had likewise choked away his life into a feather pillow in Calais Castle as Gloucester's had done, he, too, would have looked on Richard only with hatred. Yet Kings, if God were merciful, might well receive more forgiveness than other men, having more need of it. He saw no reason why he and Richard should not be friends. Already he looked to the day when his courage would come to him and he would go down on his knees to Richard to beg his father's return when the first ten years of his exile were done.

Three days following, the boys came to their evening meal. Richard usually dined sumptuously in the great hall of the castle, where the air was fresh and sea scented after the daytime heat. But this night, when they came into the hall, all things seemed amiss—the minstrels absent from their places and the King's chair, under its gilded canopy, empty on the dais. There were people grouped about the long tables, but their talk was hushed as though death walked the castle.

As Henry went toward his place, first one and then another turned to look upon him. The talk died as if blown out by a giant's breath. It seemed to him all stared upon him in silence— the pages, the carvers, the English lords and their retainers, the Irish noblemen with their fresh-skinned ladies.

He stopped, not knowing what to do. One of Richard's clerks came toward him, twitching his thick gown, for he all but ran. "Wait," he said. When he reached him he said, "You are straight-way to go to your chamber."

Henry looked at him, not finding an answer.

The man spoke louder. "Hear me," he said. "You are to keep your chamber and not to leave it. Do as I bid you."

Save for Cambridge, none had before spoken to him as less than a great-grandson of a King of England. This man especially among the clerks had ever bowed to him. Henry turned from him and went out of the hall, all men in silence watching him. He sought to bear himself proudly and to keep up his head.

XII

Gloucester soon came to him in their chamber. "What's hap-pened?" he said. "Do you think the French have landed?"

"No," Henry said. "It has to do with me."

"I know not what you've done," Gloucester said. "It must be something terrible. I'd liefer not be in your shoes."

Malbon was nowhere at hand, nor was Gloucester's faded re-tainer. They set their clothes aside and lay unsleeping in the great bed. The castle hung dark about them, quiet as the grave. So silent was it that when the latch of their door leapt in sudden rattle, the noise stiffened them in terror, Gloucester, in a school-boy's fashion, plunging his head beneath the clothes.

A pool of candlelight wavered upon the threshold of the room, and in its center Aumerle's face. He came silently round the bed, the tallow caking already upon his rings.

In the dimness he groped to set his hand on Henry's shoulder. "Lancaster," he said, "your father is back."

"Back?" Henry whispered. "In England?"

"In England, aye," Aumerle said. "He landed at Ravenspur with but six men four days ago."

Henry looked upon him with delight. He set his hand against

Gloucester's ribs and dealt him a fierce prod. "Oh, Humphrey," he said. "My miracle. It's happened."

"Cousin, cousin," Aumerle said. "Not so fast. I said your father landed with six men. So he did, but we hear Northumberland, and Harry Percy, Willoughby and Greystock, have all ridden to join him. By now he may well have twenty thousand."

"What will he do—my father?"

"He says he comes only for his own," Aumerle said. "More he will not claim. He marches westward across Yorkshire to his own duchies. It is said his army swells at every step."

"He is mad," Gloucester muttered at Henry's side. "Has your father no love for you?"

Henry asked him in a whisper what he meant.

"In faith," Gloucester said, "you understand well what I mean. The King holds you here with him. Your father must know it."

It seemed he shrank away from his cousin, as if he saw him already dead. Henry answered him in a fierce voice. "He only comes for his own," he said. "What evil is there in that?"

"Evil enough with twenty thousand men at his back. My father did much less than that, and he paid for it. Would your father see you with a feather pillow held across your face?"

Aumerle answered him roughly, "Still your tongue." To Henry he said, "The King would talk with you. Get your clothes."

Richard paced in the galleried room of the keep, and on the stairs they heard his voice raised as against their coming. Hysteria had thinned it. Hollow, high-pitched, the words incessant like the clacking of a mill, the King's voice echoed his pacing up and down the rush-strewn floor.

"By God's most precious wounds, he is our cousin, lords, and he uses me thus."

His back was to Aumerle and the boy on the gallery stairs; yet he swung at length to look upon them, his face in the torchlight bloodless as a waxen mask. He stared upon Henry, then beckoned him.

"Come here, boy," he said peremptorily.

Henry went to him and knelt, desiring Richard would not see him trembling. After a little the King spoke in a thin voice. "You know what that proud man—your father—has done to me?"

The boy answered him, "Yes, my lord."

"In truth, Henry," Richard said, "I am very sorry for you. I shall have to punish him, and it may be I shall have to punish you likewise. There will be a high reckoning to Lancaster for this day's work."

All the room was silent save only for the breathing of the assembled lords. Henry strove for words, fearing whatever he said might touch the King to fury.

"I am sorry too, my lord," he said at last. "But it was not of my doing."

Was that true? He had prayed for it hard enough, God knew. But it may be that the sages were right and men knew not for what they prayed.

Richard spoke less harshly. "I like you well, boy," he said. "I hope I may ever use you gently, but in life the sins of the fathers often fall hard upon the sons." He gestured, seeking to steady his fingers, and Bagot came forward, pallid faced and with his high laughter gone. Richard spoke with him in a sunken voice. To Henry he said, "I would have you go to Trim Castle—you and your cousin of Gloucester. Sir William Bagot will bear you thence on the morrow. It must be your lodging until yonder rebellious man, your father, learns that his King yet has power to withstand all such treasons. Now get you gone."

The boy rose and Bagot gestured him to his side. When they would have passed from the King's sight into the dark gallery, one of the Irish nobles entered and murmured to the King. Richard swung upon him, twisting his mouth. His fury was such that for an instant it seemed to his lords almost as a madman's.

"Westmorland too? God's mercy, do all men fawn on Lancaster? These are the men I cloyed with lands and favors. Ingrates and traitors—may they rot in hell."

One of the clerks stood by him, bearing an open inkwell. Richard snatched it and dashed it to the ground, where it rolled like a drunken thing toward Aumerle's feet. The sudden fire of violence broke Henry's courage. He fled up the gallery stairs and into the darkness. Behind him Richard's high voice echoed as if in pursuit. "I am very sorry for you, Henry. I am very sorry for you."

XIII

The next day the two young cousins rode northwest to Trim. Their journey lay past the sacred town of Tara, where the Stone of Scone had once rested, and into the Meath hills, where the land was green and peat scented and the hamlets unkempt yet fair. At Ath Truim—the ford of the elder tree—stood the great fortress which men named King John's Castle, rising darkly above the Boyne. This place was held in loyalty to Richard by the de Burghs, the Earls of Ulster, and it was Lady Ulster who came to greet the two young Plantagenets in the castle court. Her lord was gone from her, fighting at Richard's side, and she stood now the castle's chatelaine, the great key of the keep bound to her waist by a chain of scrolled silver.

Gloucester, throughout the day's journey, had made much complaint of the heat. At the foot of the stairs he had to be lifted from his horse; and that night he tossed in his bed in a high fever. Lady Ulster herself nursed him, bearing him to her own quarters where she and her women could better tend him. Henry was forbidden his room. Men spoke with him as if his cousin mended, but one night he came upon a tonsured priest, with a dirty surplice thrown aslant his arm, leaving the chamber where Gloucester lay.

The sight struck against his heart. He fled to the great hall, where Bagot sat at his wine, and asked him when his cousin would again be in health.

"In faith," Bagot said, and laughed, "never, it would seem."

He spoke truly, Gloucester dying at daybreak the day following.

Henry was greatly overwhelmed. Being Plantagenets, he and Gloucester had fought; yet they had well liked each other, and each to the other had been as a tower of strength. It seemed to him Malbon alone was left him. He dogged his footsteps up and down the rambling length of the castle, as a puppy might his master, setting aside all food and sleeping ill.

When on the fifth day they came to breakfast, Malbon would have served him. "You must eat, Lord Henry," he said. "You'll lose strength else."

When Lady Ulster saw that he set aside his food still, she spoke to him in a teasing voice, yet half-grave. "Lord Henry," she said, "I would come to terms with you. Sir William Bagot journeys to Dublin for this day, and my ladies and I are going to sit by the river and fish. It may be we could bring you with us. Would that please you now?"

He answered that it would greatly.

"Then hearken to my terms," she said. "Eat your breakfast."

Bagot feared to let him beyond the castle walls, and save for that day he never left them. It was intensely hot now; the grass browning, the leaves shriveling on the trees by day; even the nights arid and sweltering. Malbon slept with him in his room, for since Gloucester's death he could not easily have borne to lie alone. The dark was peopled with many horrors—of Gloucester's father in Calais Castle; of his own father who might well lie now in Richard's hands, thence to be "hanged and headed" as Richard had promised him. It seemed to him whichever way fortune bowed evil would come of it. If Lancaster failed in arms against the King, his father was marked to die; if his father seemed to be coming to success, he himself was most surely marked for the King's vengeance.

When he could bear his thoughts no longer, he spoke Malbon's name.

Presently there was much shuffling and Malbon bent over him. "Yes," he said. "Yes, Lord Henry."

Henry said, "If I do not hear from my father soon, I think I shall go from my wits."

Malbon set his tongue against his lips. He knew not what to

say and sought for an assurance he could not find. "I am sure there's naught to trouble you, Lord Henry," he said at last. "It is very hot. Will you not have a drink of milk?"

Henry looked at him in fury, but Malbon had ever served him well, and he checked it.

"No," he said. "It's no matter. I'm sorry that I woke you." He lay without sleep until the morning.

XIV

The next day men told of an English merchantman lying in the Dublin roads, awaiting the tide, and believed that she came from the King. When at midday the castle sat at meat, one of the watchmen brought word that horsemen rode from Tara. None could tell their chivalry, but they were English. Whosoever they were, all knew they would bear the King's tidings from England. The great hall grew, on a sudden, still and silent, even the servants ceasing to eat. Lady Ulster set her arm about Henry's shoulders, herself in fear for him.

"God with us, sir," she said to Bagot, "the King will send the boy no hurt?"

Bagot shrugged and set down his wine. Henry could scarce look at him. Not reasoning, he set his hand to the knife that lay beside his plate, but Bagot reached across and gained it from his fingers. Through the huddle of servants about the doors, those at the high table could discern the movement of covered heads. Then Thomas of Dorset, with his men-at-arms, came through the throng and up the hall. To Henry the sight of his uncle was as the answer to a prayer. He sprang up and ran to him.

Dorset stooped and set his arms about him. "Hal," he said, "is all well with you?"

"My father?" Henry said. "What of him?"

"Safe and in health," Dorset said cheerfully. "And praying the saints for a fair wind that I may bring you to him with all speed."

The boy gasped and said, "Is he, then, still in England?"

"He rests at Chester with Richard," Dorset said. "All's agreed on, Hal. Your father will suffer no hurt."

Henry said, "But he will go from me again. The King will send him back to his exile."

"No," Dorset said. "He will not do that, Harry. You'll not lose your father again."

"Oh, good my uncle," Henry whispered. "It is my miracle." He looked at his feet, so that no man should see he all but wept.

"Nay, now come," Dorset said, drawing him toward him. "It is done with now. We shall have you and your father together again and your feet on English soil."

Bagot spoke to them from the high table. "My Lord of Dorset," he said sharply, "am I to render the boy into your hands?"

Dorset answered him grimly, "Aye, sir."

"I do not do so," Bagot said, "save only on the King's authority."

Dorset answered, "I bear Richard's authority."

Bagot said in a sullen voice, "It were better, my lord, to say King Richard."

"I'll not quibble words with you," Dorset said. "But this I will say. Well is it for you that I find the boy in health."

He turned from him and spoke to Henry, bidding him go with Malbon and prepare for their journey. They rode from the castle the same hour, Lady Ulster waving from the gatehouse till their way hid her from their view.

Henry rode at his uncle's side, eager with questions. Dorset laughed, telling him but little.

"Nay, now, Hal," he said. "Wait. Your father will tell you it all for himself."

Smooth seas and fair winds brought them to Liverpool. Henry found it a wondrous thing to be back on English earth. The old names—Hereford, Kenilworth, Tutbury, Monmouth—lay in his mind like an enchantment, all these being Lancaster's again. It seemed to him that his own as well as his father's exile had ended.

On the last stage of their journey to Chester, he could scarce keep still in the saddle. They came to the castle at noon, the porters setting the grille wide for them. In the summer's warmth some few lords and their attendants stood about the terrace, and among them the boy saw his father, his red-gold head bent over a makeshift table. He shouted his father's name and flung himself from the saddle. Derby met with him in three raking strides. He swung his son off his feet with as much ease as he had done five years ago in Monmouth. Henry clung to him tightly, finding no words. Derby set him down at length, himself seeking speech.

Three of the great house of Percy stood with him on the terrace —men who, when he had landed at Ravenspur, had ridden straightway to him, offering him their swords. Foremost of them was the Earl of Northumberland, a man with carnivorous eyes, elderly and sallow faced; and by him his brother, Lord Thomas Percy. The third was Northumberland's son, Harry Percy—he whom men named Hotspur—younger again, broad shouldered, self-possessed and much graced by a handsome flamboyancy.

Derby set his arm about Henry's shoulders and called to them, "My lords, I pray you come and meet the eldest of my brood."

They came unwillingly, feeling themselves superfluous. Derby smiled and said, "Grant us your pardon, lords, if we seemed to wear our hearts upon our sleeves."

"Nay, my lord, nay," Northumberland said. "This is the heir, eh? A fine lad, my lord—a canny lad. Your inheritance will na fall ti the ground." He patted Henry's cheek in fulsome manner, then smiled, his teeth blackened and broken in their gums.

"These are the lords Percy," Derby said. "They are my right true friends. You'll honor them, Harry."

Hotspur broke into a great laugh. "Afore God," he said, "another Harry? We aal be 'Harry' here."

"Away wi' ye," Northumberland said. "It is a good name."

They went early to meat, the Percies dining with them at the high table. When they were done and would have left the hall, Derby set his hand on Dorset's arm.

"Thomas," he said, "what have you told him?"

"Nothing, brother," Dorset said. "I thought it best you should tell him yourself."

Derby nodded and passed on. He brought his son that night to the quiet chamber above the gatehouse where they might be alone. Now that the warmth of their first meeting was spent, they had come to a strangeness with each other, like a maid's shyness, not knowing what to say. After a little Derby leaned forward and ruffled his son's hair. "What say you, Harry?" he said. "Are you glad to have me back?"

"Oh, my lord," Henry said, "I know not how to speak of it. If Mother were here, all things would be perfect."

He asked then when they might return to Monmouth.

"Monmouth?" Derby said. "There's nothing at Monmouth. I have many plans for you, Hal. Your other uncle, Henry Beaufort, is Chancellor of Oxford now, and I thought to send you there. Would that be to your liking?"

"I think I should like it well."

"I would have you fitted for the future," Derby said. "At my death all things fall to you."

The boy said in a low voice, "I have just got you back and already you talk of death."

"God in His mercy keep me from it yet, but when it comes I would have you ready for the great titles you will bear."

This was to Henry as his grandfather's talk. Lancaster had already brought grief enough to him and to his father. Almost would he have let Gaunt's coffers and Gaunt's lands lie where Richard had scattered them.

He began to speak of other things. "I have so much to tell you," he said. "I am Knight now. The King dubbed me in Ireland. For all I was his prisoner, he was kind to me, and I pledged my sword to him."

Derby checked him, his face hardened. "Wait, Hal," he said. "It were better I had spoken of this before."

For a little he said no word, then he said, "Richard resigns the crown. He is no more King."

He saw his son look incredulous and spoke louder. "Aye," he said. "I know it all. He is our anointed King, hallowed our liege by the holy oil of his crowning. And we bowed our knees and made our oaths to him. But he made oaths to us, and, under heaven, he has not kept them." He rose from his chair and paced to the mantelshelf, where hung the great dorser, embroidered with the arms of Lancaster and Castile. "All I was promised— that if my father died during my years of exile my inheritance would be safe—broken as the goodwife breaks her piecrust. Your great uncle, Archbishop Arundel, to whom Richard swore none other would take his bishopric, exiled too and despoiled of it. Thomas of Gloucester, my own uncle and his, done to death in Calais Castle. And this poor kingdom, Hal, this beggar realm, whose laws he swore to guard and keep at his crowning, sucked dry by him to bloat the flesh upon his flatterers' bones."

Henry spoke as bewildered. "Who will be King, then? Richard's heir—our cousin, Edmund Mortimer?"

Derby laughed in hard fashion. "A boy, Hal? Even younger than yourself." When Henry gave him no answer, he said, "The whole realm is beset by perils, the French ever eager for conquest, the Scots at our backs. There's no boy's work here. It is to Lancaster that the land looks now."

Henry could scarce look at his father. He said at last, "But Edmund Mortimer is the heir. Is it that you will take the government upon you until he comes of age?"

"Hearken to me, Hal," Derby said. "When we come to London, Richard will set his signet to the articles of abdication, confessing himself unfit for all his kingly state. Then, as I know, the Lords and Commons will seek to deliver the crown into my hands. What think you I will do?"

Henry did not answer.

"I shall take it up," Derby said. "But as very King, that it may pertain to Lancaster in full sovereignty—to me and to my heirs."

He looked at his son and saw him pale as the dead. Henry whispered, "Then I—then I—"

"Aye," Derby said. "In fullness of time, and God willing, you will be King of England."

It was to the boy as if a cold and horrible destiny flapped with black wings across his face. He set a hand to his mouth. Derby saw him as a young and stricken animal entrapped by the hunters. When he would have gone to him, Henry slid from his chair and went backward to the wall.

"What ails you?" Derby said.

He said in a voice so low his father barely caught it, "We are not the Kings of England."

Derby looked at him with impatience. "Afore God," he said, "you talk like a babe. To this realm we have a triple claim. By descent—we are the male line of your great-grandfather, Edward— by the will of the people and by conquest." He spoke then more gently. "And if the crown is to be paid for," he said, "have we not paid for it already—you and I? I knew many a harsh night when I lay in exile in France; and I wonder if you slept easefully as Richard's prisoner in your Irish bed."

He went back to his chair, sitting with one leg crooked atop the arm. In the firelight the gilt of the Garter at his knee blended in fierce arrogance with his red-gold head—high-set and confident. "Come to me, Hal," he said.

The boy went to him, and he set his hand to his chin and raised it. "We reared you to be Duke of Lancaster," he said. "Now is your heritage much greater. Have you heard men speak of the title, Prince of Wales?"

Henry answered him, "Yes."

"It is a name the realm has lacked these twenty-five years," Derby said. "But your grandfather's brother, the Black Prince, bore it and carried it with honor to his grave. I would have you likewise bear it proudly."

Henry could find no words to answer him. Derby saw him wan and white, as if he ailed. He said at length, "Is all this too great for you? You're wearied from your journey."

Henry hesitated and spoke again. "My father," he said, "what of the—what of Richard?"

Derby frowned and said, "He'll come to no hurt. Go now to your bed."

XV

The day following they journeyed to London, Richard with them. Men could scarce recognize the King. Gowned as a priest, unkempt, silent as the grave, he rode at Derby's side through the land whose kingship he barely held and which had long turned from him.

He had few to call "friend" now.

Almost to the last he might have stayed defeat, but when at last he took ship from Ireland, he had come fearfully, seemingly unnerved to fight. He spent himself, kicking Aumerle's cap across the room, cursing in black fury the realm's perfidy, until those about him saw his mind was bent to yield. Disguised as a priest for greater safety and with but five men, he had abandoned the remnant of his army and yielded himself to his cousin of Lancaster at Flint Castle.

They came to London on the thirtieth of September. The city greeted them, as the rest of the land had done, joyously and with acclaim, the citizens crowding the windows and the streets to look upon them. These marked the great ones eagerly as the horses passed—Derby in splendid garb; his young son dressed in blue and white, the livery of Lancaster, riding with him; Hotspur, for long the land's idol; and Dorset, who bore in his veins proud Gaunt's blood. Richard they greeted with fury. So fierce was the Londoners' hate against him that Derby had encircled the King's horse with a double cordon of soldiers that he might bring him through in safety. With linked arms and linked bows, the escort struggled to bear the King through his city's streets. The people strove to reach him, shrieking "Bastard" as he passed; the apprentices howling that he was no son of the Black Prince, but begotten by the Princess Joan's leman; even the good wives calling for his blood.

Henry heard them with a boy's horror. If they named Richard "Bastard"—he who was their anointed King, direct descendant of the unbroken line of the Plantagenets—what would they one day name Lancaster? He could not bring his eyes to the King. He rode on, pressing close to his father's horse, until Derby spoke to him sharply, bidding him hold up his head and give the people greeting.

Thus they came to the Tower, where five months ago they had embarked—the golden King and the young cousin, his prisoner. The great walls shut out the clamor of the mob, the dusk blackening in quiet shadow St. Thomas's Gate and the arch of the Bell Tower. When Derby had dismounted, the King tried to do likewise. He was much begrimed, the dust thick in his beard and his rough priest's gown deep drenched with sweat at armpits and shoulders. Under the cressets his face gleamed with his running sweat, his golden hair streaked about his temples, so that he looked, in very truth, a man in fear.

As he gained the ground, the hem of his priest's gown caught in his spur. He strove to loosen it but could not, his fingers shaking. Derby and his lords had passed within, and the soldiers stood by watching, no man helping him. The King had before scarce even set apart the fastenings of his coats. He who had always loved finery and the gilt and ceremony of kingship saw himself now deserted by these as by all else.

After a space Henry could bear it no more. He knelt by the King and wrested the material free.

"Thank you, my boy," Richard said. "My prince—I should say."

He set his hand under the boy's chin. Its touch was moist and clay cold as the hand of the dead. "You proud Lancasters," he said. "You proud, stiff-backed Lancasters. To you on the morrow

I sign away my crown, and you think the day will never come when you will want to set your hands to it and hurl it from you."

When Henry drew from him, he stepped closer and spoke in a voice high and whispering. "I liked you well, Henry," he said. "I always liked you. And now what is it that your father has done to you? You could have spent your days in ease in your castles and manors; married some fair Englishwoman; watched your sons grow to manhood; hawked and hunted and named men your friends. And now you will be King. There'll be no man again for your friend. You will never lie of a night save with treachery and guilt as your bedfellows, and when you ride to your pleasures, death will be at your elbow. England has ever hated her Kings above all mortal men. Did I say I were sorry for you, Henry? In truth, my heart could crack wide open for you now."

Henry heard him, desiring only that he might escape from the shadowy dark and this ghostly whisper of a King. He could well have fled, but he held himself from running. The soldiers drew about them to bring the King to his quarters. The boy watched him pass from his sight into the White Tower, walking gropingly as a sick man might walk, the torches agleam on his damp hair.

He was not to see Richard again. From the Tower, after he had set his seal to the articles of abdication, Richard was brought to Pontefract Castle. Within six months the land learned of his death, he having died, it was said, of a wasting fever. Henry was himself too ill to take great note of it. Lancaster's first chill Christmas of kingship had been spent at Eltham, beset with revolt and treason, John Holland, Richard's half brother, raising an army on the captive King's behalf. On Twelfth Night, traditional night of revelry, the uprising began; one of Holland's creatures, at the same time, seeking by poison to rid the land of her new King and his four young sons.

Henry had all but died, and Derby himself had been much stricken. Still sick, he had had to fly to London, his eldest son wrapped in a blanket and borne in Malbon's arms over the frost-bound roads. Once there, Derby had delivered his sons to the

keeping of the city, himself riding out in arms to come to victory
against the rebels.

Richard at the same time had breathed his last in his prison
chamber at Pontefract, many men whispering it had fallen out
opportunely for Lancaster that he should do so. It seemed that
while Richard lived those who now bore his kingship would not
know safety; but his death brought small ease to Lancaster.

Soon it was to them as if they would not escape his ghost.

BOOK II

THE
AZURE LION

"The cognizance of the Percies was an

azure lion, rampant."

Richard had been in his grave a year when Henry left Oxford to ride northward to Chester. He had studied close on ten months at Oxford; much loving it, for it seemed to him no one troubled here whether he were prince or no. He had been as his fellows, his days filled with sport and learning, and Oxford herself too withdrawn, too busied about her tasks, to heed the troubles that beset the realm.

Malbon rode with him, and he asked him when he might return. "I hope it will be soon," he said. "Does my father want me long away?"

"I know not, my lord," Malbon said. "It is these troubles in Wales. Since it is your own principality, the King, your father, would have you there."

They came by nightfall the next day to Chester Castle, where eighteen months ago Henry had ridden out in Richard's company. The King already lodged at Chester where he had come four weeks ago. There was much trouble now in the west—all Wales in arms against England, at their head that strange man of Sycharth, Owen Glendower, who had well learned to entwine his own wrongs with those of his land. No man believed he would be quickly quelled. Derby had brought Harry Percy from the north, thereby setting against Glendower him whom all men reckoned the fiercest and finest fighter of the realm.

The King gave his son good greeting. He was graver-faced; the energy which had clothed him as Henry of Derby muted as if he knew now what it was to be sometimes weary. They had but a night together, for the King planned to return to London on the

morrow. When he was about to take his journey next day, Percy
came into the Great Hall to bid him farewell. He was as Henry
had first seen him in this same castle eighteen months back—high
complexioned, moustached, handsome, his glance swift and keen
as a lance thrust.

He made to kneel, but Derby raised him, his face lightening as
if the sight of Percy gave him pleasure. "What need of that?" he
said. "I would have Harry Hotspur my friend."

For a while they spoke together, then Derby turned to take
leave of his son. "I go now, Hal," he said. "I have set Sir Hugh le
Despenser over you to be your governor. In all things you are to
obey him as you would me. Lord Percy, yonder, is likewise to
have you in his command." To Percy he said, "I would have my
son taught to war, and I have brought him to the finest soldier in
the realm that he may learn of him."

Percy smiled, not turning aside the compliment. "God wi' your
grace," he said. "We'll teach him well."

When after Derby and his lords and servants had ridden from
the court and they were alone, he gave Henry his strange smile,
warming and deprecating.

"Harry, eh?" he said. "I hae a Harry likewise—a fine, canny
lad, just your age. I left him wi' his mother, flying his merlin, as I
doubt not, in the pastures of Alnwick." He spoke then in jest.
"There's too many to bear this name," he said. "Look at we
twain—Harry Plantagenet and Harry Percy. What's to be done
about it? We canna both be Harry."

The boy answered him shyly, liking him well. "My mother
oftentimes called me Hal."

"Did she for aye?" Percy said. "Then will it be Hal."

He spoke in robust and cheerful fashion, his speech twisted by
an impediment of tongue and given charm by it. His own shire,
Northumberland, mimicked this speech, and even London sought
to copy it, not in mockery, but out of compliment, for Percy was
much idolized. He knew it well and took it all carelessly.

After a space he said, "Do you know aught of yonder Welsh hellion, Glendower?"

Henry answered him, "Only that he has fired all Wales. We had many Welsh students at Oxford, yet none returned to us for the Lenten studies. All men believed they had gone back to Wales to bear arms for Glendower."

"Aye?" Percy said. "Better for them had they rested wi' their books." He spoke then of Oxford. "How liked you it?"

"I liked it well," Henry said. "I hope I may soon go back."

Percy smiled and spoke grimly. "I hae somewhat to teach you first," he said. "Something of a sort you didna learn at Oxford."

II

When April came, Percy marched into the Dee Valley, seeking the Welshmen, who, at his coming, melted into the hills as though into the very earth. Even the weather fought for Glendower, wind and rain beating against the attackers. The men of Northumberland had no care of it, but the men of Shropshire and Hereford, themselves half-Welsh, knew of the tales that Glendower had a sorcerer's power and fought by magic, commanding foul or fair weather. They were in much fear of him as an adversary, and Percy doubted their will to fight.

Percy brought the prince with him on this march. Le Despenser had set his face against it, desiring to keep him at Chester, but Percy would not have it so. The boy saw war now, such as he had not known in Ireland, and knew fear.

On the night they neared Flint, their guides three times failed them in the dark and the drenching rain. Glendower's hidden bowmen were always at hand to harry all their steps, and they sought shelter from them among the rocks. Henry saw the man who stood with him taken with an arrow between the shoulders. He was straightway slain, but he gave one high yelp as a dog that is trodden on in the dark, his blood spattering all the boulder where the prince clung. Henry held to it as if he would never leave go. When Percy came to him, he had to loosen his arms from round it.

He was gentle now, dealing with the boy tenderly and contriving to stay close to him. "Come, now," he said, "we'll soon gain our shelter at Flint. It isna sae far."

They had a march of yet two hours over stones and wet bracken. The boy was spent, sodden with the rain and shaking. When they drew near Flint and it was safe to ride, Percy set him on his own horse, walking beside him.

"You find it harsh now," he said. "Yet aal things soften by custom."

"No," Henry said. "I cannot watch all these things and keep my valor. I'm not like you."

"You think I was ne'er stark afeared," Percy said. "When I first came to battle I was your age—I was but fourteen. In truth, I was sae stiff wi' fear I knew not how to lift my sword arm. It was as if my blade went thrusting of itself."

Henry strove to smile and said, "It must have been Excalibur."

"Nay," Percy said. "Yet I had such good employment that day I forgot to fear." He began to speak of it reminiscently. "It was a real battle," he said. "Not such as this. The Scots sae drove upon us that they broke through at the inner wall. The Bloody Gap we named it, and sae men call it still in Alnwick. Yet there's nae fighter like a Northumbrian. My father had a squire—him whom they called Witherington. Aal the forenoon he fought alongside wi' me until both his legs were smitten off; then did he raise himself and fought upon the stumps. Thus we came to victory."

After a space Henry said, "Yet, are you never afraid?"

"Nay, no more," Percy said. "And to tell true, I think I hae nae need to fear where I stand now. There was a wise woman once in Alnwick. She it was who told me I would lie for my last night's sleep in Berwick—and she was a very wise woman and much sought to. I think well she spoke true, and I'll die in fight wi' the Scots. And if I do I hae small care of it."

He set his head back in the rain and began to sing in lusty fashion.

> Oh, when that ye hear me gie a loud, loud cry,
>   The broom blooms bonny and says it is fair.
> Shoot an arrow frae thy bow and there let me lie,
>   And we'll never gang down to the broom ony mair.
>
> And when that ye see I am lying cauld and dead,
>   The broom blooms bonny and says it is fair.
> Then ye'll put me in a grave wi' a turf at my head,
>   And we'll never gang down to the broom ony mair.

They came to Chester the next day. After le Despenser had Henry go straightway to his bed, he went into the chamber where Percy sat at his wine.

"My lord," he said, after a little, "the prince is but a boy. Will you not take pity on him?"

"Tch," Percy said. "It's naught that befell him. I knew what it was to wipe Scots' blood off my blade when I was fourteen."

Le Despenser answered him in dry fashion, "We are not all Percies."

"Afore God," Percy said, "this isna to Lancaster as a May morning Morris dance. There are many ready enough to claw the crown off their heads and to claw it off in blood. Think you there is another way for them save the way I am teaching the boy?" He set down his wine and sat brooding, staring at the coals of the fire. "Aal our fortunes are bound wi' them," he said. "Percy set the crown on Lancaster's head, and thus it rests, do I myself hae to hold it there wi' my own hands."

III

Percy, when he sat at meat with the prince, often set him questions of sieges, arranging the saltcellar and the knives in pattern on the board. "Here stands your castle," he would say. "Your river runs alongside—sae—and here a cliff. Tell me, now, where you would draw up your siege lines about her."

Other times he would engage him in mock combat with the broadsword, showing him of his skill, while the pages hung about the stairs to watch them and applaud. All that he did he did hugely, gaining the boy's heart as he had long since gained England's. The land loved him well, for he had delivered her from invasion and conquest; Charles of France, fourteen years ago, having sought to destroy her, to burn her towns and sell all—both men and women—into slavery. When Percy was named in the London taverns, men still grinned their pride of him, dubbing him "Hotspur." None had his horsemanship nor his craft of battle. He was as skilled with the bow as with the sword; versed in state and chivalry; a huntsman and a falconer, no man matching his vast and gusting courage. He fast set his enchantment upon the boy as he did on all. It seemed to Henry he had not before met Hotspur's like, seeing him as the land saw him with a name as potent as magic.

There was a tennis court at Chester, newly built. Percy was as skilled in the game as he was in all else, and Henry much desired to play with him. He spoke of it on the sixth day of their return from Flint.

"Harry," he said, "will you not give me a match this noon?"

"Nay," Percy said. "I dinna play for naught."

The prince had lately been given a fine roan stallion, Lygard, which was dear to him and which Percy much admired. He offered to set the horse for a forfeit.

"I'll play you for Lygard," he said. "He is yours if you win. If I win I'll name your battle gauntlets."

"I'll match you straight, mind," Percy said. "And when I win, keep your bargain."

Henry said, "There's my hand on it."

Percy grinned and said, "Were I you I wouldna hae provoked this match."

He summoned the pages and bade them take the rackets to the

court. The rackets were short, thick covered with parchment; and the court itself was all enclosed, its net fashioned in cords of blue silk. When it became known Percy played, many crowded the main wall behind the tambour, eager for the game.

Percy loosed his surcoat, but did not trouble to take it off. He began in careless fashion, seeking to play well within himself. After a while when he saw he was held, he pressed harder. Henry could not match the strength of his drives nor the spin he set upon the ball.

When Percy had gained the first set and they stood for a moment, each at his own side, to rest, Stafford leaned from his chair to speak with Henry. "My lord prince," he said, "he has you as you are now. Fortune your arm, and feed him with the volley."

Henry saw that he spoke true. When they fell to play again, he struck boldly for the grille and the winning gallery. Percy found he could lay few good chases, and his strokes began to fall short. The play was fierce and very skilled, so that the pages grew loud in their excitement.

Presently Stafford saw Sir William Blunt by the door and called to him. "Come and watch this," he said. "You never saw a game its like."

Blunt came and sat with him. "In truth," he said, "I think that he has Percy troubled."

Percy at last took off his surcoat and tossed it to one side. He began to fear he was to be shamed by a boy, and his face was dark. The last set was waged as grimly as if it were battle. At length le Despenser spoke with Percy.

"Will you not rest at least ten minutes," he said. "The prince is near dropping."

Percy answered him angrily, "Not unless he would hae it that I win by default."

When they fell to again, Percy drove to within eighteen inches of the dedans wall. This was named the perfect chase, for no other stroke on the floor could beat it. Henry could hope only to equal it. He drove hard at Percy's feet and seemed to do so.

The page, who marked that side of the court, screamed in high voice, "Chase off," and added the score in much excitement, "Thirty and five to the lord prince. To the Lord Percy but love."

Percy glared upon him. "Are you stricken blind?" he said. "It fell a chase short."

The page answered stammering, "In truth, my lord, I thought it fell true."

"It did not," Percy said. "It's the shadow from the cressets that move yonder upon the floor."

The boy said, mumbling, "It may have been, my lord."

Henry was spent now almost to failing. When Percy saw it he moved to the kill, raking the court with fierce shots from side to side. It was not long to be withstood and at length he came to victory.

When the prince came up the court, Percy set an arm about his shoulders. He was equitable again and gave him good praise.

"Never was I sae hard-pressed," he said. "You near drew my teeth."

Henry smiled and said, "I did not really think I could beat you." He spoke of Lygard. "My groom will set him in your stall on the morrow," he said, "if I may ride him but once more, before breaking fast."

"Aye," Percy said. "That's good enough, but see he comes to my stall after."

When the prince had gone, Stafford and Sir Hugh le Despenser came up. Percy wiped his face and took wine from one of the pages. He looked sweat drenched and much blown.

"He did battle with you to the last," le Despenser said. "You surely cannot mean to take his horse?"

"Why not?" Percy said. "'Tis a good horse."

IV

Once again while the summer held Percy marched out against Glendower. He was in ill humor, for the King sent him little money. He grumbled now that he was forced to pay the soldiers from his own pocket. Each day he came to Henry seeking the prince's jewels or plate that he might pawn them. Henry had given him all that he had—his rings, the ouches and jeweled girdles, the daggers pricked out in the hilts with rubies.

Percy took them with much complaint. "Does your father think we can feed an army from air?" he said. "We canna fight Glendower wi' naught."

He was constant at Henry's side when they ventured again into the Welsh valleys, wary for his safety, and oftentimes tender; yet he determined to teach him war. He set the boy now with a company of archers under him to command. On the fifth day of their march Glendower's bowmen loosed upon them from behind the crags, and they fell to skirmishing. One of the Welshmen was struck and fell some twenty feet from the boulders. Henry saw him lying in his own blood in the rain and striving to move, like a broken-backed insect. He would have sent his own men to bring him up that he might be tended, but when they gained the lower slopes Glendower's bowmen took aim upon them and drove them back.

When they came presently to their night's lodging, Percy came to him. He was much angered and spoke loudly. "It was a mad trick," he said. "Why did you send your men seeking that Welsh hellion?"

Henry answered him, "He was sore hurt. He was bleeding near to death."

"What of that?" Percy said. "He was one of Glendower's flea-bitten knaves. He was your foe."

Henry was spent and fret from the day's toil. He answered Percy, matching his own anger. "Oh, let me be," he said. "I never sought to come here. I was content at Oxford."

"Your father brought you here," Percy said, "that you might learn your way."

The boy answered him in a low voice, "Am I never to know peace?"

"Peace," Percy said. "You will be King. You'll know nae peace until you lie in your tomb."

Henry said, "But I could not leave him. He was Welsh. I was born among such as he."

"Learn this," Percy said. "Your own men come first. Why think you my Northumberland lads follow wheresoever I lead? Because they know if two lie smitten in the heather and one is left it willna be he wi' the lion badge on his shoulder. Your heart may bleed for the enemy, but see that your soldiers do not."

After a space Henry answered him. "You are right," he said. "I am sorry. I should not have done so."

Percy looked upon him and smiled. "One of these days we'll make of you a canny fighter," he said. "Say then that Harry Percy taught you."

V

The King himself took command at the end of the summer against Glendower, but with small success. From the north like-wise came many threatenings. Percy's own Castle of Wark had fallen to the Douglas, and in September he hastened back to retrieve it.

Derby rode again to London, taking his son with him. Few cried for Lancaster as they passed through the streets. Everywhere disappointment lay grayly on the land; even Richard now seem-ingly mourned. Yet before October was out the bells were set ringing again. Hotspur had swept the Scots from Wark, from Ber-wick and from Bamburgh. At Homildon Hill he had crushed their full might, taking as prisoner the Douglas himself.

Henry could well see Percy in imagination in battle at Homil-don. In his boy's worship of Hotspur, it seemed to him Percy had by himself come to victory there while his whole army had done no more than watch. His brothers well knew how it was with him. Tom mocked him, mimicking Percy's speech. They quarreled as they had done in their earlier childhood, coming to blows over Percy's name. Tom was thirteen now, not so tall as his brother but sturdier and broad shouldered. Neither he nor John nor Humphrey bore the title "prince"; but Henry only. It irked Tom that he should be no more than Lord Thomas of Lancaster.

Six weeks after Homildon, when Henry was in the gardens of Westminster, Humphrey came to him. He was but eleven, slender and brown eyed, thin faced, with a look that promised adult cleverness.

"Have you heard?" he said. "We are to have a new mother. She is widow to the Duke of Brittany—the Lady Joanna of Navarre."

Henry said, "It's not true."

"For sure it is," Humphrey said. "Father met with her when he was banished. The old Duke was alive then, and they were both hospitable to him."

Henry spoke no more of it. He went to his own chamber and cast himself on the settle by the window. It was eight years since his mother had died. Eight summers and nine winters for the Monmouth trees to leaf and fall, for Richard to die and Richard's realm to pass to Lancaster; and she had seen none of it. Her part in all that had befallen Lancaster had been under the stones of Leicester church. When February came, Derby rode to meet his new bride, bringing her to Winchester, there to wed with her, quietly and with no pomp. The realm was enfeebled and poor, and the King hoped by this match to gain alliances with Brittany, Navarre and Castile.

Joanna had brought two of her daughters with her, but she had had to leave her sons, with small hope of seeing them again. This had been much grief to her. She loved her sons with a fierce possession, holding them above any, so that none other's children seemed to her to approach them. She wept when she spoke of them to Derby. His own sons awaited her in London. He brought her to them the day following their wedding, as sleet and snow whipped the city and few stood in the streets to greet them. Jo-

anna was much disappointed in the land, finding it chill and
sullen, its pomp and chivalry crippled. Her wedding also had been
a poor thing to her, lacking all splendor.

The boys awaited their stepmother in the Painted Chamber.
She came at last on their father's arm, clothed in cloth-of-gold,
herself black eyed, stoutish and sallow skinned. She had suffered
much from the seas, which had tossed her fiercely five days, and
her face still bore the greenish tinge of her sickness. Derby spoke
with her in French, for she had no English. "These are my pup-
pies, sweet," he said. "Bear with them. They are unruly boys.
They well need a mother again."

He beckoned his sons, and they came forward. They were well
favored, for they had their mother's beauty, but in all else they
seemed to Joanna to fall far short of her own sons. She looked on
them, accounting Henry sullen and unbiddable, the other three
only a whit less so.

She kissed them all briefly. Only when a servant came, bearing a
tray set with wine and comfits and sugared fruits did her face
lighten. She had fasted since her sickness, and she ate heartily,
her jaw moving as to a measure against her silken barbette. Lady
Hereford sat with her, giving kind welcome to her who now
walked in her dead daughter's shoes. Joanna talked of the ten new
gowns she had brought with her from Brittany and never yet worn.
When she had done eating, she took her leave straightway to try
them on.

After she had gone, Henry asked his grandmother when she was
to be crowned Queen.

"In two weeks' time," Lady Hereford said. "We must seek to
make her welcome in this bleak, raw land of ours."

When he did not answer, she spoke again. "Aye," she said, "I
know how it is. You would have had your mother go to this hallowing. But God wills all as is best, Hal. What your father does,
he does for the realm's weal."

"But to take her after my mother," Henry said. "I know not
how he could."

VI

When April came, Henry returned to the Western Marches. He went gladly, eager for Percy's company. Westminster was to him as a foreign household now, Joanna being served by Breton ladies and gentlemen and seeming to lack interest in all things save new gowns and new hoods.

Percy was still in the north, but his father, the Earl of Northumberland, and his father's brother, Lord Thomas Percy, lodged now in the Castle of Shrewsbury. They were at meat when the prince came to them. Northumberland gave him fulsome greeting, turning his blackened grin upon him and bidding the servants set a place for him. Henry had small liking for him, for behind his constant smile it was as if the mind ever groped for a fresh compliment. Northumberland's brother, Lord Thomas, who sat with him, was much different, a cold, alert man, with eyes as hooded as a hawk's. He was governor to the prince now, Sir Hugh le Despenser having set aside the task.

Northumberland would have all news from London. He was broader in speech even than Percy, greatly active for his years but given to extremes. His jewels were many, but the vast houppelande he wore was much frayed, the dyed miniver of the collar worn almost to nothing. He ate ravenously, spreading butter on his bread with his thumb and using his jeweled knife only to slice it. Against the woven dorser at his back, agleam in its gold and silver threads, he sat stooped above the board like a carnivorous spider.

Malbon served them, bearing on his hand a gold and ruby ring Henry had given him. Northumberland recognized it and began to speak of the gift. "It lifts my heart ti see ye generous," he said. "For 'tis a marvelous thankless world. Yet I can see Lancaster willna forget them that brought them ti the crown." He set his fingers on Henry's arm. "A crown's a bonny heritage," he said. "Ye'll well kna it one day. And I kna ye ti be generous and a guid lad."

It seemed to Henry he spoke much as an old woman might ogle a maid on her marriage eve. He fell to confusion, not knowing what to answer.

Percy rode from the north three weeks later, coming straightway to Henry's chamber. He was in mighty spirits and gave him warm and boisterous greeting. "How now, Harry," he said. "Still here to plague me, you whoreson Monmouth puppy?"

Henry mocked him in return but with delight. "How now, Harry," he said. "How goes it, you old foul-mouthed Border bear?"

"Tch," Percy said. "Well enough. There's nae a Scot south of the Tweed, save those that rest prisoner to me at Alnwick, awaiting ransom." He began to speak in disparaging fashion of the Welsh wars. "I'll make an end quickly here now," he said. "If the Douglas canna wi'stand Hotspur, we'll hae small fight from Glendower and his coward Welsh."

"They are not coward," Henry said. "I hope Glendower clips your ears for you."

"What?" Percy said. "Did I not know you'd go caterwauling to your father I would clip yours and wi' a will."

"Try to do it," Henry said. "May I drop dead—may worms eat me—if I say one word to my father."

"Right then," Percy said. "You are pledged, mind."

They fell to wrestling, noisily and with laughter. Percy bore Henry back upon the settle, bidding him yield. "Ask pardon," he said. "I'll grant it. I were ever merciful."

"I'd not ask pardon of you," Henry said. "Border ruffian that you are."

"By my faith," Percy said, "nae man spoke wi' me thus."

He dealt with Henry as he had said, but in play, doing him small hurt. After a little he broke into his huge laugh. "Enough of your fooling," he said. "I know well you are glad to see me. Besides I'm athirst."

He set straight his coat-hardie and shouted for wine. When it came, he set one of the silver cups into Henry's hands, Malbon watching with disfavor. "Dinna look black at me," Percy said. "The boy isna too young to know the taste of malmsey."

When they were alone, he sat by Henry on the settle. For all his fooling his lizard's glance had missed nothing. "You were looking black also," he said. "Is your mother no Guinivere? Away wi' ye, Hal. The woman isna born who was yet worth a sour face on an April evening."

He shouted, and his squire, Raoul Harcourt, came in bearing a white-haired puppy. Percy set it into Henry's arms. "Bred is he from the finest strain in Northumberland," he said. "He'll gie you good company."

Henry thanked him with delight. He asked what he should name the puppy.

"He's named Rafe of Bamburgh," Percy said. "After my brother-in-law, the Earl Westmorland. They tear their meat alike."

He began to speak then of the battle of Homildon, talking as with an equal. That Percy should talk so to him seemed to the boy good compliment. He said, "I know not how you did it."

"It were a hard fight," Percy said. "They were well served wi' their bowmen and their French lances."

"Frenchmen?" Henry said. "But we are at truce with them."

"What's a truce to them?" Percy said. "It were a time of truce likewise when yonder mad King of France planned his conquest of England. You canna recall it, you're too young; but had I and my northern knights na set our sails for Brest and mangled their fleet as it lay awaiting the winds, they would hae been on us. We served them sae hardly they couldna make good the damage afore winter, and the next spring the French King's wits had gone, and aal his dreams of conquest were set aside."

Henry said in shy fashion, "Indeed, I know not how England would fare without you."

The compliment well pleased Percy. He waved a hand but did not repudiate it. "She called me Hotspur for it, and well might she need these hot northern spurs of mine again. The French King's dream is but set aside. Let him gain his wits or Orléans or the Dauphin power enough, and I doubt not they'll be upon us again wi' their mighty ships and their full chivalry. But your father still has a Percy to cry 'Espérance,' eh, Hal? Still a Hotspur to clip their wings for them?"

He broke into his great laugh. Though he had well drunk, the wine seemed not to have touched him, but Henry was close to sleep. He said, "I think you would never fail us."

"Not I," Percy said. "As much would I do again. Then when I ride back to Alnwick the stone lions on the bridge across the Aln will mayhap remember they are Percy and roar for me."

The curtain stirred across the door, and Lord Thomas Percy came in with Northumberland. As Percy made to rise, his father laid bejeweled and grimed fingers on his shoulder with affection and bent to kiss him.

"God greet ye, my son," he said. He turned his blackened smile on Henry. "The prince will gie us leave ti speak tigether," he said. "Yet good it is ti seek each other's company. Is it na' Harry ti Harry, in truth?"

Percy turned to look upon his uncle. Lord Thomas met his eyes with a long glance. "Welcome, nephew," he said. "You were but an hour ahead of the messengers riding from London. Their tidings were for you."

Percy answered him slowly. "Oh aye," he said. "What would they."

"They rode from the King," Lord Thomas said. "King Lancaster."

He spoke as if he had no care for the prince in the room. Northumberland checked him in agitated voice, his hands moving above Henry's sunken head. "Peace, brother, peace," he said. "The de'il take these rough, hard northern tongues of ours."

Lord Thomas gave him shrugging answer. Percy set an arm about Henry and raised him. "Away wi' ye, Hal," he said in a mild voice. "I've set you in your cups, and there'll be naught but black looks from that serving man of yours tomorrow. Come, get you to your bed."

Henry gained his feet, staggering. At the door he turned to bid them good night. They, all three, were watching him; Percy, unblinking, his head sunk; Northumberland bearing his fixed ghoul's grin; Lord Thomas, hooded-eyed as a hawk. The firelight was alick against their still figures. For a moment it was with the boy as if the old strain of his wary Norman blood stirred in him; but he knew himself dazed with the wine, his brain quick to fancy, and he set the thought aside.

He bade them good night and went, the puppy following. When they were alone and the door shut upon them, Percy spoke in a still voice. "Eh, now?" he said. "My father, and you, my uncle, what would you hae me know?"

"Nephew," Lord Thomas said, "what of the prisoners—the Scotsmen taken at Homildon?"

"They lie still at Alnwick," Percy said. "You know it for yourself."

Lord Thomas said, "Their ransoms are not yet paid?"

"Nay, na' yet," Percy said. "They canna raise these sums in a day. Yet they'll pay, never doubt it."

"They'll pay, doubtless," Lord Thomas said. "But not to us."

Percy asked him what he meant, speaking slow.

"The King sends to claim them," Lord Thomas said. "The Douglas, Orkney, Angus, Moray, Stewart—any man of rank taken at Homildon. All are to be dispatched to him without delay. He holds they are no private prisoners, but the prisoners of the realm, taken as by his arms."

Percy sat with the wine cup at his lips. After a space he drank unhurriedly and set it down. He made no answer.

Northumberland broke in, in querulous voice. "It is their ransoms that he seeks," he said. "He would line his coffers wi' the gold our blood and our valor hae purchased."

"I'll speak wi' him," Percy said. "I'll take horse this night for London."

"As well spare yourself the toil," Lord Thomas said. "This brooks no argument. Here is his letter. Read his words. He bids you do it, reckoning even delay as treason. Think you we have not ourselves sent back argument before this?"

"This is his gratitude," Northumberland said. "Was it na' we ourselves that set the crown on his head? It was the name 'Hotspur' that roused the land ti him. 'Hotspur is ridden ti the Duke of Derby,' sae they cried, aal the length of the realm, and sae they followed. Eh, my son, if you hadna set the magic of your name about him, the kingdom would still be Richard's."

"Aye, you speak true," Hotspur said. He rose and went to the casement, staring from it. "Afore God," he said, "does he think he can use me thus? It wasna for this that I knelt to him at Ravenspur."

VII

Percy sent word to Glendower that same night, desiring to meet with him. The place of tryst was set beyond Westbury, at the foot of the Long Mountain; and Percy rode for it four nights following, Lord Thomas with him. Raoul Harcourt likewise rode with them and one groom, no man else.

Gwenllian Glendower, the youngest of Glendower's daughters born in wedlock, met with them. She gave Percy calm greeting, standing among her father's bowmen, under the tossing light of the cressets. She was but eighteen, her hair bound up in a coif of dark silk, and with a dagger at her belt, as the great ladies in London might carry their jeweled and scalloped daggers; though this were plainly fashioned.

She brought them to an almshouse set aslant the hillside among trees. Glendower came presently, with him his treasurer, Griffiths ap Vaughan, and the Lord de Maupassant. This man commanded the force Charles of France had sent to further Glendower's cause, setting aside his truce with England thereby. Against their finery Glendower was garbed as a peasant, his face ridged and darkened by hard weather. Almost did he seem an Old Testament prophet, a man who might well have lived off locusts and wild honey. Yet he knew how to take his pleasure where he might find it, so that the English mocked that the valleys were peopled by his bastards.

He gave Percy good welcome. "Glad am I to greet you," he said. "We have been enemies, yet I think we shall lose no honor if we clasp hands and come to treaty this night." There were chairs set, and he pointed to them. "Come, now," he said, "sit you by there. Let us see what scheme we can compound to set the Molewarp by the ears."

"Molewarp?" Percy said.

Gwenllian gave him answer. "It is what we in Wales call him," she said. "Henry of Derby, King of England. The Molewarp he is, accursed of God's own mouth. Merlin spoke of him so in a prophecy."

Glendower brought forward Griffiths ap Vaughan and de Maupassant. When Percy saw that he dealt with a Frenchman, his face darkened. He drew Glendower aside and spoke with him.

"This can we do for ourselves," he said. "What need hae we for yon knight of France? Such as he hae dealt us too many scars."

Glendower answered him it would be as he wished. He sent both de Maupassant and Griffiths ap Vaughan from him. Only Gwenllian remained, seated on a cushion, her head against her father's knees.

Glendower spoke first of Richard. "Is it that he yet lives?" he said. "Many say he escaped from Pontefract and fled to Scotland."

"This fellow in Scotland isna Richard," Percy said. "He is a little clerk having a likeness to Richard, and feeble witted. The Scots know him for a mummer, yet from policy they keep him at his tricks."

Glendower said, "When then of Richard?"

"He never left Pontefract save in his coffin," Lord Thomas said. "That we know."

"At Flint was I body squire to Richard," Glendower said. He smiled and said, "He was an Englishman, lords, and I know not that I shed tears for him. But if Wales were mine, I had as liefer see England Richard's or his heirs, than the usurper Lancaster's."

Lord Thomas answered him, "It will not long be Lancaster's."

"So do I trust," Glendower said. "Yet more is there to this task than the deposing of Richard. Richard was childless. Four sons has this man."

"They are but boys," Percy said. "They canna do aught."

"What of the eldest?" Glendower said. "He that you have left this night in Shrewsbury?"

"Still but a lad," Percy said. "A stripling. He likes me well. He'll gie us nae trouble."

"God save us, nephew," Lord Thomas said bleakly. "I am his governor and I read him very differently. If you think he will kiss hands and come curtsying at your heels like a maid, after we have laid his father's bones in the earth, you are much mistaken."

"What think you then, my lord?" Glendower asked.

Lord Thomas shrugged and said, "I think he will never leave our throats."

Percy spoke in angry voice, his face dark. "I say he wil'na trouble us," he said. "I'll be answerable for him. I'll bear him wi' me back to Alnwick."

It was as if the talk lay sour in his mouth. Lord Thomas saw him angered and sought to placate him. "We'll not use our swords against boys," he said. "Take him to Alnwick that he might learn manners from you. Make him page to your boy."

As they talked, Glendower had set maps upon the table, pinning them with his dagger. He was eager to take what men he had and march straightway upon Shrewsbury. Percy would not have it, for he believed Shrewsbury strong and well able to withstand a siege. "My way is surer," he said. "I and my father will go back to Alnwick. Gie us some eight weeks, and we will hae ten thousand men marching south under the Percy lion. Likewise will we hae the allegiance of the Douglas."

"Yet were we to gain Shrewsbury now," Glendower said, "it would be to gain the Molewarp's son."

"It would not avail us," Lord Thomas said. "It did not halt his father when Richard held the boy hostage in Ireland." He spoke yawningly. "Why should it?" he said. "He has yet three more sons to style Prince of Wales."

Gwenllian stirred on the cushion and spoke bitterly. "Prince of Wales," she said. "Henry, Prince of Wales. Owen, Prince of Wales." She looked upon her father. "You it is," she said. "Of you was it not written that a prince should come out of Wales, bearing his people's honor upon him? The Brut said it."

Percy had no liking for talk of portents. He said to prick them, "The boy is likewise Welsh born."

She turned a white and angry face upon him. "Look you, my lord, men speak still of the night my father was born. Tell you, they will, that on that night all the horses in the stables of Glendowery were found standing up to their fetlocks in blood. And across the mountains of Berwyn the goatherds saw a comet, great and yellow it was, with a tail of fire."

They could speak but little longer, for the hour grew late. When they were about to go, Percy took leave of Glendower. "I canna come again," he said. "But I'll send men to you. You can well trust them."

"Bid them come to the abbot's house in Bangor," Glendower said. "Good greeting will I give them."

VIII

The day following, Percy came to Henry's chamber to speak with him.

"Tomorrow I ride from you," he said. "I and my father journey to London and from thence to Alnwick."

Henry heard him with dismay. "I wish you did not," he said. "When will you be back?"

"July," Percy said carelessly. He set his hand on the book Henry read, his face darkening. *Sir Gawaine and the Green*

Knight," he said. "By the Mass, why do you fill your head wi' these witless vaporings?"

"Witless?" Henry said. "They are Geoffrey of Monmouth's tales of Arthur."

"Your little monkish chronicler," Percy said, "he would hae aal his knights stainless and aal his women faithful." He put the book from him angrily. "Mark what I tell you," he said, "the world's much otherwise."

He went from them the next day. The prince heard the horses below in the courtyard while he was still abed. It seemed to him a strange thing Percy should go from him without a farewell. He went to the casement, half-dressed, with Rafe of Bamburgh in his arms, and leaned from it to wave.

Northumberland bowed in the saddle as in obeisance, so low that his great sleeves all but brushed the ground, his marionette's grin jerking to his face. Percy did not look up, making pretense that he saw nothing. He set Lygard's head toward the gates. His great shoulders, Northumberland's sparse graying locks, the blue and gold of the trappings, bearing the azure lion upon them, were soon hid from view among the curtaining trees.

IX

Percy sought to plead with the King, but had come to violence. In rage he had almost spoken his intent; yet he had played his part well, making good pretense, when he was cooler, of setting all aright. When he had reached his own castles, he sought to lure the King and his armies from the West, begging his help against the Scot. Now Derby marched to him, suspecting nothing.

Northumberland was stricken with ague and in his bed, but Percy dared not wait. He rested now at Alnwick. The castle was fair, sternly and nobly built with a great barbican set against the north. There were mock figures on the battlements; one drinking from a bottle, one winding his crossbow, another shielding his eyes from the glare. So lifelike were they that oftentimes the Scots had thought the garrison greater than it was. Beyond the walls was pasture land, quiet set with drowsing cattle, and the little Aln flowed pure and still between its banks.

Percy had marshaled his army here on the green slopes, their banners and their arms brave in the sun. The Douglas himself sat his horse in the castle court—a proud-lipped, sardonic man, bearing the armor that had been six times pierced at Homildon Hill. His left eye had been stricken from him in an earlier fight, and the socket looked out from under his helm, raw and naked. He marched willingly now with his enemies that he might strike against the King of England, but he had made hard terms. Percy was pledged to send his own son into Scotland as hostage for all he promised.

Percy came out into the court with his arm about the boy's shoulders. His wife, Elizabeth, followed, weeping. She was a Mortimer and thus one step nearer the throne than the House of Lancaster. Percy loved her well and faithfully, but for the mincings of love he had no time.

"What a farewell to gie me," he said, as she set her hand to hold his stirrup. "Come, sweet, smile on me."

"Nay, do not go," she said. "I love you, Harry. I fear for you."

He answered her with a good patience. "There's naught in this for tears. On the day when we set our seals alongside Mortimer's and Glendower's on our treaties, mayhap you'll awake to find you mothered a King of England."

She said in a low voice, "Can you use Henry of Derby as you used Richard?"

Percy answered grimly, "Aye, and wi' as much ease." He bent from the saddle and kissed her damp cheek. "Two weeks, sweet, and it will be a rich man who'll come riding back to ye."

"Mair than a rich man, lady," the Douglas said. "Your guid lord will hae half England in his pocket when he returns."

Young Harry Percy—Percy's son—spoke eagerly. "Will it be ours?" he said. "We'll rule it?"

Hotspur looked at him with affection. "Aal six counties north of the Trent—aal will be Percy. When you come back from Scotland you'll ride in here a prince of the realm." He clapped a hand on his son's shoulder. "What say you to that, Harry lad? A prince. I shall hae to teach you aal my skill now. We'll hae plenty of days together, you and I, wi' lances in our hands and horses between our knees and the butts to shoot at of an evening."

"Aye, aye," the Douglas said. "Your father has guid knowledge o' the schooling o' princes."

Percy looked at him without answer. He set his horse's head toward the gates, his face darkened. Young Harry kept pace with him, talking the while. "You'll bring back the prince?" he said. "My lord grandfather says he is to be page to me. I'll not use him ill, but he must obey me. I'll have his shield, will I not? The one with the Black Prince's three plumes?"

"Aye, maybe," Percy said, but shortly. He seemed eager to go. As he and the Douglas rode forward, Northumberland came to his casement window, in a gilded bedrobe, to wave. They saw the glint of his rings in the July sunshine.

"You'll bring back the King's armor?" young Harry shouted after them. "And the prince's shield that I might bear it?"

x

Lord Thomas Percy still remained at Shrewsbury with the prince. He sought by doing so to allay doubts, but as yet no man suspected. Percy, the stainless knight, the land's legend, the lion of the North, was set by all to be above treason.

Lord Thomas had small resemblance to either his brother or his nephew, lacking all tang of the Border. He well filled his days with hawking and his nights with drinking, though wine did not touch his senses. Henry saw him seldom. On the tenth of July he rode out, to hawk, as it was supposed, but without returning. No man troubled until it was found that the falcons were hooded and still in the mews. Then was it discovered that Lord Thomas, his groom, his body servant, his four squires, and their servingmen were all gone from the castle.

Henry had with him two more of his father's lords, Lord Stafford, who was his father's cousin by marriage, and the West Countryman, Gilbert, Lord Talbot of Shrewsbury. Neither could give reason for Lord Thomas's going. They sat with Henry, in talk over it, until, when it was near dusk, one of the Chester aldermen rode into the castle court. His horse was lathered and much blown. When he came to the prince's chamber, he spoke in halting voice that a great body of men were afoot the near side of Preston, an army, it was judged, of some twelve thousand souls.

Talbot asked the device of their chivalry.

The man said in a frightened voice. "It was the White Hart—King Richard's banner."

Talbot sent him from them. For a space he sat silent, then he broke out as if for anger he would have laughed. "We have no more wits than babes," he said. "Our peerless Northern knight, our Hotspur, brews treason under our noses and we do not even smell it."

Henry swung upon him with a boy's rage. He said, whispering, "How dare you say it."

Talbot looked upon him, his thick brows drawn together. He was of the Marcher lords, but upright, most skilled as a soldier, loyal and steadfast to Lancaster. He had small liking for such speech from a boy, but he answered quietly, "Consider it, my lord prince," he said. "Your governor has gone from you this day. I'll warrant he rides now under the banner of the White Hart."

"He well may," Henry said. "But it was Hotspur you named. Whatever Lord Thomas does, Percy is not a party to it."

Talbot gave him no answer.

Henry said, "My lord, he could not do it. He, of all men, would not betray us."

Stafford sought to soothe them. "This argument will keep," he said. "Now must we send to the King, your father."

XI

The King rested in his march to the north at Burton-on-Trent, and there Westmorland sent to him, warning him of Percy's intent. The King could scarce believe the messengers' words. All time was precious to him now, but he waited twenty-four hours that he might have the news confirmed. It looked to be time ill spent, for Percy and the Douglas drew quickly nearer to Shrewsbury. Once they gained Shrewsbury, they would gain all things.

The King sent his own messengers to his son at Shrewsbury Castle. They rode over the drawbridge, summoning the porters, before it was yet day. Henry came from his bed to talk with them, Talbot and Stafford likewise.

The spokesman told them the King had summoned the levies to him at Lichfield. "He comes to you with all speed," he said. "He bids you hold Shrewsbury against his coming."

Talbot asked where the armies of their enemies lay. When he heard they were encamped at Chester, he began to urge that Henry should return with the messengers. "It is you that they seek," he said. "They could have no better hostage than the King's heir."

"His lord father expressly bids the prince stay," the messenger said. "It is feared the townspeople will lose heart else."

When he had gone, Stafford and Talbot spoke together in low voices. "This is a long throw," Stafford said. "And unless God be with us, I think Lancaster has lost it."

Talbot answered him, "The King vows he will reach us."

"He cannot be first," Stafford said. "He has fifty miles to cover from Burton and tired men to drive over them. This race is to Percy."

When it was daybreak, the prince closed the town's gates and brought his supplies and men into the castle. All day the watchmen between the merlins of the turrets peered into the countryside, stretched golden about them. The next day it was likewise. The summer's heat lay stifling upon the castle, the flies bruising themselves against the bright panes. When it was near dusk, Stafford and Talbot sat dicing in the solar. Henry sat with them, Rafe at his feet. The whole castle was hushed, men moving quietly, their ears strained.

After a space it seemed to Henry he heard a distant sound as of marching. He bent his head to listen; then saw that Stafford had heard it likewise.

Stafford gained his feet and shouted for his squire. He looked at Henry and spoke grimly. "If we had wits enough," he said, "we would have had you horsed and away."

Henry answered him, "I am sure it will be my father."

"Are you so?" Stafford said. "God send you are right."

XII

Percy knew well that he raced the King for Shrewsbury. He came with all speed, driving on his men through Whitchurch and Wem, the great Cheshire families at his back, and with them the Cheshire bowmen, the finest in England. His uncle rode at his right hand, saturnine and silent, and with them the Douglas, his battered mail agleam in the July sun. Dearly he loved a fight, and he could smell one now. His concern, like Percy's, was all for speed. "On wi' ye, on wi' ye," he muttered as he rode.

"I doubt not the boy is still there," Lord Thomas said presently. "If we can but reach them first, this throw is won."

Percy answered him confidently. "Mark it," he said, "we'll break our bread this night in Shrewsbury Castle, while the Molewarp sups poorly at some almshouse table."

When presently the spires of Shrewsbury rose above the trees, he set his spurs to his horse and rode ahead. After a space when he did not return, Lord Thomas went in search of him. He found him sitting his horse on a rising knoll, amid the trees, the reins slack in his hands.

"God save us," Percy said gently. "The Molewarp burrows fast."

Shrewsbury lay ahead, embraced by her silvery river. Lord Thomas could see the gates were closed and soldiers moved between the castle merlins. The King's standard floated high above them, spread richly on the breeze in scarlet and azure, the golden leopards and the golden lilies proud-borne upon it.

XIII

The King brought with him his second son, Tom, and a good company of his lords and knights. His army, marching with him, was in number near the equal of Percy's but less skilled with the bow and not of the northern men's mettle in the fight. Shrewsbury gave him lusty welcome, ringing her bells and thronging the streets to cheer.

The King was much wearied after two days' hard march. He took his two sons and some few of his lords, and went to Henry's chamber that he might rest. After he had taken wine, he spoke of Percy with a chill bitterness.

"That this man should come in arms against me," he said. "It was he who sent to me in my exile and greeted me at Ravenspur. I think his heart was black with treachery even then."

Henry spoke in a low voice. "My father," he said, "how can you know it is Percy who rides with them?"

"Who else could lead them?" Derby said. "They bear the lion badge. They are all men of the north."

Henry said, "They may well be his father's men or Lord Thomas Percy's. It does not prove Hotspur there." He began to speak despairingly. "I cannot believe it of him," he said. "He would not do it."

"Hold your tongue," Derby said. "You prattle like a babe."

When it was growing nearly dusk, one of the watchmen came from the tower, bringing the King word that a party of the enemy had drawn near to the walls as if to reconnoitre.

"They meant no attack this night, my lord," the man said. "They came near the gates—almost to within a bowshot—then they withdrew down the Chester road."

Derby said, "Was the Lord Harry Percy of them?"

"He leads them, so please your grace," the man said.

Derby asked him, "You are sure?"

"Why, aye, my lord," the man said in surprised voice. "He rode to within five hundred paces of the walls. Bareheaded he was, not armed, save his cuisses on his thighs."

Derby bade him go. He said in a hard voice to his son, "Well Hal, does it suffice you now?"

Henry could scarce answer him. He sat with his head bowed, seeking to master his countenance. After a space he spoke with Talbot, asking his pardon. "Forgive me," he said. "You were right."

Talbot answered him more tenderly than had his father. "My lord prince," he said, "I hope no more than that you will one day defend me as fiercely."

Tom scrambled from his cushion on the floor, speaking eagerly with his father. "Do we join battle tomorrow?" he said. "I shall ride with you, shall I not?"

Derby answered him, "Hal rides with me, but you do not."

"Will you have me come?" Henry said. "Must it be so?"

"Are you afraid?" Tom mocked at him. "Where's your knightly valor? Lord, you can sit here tomorrow and watch the women spinning if you wish. I'll gladly ride for you."

Derby sent both him and the lords from him, bidding them await him in the great hall. When they had gone, he stood looking upon his son in silence.

Henry began to plead with him that he might not have to ride against Percy. "Let me abide here only this time," he said. "Oh, my father, I'll fight Glendower from mountain to mountain for you. I'll spend my days in the Northern Marches against the Scots or against the French in Calais or Guienne. But not against Hotspur. I cannot do it."

Derby said in a bleak voice, "Is he not the King's enemy as much as these?"

"I know Hotspur is a proud, high-stomached man," Henry said. "Yet he cannot mean to be your enemy." He went on to speak of Percy's debts which he had held against the King. "The Exchequer owes him much," he said. "All summer he was paying our soldiers from his own pocket."

"Hearken to me, Hal," Derby said. "Know you how much these men—these Percies—have received from me since I was King? Forty-two thousand pounds." He took his dagger from the table and thrust it into his belt. "What would you have us be?" he said. "The little wooden puppet Kings of Lancaster? Ruling by the grace of the House of Percy to feed them castles and lands and rents and revenues until they are surfeited—a river seeking to surfeit the sea?"

Henry gave him no answer.

"You are bounden to me," Derby said, "no less than are my lords. Tomorrow, if God be with us, we will strike these men down in their traitor blood. You, I shall have ride with me, for I still command your allegiance whether or no it is Percy who commands your heart."

Henry said, speaking very low, "You have both. I swear to do you good service tomorrow."

"Come, then," Derby said. He set his hand on the latch, then looked back. "Hotspur has a son," he said, "another Harry. He is but your age, his mother is a Mortimer and near the throne. One of you, by the grace of God, will be Henry the Fifth of this realm. Come—which is to be? Percy or Plantagenet?"

Henry said, "It will be Plantagenet."

For all his words, Derby saw him still white and in misery. He had small patience with him. He said curtly, "See then that it is."

The lords awaited them in the great hall, many bearing part armor. The westering sun lay feebly upon their mail in slants and patterns, the great peaked eaves above their heads warm hued by it to rose and amber. There were many there who well served the King—Talbot and Stafford, Sir William Blunt, Westmorland and Glendower's arch-foe, the Welshman, Grey of Ruthin.

When the King was seated, his sons one on either hand, Talbot stood to give intelligence of Northumberland. "The Earl is reported recovered from his sickness," he said. "He marched this day in Percy's wake with a further four thousand men."

Grey spoke contemptuously. "Is the Alnwick spider crawling?" he said. "He cannot be here in under four days. There is a graver peril, my lords: Owen Glendower."

The King said, "We know that Glendower marches to join with Percy. Save for the early summer flood in Carmarthenshire, he would be with him now."

"My lord," Stafford said, "how close does he draw?"

The King answered him, "We know not. Yet I think that Percy awaits him hourly."

The lords shifted and looked upon each other with anxiety. Talbot spoke at last. "Our best hope lies in this," he said. "That we bring Percy to battle on the morrow."

"Remember it is Harry Percy that we fight," Stafford said. "The English Mars—the finest soldier in the realm. He will not be brought to battle so easily."

"My lords," Derby said, "my son has just named Percy to me as a proud, high-stomached man. So he is. I think that if we offer him battle tomorrow, he will not seek to avoid it." To Henry he said, "What say you? Will he fight?"

Henry answered in a still voice, "He will fight. He never shrank from battle yet."

Derby took pen and paper to draw up the battle order, setting his army into three columns. "I have command of the center," he said. "The right wing is yours, good cousin Westmorland. The prince takes the left."

"The prince, my lord?" Stafford said.

Derby answered him, "Aye."

"Good my lord," Stafford said, "I mean no imputation to the prince. We all know how he has served you here in the Marches. But he is only a boy—he is but fifteen."

Grey raised his brows and said, "His most redoubted great uncle, the Black Prince, was no older at Crécy."

"You are mistaken," Westmorland said querulously. "The Black

Prince was some twelve months older, to my certain knowledge."

"And even he found it a hard schooling," Stafford said. "Was it not said that at the finish, standing among the heaps of French slain he could not speak when the King, his father, asked him how the battle had tasted to his palate? Nor had his ears heard the enemy cry for quarter in the English tongue."

Talbot, too, would have urged it. "As you say, it is Harry Percy that we fight," he said. "This will be no mock May-day battle."

"My lords," Derby said, "let him come. I would not have it said Lancaster held back aught from his battle."

When they saw him determined, they said no more. Stafford spoke to Henry good-naturedly to cheer him. "It is to be Harry to Harry then?" he said. "I doubt not that you will make me eat my words."

Henry answered him as he might. It seemed to him now that when Percy had first talked with him, saying, "We canna both be Harry," he had meant no less than this.

XIV

Before he rode out on the morrow, the King rendered Tom into the keeping of his chaplain that he might remain in the castle. He spoke with his lords in the great hall, instructing them in this.

"If I and the prince should fall," he said. "The Lord Thomas is your King. I charge you that Percy does not gain him."

He wore battle armor, bearing the royal arms on his jupon, the leopards and the lilies, which none could mistake. Stafford went on his knees to him, fearing that if the King fell the crown would roll from Lancaster. "My lord," he said, "it is told us the Douglas has this day bound himself with an oath that he will kill all of the King's household. Let it be that I or some man else bears this chivalry."

Many kings went into battle disguised, other men donning their arms and armor and reckoning it as honor. Derby would not set aside his coat-of-arms, but he gave leave to Stafford and Sir William Blunt to put on the royal arms, that, in the battle, men might mistake them for the King.

Derby rode between them through the streets, all three now clad alike, though only the King bore his great shield and, on his horse, the caparisons of Lancaster. The prince came some little way behind his father, his standard-bearer close mounted beside him and bearing in his mailed glove the banner of the Three White Plumes. With them rode the knights, many not yet helmed and supporting their own casques in their arms. They rode through ranks of the townspeople, women, children, and old men, agape with envy or pity; all silent, so that the hoof beats rang upon the cobbles like hail on a roof. The horses curved their great necks beneath their trappings, graceful as swans. Men saw the whole army, bright and splendid in its chivalry, bedecked for battle.

Percy, at dawn that day, had sought to force a passage of the Severn that he might join with Glendower; but the river was flood swollen and he had failed. He had drawn up his army in battle order some three miles north of the town. When the King and his lords drew near, they saw he had judged well, setting his columns upon a sharp rise of hill. Across his front lay a field of beans, close sown and thick, and before it were three ponds, encircled by rushes, as treacherous for the horses as if Percy had strewn gin-traps there. They could mark him, himself, standing beneath the lion banner, his shoulders huge in their glimmering pauldrons. Behind him rested the Cheshire men, caressing their bows.

The King sought to parley, sending his heralds across to the enemy's lines. Lord Thomas Percy himself returned with them. He did not bow to the King. They faced each other in cold hatred, silently. After a space Derby began to upbraid him. "Is this how the House of Percy keeps its vows," he said, "riding in arms against their King?"

"Do you speak of the King, my lord?" Lord Thomas said. "The realm's King is the twelve-year-old boy you hold captive at Windsor—Edmund Mortimer, him that you style Earl of March. It is not against our rightful King that we come, but against Henry of Lancaster, the usurper and despoiler of the realm."

Derby answered him bitterly, "It was not thus you greeted me at Ravenspur."

"There you vowed you came but for your own," Lord Thomas said. He looked about him at the lords, flanking the King, and spoke to them. "And you, peers of England, my message is to you. Do you follow this man at whose door lie all the present miseries of the realm—who swore at Doncaster, on the True Cross, he would have nothing done against Richard's life?"

The lords shifted and looked upon each other. Stafford muttered, "Is the King God that he could keep Richard in health?"

"Know you not how Richard died?" Lord Thomas said. "It was no natural end. Richard was starved to death at Pontefract Castle, made away by cold, by hunger and by thirst, at his cousin of Derby's bidding. So was he set aside from the path of the butcher Lancasters."

Henry broke out against him with a boy's fury. "Percy, you lie. May God send that my father's lance pins all you say back against your throat."

"Peace, Hal, peace," Derby said. He set his hand upon Henry's forearm, his own voice wearied and aging against the gusts of his son's anger. "Under God," he said, "as touching the death of King Richard you lie. We have naught else to say to each other. Get you gone, and may the English blood which this day will see spilled lie on your soul and on your nephew's. I am innocent of it."

XV

Percy had not waited to hear the outcome of the parley. When his uncle returned to him, his armorers stood with him, setting fast the rivets of his helm. All about him was bustle and clangor, the Cheshire men tightening their bowstrings, the lines restless now, as though the smell of battle lay already upon the beanstalks.

Percy shouted to Raoul Harcourt to bring him his sword. He looked carelessly upon his uncle and asked him what had passed.

Lord Thomas laughed and said, "I gave him no soft words. I named him Richard's murderer to his face."

"Good," Percy said. "Now he will fight."

"Yet do I wish we had waited," Lord Thomas said. "A few hours more might well send us the Welshmen."

"Tch," Percy said. "I have the Cheshire men and the ground lies canny. When yon heathen Welshmen come up, the work will be done for them." He took the sword Raoul Harcourt proffered him and looked at him inquiringly.

"I know, my lord," Harcourt said. "It is not yours, but it will serve, I trust. You left yours behind last night at Berwick."

Percy repeated, "Berwick?"

Raoul Harcourt answered him, "My lord—the village where you slept."

"Oh, aye," Percy said. "I knew not the name." Some of the high coloring had gone from his face, but he spoke gently, as to himself. "Berwick, was it," he said. "Has the plow reached its last furrow, then?"

He hunched his great shoulders and turned that he might stare toward his enemies across the beanfield. Their banners were shaken out now, one by one, unfurling to splash their angry color across the green—the Royal Standard, the banner of Our Lady and of St. George, the banner of Chester, of Lancaster and de Bohun, the banner of Wales. When he saw the three white plumes, he looked hard upon it. The King's knights were walking slowly back toward their horses, and he discerned one less tall than the rest, slim in his mail. He called his uncle and spoke with him. "It canna be the boy?" he said.

"He is there," Lord Thomas said. "He stood with his father."

"Afore God," Percy said. "That he should bring the boy into such a battle as this is like to be. His heart is as cold as his steel."

"The boy has as many claws as his father," Lord Thomas said. "He answered me like a fiend. You've no call to deal with him tenderly."

Percy answered him, "I deal wi' none tenderly in the battle."

Some of his northern men stood with him, and they followed his gaze, marking likewise where the prince stood among his father's knights. "Naught but a bairn," said one and spat.

Percy called for his horse. When he had mounted, he took his shield from Raoul Harcourt and looked again toward the three white plumes. "Well," he said as to himself, "let us see now how well I taught you."

XVI

The King had taken brief leave of his son, setting his mailed arms about his shoulders.

"I know you will do me service," he said. "God with you, Hal."

The knights were mounted now and in their battle order. All about them the land sweltered; the corn unstirring; the horses plagued by their flies and much fretted. The knights sat, grumbling that it was a hell-born day to be brought to battle on. Sometimes one or another would draw off his glove and try to set the sweat from his eyes. They wore jupons over their armor, sleeveless but reaching to the hips, padded and quilted and bearing each his arms, so that in battle they might be known. But for these no man could have borne the heat of the sun upon his armor. All who had known battle before dreaded the time when they must close their visors and choke for breath, airlessly and in their own sweat.

Percy made no move, for delay served him best. When the

King saw he must make an end, he bade his trumpeters sound for the attack, sending forward the main body of his army, but holding back the right and left wings that they might come later freshly to the charge. His banners moved slowly down the hill upon Percy's center.

The Cheshire bowmen awaited them, their bowstrings drawn back against their cheeks. When Percy judged his enemies near enough, he bade them loose arrows. They loosed, not only against the King's column but upon the left where the prince and his knights waited.

It was as if a black cloud fled headlong across the face of the sun, its attendant shadow racing below it, darkly over grass and hillock and the tall beanstalks. The strange hissing of the arrows filled the air—a whylie's song, sibilant and shrill as death. Many men, if they were new to battle, lifted their heads by instinct to look toward it. Talbot saw the prince seem to do so. He shouted to him fiercely, "Keep your head down. Have you not learned that yet?"

The arrows fell upon them like a rain of hail. When the screaming of men and horses was hushed, Talbot looked behind him. He saw the prince bowed in the saddle, his hands to his face. An arrow shaft stood out from between them, and the blood ran thickly through his fingers onto the spiked gadlings on his gloves.

His knights gathered to him that they might bear him from the saddle. He did not speak, but Talbot could scarce urge his hands from his face that they might tend him. Malbon set aside the helm, his hands shaking. The wound bled much, and a strip of flesh and hair hung from near the right ear where it had been torn.

"God be praised," Malbon said. "It is not grave."

Talbot took the prince's shield that he might assume the command. He spoke with him gently. "You are well spared," he said. "The battle is over for you."

They sought then to bear him out of the battle, but he struggled against them. It seemed to him that if he went now his father would most surely believe that his heart was still with Percy. He feared likewise his father might even now be dead or stricken under Percy's arrows, believing this of him. "Let me be," he said. "My father needs me."

"My lord prince," Talbot said, "there be others of us here to do him service."

"It is a head wound," Malbon said to the lords. "If he rides again, I fear he may become blinded with his own blood."

Henry answered him fiercely, "Is it beyond your wit to stanch a scratch?"

When they saw him determined, they yielded with relief, for the levies they led were not battle hardened but already in poor heart. Malbon set as much binding about the wound as the helm would allow for. He hastened with the task, for the fight went ill, the main body, which had gone forward under the King's banner, near shattered by the fire of the Cheshire men. Above the clash of battle men heard only the shouts of "Espérance"—the battle cry of the Percies. It lay on the hot Shropshire air like an echo from a northern moor.

Henry took his shield from Malbon and stayed himself on it. Talbot spoke, bidding him await the return of his strength. "No haste," he said. "Take what time you will."

Everywhere the King's columns fell back, the lion banner of Percy steady as a ship borne on the winds. Henry drew in his breath and spoke with Talbot. "My lord," he said, "can we not ride to my father?"

"All is lost if we do not," Talbot said grimly. He bade Henry order the charge. "Give the commands, lord prince," he said. "We all will hold close to you. Do what I bid you and set your teeth."

Henry spoke the first command. All about them the lance points came slowly down, as if a shiver of silver passed glinting under the sun. The knights settled each his lance into the rest behind his right elbow. Henry bade, "Forward, banners," and with his standard-bearer set spur to horse.

The charge brought them through the beanfield and onto

Percy's right, doubling it back against his center. Everywhere the lines were broken, all a desperate confusion, no man knowing whether he fought alongside a friend or an enemy. Percy's intent was to kill the King. He knew well that the scales hung even poised, and he fought with a grim and zestful courage. Ahead of him the Douglas fought on foot, hewing with a madman's fury. He, too, sought the King's life, bound by his oath to kill all of the royal household. So fierce was their thrust that it brought them to the very foot of the King's standard. The prince saw his father's knights everywhere fighting hand to hand as with despair.

Stafford lay trampled beneath the standard. Blunt had likewise fallen. Men so feared for the King that almost by force they urged him from the battle until the fury of the northern men should spend itself. From the slopes of Haughmond Hill he watched while his son's banner drove deeper into Hotspur's center —the three white plumes abob above horses and men as a symbol of hope. Then messengers came spurring to him from the west. They brought word that Glendower and his army drew close, some said but an hour's march distant. The watchman on the towers of Shrewsbury had sighted his banners beyond the curve of the Severn.

The King saw he had but one hope now. He rallied his men and drove back into the battle. His fresh charge entrapped the northerners as between two foes. They began to fight despairingly, feeling themselves at last overborne.

It seemed to the prince and his knights that they were less hard-pressed. Henry found himself alone, even his standard bearer, whose duty it was ever to stay by his side, parted from him. He set back his visor with a shaking hand that he might breathe. A single horseman rode across his path as in flight. He saw the ramping lion of the Percies clawing in gilt and blue upon the saddle trappings and knew the horse for Lygard and Percy for his rider.

It seemed to him Percy was most surely doomed. He set his spurs to his horse and drew level. "Harry," he shouted, "ride for the river. Glendower will give you sanctuary."

He sought to drag Lygard's head round to the west, scarce knowing what he did. Percy seemed in a manner to turn toward him. His visor was up and an arrow shaft stood from his brow between the eyes. At the like moment the dead man's balance which had maintained him in the saddle forsook him and he fell.

He lay cradled in the beanstalks, the shoots curled about his bloodied mail. When Henry knelt by him, some trick of the light, some quirk of sun and shadow, threw on his face a look of glassy recognition, almost of his old rough and zestful humor.

Slowly the knights and the men-at-arms gathered about them. All stared at Percy's body as though they could not believe what they saw. They stood muted until Grey fell on his knees and tore off Percy's helm. He held it aloft, shouting, "Harry Percy is dead."

The cry was taken up, tossed from hill slope to hill slope as the cocks tossed their morning shouts of triumph. The King's knights roared it as they hewed, "Harry Percy is dead." The northerners wavered, though for a space they yet fought. Then they, the men of Northumberland, the men of Cheshire, threw away their bows and began to run. A few of Hotspur's knights—not many, for most were already fallen—still strove where they stood. The King could use pity on none, for the Earl and Glendower were yet in the field, and he dared not let Hotspur's army re-form. He sent his knights in pursuit. As the runners blundered from them, ashen faced, they rode among them. Each hacked from side to side, as he came, aiming at the necks.

Henry watched them with a still face, kneeling yet by Percy's side. Talbot bade the squires take Percy up that they might bear his body to the King. He had ceased to bleed, but some of the blood which stood upon his face dripped to the beanstalks as they bore him.

From all sides the knights came toiling toward the King's standard, herding their prisoners with them. The Douglas was of them, to be used with honor, since as a Scot treason could not be named against him. Lord Thomas Percy likewise lived. He had been thrust through the thigh, and he came halting, dragging his leg after him across the trodden turf. From between the joints of his cuisses the blood welled up unchecked. When he saw the prince, his eyes glimmered at him for a moment, before he passed on, his warders with him.

When the King saw his son, he came forward and embraced him. Henry stood in his arms, still of face and rigid. Derby spoke of his wound, bidding him set back his helm that he might look upon it.

The knights that stood about them began loudly to praise the prince. They spoke with warmth, after the fashion of their chivalry.

"God save your grace," Talbot said, "none has better gained his spurs. His spirit upbore us all."

"It was his charge that delivered us," Westmorland said. "Had you not known, you would have said Harry Hotspur led it."

Henry could scarce bear their words. He feared he would come to tears before them all and so shame himself. Talbot saw how it was with him and spoke more brusquely. "Yet has he much to learn," he said. "He looked upward at the arrows, like a fool. I pray you, my lord, let me take him and see to the dressing of his wound."

He and Malbon brought Henry back to the castle. Tom met with them, loud with his questions and much excited. He followed Henry to his chamber and hung upon the end of the bed. "I should have been there," he said. "I am only eleven months younger than you. Did Hotspur try to run like a churl? Was all thick with blood?" When Henry gave him no answer, he lost patience and turned to go. "We did win this battle, did we not?" he called derisively over his shoulder. "In faith, I hope I never see you in defeat."

Malbon set aside the prince's armor and the shirt of link mail. The silken undershirt was chill and wringing to his hands, and the bandages heavy with blood. He feared to dress the prince's wound himself and summoned the women, the greave's wife and the wives of two of the porters. They worked tenderly, naming Henry "poor hinny," "poor lamb."

Presently the dog, Rafe, came bounding in to his feet. Henry thrust him away and would not look upon him. "Keep him from me," he said. "I want none of him."

"Why for sure, you do not," the woman said. "You want to sleep."

When they had gone from him, he lay wakeful in the great bed, the wound much throbbing, as though the blood strove to burst apart the bandages. When it grew dark, men began to move in the courtyard below his window, the light from their cressets flickering across the beams of the ceiling. Above their footfalls a spade rang in sharp fashion against stone. He knew that his father's men went out by torchlight to bury the dead on Hayteley Field. Hayteley Field. Well named. A hateful and a hating place.

Below the window a man walked singing, his voice West Country but the song of the north.

> *Oh, when that ye hear me gie a loud, loud cry,*
> *The broom blooms bonny and says it is fair.*
> *Shoot an arrow frae thy bow and there let me lie,*
> *And we'll never gang down to the broom ony mair.*

It was the song Percy had loved above all others, for it had spoken of the north; of the ravaged castles with their faces toward the Scots and of the stone lions, gardant on the bridge across the Aln. Henry heard it as in a foreign tongue. It seemed to him the whole realm lay empty of Percy's hugeness; the castle, likewise, which for two years had known the echo of his great laugh, lay still and hollow under the stars.

He heard Rafe at the door, and Malbon's voice, bidding him be silent. "Malbon," he shouted, "let Rafe in."

The door opened and shut, and Rafe sprang upon the bed. Henry set his arm about him and fondled him. "I know not why I blame it all on you," he said.

He spoke Percy's name in the darkness. "Oh, Harry," he whispered. "Oh, Harry." He turned on his face that he might weep.

Malbon, beyond the door, heard him and went to summon his father.

XVII

Derby came to him at midnight, a bedrobe about his shoulders. He spoke of the battle, praising Henry, though the warmth was gone from him. "The Percy estates are forfeit now," he said. "I would make them yours."

Henry answered, "I want none of them."

Derby said, "Then are they John's." He spoke on a sudden more harshly, saying, "Think you, you are the only one to weep for Percy?"

Henry said, "Is he given Christian burial? That much we can surely grant him?"

"He cannot lie in a loyal man's grave," Derby said. "He was a traitor. What would you?"

When Henry gave him no answer, he spoke more coldly still. "What did you take the kingship to be?" he said. "A thing to grow sleek and fat under? Believe me, you will know many such nights as this."

Henry looked at him with fear. He sought to ask his father of Richard and all that Lord Thomas Percy's words before the battle had meant, but he could not.

"My father," he said. "Richard did not . . . ?"

Derby stood looking down upon him, his arms folded. He asked him in a cold voice, "Well?"

"It was nothing," Henry said. He turned over on his side away from his father. "I am weary," he said. "It's been a vile day."

Derby answered him curtly, "You should well thank God for it. It was no vile day that saw the crown once more settled upon Lancaster."

It seemed to the boy the cost of kingship had ever been too high. He said in a choked voice, "I think the crown of England is a hateful and a lecherous thing."

Derby looked upon him with impatience. He bade him a curt good night and went from him, leaving Henry to his grief.

XVIII

Glendower had watched the last of the battle from the branches of an oak high over the Severn. When he saw that the northern men broke their ranks, he withdrew his own force back into Wales. The King knew that to go in search of him would be useless. On the morrow he brought the rebel lords swiftly to their sentence, setting the block in the great hall of Shrewsbury Castle. Lord Thomas Percy was brought to it first. He went unflinchingly, dragging his hacked and torn leg after him across the floor. Sir Richard Vernon and John Venerables, two of the Cheshire knights, followed him. The King and his peers watched grimly while the blood splashed upon the rushes of the floor where once the Percies had dined with princes.

Hotspur had been buried with honor the previous night; Derby granting this much to the man who had so aided him in his venture against Richard. Yet England still clutched at her legend. The land already grew loud with whispers that Hotspur yet lived, men saying that after the battle he was seen riding northward, betrayed by his furious spurring.

There was much danger in this for Lancaster. Percy was torn from his grave, his body quartered, the dead head hacked from off his shoulders to be sent first to York where it was impaled above the north gate, facing his beloved Alnwick. Then was it borne to London Bridge, that it might rot there in the fog and spray of the Thames.

And we'll never gang down to the broom ony mair.

Nor yet was Lancaster safe, for Northumberland, the Spider of Alnwick, still marched to the south. Derby sent Westmorland and an army to block his way, then himself made ready to follow.

There were men enough with Northumberland, but the Spider had loved his son, and the news of Hotspur's death broke him. He met Derby on his knees, an old and shattered man, babbling of mercy and past favors. Derby was wearied and much sickened by the blood of Shrewsbury. He pardoned Northumberland, restoring into his hands all the vast Percy estates.

(Six more years of life were left the earl. He was to spend them intriguing ceaselessly with all Lancaster's enemies—Glendower, the French and the Scots. He died at Bramham Moor as his son had died at Shrewsbury, bearing arms against Lancaster—an old man of over seventy, fighting furiously to the end, with the lionlike and bloody courage of the Percies. His lips, when he was stripped of his helm, were drawn back against his teeth in the fixed and blackened grin that had many times turned on Lancaster.)

After his meeting with Northumberland the King returned straightway to London, Tom and most of his lords with him. Henry remained yet at Shrewsbury. On the day following the battle his wound was angry, and he had a fierce fever. The King summoned two of the town's physicians to him. He set the prince in their care, knowing that he himself must march to the north.

One of the physicians, Nicholas Colnet, came to the prince's chamber on the morrow. He was not greatly over thirty, a tall man, his gray leech's gown in parts threadbare, for he tended the poor of the city without payment. When he entered, he ducked as from habit in case he should strike his head on the lintel.

There were ewers of hot water near the bed, and Colnet began to unwind the dressing. He sought to be gentle, but the blood had dried, binding the cloth to the flesh, and he had to rip it away. Henry shifted but said nothing.

"I am sorry, my lord," Colnet said. "I know it to be most hurtful to you."

Henry answered in an angry voice, "It is nothing."

Colnet bent over him and looked hard at the wound. "It is clean," he said. "It will heal well."

He began to set fresh dressing upon it, talking cheerfully. "You were lucky, my lord," he said. "If this gadfly had been another two inches to the right, it would have been a different tale."

Henry gave him no answer. Colnet said gently, "I have known many younglings of fifteen—none but were glad on a summer's morning that they lived."

Henry answered him, "It may be they were not Kings' sons."

"I well know how it is with you," Colnet said. "You bore yourself with honor in the battle—all your knights witnessed you flinched not so much as an eyelid—but now you have the reckoning. It was ever so. Any of your knights, be he the most battle hardened among them, would tell you it always comes thus."

It seemed to him Henry's wound was not great enough to bring about so high a fever. On the morrow he came to him at dusk and sat with him when he saw the night would be a bad one. Henry's breath was short and much fevered. He tossed about the bed, finding no ease wherever he lay.

After a little he spoke in a fretful voice. "I know not how they could say it," he said. "That Richard was starved to death at Pontefract."

Colnet saw his fever was such that he spoke without knowing what he said. He sent Malbon and the women from the room and sat alone with Henry on a stool by the bed. Henry went on speaking of Richard. "All that Lord Thomas spoke before the battle," he said, "it will not leave my mind. I know what the French said —that my father sent a knight named Piers Exton to murder Richard, but they ever hated us. They would say it. I never gave them any heed."

Colnet said in a soothing voice, "Why then give heed to what Lord Thomas Percy might speak?"

Henry said, "It was ever held the Percies knew all our secrets." He began to toss again in the bed. "It could not be that we came to the crown in Richard's blood," he said. "It could not be. God would require it at our hands—such sin as that. If I ever began to believe it, I should go from my wits."

"My lord," Colnet said, "you must ask your father of this matter."

"I tried," Henry said. "I could not do it. My courage left me." He drew in his breath and said, "Yet it is not so. My father would not have used Richard thus."

His fever dropped a little, and after a space he dozed. The next day when Colnet went to him, he was much mended. Henry greeted him in withdrawn fashion. At midday when they were alone together, he sat up in bed and took a little broth. At length he set the bowl aside and gave Colnet a strange look.

"I thank you," he said. "I know well I am often hard to tend. Was I so last night?"

Colnet answered, "You were very sick. It was a bad night."

"Did I talk with you?" Henry said. "It seems to me that I did."

"You'll not recall it," Colnet said. "You spoke in your fever."

"Colnet," Henry said. "What did I say? Who was there?"

"None else was there," Colnet said. "And I have forgotten what nonsense you spoke."

BOOK III

THE PRINCE

"Call thyself prince, Hal?"

In the January two years later, the Countess of Hereford sat with the King. She came rarely to Court these days, busying herself at her own Castle of Pleshy, so that Joanna might not think she interfered. She found Derby much changed, grown to fleshiness and with flecks of gray in his red-gold head. No man could say the King spared himself; yet he had become chill and wary, acquainted well with treachery.

With him was Lady Hereford's own brother, Thomas Arundel, Archbishop of Canterbury. He kissed his sister's still smooth cheek and saw her seated by the fire. He it was who had gone to Derby in his exile, desiring him to return and thrust Richard aside from the throne. He was aging now, white maned like a lion, but strong and of a furious energy, a fierce, forthright man, given to much violent self-assertion.

The King had that day signed a marriage treaty with Denmark, betrothing his younger daughter into the Royal House. Both the little girls grew pretty and yellow haired, Philippa twelve and Blanche just thirteen. Both would go to their bridals within the month, the one to Denmark and the other to Bohemia. They were poorly matched, for the great houses of Europe did not seek alliance with Lancaster.

Derby spoke of the little girls with some tenderness. "They have the Plantagenet fairness," he said. "They are as all the maids of the House of Anjou."

He had also sent his ambassadors that spring into Burgundy. Arundel spoke of this in a soothing voice. "My good liege," he said, "you will gain a daughter once we secure the Lady Anne of

Burgundy's hand for the prince. I am glad these plans are much advanced. It might well be he will have his bride in England before Easter."

"Oh, Thomas," Lady Hereford said, "if he were your son I think you would not press this matter so."

"He is my great-nephew, sister," Arundel said in a stiff voice. "I desire his weal and the land's. I think with the realm poor as it is, we will find him no better match than Burgundy."

Lady Hereford said sharply, "He is set against it."

Arundel raised his brows and said, "He has not yet met her."

"He talked with the Burgundian ambassadors," Lady Hereford said. "He has seen her portrait. It may be he knows his own heart in this."

"My good Joan," Arundel said, "is he not the prince? It is policy alone can mate him." He set his bishop's staff to the ground and leaned upon it. "I well know he is just of an age when a pretty face is the moon and the stars," he said. "But these matters can not weigh with us. Aside from which . . .

He blew out his cheeks and looked upon the King. Derby said, "Speak on, my lord Archbishop."

"The King knows I desire naught but the well-being of his house," Arundel said. "He will pardon my outspokenness. But I have long thought marriage might well be a sobering influence on Henry. He is much changed since Shrewsbury."

Derby said in a cold voice, "Yes, he is greatly changed."

"There is much incitement to riot these days for a young man," Arundel said, "especially one newly brought to a position of eminence in the realm."

Soon after he rose to take his leave, setting his blessing both upon his sister and the King. When he had gone, Lady Hereford began to speak of the prince's betrothal, earnestly yet with a cheerful humor. "Bear with me, my lord," she said. "I have poor arguments—only those of an old woman who would not have her grandson made wretched by a match he longs to escape."

Derby answered, "I was fourteen when I first wed. Mary was ten.

Did Gaunt stop to ask us if we were content with each other?"

"No," she said and sighed. "Yet by God's grace I think you were not unhappy." Presently she said, "Hal grows much like his mother."

Derby answered her bitterly. "You think I do not see it?" he said. "But your brother, the Archbishop, spoke true. Underneath that traitor likeness I have a son who is fast becoming a rioter and a drunkard."

"What would you?" she said. "He is young and his destiny will soon rob him of all his gaiety. When he was thirteen he was tasting war at Glendower's hands in the Marches."

Derby answered with impatience. "I, too, found such excuses. It had been better for him had I not."

After a space she said, "Tom was ever your favorite, was he not?"

"Tom bears me some affection," Derby said, "Hal thinks of naught but himself and his pleasures."

"Oh, my lord," Lady Hereford said, "he loves you well." She began to speak of Shrewsbury. "Think back to that day," she said. "You forced him to choose between yourself and Hotspur. It was you that he chose."

Derby said, "It would have looked strangely if he had not."

"Aye," she said. "Yet Hotspur died under his eyes. It was not a light thing."

He did not reply, and she said, "Hear me in this. For the happiness you and Mary bore each other, will you not force Hal into marriage with Burgundy's daughter?"

Derby answered shortly, "He must marry as is fit. I have the land's weal to think of."

When it was time for their meal in the great hall, he brought Lady Hereford down with him. The four boys were already seated at their places at the table on the dais, but they rose as their father entered. Henry was seventeen now, Tom sixteen, quiet John fifteen, and Humphrey but newly fourteen. They looked as they were—active, clever, and much spirited, their vitality pricked by the nerve-strung restlessness of the Plantagenets. In all things they were well favored. Almost it seemed, as in the children's tales, that every good gift had been set upon them at their christenings and likewise that the evil gift lay upon them also. Tom grew unimaginative and lustful; John calculating; Humphrey under the shadow of the weakness that had scarred Gaunt's fierce youth. Already tongues wagged against Henry. Men spoke of his growing wildness, naming him a hard drinker, young as he was, a lover of taverns and a hater of his bed.

Joanna sat at the King's right hand, her hair and coif padded hugely over the ears and encrusted with jewels. She ate heartily, her eyes ever peering at the food, so that the mountain of cloth folded about her head seemed too great for her neck. All the meal was fish, for it was Lent; the servers presenting their dishes to the King on their knees, but standing to the others and serving them from the front. Joanna when she spoke used only French, for she still knew scarce any English. The rest were silent as if they sat among strangers; Philippa overwrought by the news of her bridal and eating nothing, her fairness sometimes flushed and sometimes drained of color. Lady Hereford saw them all much changed. It was hard for her to recognize them as the same family she had known at Leicester or Monmouth.

When the meal was near ended, the King spoke sharply to his eldest son. "I meet with the Burgundian ambassadors again this afternoon," he said. "You will be there likewise."

Henry said, "My lord, have I to come?"

Derby answered him, "Must I bid you twice?"

He and the prince were with the Burgundians all the afternoon, hearing their master's proposals but without agreement. When they parted, Henry went to his brothers' chamber.

"Anne of Burgundy," he said. "I'd as soon take poison as take her."

His brothers greeted him mockingly, treating it as a jest. All men betrothed their children whereby they might come to gain, even the London shopkeepers contracting their sons and daughters in marriage, oftentimes before they could walk. Only the very poor could marry straightforwardly, as for love or lust.

"You'd not have escaped this far," Tom said, "save that the great houses of Europe think England a sinking ship."

"You have her, then," Henry said. "Have you seen her portrait? One of Burgundy's own noblemen called her a stuffed owl."

John answered, "A feathered owlet was what he called her."

"It must be much the same thing," Humphrey said, "since Burgundy threw him into prison for saying it."

"I'll never love Burgundy's Anne," Henry said. "I could not. Yet father would have me bound to her."

"Well, what of it?" Tom said, staring. "Where you marry and where you take your pleasure have naught in common. You'll be King. Haggle a dozen a day, if you choose." He got to his feet with a grin. "I knew not we were going to have you the Duke of True-Love or the good King Arthur."

"Oh, hold your tongue," Henry said.

Tom thrust his face close to his, grinning. "Try to make me, good brother."

"You might yet escape, Hal," Humphrey said, "if you can withstand father until the spring. He will want you back in the Marches when Glendower comes out from behind his mountains."

"May he come from them soon, then," Henry said. He began to set aside all the marks of his royalty, taking off his ring and the belt he wore, its clasp worked in jewels and fine gold. "I think I'll take Malbon's old brown cloak," he said. "I want to go for a stroll."

Tom laughed. "A stroll in the city," he said. "Your stroll will not take you past the Blue Dove in Fish Street, I'll warrant."

"I would not, Hal," John said. "You'll much anger Father."

Henry shrugged. "I doubt he'll care," he said. "He's too busy with Burgundy."

II

Everywhere Lancaster was beset by troubles, with rebellion in the north, in Ireland and in Wales; the Scots ravaging the Border lands; and the French marching into Guienne until the whole province looked like to be lost. The King himself prepared to march north to deal with the revolt of Mowbray and Archbishop Scrope, both leaguing with Northumberland. On the night before his setting out messengers rode to him from the west, bringing him news of Glendower. When he heard it, he sent for his eldest son, but Henry was nowhere to be found about the palace. He came at last to his father's bedchamber, where Derby worked by the light of one small candle. Henry had been drinking, though it marked him little, only his cheeks flushed, so that he had more than usual his mother's likeness.

Derby spoke with him in cold anger. "So you have come," he said. "I'll not ask where you were." He spoke shortly of the messengers from the west. "Glendower was enthroned three weeks ago at Machynlleth," he said. "He proclaims himself Owen, as by the grace of God, Prince of Wales."

Henry said in a low voice, "Does he so, my lord?"

Derby gave him a bitter look and said, "Men name him loose in his living. They say he has scattered more bastards after him in the hamlets of the valleys than another would scatter oaths. Yet he bears the title, Prince of Wales, more fittingly than does my son."

Henry gave him no answer. Derby went on. "He signs himself with the signet of Llewellyn, swearing he will stamp out the English tongue from Wales. He has summoned to him a parliament of all the Welsh shires. Every week, it is said, his armies gain in might." He set the despatches into Henry's hands. "I am sending you back to the Marches," he said. "In full command. Think you that you can quit your tavern crawling long enough to bear the King's arms in some sort with honor against this Owen?"

Henry said, "I do not think I have failed you in that, my lord."

"You know not all yet," Derby said. "We fear Glendower has

sent for aid to France. The truce notwithstanding, it may be Charles will grant him both arms and men. If he does, then is the peril in Wales great."

He spoke wearily, as if his burdens grew too harsh for him. Henry looked upon him with compunction and began to speak earnestly. "My lord father," he said, "will you not judge me by what I am here? I shall serve you well against Glendower. I swear it."

"I can spare you but few men," Derby said. "At most three thousand. I well know it is not enough."

"It's no matter," Henry said. "I can make shift."

Now that there was again much danger to Lancaster, they had grown closer, as in their perils in the past. The next day the news from the north was very grave. Derby made ready to hasten there, the prince preparing to take his journey to Wales. Both had their horses and their baggage in the palace yard, the men-at-arms by them, bearing bill hooks and in link mail.

Derby took leave of his son, charging him gravely with his task. "All rests upon you," he said. "Hold Glendower back in his mountains. Else will the wolves be upon us in their packs."

Henry answered him that it would be well. "Will you not look to your own faring, my lord," he said. "There's naught to trouble you here."

"You're a cheerful fighter, Hal," Derby said. "You do my heart good, though I could well deal you many a good box on the ear."

Henry laughed and did not answer. Derby set his arm about him and brought him out to where the horses stood. When he would have mounted, he turned and spoke again. "The matter of your marriage rests for the present," he said. "I would not have you troubled with it now."

Henry thanked him with joy. They parted more tenderly than for many months, each to his own enemy.

III

The prince went back to the Marches this time no more under tutors and governors, but in full command of all his father's armies in the west. All Wales was Glendower's now, the dark magic of his name flooding the valleys and bringing all of his blood to his banner. With the spring he marched into Shropshire and Hereford, where lay the vast de Bohun inheritance. He used it roughly, sparing nothing that pertained to Lancaster. The Castle of Hay, where Henry had played as a boy, was left with scarce two stones together. Everywhere the prince found his lands ravaged, his barns and his manors gutted, his own and his grandmother's tenants seeking shelter in the Worcester villages. Yet he knew himself dealt with justly, as within the rules of war.

There was much here to fire men's imagination in the duel between the Welsh knight of fifty and the boy of seventeen, each by his own conceit naming himself Prince of Wales. Many of the Marcher lords awaited Henry in the manor house where he was to lodge, their men-at-arms, their heralds and bannerets thronging the sheltered court. They had ridden from their lonely Marcher castles where each was to himself as a king, united in hatred for the Welsh but resentful of each other and oftentimes of the royal restraint. Many chafed that they should be set under the command of one as young as the prince. Talbot warned Henry of them as he brought him in to them.

"They are as baited bears," he said. "Stand foursquare against them, my lord, or will they be at your throat."

It seemed to Henry he must first do battle with his father's lords before he could come upon Glendower. They gave him indifferent greeting, many not rising. When they heard of the force he had brought with him, they looked upon each other with dark faces.

"Afore God, my lord," Grey of Ruthin said, "does the King, your father, not understand how great is the peril here on the Marches? You cannot hold Glendower with a few raw farmhinds dragged from the Kentish wealds." He began to speak of the ill Glendower had done him, for they were ancient enemies. "Three of my manors razed, my own castle—the Red Castle—gutted, my serving sluts carried off that they might bed with yonder Welsh hellion and people the valleys with bastard traitors. It would please me well if the King had sent twenty thousand men that we might strike across into Radnor and burn every Welsh hamlet we came to."

"You cannot lay it all to Glendower," Henry said. "His own home, Sycharth, was burned by Hotspur three years ago—a most fair manor, beloved by him."

"One manor," Carew said. "That is little enough for an attainted traitor."

Grey joined answer with him. He was a high-humored, choleric man, violent and ever eager for a quarrel. "You speak true," he said. "For my part if I take a man who so much as babbles three words in the heathen tongue of Wales, I'll hang him in lieu of Glendower."

Henry said, "Nay, my lord, you will not."

"I'll hearken to none at seventeen," Grey said. "I was driving these Welsh pirates out of my lands before you were breached."

Henry answered him that he bore his father's authority. "Do as I bid you, my lord," he said. "It would ill serve us both if I had to set you under armed restraint here in Worcester."

Grey looked hard upon him and did not speak.

The lords began to ask the prince how he would deploy his forces. Most had their estates and castles in the north, and they urged that he set them there. "Look to the north," Carew said. "Glendower is a man of North Wales, both Sycharth and Glendowery lie there. It will be from the north that he'll strike."

"I do not think so," Henry said. "He fights for all Wales now, not for Sycharth and Glendowery."

"Your estates lie in the south," Grey said. "Ours are in the north. Are we to sit here with you while Glendower makes our manors ashes and our castles piles of rubble?"

"Afore God," Henry said, "Glendower hunts higher prizes than a Marcher castle. He looks now to France. If Charles renders him the men and supplies he asks, he seeks to overrun all England. Thus great is our peril."

After the lords had gone from them, he and Talbot stood together scanning the map upon the table in silence. After a little Henry said, "I am sure it will be the south."

Talbot answered him, "I think you judge rightly, my lord."

"But if it is not?" Henry said. "Talbot, what if I cannot hold him? What if he gets past me?"

"My lord prince," Talbot said, "what more can you do save your uttermost?"

When they were mounted and ready to ride, the servants brought them stirrup cups, strong brewed and very bitter after the fashion of Shrewsbury ale. Henry drained his and gave it back to be refilled, taking it again. When he saw Talbot's glance upon him, he flushed and set the mug aside. "You're right," he said, "I drink too hard."

"You will need your wits clear," Talbot said, "if you would break a lance with Glendower."

"It will be different here," Henry said. "I promised my father."

IV

The prince moved from Worcester to his own castle of Monmouth, and from thence to Caerphilly Castle, one of the great fortresses of Wales. On the last day of the month messengers rode to the castle court bringing word of a fleet beating westward. Henry took horse and rode to Porthcawl, Talbot with him. When they had dismounted, they lay alongside each other in the deep eel grass of the cliff face so that they might look across Swansea Bay. There were wild geese here, on the wing, stiff-necked over the broom, and the bay was sweet and rain washed as watered silk, the Gower coast and Mumbles Head blue as a bruise upon the skyline.

There were many ships in the bay, beating slowly in toward Neath. They bore the Cross of St. Denis on their pennants without concealment, for the King of England had no navy and there was nothing to hinder them save contrary winds. The brilliance of their chivalry loaded their sails and masts and timbered sides. Against the fair muted face of Wales the brightness of each ship was as a daub of paint from a giant's palette.

Talbot named them French. "So they have come," he said. "Our luck runs thin."

Henry said fiercely, "In truth, Talbot, I cannot lie here and watch them come in. We have six hundred men. By hard marching we could reach Neath by fall of dark."

"My lord," Talbot said, "were you to take your six hundred into Neath, you would not bring them back. What more could the French desire of this enterprise?"

"Aye, you say true," Henry said with bitterness.

Their escort stood a little back from the cliff by the roadway; mostly Monmouth men of the prince's service and with them a few men of Caerphilly. All stood uneasy and muttering. When Henry and Talbot returned to them, one spoke to his fellow in a distinct voice. "Did you not see the sea, bach? Beautiful she was, and smooth as glass. Not all spring have I seen such a sea. Owen sends the French ships good sailing."

"You speak as a fool," Henry said sharply. "Glendower can use naught against you save flesh and blood."

The man answered in a stubborn voice. "There's no disrespect I mean," he said. "But English is my lord, and these matters are hid from him. Much sorcery is known to Owen. Likewise has he a prophet, Crach Ffinnant the Scab, a strange man and evil, who has many mighty spells."

Henry said, "He would have you think it. These tales are for old women."

The French marched with Glendower now, fine armed and bearing splendid accoutrements. Of all nations they were held to be the most skilled in battle, and with the Welsh bowmen alongside them it was as if nothing could gainsay them. In two weeks Glendower broke his bread in Caerphilly, marching from thence on Cardiff to set the whole town to the burning. In the west Aberystwyth fell likewise, and fair and mighty Harlech, the guardian fort of West Wales, her ravaged face seaward. No English withstood him now within his realm save only Carew at St. Clears, and he who was his own son-in-law, Scudamore, at Carreg Cennen. Both these lay under siege and close to despair.

Glendower moved next upon Chepstow. Henry sought to check him there, sending Talbot with a force to strengthen the castle. Talbot drew near in darkness, many of his soldiers fearful and murmuring. When they came close, they were deafened as by a clap of thunder. On a sudden the night sky was riven across the tops of the mountains, the hills themselves glaring out upon them, black and fiery, like the very caverns of hell.

There were not many in Wales who could recognize the sound straightway. The men cowered from it, one raising his voice in terror. "It is the devil," he screamed. "Glendower calls out the devil."

"Jesu, mercy," moaned another and crossed himself.

Talbot saw half his force break and run. He sought to drive them back, his knights laboring with him. In the midst of all, one of the squires turned staring eyes on him. "He has guns, my lord," he said. "Owen has guns."

v

Henry was now all but driven from Wales. He drew back to his own Castle of Monmouth, his two Yorkist cousins, Aumerle and Cambridge, riding to him there. Aumerle was Justiciar of Wales, but his allegiance went ever to the winning side. Henry knew it well, but he had still affection for the cousin who had shown him kindness in the coldness of Richard's Court.

Cambridge was yet handsome and cold of face. Between him and the prince there was much formal courtesy and small liking.

Each always recalled the time on Tower Wharf when Cambridge had set Henry from his path like a puppy that had strayed there. Both the brothers took meat with the prince in his own chamber, Talbot with them. All were grim faced, fearing Glendower's next advance. Henry told them of the guns.

"I know not how they came by them," he said. "They have no means of casting them here in Wales."

"Not unless friend Owen cast them in a clap of thunder," Aumerle said. "No, cousin, I have knowledge of those guns. They were a gift to Glendower from the King of France." He spoke as between mouthfuls of food. "Friend Owen was in Paris himself this spring. King Charles received him as he would any prince of the blood. They are bond brothers now, the truce with England thrown under the table and a treaty of friendship between them."

Cambridge said, "The French must have found yon bastard Welshman barbarous enough."

"No, no," Aumerle said. "They wondered at his courtliness."

"He is a great man," Henry said. "I'm fast learning that. He has fired Wales as a spark among tinder."

Cambridge raised his brows and said, "Leave his courtliness, cousin. It is more to the point to consider where he will next strike. Is it that we sit here while he moves past us to the north?"

Henry looked at him in troubled fashion and did not answer. He bore half-mail, yet he seemed to have few years, with a boy's cap of hair, short cut in the new fashion, and a boy's anxiety at a mistake. Talbot spoke to ease him, saying he himself would have made a like choice.

All men feared now that Glendower was beyond the prince's holding and that he would move against the undefended north to overspill his own land into England. For three days was there no word, but on the fourth messengers rode into the castle court. Glendower had crossed into Monmouth, falling upon Lancaster's own town of Grosmont and partially burning it. He moved now upon Usk. Henry and his knights snatched their armor to them and rode out to meet with him, almost with thanksgiving.

VI

Glendower had brought with him on this march many of his own household. Gwenllian rode at her father's side. She was nineteen now, straight and slender as the pines that had stood about Glendowery and eager for the battle. When she saw the flames that lit Grosmont, she spoke in pleasure. "There's back we have served him for Sycharth," she said. "I would we could do likewise to all Monmouth."

Her father smiled upon her. "Little hellcat that you are," he said, "I know not how your gentle mother bore you."

With them rode Glendower's brother and two of his sons—Meredith who was his heir, and Griffiths, who was but a year older than Gwenllian. Griffiths was standard-bearer to his father and carried against his thigh the banner of a maiden, her hands worked in scarlet. He was boyish in his spirits and as jubilant as his sister.

"A good day's work it is," he said. "There's something for Derby's whelp to remember us by."

"Oh, Father," Gwenllian said, "almost is he sent from Wales."

Glendower answered her grimly. "Maybe it is so," he said. "But I do not cry victory yet. Boy as he is, he is a clever fighter."

They drew near to Usk, Glendower setting a hard march, for it was well after noon. His army was mostly bowmen, barefoot and in their ragged brown; behind them rode Crach Ffinnant the Scab, Glendower's prophet; and his bards, their scarlet bardic robes staining the gray hills. All these were white haired and white bearded, some bearing harps and some bent bows to show that there was war. Chief of them was Iolo Goch the Red, who had been with Glendower since his birth. This man turned to song more easily than he spoke, clothing all his thoughts in music.

Presently one of the scouts came hard riding to Glendower. He spoke of a force of English ahead in the valley. "Not very great is it," he said. "Two thousand, as we judge. Saw their banners clear we did from the crest of yon hill."

"Whose banners were they?" Glendower said. "The boy's? The three plumes?"

"The bear it was, my prince," the man said. "Lord Talbot's."

Griffiths began to urge his father to attack. "It is your day," he said. "Give them another buffet in the teeth."

Glendower set his men, both French and Welsh, in their battle stations and unfurled his banners. When they rode upon Talbot, his small force met them steadily.

Griffiths cleaved close to his father, so that all men, seeing the banner, might know where Glendower fought. Suddenly he looked over his shoulder and cried out. "There's more," he said. "Look you behind you."

One of Glendower's squires thrust close to them, pallid faced and gasping. "It is the Dukes," he said. "Aumerle and Cambridge. They lay concealed behind the hill's spur."

The Welsh found themselves now most sorely pressed. Glendower himself was unhorsed. When Gwenllian saw it, she set her spurs to her own mount and rode to him. "Look to yourself," she said. "As you love me—as you love Wales—will you not go?"

He spoke with her tenderly even in the clash of battle. "Little goose," he said, "think you I would take your mount?"

She answered him, sobbing, "All is lost if you are taken."

Iolo Goch, the Bard, spoke then, echoing all her words. He had much influence with Glendower, for he had ever given him his counsel and sung of the strange tales of his birth. "Do this bidding," he said. "It is for Wales. It is for the Cymry. Once you are taken and in chains what hope have we?"

So they both pressed upon him, urging him.

VII

Henry came late to the field, for he had set a third body of men to the west of Usk, fearing Glendower would march upon the town from that side. When he heard the battle was joined, he rode straightway to Talbot. Aumerle met with him, setting the sweat from his eyes and in high humor. "All fell out as you planned, cousin," he said. "This was a mighty good day's work."

Henry asked him of Glendower.

"It may be he lies among the slain," Aumerle said. "If not, we'll have him before he reaches the hills."

Four siege guns lay in the bracken alongside the Welsh sumpter horses, and he brought Henry to them. The guns were well cast, each bearing a fleur-de-lys scratched beneath the linstock and under it the name "Rouen."

"These come from Charles of France to friend Owen," Aumerle said. "They cast them in the foundries of Rouen and ferry them down the Seine that they might ship them from one of the Normandy ports. You would not know it. A place called Harfleur."

Talbot had brought his prisoners to the manor house of Usk. Meredith and Griffiths had both been taken, and three of Glendower's daughters, the ladies Katherine, Alice, and Gwenllian. Katherine was great with child. The soldiers had set a chair for her, and she sat before the empty hearth weeping.

The others looked upon Henry with hate, Gwenllian speaking loudly and in English. "It is Derby's whelp," she said. "Son to the Molewarp."

Katherine bade her be silent in a shaking voice, saying, "Mad are you to talk thus."

Meredith asked of his father. He was a gaunt, hollow-cheeked young man of some twenty-eight years, his English, unlike Gwenllian's, falling haltingly from his tongue. "If you know, lords," he said, "it were charity to tell us."

Aumerle answered him in light fashion. "If he lies not dead," he said, "we shall have him in chains by nightfall."

"Saxon bastards that you are," Gwenllian said. "The whole land is ours. Wales is ours and England is ours. What were the Plantagenets themselves save Norman scum bred from the loins of a Falaise washerwoman?"

She went on speaking that they might keep their eyes upon her, her hate dark glowing and magical. Griffiths still bore his dagger, thrust into his belt beneath his jupon. While she spoke, he sought to draw it quietly, stepping forward upon the prince. But the soldiers had read his intentions. One spun the dagger from his grasp, dealing him a hearty buffet on the face. He fell full length across the prince's feet.

Henry began to speak to them in a calm voice. "I must deliver you to my father," he said. "Yet I do not think you will find him overharsh."

He brought them to his own Castle of Monmouth. Joan Waring greeted them joyously, hugging the prince, for she had feared for him.

"There's safe you are," she said. "The Good Lord be praised."

Henry set Glendower's daughters in her charge, bringing them to a wide chamber above the castle court. Joan served them with an ill grace, thrusting the food she brought them before them as if she could well have poisoned them. They knew her to be Welsh like themselves and looked upon her coldly as one taken in treason.

There was a great bed in the chamber, fresh made with clean sheets and down pillows. When they were left alone, Gwenllian and Alice made Katherine lie down upon it, taking off her shoes and coif.

"Oh, Katti," Gwenllian said, "I feared this ill day would bring the babe before its time."

Alice said in a frightened voice, "Will they bring us through the streets of London as whores to a penance?"

"I care not," Gwenllian said, "if only Father is safe."

While her sisters rested, she sat long by the casement, watching the trees about the garden grow blue and soft etched. There were still many soldiers about in the castle court, and she could sometimes hear their speech.

"Think you it was Owen?" one said as he passed.

"It looked like him," his companion said. "They're bringing the carcass now to the chapel."

Gwenllian turned white as one dead. She looked back at her

sisters, but Katherine slept and she did not speak. Presently, when it grew late, Henry sent word by Joan Waring that he desired to talk with them. Katherine set her coif about her hair and tired it, then bade Joan admit him. Henry came in with Talbot at his side. He bowed to them, doing them honor as he might the great ladies of the realm.

"I would have you know it, ladies," he said. "Your father is safe. We have searched these past five hours, but without taking him. Now is it dark, and we'll not do so. He is out of our hands."

Gwenllian said, trembling, "Not dead is he?"

"Nay, he lives," Henry said. "We thought he lay among the slain, but it was your uncle, Tudor Glendower. He had no mole under his left eye such as your father bears. Him will we bury with honor."

The next day he brought them on their journey to London, riding with them part of the way. The road was rough, beset with hills and stone strewn. After a little Talbot rode to the side of the litter where the women sat, and took Katherine up behind him to ease the jolting. Gwenllian had sung when she first had left the castle in joy that her father did not ride with them, but now she sat silent beside Alice, white and straight backed. Presently Henry offered to take her up on his horse, as Talbot had Katherine. She gave him angry answer, saying, "I am not with child, my lord."

"Are you not, lady?" he said. "I knew you lacked a husband."

She saw he mocked her and turned away her head, but after a while, she called him and said she would come up. They rode together as a knight and his lady, Gwenllian's torn skirts spread about her across the horse's flanks.

Henry spoke with her, praising her singing. "I know the air," he said. "It was 'Mentra Gwen.' I never heard it sung sweeter."

She answered in a chill voice, "There's flattered I am."

"You've naught to fear," Henry said. "My father will not keep you long in London. He'll send you home—you and your sisters —as I doubt not."

"What of Griffiths?" she said. "What of Meredith?"

"They were taken in arms against us," Henry said. "We can but hold them till the war ends."

"Aye, you would do so," she said. "They will be as eagles caged. But you're a Saxon. You care not."

He said fiercely, "Can no man love Wales save Owen Glendower?"

"No man," she said; saying presently with more condescension, "you do not understand these things as I do. I am nineteen; you are but seventeen and of England."

He answered, "I, too, was born in Wales. The day will come when I'll have the Welshmen marching with me under the banner of Lancaster."

"Never," she said. "Set me down."

He dismounted, seeking to help her, but she would not have it and slid to the ground all but on top of him. He held her that she might not fall, then set his lips to hers. They stood alone, screened by the trees, no man observing them.

They went from each other, speaking no more words together for the rest of the journey. Henry went with them no further than Gloucester, turning from them there. Both he and Gwenllian looked back twice upon each other as the women and their escort rode on.

Glendower yet lived and would fight again, but England, for a summer's space, was delivered from him. Men knowing how slender had been the prince's might named it as a miracle. But Lancaster had small space for rejoicing. The King after his quelling of the northern rebellion was stricken at Stamford, lying for four days close to death. When it was thought he could be moved he was carried to London, and the messengers riding in to the prince summoned him to his father's bedside there.

VIII

Henry rode all the night that he might come to his father with all speed. There was much alarm in the palace. When the prince came to his father's chamber, the King's physician, Dr. David Nigarelli of Lucca, barred his way. "I would not have you enter," he said. "It may be the King, your father, has leprosy."

Henry would not heed him and went in. Only his uncle, Thomas of Dorset, and one servant stood in the room. Dorset greeted him and spoke to reassure him. "He mends, praise God," he said. "They tell us he lies in no danger now."

He brought his nephew to the King's bed, bearing the candle in his own hand. Henry looked down upon his father's face, seeing it as a stranger's, fouled with sores, the nostrils ravaged by boils. Scabs clung everywhere to it—his eyelids, his cheeks, the hairs of his beard, the swollen lips. His hair lay gray matted on the pillow, with here and there a fleck of red-gold to gleam in the candle flame in ghostly mockery of what had once been.

Henry drew in his breath, turning away his head. Dorset took his arm and led him to the chair by the fire. "Where are my wits?" he said. "I should have warned you, Harry. But it is certain he will mend."

The King did not know his son. Henry bided with him for three days, sleeping in the sickroom and scarce leaving it. He much feared for his father. At length he sent for Nicholas Colnet, the young West Country physician who had tended him after Shrewsbury and whom he well trusted. Tom had likewise been summoned from Ireland, he and Colnet arriving the same hour. While Colnet went to the King, the two boys sat in the anteroom; Tom begrimed from his riding, Henry disheveled and wearied. Tom, for all his journey, was yet boisterous. That the King would live was beyond dispute now, and he shrugged away the fear of leprosy. He was eager to talk of other matters. He spoke of his uncle, John Beaufort, who had died six weeks previously, and his widowed aunt—she who before her marriage had been Margaret Holland, Richard's half-sister.

"She'll be a mighty rich woman now," he said. "You know how old Gaunt fawned on his bastard sons—castles, lands, rents, revenues. All that huge Beaufort estate—hers now." He fingered the gilt tassel of the cushion at his elbow and looked upon Henry as if in apology. "It were a shame if that fortune went out of the family. The Pope is lenient with such matters, provided the thing is gone about rightly. If I should care to fill my uncle's place, I need but send a gift to Rome."

"You? You want to marry her?"

"Why not?" Tom said. "She likes me well. I've but to ask her."

Henry said, "She's your aunt."

"She is the widow of our bastard uncle," Tom said. "I told you I would need dispensation, and I told you I would get it. Afore God, you look as though I were talking of bedding with the witch of Endor."

"She is a Holland. Half-sister to the—half-sister to Richard."

"Well, what of it?" Tom said, staring. "The more reason for me to step in before her family marries her off to some slobber-degullion like Harry Percy who'll use her wealth to raise an army against us."

"In truth, I think you are mad," Henry said. They sat glaring at each other in prickly opposition, on edge and angry. Tom rose at last and moved away. "No need for me to make my mind up yet," he said. "And when I do I'll do it without thanks to you. Are you waiting to see this country leech of yours? I'll go have a meal and change. What Nigarelli says is of more import to me."

After he had gone, Henry sat on in the glow of the fire. Colnet came to him at length, rolling down his long sleeves, his hands freshly rinsed. He talked with Henry reassuringly, sitting with him. "I do not think it is as you fear," he said. "In these days no physician can look at a scab or a skin irruption without wringing his hands and naming it leprosy. It seems to me God has not laid that upon the King."

Henry asked him what it was that had stricken his father.

"It may be he has had ergot," Colnet said. "At Stamford, it is said, he raved at his servants that they had thrown burning brands over him. I have seen other men, after they had eaten infected bread, taken thus."

"You cannot tell me he mends," Henry said. "His face, Colnet —I could scarce look on it."

"The scabs are St. Anthony's Fire," Colnet said. "I do not disguise to you, my lord, that the King, your father, has been and still is a very sick man. But, by my faith, I believe him to have some years of life yet."

Henry looked past him through the half-open door of the sickroom. The great bed stood there, shrouded in its tester, and alongside it, on a stool, resting on a velvet cushion, was the crown, to signify it was the King who lay there. In the darkened room it glimmered like a mariner's lodestar, but evilly.

"This I know," Henry said, "the source of all the evil that has come upon my father lies beside him on the cushion yonder."

Colnet sighed and said, "I do not quarrel with you. Your father has seen little ease these last six years. Yet does he mend."

After he had gone from him, Henry walked alone to the river bank to gain the night air after the stench of the sickroom. Others passed that way, muffled in their hoods, not observing him, for he stood in the shadows near the great wall of the palace. Presently two came near and he heard their soft speech.

"How fares Lancaster?" said one.

"He mends," the other said. "But he was sorely stricken."

His companion broke into quiet laughter. Henry judged him a Lollard, by his plain habit and his pleasure at all that had befallen the King. "Did he not murder Richard?" he said. "Now God has smitten him, and his toes and his fingers drop off. God is not mocked, brother. These usurpers will yet find their bloody crowns heavy on their heads."

Henry turned from them that he might hear no more. He felt himself in horror. When he came again to his father's chamber, it was as if the crown winked upon him, echoing all he had overheard. He called for the servants and bade them take it away. They looked at him in much astonishment.

"My lord," said one, "where shall we bear it?"

"Anywhere," Henry said. "But take it from here."

The day following, the King's senses came back to him. Tom sat with him, and he asked him what had become of the crown.

"Did you not know, my lord?" Tom said. "Hal took it. I thought it would be at your bidding."

The King said, "Is he thus impatient?"

When his eldest son came to him, he spoke with him coldly, remembering nothing of Henry's long vigil. They had short time together, for Henry was soon returned to the Marches and Tom to Ireland. The storms yet raged about Lancaster, with only the failing King and three of his four young sons to toil against them. In March the French fell upon the realm, burning both Plymouth and Falmouth and ravaging the coast between. Only by the death of their leader, the Count St. Pol, was the land delivered from invasion. Many other perils threatened. Yet by their finger tips Lancaster clung on, until it was as though the patron saints—the champions of Christendom, in whose hands lay the destinies of kings—had blessed their arms and their courage.

IX

Six months had gone when Henry rode to his grandmother's house in the Strand. She stood in the garden, cutting autumn blooms from the rose trees, but when she saw him she let the scissors fall dangling from the chain at her waist and went to meet him.

When they had come to the solar, she said, "Your father is ill pleased with you, and I blame him not. I am ill pleased likewise."

He set his arms about her and kissed her, hugging her hugely. "There," he said, "now we be friends again."

"We be no such thing," she said. "Harry, set me loose. All men tell me I have a rioter for a grandson." Presently she said, "Now that you have your own fine city house and your own household, I would have you do something for me. I have a young man here with me—the son of Gaunt's steward, Walter Hungerford. He bears his father's name, and he seems to me as honest and careful as his father was. Will you not take him into your household?"

He said, "If it will please you."

"It would please me well," she said. "These young men that you have hanging about your sleeves, I like none of them. How is it you can bear with them daily as your companions?"

"Dear my grandmother," he said, "I know them for what they are. At least they ride under their own colors."

"And who did not?" she said. "Harry Percy?"

After a little she said, "What ease does your tavern crawling bring you?"

He half-smiled and said, "There's much ease in wine and company. It drives your thoughts from you, and I would not think."

She asked him, "Of what would you not think?"

He sought to give her answer.

"Nay, do not fear," she said. "God is faithful. He will not set the crown upon you and leave you lacking strength to bear it." When he still was silent, she said, "Well, get you back to your boozing. You'll not escape your hour, Hal, run from it as you will."

When Henry rode from the house, Walter Hungerford rode with him. He was twenty-two, some four years older than the prince whom he now served, but against the battle, intrigue and violence of Henry's youth his own seemed to him a colorless thing. Henry scarce troubled to speak to him save that he asked him carelessly where he had read. When Hungerford told him Cambridge, he repeated the word derisively. It seemed to Hungerford almost as though he were expected to ride ringing a bell and crying "unclean."

There were many taverns in that part of the city, flanked by Bread Street and the Standard. Henry sent his men-at-arms from him, but he desired Hungerford and another of his gentlemen, John Gornot, to stay. They drank together up and down the Chepe, where there were slatterns to serve, their hair bound up in greasy coifs, and their fellow drinkers were ratcatchers and rakers; thieves crept out of sanctuary for the night; pardoners, their pouches bulging with pardons from Rome which might be any man's at a price; and the city bawds, in their rayed hoods, defying the law which confined them to Cock Lane. None knew the prince, for he bore no finery. It seemed to Hungerford he well liked the company, playing hazard with any and as eager as an apprentice to sing when a strolling jongleur unslung his lute and plucked witchery from its strings with filth-encrusted fingers.

He and Gornot drank hard also, Gascon or Rhenish or expensive Tyre which was thirty-two pence a gallon. Hungerford knew better than to try to keep pace with them, but, when Henry proposed they should dice for who was to pay, he found that he lost in every tavern that they came to. By the time it grew late his purse was well-nigh empty, and it was much relief to him when Henry at last spoke of returning.

Curfew had long gone and chains lay across the street corners to snatch at the feet of lawbreakers, witches and ghosts. Hungerford marveled they were yet sober enough to avoid them. His head was near bursting, and he followed laggardly behind Henry and Gornot through the narrow streets. Henry had his own house now, as befitted him since he was eighteen. It was Sir William Poultney's fair mansion, Coldharbour, set at the end of the Chepe, its gardens of pleached pear trees and lawns, walled about and fluting down to the Thames. Henry could not have afforded it; but Sir William had much fondness for Lancaster, and for his rent asked no more than a rose on midsummer day. Malbon came to admit them, his face disapproving.

"I was growing anxious, my lord," he said. "The city is an evil place at nights—so many rogues—and it is very late."

"No later than last night," Henry said. "Malbon, you cluck like an old hen."

When they entered, Henry went from them to his chamber. Hungerford found himself alone in the great hall, dim and firelit, the tapestries shadowing the walls. Already he seemed to himself as a fool, bound now in service to a wastrel prince bent on riot and pleasure. He had small liking for either Gornot or Henry. He would gladly have set aside his bargain and gone from them back to Lady Hereford's. Presently he was summoned to the prince's chamber. The dog, Rafe of Bamburgh, lay on the bed foot. When Hungerford came in, it was as though he sensed antipathy to Henry and fell to growling low in his throat.

Henry cuffed him as in play. He looked carelessly at Hungerford and began to speak of his father. "He served old Gaunt for many years," he said. "Is he still in health?"

Hungerford answered, "He died at Tutbury four years ago."

"Did he in truth?" Henry said. "Service to Lancaster is a killing thing."

Hungerford answered in a chill voice, "So it would seem, my lord."

"Look, Hungerford," Henry said, "I took you to oblige my grandmother—I much love her. But I do not think you and I sort together. What say you? Do you want to stay?"

It seemed to Hungerford that if he went now, it would be to them as though he grudged the loss of his purse. He said coldly, "I can stay the winter, my lord. Your grandmother much desired it."

"As you will, then," Henry said. When Hungerford would have gone, he called him back. There was a purse thonged in scarlet leather set on a stool by the bed, and he picked it up and tossed it to him.

"This is to make good your loss," he said. "It's what we took from you."

"My lord," Hungerford said, "it is yours. You won it."

Henry looked at him in mockery and said, "It was not fairly won. Gornot and I were palming the tables—a trick of the Lombardy moneylenders."

Hungerford scarce knew what to answer. Henry lifted his brows and smiled. "I know well what you think," he said. "Old Gaunt never cheated your father out of his purse; but times change, Hungerford. If you stay, I'll warrant you'll see much difference in Lancaster."

X

Hungerford found he was set as steward to the prince as his father had been to Gaunt. It was a harsh task, for Henry had no care for money and was ever spending or dicing or giving it away into the hands of the members of his household. Hungerford could abide few of them. He liked, as did all men, quiet Lord Scrope, who was Henry's treasurer, but the rest were to him empty gallants—elegant young men who leaned over Henry's shoulder when he diced or drank, flaunting all the extremes of fashion with their long-toed shoes, dagged hoods and padded shoulders. It was not an easy household to control, but Henry, who had stood foursquare against the Marcher lords, scarce seemed to trouble to try. Hungerford thought all preyed much on the prince's profligacy. It puzzled him, for Henry did not seem gulled by them, yet he had them ever with him.

The King ailed much these days, and there was little revelry at Court. At Michaelmas there was the traditional dancing, but all was drear—the musicians scraping and plucking wearily from the gallery and the dancers moving as by rote. At nine the King went from the hall with Joanna. Almost straightway the atmosphere was easier for his going. Henry spoke with the minstrels, and the music began again, light and lilting, an air to set the feet atapping. The dancers swirled about the floor, their sleeves whipping color across the gray walls in flicks of emerald, ivory and flame. The laughter of the women grew shriller. Hungerford saw Gornot stagger as he pawed the silk scarf across his partner's throat, the silk ripping. He stepped back beneath the arch of one of the oriel windows where the night air was cooler. Two others stood there,

Margaret and Isabella Holland—hidden from him by a pillar. Both these were of the great family that had been kin to Richard and were therefore suspect. They did not see him and he heard Isabella's voice, speaking low and angry. "And he will rule us," she said. "A drunkard and a lecher for a King. It turns me sick."

Her sister Margaret answered her fiercely. "Hush, are you mad?" She was older than Isabella, gentler and less fair. She it was who had married John Beaufort, Gaunt's bastard son, and was thus sister-in-law to the King and aunt to his four sons. She was in white, in mourning for her husband, and her eyes clung to the second of her young nephews, Thomas of Lancaster, as the dance swept him past.

"Aye, mad to see them here," Isabella said. "Holding their bastard court in my sweet Richard's hall. Margaret, you cannot take Tom of Lancaster, a boy not yet eighteen, your own nephew, the son of Richard's murderer."

Margaret answered, "My first marriage made me half Lancaster."

"But to take him for husband," Isabella said. "You are eight years older than he is."

Margaret answered her, "I know."

"But you are also an heiress," Isabella said. "Your widowhood has made you of the richest in England."

"I know that too," Margaret said in calm fashion. "I am not blind. I know why he wants me. I am not young or desirable to him, yet I'll take him. Leave it so, Isabella. It's not in me to reason it."

"Well," Isabella said. "It could yet be worse. It could be that you sought Prince Hal."

XI

Tom's betrothal fell within the forbidden limits of the Church, but by spring he had sent to the Papal See and gained dispensation. Henry much opposed the match, and the two brothers quarreled fiercely almost to the wedding eve. Only then did the

prince seem to admit defeat. He did so with a show of grace,
standing for Tom at the ceremony and loading him with gifts of
horses, gerfalcons, jewels and loving cups; yet between them bitterness lingered. After the wedding Tom sought possession of his
wife's fortune. He learned that his uncle—he whom Gaunt had
once named "his prudent lad"—had left a will setting all in the
hands of the Bishop of Winchester and under his seal was tied
down the whole estate. No man taking John's place in Margaret
Holland's bed could touch a penny of the vast Beaufort fortune.

Henry treated this as wondrous jest, and for days Coldharbour
rocked with it. Tom was in fury. He talked wildly of litigation,
and when his brother would give him no support came near to
blows with him. He knew well now what he had done. At eighteen
he was tied to a woman, not counted fair by him, with more years
than himself so that he reckoned her middle-aged. He quickly
sought other consolation. Margaret might be smilingly gentle with
him, whiten her cheeks with fard, wear her richest gowns, but
she still spent her days spinning with her ladies in the Palace of
the Savoy and oftentimes her nights alone in the great bed. Tom
turned to the sister of one of his father's knights. By the time
another spring had come around, she was three months gone with
child by him.

Yet was Tom still his father's favorite, and the ailing King,
cold and suspicious, resenting the rest of his brood's health and
animal spirits, set much store by him. It was a weapon Tom had
not before used, but he was in much fury over Henry's laughter
and he did so now. Men marked how all his brother's misdeeds—
and there were many—were brought to the King's ears. Soon
Henry found himself received at Court as a stranger and turned
to his own pleasures more waywardly than before.

XII

When summer came Hungerford did not go with the prince into
Wales. It was the eighth summer Henry had spent matched against

Glendower, and Hungerford parted with him, vowing himself glad to be gone. It seemed to him that again to offer his service to the prince would be madness, but in seven months, when the summer campaigning was over, he found himself again at the postern gate of Coldharbour, naming himself a witless fool. Malbon admitted him and brought him to the solar. None else was there save a young boy polishing the sconces. He was wrapped in a surcoat greatly large for him, and his aspect was one of patched dirt, as though his face and hands had been newly washed and the rest left. Hungerford did not know him and spoke with him.

"You are but new here, boy, are you not?" he said. "What's your name?"

The boy answered him, "Edward Bryce, so please you, sir."

Malbon spoke then, saying, "He is a lad apprenticed to one of the goldsmiths down the Chepe. The prince was returning last night and, in a manner, stumbled over him in one of the alleys. The boy had seemingly run away from his master's shop and feared too greatly in the dark to move."

Hungerford asked if the prince meant to keep him.

"The boy is apprenticed," Malbon said, "bound by his indentures. He must be returned to his master."

"I'll not go," the boy said. "Sooner I'd starve in the streets." He drew the sleeve of his surcoat across his nose and glared at them in half-tearful defiance.

Malbon dismissed him and when he had gone sighed. "The prince would buy him if he could," he said. "Yet he cannot. He has been back from Wales but a week, and already much of the plate is in pledge."

Henry drank that night in the Blue Dove, a tavern much favored by the Chepeside apprentices. Hungerford sought him there, finding it crowded with journeymen and apprentices, their sleeves gay with the girl's favors they wore pinned upon them. A fat friar sat back against the barrels, balancing his drinking pot against his paunch, and the serving wench plucked her brows before a cracked mirror, that she might be as the great ladies who would not countenance a hair showing.

Henry and Gornot sat together on a bench across the room. The candles glinted on Gornot's finery, jeweled belt and dagger, ermine-trimmed cote-hardie, and long shoes thrust into the rushes of the floor. Henry wore a plain jerkin belted in leather. Against the peacock splendor of Gornot, he might have been another apprentice boy. He looked lean and hard after a summer in the field, but his brows were lowered.

He gave Hungerford careless greeting. His casual acceptance of him pricked into life Hungerford's brooding resentment. He sat glumly silent as Henry called over the drawer. When Henry would have paid the price of his ale, he forestalled him.

"You have the price of a drink, Hungerford," Henry said. "I would you had the price of an apprentice." He spoke of the boy Hungerford had met with at Coldharbour. "He's a good boy," he said, "and his master used him with much hardness. I should well like to keep him."

"He's a sniveling bastard puppy," Gornot said. "It passes my comprehension, Hal, that you, a prince, should want such with you at Coldharbour."

Henry gave him a hard look and said, "I have you there."

Gornot's eyes snapped at him, but he made no retort. Hungerford asked hastily who held the boy's indentures.

"The goldsmith at the corner of the Chepe near the Poultry," Henry said. "Him they name Whaplode. I sent Malbon to him this morning, but he says young Ned is a good craftsman and he demands him back."

"Demands him?"

"He's in his rights. I owe him money already, and I could not take a lad apprenticed to a master without buying up his indentures. But he puts the price high. He wants twenty crowns."

He began to speak more bitterly. "If my father would but pay me my dues, I could do it," he said. "He knows well that all last summer I paid my soldiers from my own pocket. The Treasury owes me seven hundred crowns—two hundred more than it does Tom, yet he is paid. Another payment is made to him tonight for the debts he incurred in Ireland."

Gornot broke into noisy laughter and said, "In faith, Hal, your father loves him better than he does you."

Henry made no answer, toying with his mug as in thought. Hungerford saw his eyes agleam. He began to fear what would come next. At length Henry spoke of the retainers who would bear the Treasury purses to Tom at the Savoy. "I know which way they come from the Tower Mint," he said. "The Chepe, Bread Street, Cordwinder's Street, the Standard. There is a dark passageway off the Standard—they can only come through it but one at a time. Should we be awaiting them we could have the Treasury purses out of their belts before any had the wits to raise a hand for himself."

"You mean to rob them?" Hungerford said, finding breath. "You?"

"It's no robbery," Henry said. "I told you the Treasury owes me seven hundred crowns."

"I'll have none of it," Hungerford said. "You're in your cups, my lord, or you would not think of it."

"Well, drunk or sober, I have to have the money by tomorrow," Henry said in cheerful fashion. "Or Ned goes back to Whaplode."

As they talked one of the ratcatchers came upon them, seeking company to drink with. He was a large man, red faced, with his scarlet bonnet knotted at the end and the dead bodies of the rats he had raked from the gutters roped together and slung over his shoulder.

"Cold night, my masters," he said, sinking down as Henry made room for him on the bench. "But plenty here to warm the guts. Eh, but the price goes beyond an honest man's purse."

Henry asked him if he desired to earn a noble. "I have an argument on my hands," he said. "There are those that bear a purse I reckon to be mine. I would gain it if I could, and I seek an honest fellow or two to help me."

"Why bless you, sir, willingly," the ratcatcher said. "But you'll not say no to a half-groat now? An earnest, as you might say—by way of account."

Henry gave him a coin, and he thrust it away into a bag slung round his neck, under his shirt. Though all was done swiftly others watched and drew nearer, drawn by the smell of money. There were few left drinking now, for as night had closed down the tavern had emptied. Most of the apprentices had gone. Only a handful came about the prince—two apprentices, a rat-faced journeyman, an archer, carrying both his pouch and his mug in his left hand, for he had been prisoner and his right was smitten off.

"Have you no sense?" Hungerford muttered at Henry. "Send them off while you have time."

Henry grinned at him and gave him no answer. He spoke with those that stood about him, telling them no more than he had told the ratcatcher. All were ready for gain to follow him, the archer eager to be gone and about it.

"Not you, friend," Henry said. He rose and slipped a coin into the archer's mug.

The archer answered, "I'll earn it, so please you."

"Drink up then," Henry said. "For we must go. John, do you come?"

Gornot answered that he would, in hurried fashion, yet it seemed to Hungerford he followed Henry laggardly.

When they had gone, he himself returned to Coldharbour, through shadow-ridden streets where shuttered inns creaked their signs at him and cats fled about the gutters. Few yet remained afoot in Coldharbour, but Scrope still sat at his accounts. Hungerford told him of the night's work, Scrope hearing him with laughter and amazement. They sat together awaiting the prince's return.

Presently Gornot came to them, alone, saying he had lost the rest in the dark. He spoke with his eyebrows uplifted at Hungerford, but he was foul tempered, sending Ned with a cuff for wine and aiming to kick at Rafe. Henry followed some forty minutes after curfew had rung from St. Martin's le Grand. He bore a Treasury purse thrust into his belt and likewise many signs of battle.

When Gornot sought to give his tale, he answered him with contempt. "One of the apprentices likewise had second thoughts," he said. "And the journeyman lost all use of his legs before we were half-way down the Chepe. At the finish there were but four of us. It was well their leader kept well out of it. He was a fat, dough-faced man, button mouthed. I never saw such a craven."

"And you took no more than one purse?" Gornot asked.

Henry answered, "It was not easily come by."

"Nor was it," Scope said. "Your eye turns a most princely black, my lord."

Henry laughed and said, "May it mend before the Council meets."

"By the saints, I should hope so," Hungerford said. "What will you tell your father otherwise, my lord? That you go brawling along the Chepe like a common apprentice?"

"Don't prate at me, Hungerford," Henry said dangerously. "Hold your tongue until I ask your counsel."

Malbon entered as he spoke, saying there were messengers come from the King. "I told them it was very late, my lord," he said. "But they greatly desired to speak with you."

Two wearing the antelope badge of Lancaster followed him into the room; a fair-haired young man, much disarrayed, and another, meticulously garbed by contrast, with fat cheeks and a mouth as small and neat as a woman's. After Henry's words all knew him. Scrope prudently set the candles in a corner distant from the prince.

The fat man bowed very low. "You will not know me, my lord," he said. "My name is Francis Fauconer—vastly privileged to serve your most redoubted father and your princely self."

Henry asked him what had brought him.

"My lord, you have suffered some loss this night," Fauconer said. "It was outside the Standard. A pack of arrant ruffians set upon us there. We did all that men could do, but they got away with the Treasury purse we were conveying here to you."

Henry exclaimed and said, "To me? You were bringing it to me?"

"A hundred crowns," Fauconer said. "It was thought at first to send this sum to the Lord Thomas, but before we set out the King, your father, bade us bring it to you. It is somewhat toward the many debts incurred by you last summer in the Marches."

Henry answered him, speaking feebly. Fauconer mistook his tone and took on an air of injury. "We gave blow for blow, my lord, so far as we could, yet were we greatly overmatched. There were some twelve of the scoundrels—sanctuary men, unless I mistake it."

"I do not think there were so many," the fair-haired young man said. "The truth is that they surprised us."

"There were not less than a dozen of them," Fauconer said sharply. "I myself engaged the leader. A man somewhat of your own height, my lord. An arrant ruffian, black-bearded like a gypsy."

Henry smiled and said, "I don't doubt you made good account of yourself."

Fauconer gestured with his hand, saying, "I carry many bruises from the encounter."

"In truth," Henry said, "you must show us of the bruises."

"I make no complaint," Fauconer said hastily. "They were received in your service, my lord, and willingly borne. Would you have us inform the watch?"

"My servants can do that," Henry said. "I thank you, sirs." He groped in his belt for some coins, remembered in time they were freshly minted and might be recognized and asked Hungerford to lend him his purse. To the fair-haired young man he gave five nobles, with another five to be divided among the rest. It was handsome reward. Fauconer watched with a look of pleased anticipation which turned into one of much agony as Henry pressed fourpence into his palm and waved a hand in dismissal.

When the door was closed, Hungerford spoke in mockery. "Not much gain for all your trouble, my lord," he said. "The purse was yours from the start."

"What a night," Gornot said with a drunken whoop of laughter. "Hal, you robbed yourself."

Henry looked at them, seeing them all close to laughter. For a space he looked dark-faced, then he too set back his head and began to laugh. Their laughter grew so loud that Hungerford feared it would carry to Fauconer's ears.

"You've been well served, my lord," Scrope said.

"Aye, maybe," Henry said. "But I've gained the boy."

On the morrow he sent Malbon round to Whaplode's shop that he might buy up Ned's indentures. When the boy heard he was to stay, he came near to tears in joy. He was a good boy, alert and most biddable. He could not tell how old he was, for his mother had died at his birth and his father, a seagoing man from the south country town of Hythe, had been taken by French pirates off Brest and cast into the sea with the rest of the crew. Henry made him page to him, though all men held a prince of the blood must be served only by boys of noble houses. Ned sought to please him in all that he did, ever at hand and eager for any bidding. He had much love for his master. Soon he was toward Henry as Henry himself had once been toward Hotspur.

XIII

Archbishop Arundel walked four days later in the corridors of Westminster, with him Henry Chichele, the Bishop of St. David's. The prince was much on his tongue. When he saw Henry passing the casement below them, he broke out in anger. "In truth," he said, "he has every tongue in the city clacking."

"The prince?" Chichele said. "Yes, a most engaging young man, is he not?"

"As shallow as water in a gutter," Arundel said. "The matter is of great grief to me. It was I who went in disguise to the King, his father, during our several exiles and begged him to pluck the realm from Richard's grasp. Yet for England's sins the father is broken in health and the son is no better than another Richard."

Chichele answered him in calm manner. He was a quiet-spoken man, alert eyed, with a gentle and humored mouth, a Saxon, bearing no Norman blood in him. That he had risen in the Church had much surprised him, for England looked for her prelates to the fiery prince-bishops of Normandy—men like Arundel, in whose veins ran the blood of the great houses of Howard, Fitzalen and de Bohun. "It is true that he is wild," he said. "But it may be we demand of him too much."

"I demand nothing of him," Arundel said, "save some slight awakening of kingly dignity. I am an old man, Chichele. Praise be to God, I shall doubtless not see the ruin which I strove to avoid come upon us."

"He drinks as he fights," Chichele said, "with a young man's vigor. You cannot throw him summer after summer against Glendower and expect him to remain but a boy."

"Yes, yes," Arundel said irritably. "I have heard Glendower pleaded before in excuse for him—so often that I grow wearied of it. In Wales his personal courage is not in question, nor will be, I trust; these are not times for cravens. But here in London he gives pleasure to none save the wastrels and tavern keepers."

"He has a liking for humble folk," Chichele said with his calm smile. "Not taken to excess, it may be no bad thing."

"He will be the King," Arundel said sharply. He was talking to one whose own beginnings among the Gloucestershire cornfields were humble, but he had forgotten it. "The boy has no two thoughts in his head save reveling away his life in taverns and this modern music which I do not understand. He is kin with me —my own sister's grandson, as well as heir to the house into whose hands I guided the scepter and the sword. It is hard for me to stand by idle while all tongues clack over him."

"My lord," Chichele said, "we cannot convict him on rumor."

"Yet is there enough here," Arundel said. "It affrights me that if death were to claim the King tomorrow, it would be incumbent on me to place the crown of England on the head of one no more fitted to bear it than some drunken lout of a Chepeside apprentice."

When he would have gone, Chichele checked him. "My lord," he said, "must it be that you speak of this matter to the King? It were a sad thing to see them estranged."

"They are that already," Arundel said. "The boy has alienated his father, and I wonder not at it. No words of mine can worsen it."

He went from Chichele to seek the King. Derby awaited him in the Painted Chamber, resting on his stick before the hearth. Two winters had passed since the illness which had almost carried him away at Stamford, and the pollution of his face had never healed. He rode but seldom and never walked even along the passageways of Westminster without a stick. With him were his half-brother, Thomas of Dorset, and Queen Joanna sat by the window spinning, her four handsome stepsons ranged about her. It looked a picture of much charm, as of the reigning house, but no peace lay there.

The King sent his three younger sons from him, but he kept Henry.

Arundel spoke first to the prince in a chill voice. "It pleases me well to see you here," he said. "Your company has been much otherwise of late."

Henry gave him no answer. Arundel went on in deliberate fashion. "I do not lightly say these words before your father," he said. "Doubtless he also rebukes you."

The King sighed and said, "My lord Archbishop, I have already spoken with him."

"My dear lord," Arundel said, "he listens, I trust. The matter of his conduct is of much import to the realm."

He stood by Joanna's side, and she broke out to him in her guttural French.

"I mean no ill to the dead," she said. "The Lady Mary de Bohun was doubtless a pious woman. Yet her sons are small credit to her wisdom. I came to this charge too late."

Her voice rose and fell behind the hum of her spindle. She did not mean Henry to hear, but he did so and looked upon her darkly.

The King said sharply, "Hear me, Hal. Have you no care what men speak of you?"

"My lord, they will say it, anyway."

"*Eh bien, Henri,*" Joanna exclaimed. "You are heir to England. The sons that I bore will find their inheritance only in dukedoms, yet they bear themselves with far more princely grace."

Henry said in a fierce voice, "Madam, this is none of your business."

"In truth, Harry, you'll not speak so," Derby said in cold anger. "Ask your mother's forgiveness."

After a space Henry said, "I ask your pardon, madam. I spoke too roundly." He had with him the Council's report on the spread of Lollardy in the universities. The King bade him read it, for he desired the Archbishop to hear it. Arundel and the prince were opposed on this matter, Arundel desiring to suppress Oxford's charter and Henry, much loving Oxford, that she might keep it.

When the prince spoke the name of Roger Courtney, the Chancellor, Arundel halted him. "I know not if he is to be trusted," he said. "Did he not once bear arms for Richard?"

Henry answered that he did so for honor's sake, saying, "He had taken an oath to Richard."

The King said, "All oaths to Richard are accounted treason."

Henry answered, "We swore ourselves."

"We took an oath to a man unfitted by his misuse of kingship to exact it."

"By whose judgment was he dubbed unfitted? By ours? By Lancaster's?"

"By the realm he broke and despoiled," Derby said. "This is a schoolboy's babble, Harry, and I grow sick of it. I grow sick of hearing in your mouth the name of a man who became fat and besotted on his own subjects' hatred."

Henry said, "Are we so greatly loved?"

They stood thus, snapping their angry jibes at each other like two common journeymen bent on a Chepe quarrel. Joanna had ceased her spinning, even Arundel hushed. Derby spoke with a raised voice, "England is ours by right of conquest and by free election. If Lancaster's name is tarnished, your own rioting has tarnished it. You are no more deserving of love than was Richard." He looked at his son and spoke with bitterness. "My poor broken realm," he said, "at my death to be thrown into your lap. I wonder at her fate."

"It may be you should have thought of that, my lord, before you laid your hand to Richard's crown."

The King lifted his stick and struck him across the face, making to strike again. There was much weight in the blow. Henry drew in his breath as with surprise, then stood like a rock.

The King lowered his stick, coming again to control. He and his son met each other's eyes with much cold anger, Henry setting back the blood from his cheek with his hand. Arundel watched with satisfaction. Even Dorset, oftentimes stanch in defense of his nephew, was angry with him now.

"You should have done that more often, my lord brother," he said to the King.

"Read on," Derby said curtly.

Henry bent his head once more over the Council's report. Anger shook his voice for a line, but he sought to steady it. When he had done, Derby bade him go. He bowed and went from them.

Tom met with him in the passageway. He and Henry still scarce spoke to each other, save with a raillery, often bitter. "How now," Tom said, yawning, "has Father beat you?" He stared at the rage that leaped into Henry's face, then broke into a roar of laughter. "It is not true?" he said. "I spoke in jest." He raised his voice that he might call his brothers. "John, Humphrey—here to me. Hearken to this."

He affected to stagger down the passageway, helpless as from laughter. Henry went from him furiously into the cold March air, where Gornot and Hungerford stood beside the horses in the palace court.

"Where to, my lord?" Gornot asked as Henry jerked the reins free and swung into the saddle.

"The Blue Dove," Henry said. Hungerford desired to protest but he checked himself. Henry's mood showed in his face. It was like to be a wild night.

XIV

Hungerford and Ned dragged Henry to his bed that night in much anxiety in case their way through the city streets was noted by the King's servants or those who served Arundel at Lambeth. Hungerford did not rouse Malbon but brought the prince to his chamber himself. Henry lay as one dead, only his breathing heavy and wine laden. While Hungerford held the candle above the bed, Ned sought to drag off the prince's clothes, setting purse, pouch, dagger and signet ring on the stool. Only the ring was in princely character, bearing Henry's crest. Hungerford picked it up and looked upon it—the chained swan of the de Bohuns halved with the Cross of St. George, all delicately wrought in silver and crimson enamel.

He tossed it from him and spoke in anger. "And he will be King," he said. "I know not what will become of us."

Ned lifted his head and looked at him darkly. "I'll hear no ill of him," he said. "But for him I would have starved in the streets."

"It contents you, then," Hungerford said, "that you'll one day have a drunken rioter for a King?"

The boy said in a fierce voice, "He is not as you think. I would go anywhere with him. In truth, I would die for him."

"Peace," Hungerford said. "I did not mean to anger you."

He went from them to his own chamber, casting aside his clothes in anger and weariness. He had small time to sleep, for at six the bell of St. Thomas of Acon rang out prime. The church stood at the corner of the Chepe, and its great bell was such that none at Coldharbour could sleep through it. The city began to awaken then, the narrow wicket gates set open in London's walls to admit foot travelers and the country folk with their baskets of produce. The Chepe woke also, so that those still abed could hear the rumble of the first carts, while the early traders began to set up their stalls and the apprentices would start shouting, yawningly, "What lack ye, my masters? Combs for the closets, jeweled buckles, damasks and silks, a fine fair necklet for your lady? What lack? What lack?"

They had scarce begun their cries when Malbon came to Hungerford's chamber and bade him go to the prince. Hungerford roused himself and began to dress. He asked Malbon what was amiss.

"There is ill news from Wales," Malbon said. "The Lord Thomas has come with the messengers but five minutes ago. The prince is bidden back to the Marches."

Hungerford said, "He'll not make his journey today."

When he went from his room, Tom stood by the dead hearth in the hall, sprucely garbed in green surcoat and cloak, the white boar of the Hollands, his wife's badge, embroidered in silk on his sleeve. He spoke mockingly of his brother. "Is he still abed?" he said. "I doubt not he's dog-sick this morn."

"If you'll wait, my lord," Hungerford said, "I'll rouse him."

"Rouse him?" Tom said and laughed. "It will take more than any one to rouse my brother after a night's riot. I'll come and give you aid."

Malbon already had drawn back the shutters of the prince's chamber so that the sunlight flooded in. Henry had set an arm across his eyes to keep the light from them, but he no more stirred. When Tom saw it, he flung back the door and went to the bedside boisterously. "Good morrow, good my brother," he said. "You're for horse and the Welsh mountains. Friend Owen is on the march again. Aberystwyth has fallen to him."

He set the papers he had brought with him on the coverlet. Henry struggled up in the bed that he might sit. He sought to read, screwing his eyes against the light and with a hand to his head.

Presently he said, "None expected he would march until April."

"I warned you, brother," Tom said. "I always said Glendower would catch you with your shield down one day." He looked upon Henry with mocking enjoyment. "Mayhap one of his bards looked in a magic mirror and saw it all—you drinking yourself dog-sick with a sanctuary man in a Bread Street tavern. That would bring Glendower from his mountain foxhole."

"Get out," Henry said. "I want to dress."

Tom raised his brows and grinned. "Dress?" he said. "You could not stand. You'll need a day to cool your head."

Henry again bade him go in an angry voice. Tom rose, hitching his cloak about him. "I'll go," he said. "Though it would be sport watching you get to your feet. What do I tell Father? That you are sick? That you have a fever?"

Henry said, "Tell him what you will."

Tom answered in mockery. "I'll let you down lightly since you already took one blow from him. I shall tell him you lie abed, but no more. Fare you well."

When he had passed into the corridor, he swung the door shut with a crash that had the windows leaping in their frames. Henry set a hand to his head and groaned. "I know not what I drank last night," he said. "It must have been poison."

Hungerford saw him white-faced and deadly sick. It seemed to him Tom was right and that the prince would not this day be on his way, but Henry set aside the sheets and gained his feet. While he dressed he spoke with Malbon, giving him many orders, forgetting nothing. Hungerford saw him for the first time as changed, as though the rioter and carouser were set aside and the knight stood in his place.

Henry caught his look and strove to smile. "Friend Owen has moved fast this spring," he said. "Would God he had chosen another day for it."

"My lord," Hungerford said, "you're not fit to ride this morn."

"In truth, Hungerford," Henry said, "I'd better be. Glendower will not wait on my night's drinking."

XV

Henry was at Oxford by nightfall and came thence to Chester. Talbot gave the prince curt greeting. He had heard the tales of Henry's London wildness, and he was put from patience with him. His manner swift-pricked Henry's resentment, and men marked that their old ease of association was much chilled.

Yet soon was there much cause for gladness. It was as though the taking of Aberystwyth had been Glendower's last funeral gleam of triumph, and his might now lay spent and burned out. It was to Henry that the men of the valleys now came; the ragged Welsh bowmen, black browed and bitter, with never a word of English; the chieftains, proudly bearing on their shields the ancient insignia of Llewellyn but ready to make terms and swear fidelity. All came claiming the pardon Henry had offered them four years previously.

Men whispered that in all the western harbors the Frenchmen hoisted their painted sails and crept out with the tides and the fair winds back to their Normandy ports. By August Glendower himself was a fugitive, his armies shrunken to a tiny handful, seeking the safety of the mountains. Henry came in full cry after him down the Dee Valley, which oftentimes had flung its gentle mists about him in the past. Few doubted now that Owen was doomed. Aumerle spoke with Henry jubilantly, scanning the distant hills as they came to their night's lodging. "You have him, cousin," he said. "Welsh fox that he is. When you bring him in chains to your father in London and the gallow's rope is about his neck, there'll be no man to dispute Wales with you."

Henry made no reply. Aumerle raised his brows and broke out laughing. "By cock and pie," he said, "I believe you hope he'll get away."

Henry answered him calmly. "If he falls to me," he said, "I'll take him."

Glendower's case was indeed desperate. On foot, attended by four only, he used the night to creep like the wounded fox Aumerle had likened him to, past the English camp into the Berwyn hills. By morning the English were hot upon him, the bowmen beating the bracken yard by yard. The English knights watched, standing together by their horses. So certain were they all violence had passed that they had not troubled to don mail. Henry stood some small way from the others. A brook raced by him, crystal-clear over brown rocks, and he heard a pebble plop into it as from a great height. He lifted his head and looked up, seeing high above him four figures seeking the shelter of the next crag as a hunted rabbit might dart from tree to tree. He looked back at Talbot and Aumerle, but they stood intent on the soldiers' searching and did not turn. When he knew no man observed him, he raised his sword blade to his lips and lowered it. Glendower answered him with uplifted hand in knightly fashion, so they might well have ridden from the lists dipping their lances in homage to one another, their combat done.

Thus, three weeks before his twenty-first birthday, Henry came into his Welsh inheritance. He had fought with Glendower seven years that he might attain it.

"It passes my knowledge how he got away," Aumerle said when they were returned. "Yet he'll trouble us no more, for all he gained his sanctuary."

Talbot answered grimly, "When winter comes, he'll find the mountains no gentle resting place."

"Nay, he will not, but on earth he'll know no other," Aumerle said cheerfully. "For his life he will never dare set foot beyond them." He looked at Henry. "So it's done, cousin," he said. "Your father will mend the quicker when he knows."

Henry had not known his father was again sick. Aumerle made haste to tell him all was well. "It was but that he fell to swooning when he rode to Mortlake," he said. "He mends again. This news will be to him as excellent medicine."

It was Talbot who had received from the Council the tidings of the King's sickness. Henry spoke with him in an angry voice, saying, "Am I the last to know how my father fares?"

Talbot answered him coldly. "It seemed to me you would have had but small interest in it."

Henry gave him a lowering look but said nothing. They spoke no more words to each other until, at nightfall, they lay down on the straw pallets which the serving women had spread for bedding on the floor. Under the window Aumerle fell to snoring in subdued fashion.

"Talbot," Henry said softly.

Talbot answered him, "My lord?"

"You think me a poor son of my father?"

"I do not judge you, my lord."

"All other men do. It is freely said."

"You are their prince," Talbot said. "A fierce light beats upon you. I have seen you here in the Marches. Since you were seventeen, when you first took up your command, I have watched you match lance with lance and blow for blow with Glendower. But other men know you only from the tales of the London taverns."

"Talbot," Henry said, "in truth I know not what is the matter with me. I would have gladly rendered my life here in the Marches for my father. But in London I stifle."

"Aye," Talbot said. "You are not the first to find a King's robe heavier than armor."

XVI

The King knew much ill-health now and but rarely sat at the meetings of the Council. He had dispatched a force into France, under Sir John Cornwall, to serve the French King. Charles de Valois rendered good payment for them, for he lacked men to quell his troublesome nobles and bought them where he might from friends or foes. Henry much loathed this, seeing his soldiers as mercenaries, their service and their lives spent in the cause of their ancient enemies. When his father lay abed of his winter sickness, he sent letters to Cornwall under the King's seal, bidding him make peace and return home. Cornwall obeyed, believing that they came from the King, and withdrew all his men from Paris.

The news that peace was made reached England when the King was somewhat recovered. When he heard it he was brought to the Council Chamber, his servants bearing him in his chair, for, since his attack at Mortlake, he had not set foot to the ground. The Council sat about the great oaken table alongside the casement windows, where on the stone sills outside the pigeons cooed and lichen overhung the buttresses. The chamber was wide and light, the table polished and set with long goose quills and silver ink wells. Henry sat at its head where, since his father's illness, he had presided. All rose when they saw the King, and the prince moved from his place.

Derby began to speak in bleak anger of Cornwall's action. "Did he presume me dead," he said, "that he should set his hand to a treaty without our authority? I would have him answer for it, my lords. I am not grown senile, nor do I yet lay aside the weight of government."

It seemed to Henry that he must speak before, in a manner, Cornwall's head lay before them on the table. "He is not at fault," he said. "He did this at my commands."

"It does not excuse him," the King said. "Wherefore should he obey you?"

Henry answered, "I wrote under your signet, my lord."

"Afore God, Harry," Derby whispered, "I should have you in the Tower for this."

His anger had sent the scabs that clung to the underside of his nostrils a livid purple. For a space it daunted even Henry. He began to speak uncertainly, saying, "You fell sick, my lord, the day the matter was discussed. I thought you inclined toward a treaty."

Derby looked hard upon him and said, "Do you speak true?"

Henry stood flushed and in silence. After a space he said, "No, my lord."

"I do not think harm will come of it," Dorset said. "Much English blood was spilled in this quarrel."

The King made a weary gesture for silence. He looked upon his son no more with anger but in chill hostility. At length he beckoned forward the clerk. "The prince has served on many meetings of the Council," he said. "What sum is owing to him in lieu of this?"

The clerk looked startled. "Quite a considerable sum, if it pleases your grace," he said in a flustered voice. "Some twenty-five or thirty pounds. If your grace would but grant me a moment, it can be reckoned with exactness."

"Reckon it so," Derby said. "And have the prince paid before he leaves our presence." He took a quill and scored through Henry's name heading the rolls. "Doubtless you think as I, my lords," he said, "that my son is not fitted to serve me longer in the office of a councilor."

To his son he said, "Go then. You will be paid in full for what service you have rendered."

Henry answered that he had no care for payment.

"Have I not told you to go?" Derby said. "Must I bid you twice?"

Henry set back his chair. He bowed to his father and went from him, the room silent. He well knew all watched him and that they looked mostly upon him with anger.

When the day's business was done, the King was borne from the Council Chamber. "Well, in truth," Westmorland said after the door had closed upon him, "this is most disappointing. The boy seemed to promise so splendidly for a time."

"The effect of a sudden access to power," Suffolk said. "How often have we seen it?"

"You judge him early," Chichele said. "There is no more humbling thing than the crown of England. Let him first feel the weight of it."

Arundel made a singular, strangulated sound in his throat. "The weight of the crown," he said. "I had rather he felt the weight of his father's sword strap—prince though he is."

"Not gracious thanks," Dorset said dryly, "to one who for seven years held Glendower back with his bare hands."

"Likewise witness his charge at Shrewsbury," Westmorland said. "A brave thing. I was there," he added as though to make all things clear.

"Any man can go roistering into battle," Arundel said sharply.

"Nay, he did not go roistering," Westmorland said. "They do say he wept over Hotspur."

Arundel gave him an impatient look. "Now do not ask me to believe that," he said. "The boy will be in his cups again in some Thames-side hovel tonight, doubtless with a whore on one side of him and a sanctuary man on the other. Nor will it be the memory of Hotspur that has driven him there."

When he had gone from them, Dorset and Bishop Chichele sat alone together. Dorset spoke in a troubled voice of the prince. "I know not if we can expect other from him," he said. "He knew a harsh schooling at Glendower's hands and at Percy's. Oftentimes it seems to me his is the roistering of a young man who fears he may not be alive tomorrow."

Chichele sighed and shook his head. "No, my lord," he said, "it is somewhat sadder. It is the roistering of one who fears he may well be alive tomorrow."

XVII

Henry came back to Coldharbor in much anger but seeking to shrug it away. "So much for the Council," he said. "I am dismissed it."

"Well, my lord," Hungerford said with forced joviality, "I know not how you are going to fill your days."

Henry laughed as with bitterness. "Oh, don't fret, Hungerford," he said, "I shall fill them."

He did in fact fill them with all manner of escapades, and his wildness was once more the talk of the city. The King was ailing more than before, being, it was said, troubled in his conscience and unable to sleep. It was said by his enemies that the shadow of Richard of Bordeaux lurked at his elbow. He talked oftentimes of a pilgrimage to Jerusalem, seeming to recall the prophecy of his youth that he would die there. Rarely did he show himself to his subjects, and the toil of government fell more and more upon his four young sons. Men marked them with both joy and despair, seeing them all brilliant, all wayward, all with the dark physical beauty of the de Bohuns, yet it was as though the prince in all things had the edge of his brothers. He gave much disquiet to those who wished Lancaster well, ever surrounded by his bejeweled and swaggering young men, drinking in the noisy parties Lewis Hall held nightly at the Vintry or kneeling that he might toss for hazard among the rushes of a tavern. Yet he had other diversions. He much loved music and wrote it—descants and airs, haunting and charming to the ear and of much merit. Oftentimes when the clamor of the Vintry was at its height, Lewis Hall or Hoccleve or Geoffrey Chaucer's son, Tom, would draw him aside that they might talk poetry with him. And when Hoccleve penned a rondel, Henry set it to music with an air that had about it a summer's day enchantment to ripple through the lute strings.

Yet few men marked him when he was thus. He got no more sleep than his father did. Nightly Coldharbour stood ablaze with lights as the single candle of the sleepless King flickered in darkened Westminster, and there were many to point to the contrast and shake their heads over Lancaster.

XVIII

When it was spring, the King walked a little on his stick in the gardens of Westminster, Joanna with him. Archbishop Arundel sought him there. "God greet you, my liege," he said. "It is a pleasant morning. I fear what I would say may darken it for you." He spoke the prince's name.

"He must go his own way," Derby said. "I have outfought many foes, my lord Archbishop, but against Harry I couch my lance."

"My liege lord," Arundel said, "you use him too patiently. It was not thus that the Book of Deuteronomy instructed the Israelites to deal with their stubborn and rebellious sons."

Derby made a weary gesture. "Come," he said, "what would you have me hear?"

Arundel began to speak of the payments made to Henry in his capacity as Captain of Calais. "These moneys were for the wages of the English soldiers in our French possessions," he said. "Yet we of the Council have had no receipts for them."

"Good my lord Archbishop," Derby said, "I have a rioter and a drunkard for a son—that much is admitted. Would you have him also a thief?"

"I do not accuse him," Arundel said stiffly. "But I would have these sums accounted for. Rumor is quick to say they have gone on private debts not public ones."

Derby spoke in a still voice, saying, "Could it be so?"

"Nay, why not?" Joanna said. "He owes money, does he not?"

"Madam, his debts are the talk of the city," Arundel said. "There is not a merchant in the Chepe to whom he does not owe money. It is freely said more than two thousand crowns would not discharge them."

Henry was yet in Calais. When he returned, it was to find his papers seized and his treasurer, Lord Scrope, lodged in the Tower.

He sought immediate audience with his father, but the King, sick again and near convinced of his guilt, would not see him. Henry went back to Coldharbour and his revels as with indifference, bent, it seemed, on joining Scrope in the Tower. He would in truth have done so if Hungerford had not searched the length of Cold-harbour for the receipts, finding them and bringing them to Dorset who himself took them to the King. All was in order and not a penny had been misapplied. Henry could have well proved the charges against him baseless as from the first, but it seemed he had had no care to do so. The King remained much angered with him. He summoned the prince to Westminster that for a time he might be lodged under his roof, but he himself kept his bed and barred him from him.

One night when Hungerford returned to the palace, Ned met with him. He was shivering and close on tears. "Oh, sir," he said, "what a night we have had. The prince was all but murdered." He began to tell Hungerford of it, his voice shaking. The attacker had lain hidden behind the tapestry in the prince's bedchamber and when Henry had come there alone had sought to set a knife between his shoulders. They had grappled together silently. Only Rafe's furious barking had roused the servants to the prince's aid.

Hungerford went straightway to the bedchamber. With Henry was his uncle, Thomas of Dorset, white faced, for he had much love for his nephew. Henry sat clad in a bedrobe, pale likewise but much composed. "Some crazed Lollard," he said. "He did me no hurt."

"Praise God we reached you in time, Hal," Dorset said. "Yet I know not why you never cried out."

Henry sat by the fire, his head turned from him. "Uncle," he said presently, "was that how Richard went—alone and in the night, with never a dog to bark?"

"Harry, Harry," Dorset said, "what do you speak of?"

Henry said, "I thought it may be I went for Richard."

XIX

When the King heard of the attempt on his son's life, he summoned him to him. Henry went on his knees to him, speaking first of the payment to the Calais soldiers which had first estranged them.

"My lord," he said, "did you in truth think I had stolen it?"

Derby answered, "Is it so long since you laid hands on a Treasury purse?"

"I do not rob my soldiers," Henry said in a stifled voice.

"No?" Derby said. "It is a fine distinction." Presently he said, "What am I to make of you, Hal?"

"Oh, my lord," Henry said, "I am often at fault—that I acknowledge—but I have much love for you and I would not rob my soldiers. It was past my belief that you thought I had. When you would not see me, I did what in truth I seem to do many times—I lost grip of my temper."

He yet knelt with his head bent. Derby, looking down upon him could see the scar of Shrewsbury under his hair, and his face softened. "You provoke me much," he said, "even to blows. Did I give you much hurt, Hal?"

Henry said, "Why nay, my lord. It was deserved. Even my uncle thought so."

It was as though they came nearer to each other than for many months. Henry felt them returned to the warmth of his boyhood. He said, "My lord, will you not come with me tomorrow for a day's fishing? We can cast for salmon as we used to in the Wye."

Derby answered, "There are no salmon in the Thames."

"Yet there may be for us," Henry said. "Will you not come?"

"If I have health enough," Derby said, smiling, "and the day is fine. Get you gone from me, Hal. If I am to bear with you all tomorrow, I have had enough of you now."

On the morrow Derby was carried down to the water's edge in his gilt chair, while Henry cast from the bank, with but little success yet eager and glad in his father's company. The day was sunlit, and the river flowed silver sweet between its trailing willows, much apple blossom and wild cherry tossed about it. Yet Derby was chill again. It was to him a hard thing to watch his son's vigor, himself lacking the strength to rise from his chair. That day the city had rung its bells in thanksgiving for Henry's deliverance. The King had heard them, well knowing few would ring for himself in like circumstances. He saw the love of the Londoners set no more upon himself but upon his son.

Presently Henry came to him and laid his line on the grass beside his chair. "You were right, my lord," he said, "I'll hook no salmon here. It is not as Monmouth."

The King said, "Is Monmouth never to be off your tongue?"

Henry looked at him in puzzlement. "My lord," he said, "I did not mean to anger you."

Derby said, "Whether or no you angered me has not weighed greatly with you before. Witness the company you keep at Coldharbour." Presently he said, "Your mother would have you married, Harry, and I begin to think she speaks wisdom. The hand of Anne of Burgundy is still yours if I asked it."

"My lord," Henry said, "when I went to engage Glendower you promised me that match would not again be thought on."

Derby said, "Your mother urges it on me."

"She is not my mother."

Derby looked at him with cold disfavor. "She is the Queen, your lady. She should have had you earlier, Harry. Mary—God assoil her—so cloyed and pandered you, as Richard's mother did him, that you grow as he did."

"My sins are my own," Henry said, with a tremble of anger, "much as that woman who shares your bed would like to lay them to my mother's charge."

He remained on one knee by his father's chair, in expectancy of a blow. The King looked upon him, then turned his face to the trees where his attendants waited beyond earshot. He beckoned and they came to bear him off in his chair toward the palace.

Hungerford came to the prince, seeing him, for a space, with the same look of tormented bitterness as his father. Henry lifted his head and spoke in a hard voice. "It's of no use," he said, "I know not why we try."

XX

That night be changed into unaccustomed finery and hounded both Gornot and Hungerford out with him. They rowed across the river to Southwark, going from the river stairs on foot to the Vintry. Among the hovels and brothels of Southwark it was a queenly building, timbered in black and white, with jalousied glass windows and painted shutters. Bunches of herbs, freshly dried and sweet smelling, hung inside the door; nor was there smoky tallow to foul the atmosphere, for Lewis Hall lit his great room only with candles of perfumed wax, like a noble lady in her bedchamber. Already the minstrels played softly behind the screened gallery. Tom was lounging at the end of one of the long tables, a drinking pot at his elbow. He caught at his brother's sleeve and spoke in mocking delight, saying, "For the love of Lucca, Hal, not another lance broken with father?" When Henry did not reply, he said, "It was all kiss and handclasp yesterday. What went wrong today? A payment to the Calais soldiers gone astray? Or a purse snatched off the Standard?"

"The Calais garrison were paid," Henry said with threatening calm.

"Oh, for sure. But you have made Father mad. He talks again of having you bedded with your horse-faced Burgundian lady."

Henry said fiercely, "I have his promise. He'll not do it."

"Nay, don't be too sure. Policy binds kings and their promises together with a mighty slender thread."

"What if you have to take her, my lord," Gornot said. "Bed with her once. Give England an heir. Not even your father can ask more of you."

"True," Tom said, grinning. "Hal, your fellow talks sound sense. But let's have a song." He gestured to one of the jongleurs standing by the window, his lute slung over his shoulder. "Hi, fellow, we want a song."

"What, my lord?"

"Greensleeves," Tom said, and roared out:

> Chepeside jill or noble dame,
> Why, in the dark, are both the same.
> Bed with her, where e'er she be,
> In Cock Lane, cold, or Bungundy.

"For shame," Lewis Hall said, coming up behind one of the servers with a platter of venison. He was a little, misshapen Welshman, black browed but with a manner of singular sweetness. He knew well the signs of tautening tempers and as exactly how to placate them.

"For shame," he repeated. "A tune as sweet as a May morning and you set your bawdy words to it. Have you not lewd songs enough?"

He set the lute into Henry's hands. The prince was skilled in the playing of it, and his voice had a young man's purity and strength. He sang a song the Welshmen ever sang when they drank together.

> Y deisen fras, felus, a phob sort o spices,
> O torwch hi'n radus—y gwyliau.

When he came to the last line, another voice took it up in loud and confident relish. Thus singing, a man came in through the door, tugging off his shabby brown hood. He was a squat, bustling coxcomb, horribly squint eyed, with hair so red a man might have sought to warm his hands by it. "A brave song, my masters," he said. "Bravely sung—and by a Saxon, look you."

Lewis Hall spoke in embarrassed fashion. "Another of our nation, my lord," he said to Henry. "Daffyd ap Llewellyn ap Ivor of Gwent. He is but lately come to London and knows no other but myself. Whether he will be welcome by you, I know not."

"Why should I have aught against him?"

"He followed Owen," Lewis Hall said. "He boasts that his sword is red with the blood of Glendower's enemies." To the stranger he said, "It is the prince who honors my table this night."

The stranger scowled at him, his eyes turning much inward. "No prince had Wales save Owen," he said. "Though at the end many Welshmen turned aside from him to kiss the hand of Harry Monmouth."

"By all the saints," Tom said, staring. "He stands and talks treason to our faces. Harry, call the watch and have him up before the Star Chamber in the morning."

"Nay, he's my companion in arms," Henry said. "Daffyd ap Llewellyn—I know of you. You were he whom Glendower called 'Gam' and boasted you were the equal of three men in single combat."

Gam's crossed glance swung toward him. He recognized at last that he was in the presence of the sons of the King of England and he looked wary. Yet he made Henry a bustling bow, a bow of courtesy only, without homage. "Know my name you do, my lord," he said. "Better for me had it been had I known yours. Yet I did not look for Harry Monmouth behind a boy's face. So please you, my lord, I'll go now. Seven years I bore my lance for Owen, and that will find no liking from you."

"Sit you by there, Davy," Henry said, as in the Welsh fashion. "Will you not drink with me? Our lances are couched and no man quit the field with more honor than Glendower."

"Well," Tom said, pushing back his chair. "Sit and break bread with a traitor follower of Glendower, if you will, Hal."

"Oft have I heard Owen speak of you, my lord," Gam said to Henry. "Stubborn, he called you, saying that a stubborn Englishman was worse than a stubborn Welshman, and a Welshman was bad enow."

Henry asked him if he had taken the oath of allegiance to his father and he answered as by a grunt. "By the sacred feet of St. Wilfred, no. Rather would I lose my goods, my land, aye, my right arm even. Yet for my children's sake my wife has so sworn."

"You have many children?"

"Indeed, yes," Gam said pridefully. "Seventeen of them there are, and eighteen will it soon be."

"In truth, we must drink to them," Henry exclaimed. "A toast to each."

"Indeed, my lord," Gam said. "Does it please your highness to drink now to my first-born, Daffyd ap Daffyd ap Llewellyn?"

"It does," Henry said. "And I like you, too, Davy, in truth. We must get drunk again together."

"My lord," Hungerford said, "your father is already wrath with you. Stay sober this night."

"Oh, peace, Hungerford," Henry said. "You're crab-apple company."

Curfew sent all the boats to the north bank for their night moorings, and not even for a King's son would a Thames waterman dare remain at the Southwark side. When it drew near, the prince called his gentlemen and walked to the stairs. Tom came with them, lurching along in the van of his four besotted retainers. He was in his cups and likewise quarrelsome. All the way back across the night-misted river he and Henry snarled at each other in the bows of their wherry.

Curfew was pealing from St. Martin's le Grand as they scraped against the stone stairs of Fish Street. One by one the wooden shutters of the houses leaped darkly across lighted windows, blotting out the city, but many folk still strolled the streets. Of them were John and Humphrey returning from dining with the mercers at the Guildhall. Tom as he came ashore saw them go by, with them their young torch-bearing pages and a handful of retainers in the blue and white of Lancaster. He sought to catch up with them and broke into a lurching run. A ragged journeyman loitered with others at the top of the stairs and was all but knocked off his feet by him.

"Ho, friend," he said, gripping the tassels of Tom's surcoat into one fist, "would you knock an honest man into the river with your drunken amblings?"

"Out of my way," Tom snarled at him. "Damn you for a misbegotten drunken lout."

The man tightened his grip and answered, "You crow mighty loud for a young cockerel."

Tom struck at him with a drunkard's fury. The journeyman took the blow grunting, but he was a tough, weather-hardened man, and he came back at Tom like a bull bearing down on a terrier. As they fell to grappling, Tom set back his head and let out a ringing howl, "Lancaster. To me."

The prince's wherry had put out again from the stairs, but Henry would at once have his wherryman pull back. Hungerford laid a hand on his arm. "My lord," he said, "have you not already angered your father enough. Pull on to Coldharbour."

Henry set his hand aside with impatience. He sprang for the stairs and scrambled up them. Already there was much furious scuffling atop them, for John and Humphrey had likewise heard the battle cry of Lancaster and come to answer it. All about the taverns were spilling out their occupants. Hungerford saw two apprentice boys come up, their cudgels at their waists. After a space they swung at each other as if they were mortal foes.

"Looks like a jolly night, my masters," the wherryman said gleefully. He went grinning up the stairs, rolling back his sleeves.

"Sit down, you fool," Gornot said as Hungerford made to follow. "The watch are yonder."

"We should warn him."

"Much thanks you'll get for your warning. I like his service well enough when it leads me among the wine casks of the Vintry, but here it grows too rough. Let him get his head broken here or by his lord father tomorrow, if he will."

Hungerford scrambled from the boat, seeking Henry's side. The watch was near, but when Henry knew it he went back that he might warn Humphrey. Of Lancaster, Humphrey only escaped, making off down Thames Street which the watch had failed to cordon. In the confusion and darkness the watch seized on those they could, dragging all to the King's Bench. Chief Justice Gascoigne presided there, and though he well knew the three young lords of Lancaster he held them in ward with the rest.

When it was morning the King sent word commanding that the lords Thomas and John be set instantly at liberty, and Gascoigne, reluctantly, for he was a cold, fearless, precise man, submitted. Of the prince there was no mention. Plainly the King had no care what happened to him. But the officers of the court were still too faint hearted to prefer charges against the heir to the throne. They proceeded only against the lesser fry, the apprentices, the journeymen, and Henry's wherryman, for all the prince pleaded the man had but come to his defense. There was a furious scene between them, the contained, stern, cold-voiced old man and the angry heir to the realm.

It was late evening before Henry returned to Coldharbour, and he came in defeat, dirty and bedraggled. Dorset awaited him there and his three brothers. Henry took no heed of them but shouted to Ned for wine.

"Well, you are back," Dorset said gruffly. "I have to speak with you."

"Not now, good my uncle," Henry said. "I am half-dead with thirst. I want no more but to drink and wash. The rest can wait."

"Your wine bibbing can wait," Dorset said. "Now, dismiss your minstrels unless you wish them to hear what I have to say to you."

The musicians were in their places in the gallery, ready to play out the night. For a space Henry hesitated, then he clapped his hands and bade them leave. Only his brothers remained, with Hungerford, Gornot and the boy. Henry looked upon them with anger.

"Well, Uncle," he said, "is this private enough for you?"

"For me, yes," Dorset said: "For you, I doubt it. The King, your father, has no more to say to you but this—you are to go."

Henry looked at him, not speaking.

"You are banished London," Dorset said. "Your father gives you grace until tomorrow to make ready."

Tom began to speak for his brother, fingering a tooth which the night's work had loosened. "We were all in it," he said mumbling. "Father excuses us. Why is he so mad with Hal?"

Dorset answered him, "Your brother has more years than you. He must learn a harder lesson."

Henry said, "My father gave me solemn promise that he would not again condemn me unheard."

"Then has he thought better of it. The guards are bidden to hold you should you try to force your way to him."

Henry shrugged. His anger was glinting in his face, but he tried to mask it. "I should have recalled," he said, "it was a king's promise. Have you done, Uncle? I am parched and I want some music."

"I wish my doing could bring a glimmer of wit to you," Dorset said. He strode to the great fireplace and looked up at the carved crest of the three white plumes above it on the wall. "*Ich Dien*," he said. "The motto beloved by your great uncle, Edward, Black Prince of Wales. You are the first to bear his title after him, and the words are as meaningless to you as an infant's babble."

"Oh, for the saints' sweet sake, Uncle," Henry exclaimed. "All that have I heard from Gascoigne and more. Let me be."

Dorset said, "Have you let your father be? Ten years ago you would not have found him so poor an adversary, nor your grandfather of Gaunt. Did Gaunt still live, he would have so dealt with you that you would have had no breath left for your carousals."

"In truth, Uncle, you do well to prate Gaunt at me," Henry whispered. He set back his head and broke into hard laughter. "Gaunt," he said. "Was he not twenty years begetting bastards by his squire's wife?"

"By my right hand, Harry," Dorset shouted at him, "you'll not say it." As by instinct he laid a hand to his dagger. Rafe sprang upon him, with fierce barking, but Henry caught him and dragged him back. Dorset turned and went from them. Presently they heard the hoof beats of horses riding from the court.

Henry stood silent for a space, then turned to the door and shouted for Malbon. "Take horse and ride after my uncle of Dorset," he said. "Tell him every word he said to me this night was just and I acknowledge it. Ask him of his charity to forgive me."

Malbon presently returned. The pinpricks of sweat glistened on his face, and he looked distressfully at Henry and the silent young men about him.

Henry said, "You spoke with him?"

Malbon answered, "Your lord uncle bids me say he asks only that, as you must keep your distance from the King, your father, so you will from him. He wants no more to do with you."

"No blame to him," Henry said. "My thanks, Malbon. You did all I asked."

Hungerford feared he would get well drunk that night, but he did not. He sat by the fire in his stained and crumpled clothes, coaxing a smile from Ned and making many plans for the morrow. Among the gloom that lay upon the household Hungerford saw him cheerful and composed. Presently when they sat alone, Henry said in a quiet voice, "What would you say if I told you I well loved my father?"

"I should acknowledge it, my lord."

"Would you, in truth? Or would you think me the veriest hypocrite in the realm?"

"My lord," Hungerford said, "I know not what it is you run from."

Henry sat silent. After a little he said, "Since I first learned twelve years ago in Chester that I was the heir of England—I have been seeking to gain my feet."

"Some would hold you greatly to be envied."

"Oh, for sure," Henry said. He spoke on a sudden with a bitterness Hungerford had not before seen in him. "Consider the kings you envy—King Edward, a man fine in his youth, turning to a slobbering, senile old man, not able to feed himself, his mistress at his death tearing the rings from off his fingers. Or his father, the second Edward—dragged by his wife and her paramour through the storms of winter in scant clothes so that he might haply perish of cold. And when he yet lived, beaten to death in the dungeons of Berkeley Castle. Or John—poisoned, it was said, by the monks as he rested in the orchards of Swinestead. Or the second Henry, deserted by his wife, at war with his sons, dying among servants who stripped his body of its jewels and garments and left it four days naked and unburied. These are the kings, Hungerford. This is how they were used."

Hungerford scarce knew how to answer him. He had served Henry for four years with small liking, but he saw him now stripped of helm and armor as a knight in the hands of his enemies, seeing him much otherwise to what he had ever been. "You read too much, my lord," he said at last. "Shut your mind against these tales of the past."

"Nay, you're safe," Henry said. "I thought I were safe likewise —for twelve years, shut in by my Monmouth hills." When they drew near his chamber, Hungerford lighting him, he yawned and spoke indifferently. "I know not what I've been babbling to you about, Hungerford," he said. "I must yet be in my cups."

XXI

Henry chose to go to his own manor at Coventry, because of all his possessions it lay nearest to London. He had ever known such activity that to be on a sudden bereft of it was near to torment. Oftentimes he could not sleep, lying till he could bear with it no more, then summoning his gentlemen to ride by moonlight with him or even for tennis in the base court where the pages yawned under their flickering cressets and the ball was beyond sight against the shadowy hazards. Any of his household who desired it he would have freed from this exile. Yet most stayed, for the pickings gleaned in his service were yet splendid. Gornot fell nightly to an incessant grumbling, acting the part of the veriest prisoner.

"Not wine so much as to sting your throat," he said. "Not a jill but looks like a plough mare and beds like one. Would I get back to Southwark before yawning slays me here."

"For the love of heaven, go," Henry snarled at him, "or hold your tongue and give us rest."

Next day brought Cousin Aumerle riding from London. "I have a message for you, my hot-blooded young cousin," he said after he had greeted Henry. "Go get you back to London. Your lord father has need of you to ply your lance again."

Henry said, "Does my father seek to aid Burgundy?"

"In truth, I know not, Harry," Aumerle said. "Only that a force is to take ship to France and you are to lead it."

Henry was mounted within an hour and on his way. He was delighted beyond measure. "It must be Burgundy," he said to Hungerford as he rode. "The saints keep me from his daughter, but we have no other friend in Europe and my lance is his to command."

He was full of plans. He would be reconciled to his father and once more beg his uncle's forgiveness. No more taverns for him; no more drinking or rioting. If they would but trust him, he would show himself truly knight.

When the next day they came to Westminster, he was out of the saddle before they drew rein and passed the guards at the door of the Painted Chamber. His gaiety flamed across the graying room, chilled by the feel of the King's perpetual sickness, as though a torch had been lighted there. Yet the King drew no sparks from it.

Henry went down on his knees to him and asked him how he fared. Derby gave him no answer, speaking briefly. "You are to France," he said. "The expedition is small and poorly furnished, but my Commons have urged you on me. They tell me they wish no other leader for this venture save you."

Thomas Chaucer, Speaker of the Commons and the son of Geoffrey, stood behind his chair. The King looked back at him as with resentment. It was no light thing to him that his son should be thus preferred. Fifteen years ago in his fierce and splendid youth, it would have been Henry of Derby who was so named. It was to him that his youth and body's strength mocked him in his eager and vigorous sons.

"I'll most gladly go, my lord," Henry said. "And for my misdeeds I most humbly crave your pardon. I would have so said before save that it might have seemed a begging off for pardon." He asked the size of the force to be dispatched.

"Two hundred archers," Derby said. "And eight hundred lances. No more."

"It is very small, my lord," Henry said doubtfully. "Not sufficient for my needs. Nor do I think it will content the Duke of Burgundy."

"Burgundy?" the King said sharply. He spoke with impatience. "You are too hot upon the scent, Hal. It is to the aid of the King of France that you sail."

Henry looked upon him. His father asked, "You do not like it?"

"To Charles of France, my lord? He who fed Glendower with guns and men these seven years while his signet lay to the articles of truce?"

"Think you I do it for love of him?" Derby said. "He had offered me Aquitaine in return. A good price. I would take it."

Henry said, "But, my lord—"

"In truth, Hal," Derby said, "does Aquitaine mean naught to you? Did not your grandsire and your great uncle, Edward of Wales, give their youth and manhoods in seeking to restore it where, in right, it lay—to England?"

"I do not believe their words," Henry said, his voice trembling. "If they promised to restore Aquitaine, they're lying."

"I shall judge that," Derby said in cold anger, "not you. You are here to do as you are bidden—to take ship for France with the force I have pledged them."

Henry answered him, "I do not clasp hands and ride under the banner of Charles of France. Many of my soldiers lie dead in the Welsh valleys because of his guns."

"I do not force you to go," Derby said. "Get you back to Coventry, if that is your choice." He spoke with Chaucer. "Lord Thomas of Lancaster leads this expedition," he said. "Go tell my Commons the prince fears the force available too small for his personal safety."

Henry said in a fierce voice, "I did not say that."

"All present heard you," Derby said in bleak mockery. "Too small for my needs. Was it not so?"

"I do not think the prince was mindful of his own safety, if it please you, my lord," Chaucer said. "It would seem strange after Shrewsbury and Wales if he were."

Derby bade him do as he was commanded. "The prince returns to Coventry," he said. "Doubtless there is drinking and whoring aplenty for him there. His brother will bear his lance to France." To Henry he spoke brusque words. "Well, get you gone. I would have you again ten miles from me by nightfall."

There was a stirring of discomfort among the lords. Many feared anger from the prince, but Henry withdrew with no word. When Chaucer came to him, he spoke with him. "You are bound for the Commons, Sir Speaker," he said. "Must it be that you give them my father's message?"

"I must do as the King, your father, bids me," Chaucer said. "But, my lord, we know you and your record in the Marches. No man will name you craven."

Henry spoke but little during the journey back. The first night when they lodged in an almshouse, he ate nothing yet drank furiously as with the fixed deliberation of a man intent on a drunkard's release. It was hard to gain, he complained to Hungerford. The more he drank the more did he seem to remain chill and sober as the grave.

Thus they came again to Coventry. The chill autumnal days, empty of purpose, crept haltingly away. Even Hungerford, bred in the quiet Berkshire downlands, found them beyond measure drear, and Henry existed as in durance. The November seas bore Tom and his force to France. His preference over his elder brother much delighted him, and he had gone high in confidence and impatient of advice. The King had heaped honors upon him.

He was Duke of Clarence now, Seneschal of England and Knight of the Order of St. George. There were whispers almost straightway of fighting at St. Cloud, but none knew whether or no the English were engaged.

Before Tom's sailing Henry had sent to him, bidding him Godspeed, but he spoke of him seldom and of his father never at all. Both now had dealt deep wounds to the other. It was to Hungerford as though Richard's ghost had triumphed and that the wizened skull of Hotspur, grinning from London Bridge, mocked Plantagenet. When the New Year came Henry was permitted back to London, but he gained no office or responsibility, neither the King nor his uncle speaking with him. He pretended indifference. If they deliberately conspired to keep his days empty, he would fill them as he had filled them before. Again the lights blazed at Coldharbour and the music floated over the river on the night air, the Chepe journeymen nudging each other that Hal of old was back, ready to drink or brawl with any man.

Hungerford wearied of it as he had oftentimes wearied of it in the past. It seemed to him he had given enough days in the prince's service. He came in one March evening, vowing there would be few more of them. Many young men knelt among the fresh-strewn rushes, the prince at their center. They rolled dice, the drinking mugs piled high about them. Hungerford watched idly until presently Malbon came in, thick hooded as against the winter chill and spoke with Henry. The prince hearkened to him, then gained his feet, snatching his cloak from the settle.

Gornot was all but knocked from his feet as Henry flung past him. He came unsteadily over to Hungerford, grumbling as he came. "Why the haste?" he said. "Is there a fiend at his heels?"

Hungerford raised his voice above the noise and shouted for Malbon. "What is it?" he said. "Where is the prince bound?"

Malbon gave them a white look. To his father, sirs," he said. "He is ill—he is very ill."

"What, again?" Gornot said and yawned.

"He has been summoned before, Malbon," Hungerford said.

Malbon answered, "Aye, as you say. But this time, in truth, I think it is the end. This time the King will surely die."

XXII

Henry rode with but one groom, spurring as furiously as ever Hotspur had done. It was in the Abbey that his father had been stricken. He came there, through the park land where the red deer grazed under the leafless alders, the monastery hard by, where the black-robed monks scurried to and fro. The abbot met with him, much agitated and clasping his hands.

"Oh, my lord," he said, "this is a hard day for you. The King, your father, he is very grievously sick."

Henry asked where his father lay.

"In a chamber in my house," the abbot said. "He was at his devotions, my lord, in yonder chapel, today being Friday. His servants say that suddenly, with no warning, he groaned and fell forward. They summoned me and we carried him thence. His senses came back to him only once, my lord. He asked where we had borne him, and we told him the Jerusalem Chamber, for it is so called because of its tapestries. He said he had been told he would die in Jerusalem. I do not know whether he spoke in full consciousness. I summoned the Queen and yourself straightway."

He brought Henry into the Abbey. Stonework like lace clothed the pillars and the dim tracery of the roof—all even now so old that the centuries breathed coldly against the cheek. The King lay in a stone chamber in the abbot's house, its walls draped in fair tapestries, pricking out the shrines of the Holy City, each stitch bright as a jewel where the tapers struck against it. At the bedfoot the priests knelt in prayer, Dorset and Humphrey with them, and Joanna wept noisily, supported by her women. The smell of death lay on the room, not to be mistaken though the King's ravaged face seemed but little changed. The crown had been set from his head on a stool by the bed. Freed of it, it was as though he lay easefully, only his breathing a thing of labor.

Henry went on his knees by the bedside. It seemed to him small time was left him. He turned on the company, bidding them go in a hard voice. "All of you," he said. "I would be alone with my father."

They looked gapingly at him, but they obeyed. When the great door was shut upon them, he set an arm under his father's shoulders, seeking to raise him. "Oh, my lord," he said, "hear me, I beg you. There is one thing I must know. How did Richard die?"

The eyelids, thickened by the clinging scabs, did not twitch, yet it seemed a faint flicker of consciousness stirred beneath them. Henry spoke again as in despair. "There is none other here save ourselves. I will keep troth—I swear it. No man shall hear of it. But unless I know, I cannot keep on."

His intensity pierced the armor of Derby's dying. He saw his father's lips part and bent his head that he might catch what they said. "Jerusalem," Derby whispered. After a space he said, "Hal. Bless you, Hal."

One of his hands moved outward feebly as in benediction, then striking the crown toward Henry off the stool. He started from it as a man might start from his murderer's sword. The room was still save for his own panting and his father's gasps. He well knew the King would not speak again. It was as though Jerusalem were opening her gates that the crusader might fast ride home. Henry could scarce look at him, seeing the steadfastness which had borne the befouled and stricken body through the weary years of kingship. For the space of that moment it was to him impossible that his father should have murdered Richard.

He feared that his father might die while he alone was with him. He shouted, and all came filing back, their eyes going straightway to the shadowed bed. The King was now close to death. His two sons went on their knees, each at one side of him, still as carved saints, their brown heads bowed. Thus they remained at vigil a full hour until it was seen the King had gone.

Joanna broke into a loud weeping and was borne out by her ladies. Henry would yet have knelt, but Dorset raised him. He brought him to the abbot's dining hall, where all was deserted and quiet, pressing wine into his hand. For a long time Henry sat without speech. Dorset saw him so drawn and ashen of face that he feared for him.

Presently the abbot came to them, soft-footed and timorous. "My lord," he said, "your grace, as I should say—does your father—God assoil him—lie here this night or would your grace have him borne back to Westminster Palace?"

Henry looked upon him as though he scarce understood him. Dorset, seeing him without words, answered for him. "My brother's body will lie here tonight," he said. "Later the King will make known his desires to you."

Henry now heard himself named King. It seemed to him that as it had been with Job so was it with him. *"For the thing which I greatly feared is come upon me, and that which I was afraid of is come unto me."*

XXIII

There was but little grief in Coldharbour. Only Ned when he plucked at Hungerford's sleeve looked to have been weeping. He said, "He is King now?"

Hungerford answered, "Aye—God help us."

"He'll not want me," Ned said. "I know who serves the King— only the primped-up sons of the great lords. I'll be no more page to him."

He came then to tears. Hungerford went into the solar, not knowing how to comfort him. Gornot sprawled there before the fire, wine at his elbow. He waved a bejeweled hand and called to Hungerford to join him at hazard. "Is it seemly, think you," Hungerford said coldly, "with the breath barely left the King's body?"

"I never knew a better night for it," Gornot said and hiccuped. "Fill up, friend. Drink to the new reign. Hal is King. The crown on his head and the coffers of England open at his feet." He wagged his head owlishly at Hungerford. "Were we not good friends to him? Have we not dragged after him through the taverns of the Chepe drinking beggar's brew. We're worthy of our reward."

"You've had good return," Hungerford said. "Is there a ring on your hand that was not his?"

Gornot scowled at him. "Say so, if you will. It may be he was a princely master. I'd not have suffered his damned high-stomached ways else."

It was to Hungerford as though the room had caught the ghostly rustle of Richard's robe and the empty laughter of his gallants, Bushy, Bagot and Green, the nest of leeches that had fastened on the realm's throat. He felt chill and turned to the fire.

"Let's have some music," Gornot said. "Where's that sniveling page? Tell him to bring on the minstrels."

"Oh, have done," Hungerford said. "What if the prince returns? It's likely, is it not, that he may be in grief for his father?"

"What, Hal?" Gornot said and guffawed. "Not he."

Henry returned presently, with him his groom and two lay brothers from Westminster. He was wrapped in his cloak, the hood drawn over his head. Thus muffled he would have gone past if Gornot had not plucked at his lute strings and roared out,

> We shall have Spanish wine—wine of Gascony,
> We shall have Rhenish wine—and Malvoisey.

"Hold your peace," Henry said furiously.

"Why, my lord," Gornot said, "I looked to sharing wine and a song with you this night. Have we not cause?"

"Cause? My father lies dead."

"Oh, for sure," Gornot said. "Yet you're home now, Hal. What need to go about sour as a priest and wringing your hands?"

Henry jerked his head to his escort, and they went from him. To Gornot he said, "What mean you?"

"Why, nothing. The city's full of sentimental fools who would have you shed tears over your father's bier. Oblige them if you will."

Henry stood still, his face shadowed by his hood. "I deserve that

on your tongue," he said at last. "Did I not know you for a fool
to think it and myself as the greater fool to give you cause. Only
keep out from under my feet."

He would have gone on, but Gornot caught at his sleeve.
"Wait," he said. "I am your man, Hal. I served you well. England's
a lean realm, yet her purse is still deep. You'll not forget your
friends."

"You? My friend?"

"Be not contemptuous of me, my lord," Gornot said in an ugly
voice. "Lancaster was not so high-stomached once. They would
stoop to snatch a purse or a crown."

Henry seized him by the throat, setting him backward against
the table. It seemed to Hungerford he would do him much violence, and he sought to come between them. "My lord," he said,
"he's drunk. He knows not what he says."

Henry flung Gornot from him as a sack of oats. He fell from the
table to lie among the rushes of the floor, gasping and mumbling.
"Get out of my house," Henry said. "I'll not bid you twice." He
would have gone from them up the stairs, but he turned and
tugged the purse from his belt. It was weighty, and he cast it at
Gornot all but on top of him. "Take it," he said. "Then go."

Presently Hungerford went to his chamber, bidden there. Henry
stood by the bed, still wrapped in his cloak. Almost he looked as
if he had wept, but Hungerford could not be sure. He asked if
Gornot had gone.

"He goes, my lord," Hungerford said.

"I would have them all go," Henry said. "Yet see they are well
paid. They were much deceived in me." Presently he said, "I
would keep the boy."

"And I, my lord?" Hungerford said. "Do I go too?"

"I need you, Hungerford," Henry said. "If you will, stay by me."

XXIV

That night, Bishop Chichele, having said Mass for the soul of Henry of Derby, offered his gift by the high altar of the Abbey. He was alone, for it was after curfew, and save for the King's death the doors would long since have been bolted and barred to protect the relics and the holy vessels from thieves. It seemed to him something stirred as a shadow among the great pillars. He said sharply, "Who is there? Come—I know of you."

None answered him. Chichele came down calmly from the altar bearing his lanthorn high. It was as if a shadow moved by a pillar, and he saw that it was the King. He had much pallor in the gloom. Almost it might have been the son and not the father out of whom the quickening of the spirit had gone.

"Your grace," Chicele said, "you are wet with the snow. I would not disturb your devotions, but I beg you come and sit for awhile by the fire in the abbot's parlor. There is none there."

The King gave him no answer but followed him. Chichele led him to the abbot's parlor. A fat lay brother sprang to his feet and edged toward the door. "More logs for the fire, Brother Thomas," Chichele said. "And some wine. Then his grace will no more require you."

Henry set aside his drenched cloak as if he yet slept. Chichele made to pour the wine, talking the while. "The Abbey draws your grace as it does myself. Each time I come there is something fresh to delight my eyes. I beg you look at what I found but this morning."

He went to a corner settle, on which lay something draped in a tapestry curtain and drew aside the cloth. Beauneveu's picture of Richard of Bordeaux looked solemnly out upon them.

"Oh God, Chichele," Henry whispered, "would you drive me from my wits?"

"Is that what haunts you, my son?" Chichele said. "I have long thought so. It may well be speaking will ease you."

After a space the King said, "I do not know how Richard died. That is the truth—I swear it."

"Then has God purposely closed your eyes against this thing," Chichele said. "Do not force sight on them. It will not be the first time a King of England has walked blindly."

Henry answered, "I am not the King of England. The King of England is Edmund Mortimer—he who lies in the Tower. Would God I lay there in his place and he in mine."

"Yet, my son," Chichele said, "you were but a boy when this thing was done. You were no more than twelve."

The King said in a still voice, "Is it less Richard's crown when it lies on my head than when it lay on my father's?"

Chichele sighed and said, "I am very sorry for you, Henry."

"That was what Richard said. 'I am very sorry for you, Henry. I am very sorry for you.' Father," he said, "is it sin to hate one's life?"

"It is sin, my son. Life is the breath of God."

"Then God forgive me," he said and turned away his head.

"Rouse yourself," Chichele said. "This is yet a proud heritage."

"The crown?" Henry said. He broke into hard laughter. "I have ever hated it. It murdered my father—killing him as by inches. I remember him the day he rode out to fight Mowbray. A more splendid man never trod God's earth. And I remember him as he was in kingship—so feeble that he could only be borne in his chair, his face so scabbed and fouled I scarce could look upon it." He twisted in his chair as though he felt the torturer's brands near his flesh. Chichele gave him no answer. "And Richard," he said. "I never saw a man in mortal terror until the day I rode with Richard back to the Tower. Yet Richard once was a man of courage—a man who rode alone to quell the peasants on Blackheath. That was before kingship ate it from him and he no more knew rest nor stillness of mind."

Chichele said, "Yet did Richard bear the burden of his kingship lighter by far than do you."

Henry answered him, "Richard was very King. I am not. I love fellowship, father. I wanted no more than to stand toe to toe with my Londoners, to drink or talk or fight with them. Yet I'll be set apart from all men as if I were leprous."

"It is of yourself you talk now, my son," Chichele said. "No man worth his soul's salt demands ease in this world's travail."

Henry said, "As you say. Yet I cannot take this crown, Father, I cannot. Besides all else, I am not fit. Ask any man."

"You have many doubts, my son," Chichele said. "It may be as you say—that other men share them—yet it could be both they and you are wrong."

"Father," Henry said, "was it not Abraham in the Scriptures upon whom came a great horror of thick darkness? That is upon me now. If I take up the crown, Richard's ghost will never leave my heels. Yet in me rests the hope of my house. Which way can I step?"

"Only you yourself can answer that."

"In God's mercy," Henry said, "you can advise me."

"No," Chichele said sharply. "This must you do for yourself." He went to the fire and stirred the embers with his foot, his head bowed. "It is hard for me, my son," he said at last. "I am but English. I have no proud Norman blood. Yet it is told me that scarce a knight when he is struck down wounded in battle lacks a comrade to bestride him till he can rise again. It seems to me most strange that among our high-stomached Norman princes there is none ready to bestride this crippled and bleeding realm to ward off by his own body the blows of her enemies."

Henry sought to answer him. "Father," he said at last, "I tell you true, I am deadly afraid, not for my body but for my soul's sake. The sins of kingship would be enough for me to bear were I rightful King. I cannot bear them and Richard's bloodguilt too."

"You know not what you can bear," Chichele said, "until you have tried. I have long thought the man who takes the wrong step is more justified in the sight of God than the man who, counting his own soul above all else, takes no step at all."

Henry spoke with him in a still voice. "It may be I have had no way but this," he said. "I was not my mother's first-born, but the brother who would have been my shield and buckler against this day died as a babe. So has it come upon me." After a space he said, "Yet will it not be for long."

"Nay now," Chichele said, "you are no more than in the morning of your youth."

The King said, "I think that neither I nor my house is long for the throne. Not only the good God, but England herself will exact retribution for Richard's blood." He added, "When that happens, Father, when the crown is hacked from off the head of Lancaster, pray that it falls not into the lap of the King of France."

"My prayers have long been toward England," Chichele said, "and toward her Kings." He sat silent for a long time, only rousing himself as the fire's embers stirred. He said, "It grows late, my son."

Henry answered, "Aye, Father. I must go back."

He knelt and kissed the bishop's ring. Chichele signed him and spoke a blessing. "God guide you to a right decision," he said. "When it is made bring me word."

The King looked at him in fear. Chichele said, "If there was guilt here, your father bore it nobly. Let it be so with you. Do what you must and leave Lancaster's punishment in the hands of God."

It was as if his words gave the King strength. He took his cloak and went from him.

XXV

The King would make no plans for his coronation. He moved about Westminster as with a masklike face, speaking and eating little and sleeping not at all. Only two commands were his—that Edmund Mortimer, the young Earl of March, who had lain Lancaster's prisoner twelve years, be released from the Tower and that Richard's body be brought back to the Abbey to lie in the grave he had so tenderly prepared for himself in his lifetime.

It was Dorset who brought Richard's coffin from Pontefract. When he had done with it, he came to Henry. He said, "Today I took your physician, Nicholas Colnet, with me. There was also one of the squires of my body—a man I can trust—but no man else. We opened Richard's coffin."

Henry turned his head to face him. Dorset said, "However Richard died, Harry, he did not die by violence. Piers Exton was a lie that crawled from a Frenchman's brain. There was not a mark."

Henry said, "Yet could Richard still have starved to death?"

"He could," Dorset said reluctantly. "There are no means of telling."

"Uncle," Henry said, "your own half-brother, Thomas Swynford, had the keeping of Richard at Pontefract. Was he a man who could have watched his prisoner die thus, by inches?"

"It's possible," Dorset said after a long silence. "He was a rough, harsh, violent man. I never liked him."

"He never spoke to you of it?"

"No. We had no care for each other. My mother bore him in wedlock. I and my brothers—as you last reminded me at Coldharbour—were bastard born."

The King said, "I have no pride in what I said to you that night. Of your charity, can you forgive it?"

"There's naught to forgive," Dorset said. Presently he said, "Harry, Harry, what would you have us do? Prop Richard's bones on the throne and press the crown upon his skull?"

Henry exclaimed in horror. Dorset turned to him and laid a hand on his arm. "I tell you true, there is no other way for you. Were you to set aside the crown today and place it on the head of Edmund Mortimer, there would yet be men ready to tear it off again at the sword's point. More would bleed than Richard. Would you bring Lancaster down in ruin?"

That night Thomas Chaucer and others came from the Commons. They bore a petition desiring Henry to assume the crown as his father had done, no man dissenting. When the King heard them, it was to him as though his way had been made clear. He steeled himself and sent to Arundel to set all plans afoot for his hallowing.

XXVI

The day set aside for the coronation was Palm Sunday, thereby sending Henry to his hallowing less than three weeks after his father's death. The workmen labored throughout the nights under the hissing cressets to raise the tiers about Queen Eleanor's Cross and along the Conduit. The Abbey knew no stillness under the crash of hammers. The King went there two days before his anointing that he might see how the service would be ordered. All was uproar, the scaffolding half-raised and naked as the ribs of a dead man, and huge lengths of draperies strewn about the chancel. Many of his lords moved there, some bearing falcons on their wrists, and snarled at each other over precedence. Between them the Master of the King's Musick scurried back and forth between the organ and the trumpeters, saying, "Sirs, it is much too fast."

It was beyond what the King could bear. He went from the din of the carpenters and the quarreling nobles into the abbot's garden that he might walk among the cloistered walks and the flowering currants. When Arundel desired him to return, he would not. He went from Westminster that night riding to the Tower, where by custom he must lie before his hallowing among his prisoners and his enemies.

Tom rode there likewise from his landing at Southampton. He came in defeat, both angry and quarrelsome, for the promise of restoring Aquitaine had not been kept. "They lied," he said. "It was never meant that Aquitaine should be returned. Thus was my dear brother right. Where is he? At play at hazard with some sanctuary man in a tavern in Bread Street?"

Humphrey answered, "In his chamber."

"I'll see him," Tom said. "He can preen himself he read the French aright, and I am come empty-handed."

"Guard your tongue," Humphrey said. "He's much stricken. We know not where we are with him. He took no food yesterday or today."

Tom looked at him in disbelief. When he came to the stone-fashioned chamber, it was in darkness save for its brazier. The King sat by the window, and against the jalousied glass glinted the shadowy buffets of the snowflakes.

"Why no lights?" Tom said and raised his voice. "Here, boy. Bring us a light." When the tapers were lit, he spoke in mockery. "Your pardon, my liege," he said, "I had forgot it is for you only to command." He stopped and looked hard upon Henry, then said, "What ails you?"

They fell to talking of their father, that Tom might learn of his last hours. Presently the King spoke in a constrained voice. "You were ever closest to father," he said. "Did he speak to you of Richard's death?"

"Richard?" Tom said. "He but died, did he not?" After a space he said, "Well, what of it? I was never told so, but what if he was made away with? It's no gentle game—kingship. Smite first or you are stricken down."

Presently he spoke again, "Know this, Hal. We've quarreled aplenty in the past, you and I, but it's done. I am your man. I will bear faith to you and allegiance and to none else. This I swear."

Henry strove to smile and said, "Since Father died, nothing has sounded so well to my ears."

They sat in talk, warmer to each other than they had been for many years. Presently Dorset came to the King, desiring him to think of the long hours of the morrow and get to his bed. When all had gone, Henry lay far from sleep. Others likewise watched. He knew his knights knelt in vigil in the Chapel of St. John to pray for him in the hour of his anointing. With them knelt also Edmund Mortimer. It seemed to the King most strange that he should do so, since Mortimer was Richard's true heir of the blood and his rightful place was here in the King's bed. Had Mortimer lain here this night, he himself would have knelt in the Chapel of St. John—Henry, Duke of Lancaster, at prayer for the King's soul. It was to him now as though no mortal prayers could deliver his own soul—the bloodguilt of Lancaster upon it and the sins of kingship.

And all this had come upon him because, fourteen years ago, two Dukes, Mowbray and Henry of Derby, had stood in quarrel on Brentford Bridge. When he could bear his thoughts no more, he rose and went to the casement. The lights of Southwark still beckoned him from across the river. He thought as with hunger of the sweet smell of the ale and the ease of laughter, which made nothing on God's earth so friendly as a London tavern. He had looked his last on such. *Adieu, ma jeunesse. Adieu, Hal.* From the darkness it was as if Richard's voice whispered again, "I am very sorry for you, Henry. I am very sorry for you."

XXVII

At six when the King was roused, Dorset went to him. Ned came from the chamber bearing a covered tray, and Dorset asked if the King had broken his fast. "No, my lord," Ned said. "He would not touch aught."

"Afore God," Dorset said, "he has eaten nothing for two days. He cannot go fasting."

"I begged him," Ned said. "And the Lord Humphrey did likewise. He would not."

Henry bore already his robes about his shoulders. When the Lord Great Chamberlain, the Earl of Oxford, brought the Garter to set it in its place, he thrust out his right leg. Oxford clicked his tongue and said, "No, no, sire, the other."

Cambridge raised his fine brows, as if he mocked, and the King turned from him.

Dorset saw him white and drawn as a sick man. Humphrey

plucked at his sleeve, speaking in troubled voice. "Good my uncle," he said, "bid him take sup. He cannot go as he is, fasting now into the third day."

"You must eat, Hal," Dorset said. "You will be six hours in the Abbey. You'll not get through it else."

All fell to urging him to break his fast. The King would give them no need. He rode now to Westminster Hall where the clergy awaited him, and the regalia was delivered into the hands of his nobles that they might bear it before him into the Abbey. Here all the procession formed about him, his shoes taken from him under his robes, for by custom the King must go barefoot until at the crowning the royal and splendid vestments were set upon him.

"Soon it will be done," Tom said and pressed his brother's arm.

Chichele and Thomas Langley, the Bishop of Durham, came forward to stand on either side of the King. Handsome and stately men both, they looked in their jewel-studded copes as the sons of light.

Henry spoke with Chichele in a still voice. "Father," he said, "I think I will never get there."

"Come," Chichele said. "There is One there who bears more than you. You do not go in your own strength."

The royal ladies came first to their places in the Abbey; Joanna, most richly bedecked and bearing the Queen's crown, her trumpeters and her pages preceding her; Lady Hereford, the King's grandmother likewise; and Tom's wife, Margaret Holland, now Duchess of Clarence, and therefore second lady of the realm.

Margaret's sister, Isabella, bore her train for her. Margaret spoke of the King in a whisper and how he came fasting. "I hope it will not be with him as it was with Richard," she said. "He swooned at his hallowing."

"God send Lancaster swoons," Isabella said in a fierce voice. "May he drop dead. May God strike him down."

Margaret said sharply, "He is my brother and the King of England."

"He is the Duke of Lancaster," Isabella said. "It tears my heart from me to see the crown set on yon usurper's head when it should rest on Mortimer's."

The great doors of the West Front were set wide and all awaited the King. Those who had seen the Abbey littered and in chaos marveled to see it now, fair and bright as a jewel, set with crimson draperies and the faint-moving banners of chivalry in azure, purple and gilt, so that all seemed afloat in color. Much plate weighed the side altar—sconces, dishes, anointing spoons and ewers, all fashioned with skill—so that the altar seemed afire in silver as if it burned. Before it stood King Edward's Chair—the chair carved in English oak for a hundred English shillings. The years had much bruised it, and it rested squarely upon its four gilt lions in empty grandeur.

They were coming. The people in the Abbey, bright clad as the saints in the stained-glass windows, craned forward the better to see. The nobles came first, bearing the regalia on velvet cushions—the sword, symbol of justice and mercy; the spurs of St. George for chastity; the sceptre for equity; the gold bracelets for duty; the Orb for the dominion of the Cross over the world. Edmund Mortimer bore the bracelets. He was of Henry's age, a tall thin young man, hesitant and quiet of speech. The red-gold hair of the Plantagenets was his, and he had likewise the Plantagenet fairness of skin, brought to a prison pallor by his long years in the Tower. Many, looking at him, remembered that through the centuries the Kings of England had been blue-eyed, fair-haired men, as was right they should, since blue was the color of heaven and gold, beloved by the saints, stood for righteousness and wisdom.

The King came last. Few could glimpse him, for he was hedged about by his lords and bishops, the great cloth-of-gold canopy borne low over his head by the Barons of the Cinque Ports, their mantles of velvet, most deeply blue and lined in white silk. After he ascended the steps to the shrine of St. Edward, the canopy was withdrawn, and he stood alone that all the people might see him.

Isabella drew in her breath and whispered, "How white he is. I think he'll not get through it."

Arundel four times spoke the words of the Recognition, as to the East, South, West, and North.

As the voices and the trumpets answered, the King himself returned answer with a bow. England crowned her Kings cruelly, bent on teaching them humility before she exalted them. After the oath, the nobles came forward to strip him of his splendor. He knelt for his anointing, barefoot and almost naked, to receive the Holy Oil. The Abbey grew airless and stifling as a cloak. Occasionally a woman was borne out. Men marked that sweat touched the faces of Arundel and the King, though they moved as with calmness through the blaze of candles.

When the Crown of St. Edward was held above the King's head, Isabella would not watch and turned away, close to weeping. Now was the King brought to his throne, the bishops and the peers coming forward to render homage and swear fealty. They swore on their knees, their folded hands placed between the King's palms. When he had done, each man touched the crown and kissed the King's left cheek. The ceremony took much time, for each bishop and lord swore separately, and the King, weighted with his great robes and all the vestments, the crown bearing upon him, could scarce so much as turn his head. Only Chichele and Thomas Langley stood by him in this, seeking to ease the weight of the robes from his shoulders.

The King's three brothers swore first; then his uncle, Dorset, and his cousins, Aumerle and Cambridge. Men marked that Edmund Mortimer came next, and there was much stirring among the people. Mortimer sought haltingly to speak the words of the oath, for he was afflicted by stammering. In the midst he fell to silence. Men began to fear he could not go on. They stood stiff

as with horror, the King white as the dead. Presently Mortimer began once more. "I, Edmund, Earl of March, do become your liege
man of life and limb and of earthly worship; and faith and truth
I will bear unto you, to live and die, against all manner of folks.
So help me God and All Hallows."

From the Abbey the King and the Court came to Westminster
Hall that the coronation feast might be served them. The King sat
alone, raised high above the rest on a draped dais and wearing the
full regalia. He touched none of the seventeen courses, kindling
his waning strength with sips of wine. The heavy crown bore with
much weight on his temples. He did not dare ease it, knowing that
to set a hand to it would start tongues clacking that Richard's
crown sat ill and guiltfully on the head of Lancaster.

His nobles marked that he ate nothing. Suffolk said softly, "I
marvel that he had got this far through it."

"He takes it gravely in all conscience," Surrey said. "I thought
we would know some high sport when the crown was young Hal's
—Gascoigne's head on London Bridge or Archbishop Arundel
coming to the Abbey with one foot pointing the other way."

Suffolk had been in France with the English forces there, and
he asked Hungerford now how the King had done since his accession. "Not a night's riot?" he said. "Not a purse snatched by
the Standard or a brawl along the Chepe?"

Hungerford answered, "No, my lord."

"Afore God," Suffolk said, "what's come upon the boy?"

Hungerford said, "The Crown of England."

The banquet came to an end within five hours. When all was
done, the clergy filed out of the hall by the north door, followed
by the nobles and their ladies, the King, by tradition, coming last
of all. In the Painted Chamber his knights disrobed him, leaving
upon him only the ring of England from all the insignia he bore.
When they had done, he went to the casement and stood looking
from it, wrapped in a bedrobe.

Presently Dorset came to the King, urging him to take a little
food and then to go to his bed. Ned brought a tray set with brawn

and bread and ale, all fare such as any traveler might sit down to in a London tavern, and simply prepared, lacking all ceremony. The King smiled a little and began to eat.

"Well," Dorset said, watching him, "it is done."

The King set his hand about the ring of England on his finger. "Yes," he said, "it is done."

BOOK IV

THE

CALAIS ROAD

Go tell the Constable,

We are but warriors of the working day.

Our gayness and our gilt are all besmirched,

With painful marching in the rainy fields.

A year later Archbishop Arundel walked in the Tower Gardens. The King sat at work there in the open, three gray-robed clerks scurrying back and forth across the grass to him and a table set before his chair. There were many quills and parchments strewn about the table, and with them a silver-gilt hand bell and the Seal of England.

Arundel spoke saying, "Your grace is very assiduous."

"Sit down, my lord Archbishop," Henry said. "The sun drew me. I could not work inside."

"I, too, came out to walk in the sun," Arundel said. "A whole spring's splendor in the day. I shall not see many more such."

He had become changed of late, all the vigor gone from his stride. Henry knew he spoke no more than the truth. "Why, my lord," he said, "you have many more days yet."

Arundel shook his head. "I do not grieve," he said. "I am an old man."

He fell silent, the King likewise. They were not yet at ease in each other's company, still shadowed by their former enmity. "One thing I have thanked God for most heartily," Arundel said at last. "I have thanked Him that I was wrong. I trembled for the day the crown would lie on your head, my lord; yet you have shown yourself a King in very truth when once I would have attributed to you no virtue save valor. It has warmed my heart, my lord, to see you thus, and especially in your care for the Word of God. It seems to me you have set that above all else."

The King's own friend, Sir John Oldcastle, lay even now in the Tower under sentence for heresy and marked by Arundel for the burning. Henry had sought with desperation to deliver him from his sentence, now at the last planning to free him secretly. At Arundel's words it seemed to him he were duping a dying man. His shame flooded into his face, and Arundel mistook it. "We shall not speak of the past, my lord," he said. "Other cares surround us now."

He turned that he might look at the ships in the Pool. One slipped her moorings and began to creep out to midstream, her rigging creaking as she braced her painted sails to the wind. When she came abreast, she dipped her standard in salute to the King.

"One of Whittington's, is she not?" Arundel said. "They are brave men. The claws of France reach out to the Narrow Seas."

"We have not had a ship safe through these seven weeks," the King said. "Whittington himself has lost three. I know not where to turn."

"I would we could speak to France with your great-grandsire Edward's voice," Arundel said. "I have heard tales enough of how the wool lies stacked in the Medway ports for want of a safe passage while our own people and the Flemings starve." He drew his cloak about him. Henry asked if he grew cold. "I shall go in presently," Arundel said. "But there is one thing more. Think me not blunt, my lord, if I say I would see you wedded. The times are perilous. No King walks in safety. It grieves me the succession is not secured."

Henry answered that he had three brothers. "Should I fall tomorrow," he said. "Lancaster would not lack an heir."

"That way lies thick of pitfalls," Arundel said. "Your brother is childless in his marriage, and like to remain so. It is an ill thing when the crown falls from brother to brother. Set the matter afoot now, my lord."

Henry smiled and said, "It may be we must first make the seas safe for my bride."

"My lord," Arundel said, "it must be done, and for England's weal it must be done with no carnal thought."

Henry answered, "I know it."

"So be it," Arundel said. "Twice have I set the crown on the head of Lancaster. I shall not do so again."

When Arundel had left him, the King set aside his papers. His first year of kingship had rested coldly upon him, and with much danger, the Christmas one of rebellion and violence, as his first Christmas as prince had been. The Lollards had risen against him, all but taking London and threatening wildly that they would bring him to their faith or send him and his brothers to the faggots' flames. He had quelled them but between him and them now lay only death and a hatred such as the battle field had never shown him. His friend and comrade-in-arms, Jack Oldcastle, had been of them, and stood yet defiant in his brave new faith, awaiting the burning to which Arundel would deliver him. That Oldcastle should suffer thus was more than the King could bear. He had sent to Oldcastle that this night the door of his prison would be left unbarred and that he might with safety make good his escape. All was well-planned to make it seem to men's eyes as a mischance.

When the dark fell upon the city the King himself waited beneath the arch of the Bell Tower. All was silent here, with but one cresset clamped in the wall, and the shadows crept and wavered over the cold stones, bruising their grayness. After a space there were footfalls down the dark passage, soft and swift as a man's hurried breathing. Oldcastle came under the arch. He was muffled in his cloak, the hood drawn down, but his face, chalk-white with its prison pallor, was unhidden. Henry saw him as he had oftentimes seen him in the Welsh Marches, a man of fierce courage, stout-built, with a painted smile, and eyes never altogether fixed on God's earth.

"Is it you yourself, Harry?" Oldcastle said. "I had not thought to be bidden farewell by the priests' prince."

The King said, "One of Whittington's craft lies by the Tower Wharf—the *Cog John*, bound for Barbary. Her master will ask no question of any knight of Hereford who boards her this night."

Oldcastle looked upon him, smiling. He spoke softly as he was ever wont to do, his speech of the West, where lay his lands.

"Take heed to your soul, Harry," he said. "Did your priests but know of this they would impute much sin to you."

The King knew that even thus with the Tower walls still about him, Oldcastle yet mocked him. He said, "Against Glendower you were my brother-in-arms. I ever held that, on the night we forded the Severn in flood and my horse slipped from under me, it was you who saved my life."

"And so you would grant me mine," Oldcastle said. "Then are we quittance, Harry. All is paid. Now can we each fashion a dagger for the other's back."

The King said, "Must it be thus between us, Jack?" When Oldcastle gave him no answer he began to speak as if he would plead with him. "You were ever a good soldier," he said, "and a good comrade. Do you not remember the nights when we lodged in the Marcher manors, and you taught me of your skill with the broadsword, and fooled with me? I think we each counted the other a friend then."

"By all your saints," Oldcastle said, "are you not Arundel's man? Can there be naught between us now save death?"

The King said, "What madness has come upon you?"

"It is God's Word," Oldcastle said. "Soon shall we sweep the land fresh of Arundel's priests, his popes and his images. Mark it, Harry. It will be my faith and your realm that will yet stand wedded."

Already much Lollardy lay on the land and the King feared for it. "Get you from my realm," he said. "Leave it this night."

"And if I should not go?" Oldcastle said. "What follows?"

The King hardened his mouth and said, "You'll burn."

"Aye," Oldcastle said. "Did I not say we were quittance? Now if I again fall to you you'll toss me to the faggots, and if you fall to me I shall do likewise."

The King had set his confidence on no man in this matter save Whittington. He let Oldcastle go from him, knowing Whittington had men of his livery waiting beyond the Tower walls by the bailey gate. These were there to bring Oldcastle aboard the *Cog John*, in case he sought to slip past them to his friends in the city.

That night when Henry worked in his chamber one of the men came to him. He bore Whittington's arms on his livery, under the arms of the city of London, for Whittington yet held office as Mayor. "Your grace," he said, "it is yonder knight of Hereford. He escaped us."

Even with the great thicknesses of the Tower walls about him he did not dare to speak Oldcastle's name. Henry asked him what had chanced and he went on to tell all that had befallen. "We kept ward on Tower Hill as your grace bade us," he said. "But there was much fog on the city this night. While we waited there was scuffling and shouting and presently a man came out of the fog, hard running. He was of the Hereford knight's height and stature, and we followed, but when we gained him it was not he."

When the King sat silent, he feared he was angered. "The knight of Hereford has many friends in the city, as your grace well knows," he said. "All this was planned by them. I doubt not that he lies in hiding in some Lollard's grain loft."

He asked what he should tell the master of the *Cog John*. Henry said, "Bid him wait another tide."

He yet sought to hope that Oldcastle, of his own choice, would take ship, but his reason gainsaid it. In the morning he rose early, before it was scarce light. From his casement he could see that the *Cog John* had slipped her moorings and even now stood out to the river with the tide. He well knew in his heart that Oldcastle was not aboard her.

Oldcastle's escape raised much ferment in the city. The King set a thousand marks on his head, as Arundel desired him to do, but presently it was established that Oldcastle had eluded all his hunters and was fled to Wales. Henry scarce knew whether he had joy or grief in the news. He yet shrank from delivering Oldcastle to the burning; yet it was to him that the ancient faith of his fathers' lay menaced and in freeing Oldcastle he had set a black canker to grow in the land's heart. It seemed to him that pity and weakness walked ever hand in hand. He well saw that pity was not for Kings.

II

The week following the King walked between the merlins of the Bell Tower. Below, the grass between the baileys was green as an emerald in a stone casting, and the climbing figs crept freshly up the southern side of the Beauchamp Tower. Little joy to be had here, but much shadow. Oldcastle lay coldly on his heart, and France, and the cloud of a political marriage.

Below him walked one of the prisoners with his guards. The King saw that it was Meredith Glendower whom he himself had taken with his brother, Griffiths, after the battle of Grosmont, nine years ago. Three years previously Griffiths had sought to escape, knotting his bed sheets and climbing from his window by night. The sheets had broken under his weight, and the guards, in the dawn's light, had found his bruised body below the battlements. Henry had much pitied him and his brother. He would have granted Meredith pardon, as on his accession he had granted a general pardon to all Wales, but Meredith would take no oath to him. Presently he bade the soldiers bring the prisoner up and when he came spoke to him of his father.

"I do not doubt that he lives," he said. "Yet the mountains of Wales can be a cruel haven."

"Cruel, think you?" Meredith said. He met Henry's eyes with hate. "Kindlier they be to my father than yon gentle Thames and these captive towers and the tongues of the English about him in his dying."

"I would make terms with you, Meredith ap Owen," Henry said. "I would have you go to your father and tell him the King of England salutes him and offers him a free pardon."

Meredith answered, "My father lies hidden in the mountains."

Henry said, "But you could reach him."

"Yes, indeed, I do not doubt it," Meredith said. He broke into loud laughter. "Yet it is a simple Welsh fool that you take me for. The King of England talks of free pardons, yet I think that the true desire of the King of England is that I may lead him to my father."

"Do you speak so?" the guards' captain said and glared at him.

"You are more fool than you know," Henry said. "I have long honored Owen Glendower, but get you back to your pacing if that is your choice."

Meredith gave him a fierce smile and turned away. Yet presently after a few steps he looked round upon the King with an altered face. "Oh, my lord," he said, "is it that you speak true?"

The King answered, "I do not lie to you."

"You are a Welshman by your birth," Meredith said. "Swear by the most sacred staff of St. David that you mean my father no hurt."

"I swear it," Henry said, "as by my honor. As by the True Cross. Does it content you?"

"Content am I," Meredith said. "My lord, forgive me. Much hatred can fester in durance. If my father still lives, most gladly will I seek him."

"Lord Talbot will ride with you to Welshpool," Henry said. "From thence no Englishman will follow you—I swear it. But yield yourself back into Lord Talbot's hands by the last day of July."

"My lord," Meredith said, "how do you know I shall come?"

"I count you a keeper of your word," Henry said, "as you count me a keeper of mine."

III

On the first Monday in May, the day that Arundel died, Dorset reached Southampton from France. He brought little news that was good. Charles of France lay captive to the insanity which, it was said, the debauchery of his youth had caused to creep upon him step by step. Policy lay in the hands of the Dukes of Armagnac and Orléans and of the Dauphin, who was said to be as wild a prince as Henry but eager to rule. Armagnac was straight dealing after his fashion, an inveterate hater of England with one considered aim—to drive her from Guienne and add it to his own provinces. Orléans it was who had accused Henry's father of the murder of Richard at the hand of Sir Piers Exton. Much bitterness lay between his house and the House of Lancaster, the more since Orléans had sent vast help to Glendower and laid waste Plymouth and Newport with the fleets of France. Few men believed now that the truce would be renewed, though the French nobles professed themselves willing to talk and to send an embassage.

Dorset came home gravely, to add his voice to the others that were urging Henry to seek alliance by marriage. He greatly favored the Burgundian match, since without it Duke John might yet offer his sword to the Dauphin. Burgundy offered the hand of either of his daughters—the Lady Anne, who had long seemed to be Henry's intended bride, or the Lady Catherine.

"Well, let it be done," Bishop Chichele said when the King spoke to him of it. "Yet I wish your heart lay in it."

The King half-smiled and said, "I likewise." He began then to speak of Arundel's death. "I have written to Rome, Chichele," he said. "It is you whom I would have elevated to the See of Canterbury."

"Nay, my lord," Chichele said, "this office is too high for me."

The King looked upon him and broke out laughing. "In truth," he said. "After your words to me at Westminster, I know not how you dare say it."

Chichele smiled and said, "Yet, my lord, I speak in truth. Would you set the great See of Becket into the hands of an English yeoman?"

"My beloved yeoman," Henry said, "I would none other."

After Chichele had left him, he worked late. There were many petitions for his signature, and the documents rose thick on the table among the leather caskets of the ambassadors. A portrait lay among them, worked on vellum, such as were all the portraits the courts of Europe sent to tempt him into marriage. He looked upon it, seeing one he had not seen before. The maid was very young, no more than fifteen, he judged her, with a pointed face, fair as a flower in its clinging coif. The artist's brushes had set gravity upon her; but he knew it for a mask. Once were it kissed away she would be all laughter. It seemed to him he had not known how greatly he longed to laugh again.

As by the strange ways a man might lose himself to a woman, he knew that, out of all Europe, he looked now at the one who would ever have his heart. It was to him as the song his minstrels sang.

> *Je vous aime, je vous désire,*
> *Je vous vueil doubter et servir.*
> *Je suis votre ou que je soie,*
> *Je ne puis sans vous avoir joie,*
> *Je suis par vous vivre ou mourir.*

"Richard," he said, and Richard Holme, his secretary, came gliding out of the shadows, ghostlike in his gray gown. Henry said, "Whose portrait is this?"

"The Lady Catherine, your grace, the Lady Catherine of Burgundy."

"Could hook-nosed Burgundy have sired her?" Henry said.

He went on working, but first he set the portrait against the candlestick where he could see it. Holme returned to his table, but he quickly rose again, clicking his tongue. "I have misled your grace," he said. "Forgive me. It is not the Lady Catherine of Burgundy, but the Lady Katherine of France. It was the like name that confused me. But I recall now—your lord uncle brought it back with him from the French Court. The Dauphin's youngest sister, is she not—the youngest of all the de Valois?"

"And seemingly the fairest," Henry said. He spoke no more of writing to Burgundy. When they sat at meat, he asked Dorset if he had met Charles's youngest daughter at the Court of Paris.

"Why yes," Dorset said. "A lovely child—like a May morning."

"Uncle," Henry said, "why did they give you her portrait? They refused me her sister, the Lady Isabelle, when my father sought to strengthen the truce by having me take a French wife. I was thirteen, yet I remember it well. Did not Charles say there were Dukes enough for his daughters in France?"

"He said more," Dorset said. "I tell you straightly, Harry, I think you can have no hope of her. I had her portrait at the Dauphin's hands. Yet if she comes to you, she'll come so set about with terms that they will choke us."

The French ambassadors were to come to the King that May, and he set much store by them. He kept his own counsel, even from Dorset and Chichele, but he set his face resolutely against the Burgundian match, and when he worked or lay abed the Lady Katherine's likeness stood between the candles where he could turn his eyes on it. It seemed to him Dorset had spoken true and that all April and May lay upon her. It was with her as it was with the air men sang—the air "Greensleeves."

> *She was all the King's joy,*
> *His pleasure untold. . . .*

In his thoughts he named her Greensleeves—la belle Katherine —fair Kate.

IV

Meredith Glendower, after his parting with Talbot, rode first to his sister Gwenllian. She was wed now to a knight of Cenarth, Philip ap Rhys. When she saw Meredith through her casement window she ran to him, flinging her arms about him and seeking not to weep. The house was well fashioned in stone and timber, and Meredith saw a cradle standing before the fire of the solar.

When he told her his mission, she looked upon him with much fear. "Follow you, they will," she said. "Why came you here?"

"Nay," he said. "He'll keep faith."

"Mad are you to believe so," she said. "It is the Molewarp's scheming."

He answered, "He has lain in his grave these eighteen months."

She said, "Who then is King?" When she learned she said in a strange voice, "Monmouth Harry."

She knew the secret hiding place where Glendower lay, and on the morrow, with but two men-at-arms, set out that she might bring him to it. As they rode, Gwenllian spoke of her father with a lightened face. "God has sent you in time," she said. "Had he lain there in the snows of another winter, I think he would have seen no spring."

Presently the mountain path grew too rough and steep for the horses. Gwenllian led Meredith on alone, climbing upward, the way so hard that oftentimes they had to sit and rest. At length she stopped, calling her father's name, and Glendower came out to them from a shelter in the rock hidden by fern and boulder. When he saw Meredith, he embraced him with tears. Meredith well saw that Gwenllian was right, and that if his father abided in the mountains he would swift come to death. He began to tell him of all that had befallen in London. Glendower, no more than Gwenllian, knew of Derby's death.

"Then is it the son?" he said. "Is the crown long for his head?"

Meredith answered him, "All men doubt it. France overhangs him. The Lollards fashion daggers for his back. The whole country lies sick and still about him, as a storm lies black across the mountains before it breaks. Known is it that the messengers who brought the news of his succession to the Dauphin said he would reign but a few months."

"Think they this?" Glendower said. "They know him not. It was no shallow, brawling youth who so chained me here in my mountains that I move not hand or foot."

"I watched him go to his anointing," Meredith said. "So set and white you would have thought he went to the faggots at Smithfield. Yet, my father, he honors you. He would see your outlawry ended!"

Glendower sighed. Presently when Meredith had spoken all the King's words to him, he set a hand upon his knee. "Go back to

him!" he said. "Tell him what I shall bid you. It may be he is
Welshman enow to understand it."

V

Henry received the French ambassadors at his grandfather's castle
of Leicester. They came with a most splendid retinue, dazzling
the eye with the colors of their chivalry, their horses barbed in silk
and damask and even the pommels of their saddles jeweled. The
King held great hopes of this meeting, though the embassage was
led by the Archbishop of Bourges, a man said to be much wanting
in tact. He brought with him his secretary, Monsieur Capon, an
alert, quick-witted, ever-smiling man, mistrusted by Dorset. Yet in
all matters they seemed reasonable, implying they bore conces-
sions.

The King received them in full state, as by custom he was
bound to do, in the great hall of the castle. He set into their hands
many costly gifts, his nobles standing about him. Likewise present
were lords from the Royal House of Portugal who were seeking
to tempt him into marriage with one of his cousins, the daughters
of their King. When the Frenchmen were seated, the King spoke
of the loss of his shipping in the Narrow Seas; and of Aquitaine,
promised to England in lieu of her help against Burgundy but
never rendered.

"Well, well," Bourges said. "That we can discuss when we come
to deal with the question of the English possessions. But now,
sire, in earnest of my master's intentions toward you he bids me
give you this."

He clapped fat hands, and one of his servants came forward,
bearing a gift. It was a loving cup set with rubies and aquamarine.
Henry thanked him and enquired after Charles's health.

"God has seen fit to afflict him," Bourges said. "Yet from time
to time he has full health, and the Dauphin takes from his shoulders many burdens of state."

"Our thanks to your master," Henry said. "His gift is generous."

"Less princely, I fear, than those your grace has already pressed upon us," Capon said. He lifted his eyes to Bourges, and a swift glance passed between them, affirmatory and sweet. "One other gift we bore from Rouen for you, but it lies still in London. We lacked a pack horse to fetch it hence to Leicester."

"Enough, enough," murmured the archbishop, but he looked pleased. Capon leant forward in his carved chair, his constant smile turned toward the King. Henry asked if this gift came likewise from Charles.

"From the prince Dauphin," Capon said. "Your grace—it is nothing. I had not meant to speak of it yet."

It was to the King as if he drew near to a trap as a stag in the forest might sense the hunters, yet knowing not where. He asked what it had pleased the Dauphin to send him.

"It is a gift of small value," Capon said. "Yet it was thought your grace might find a use for it. It is a packing case of tennis balls and some several embroidered cushions."

The room had grown still and heavy, even the pages bearing the wine no longer making their way up and down. The King said at last, "The prince Dauphin sends a strange gift. How is it that he would have us take it?"

"I bear a message from him," Capon said. "But I would postpone the telling of it. Do not press me, my lord."

The King said in a still voice, "Let me hear it."

Capon asked, "You would have it straightly, my lord?"

"Straightly," Henry said.

Capon sighed and spread out his hands. In his long gray gown he looked like a tutor eager to make all things clear to a dull scholar. "Since you would have it so, my lord," he said, "it is this. The Dauphin greets his cousin of England and sends you, since you are but a youngster, little balls to play with and soft cushions to lie on until you shall have reached man's estate. Further, my lord, he bids you be a good boy, amuse yourself with what he sends and do not presume to quarrel with noble princes like himself and his father."

Henry twisted in the great chair of state as from a wound. Many of the lords came to their feet, Tom with a hand to the dagger in his belt and speaking an oath. Henry turned that he might look upon the two Dukes of Portugal. They met his eyes, the one with pity and the other with much amused cynicism.

"In God's truth," Henry said, "go tell the Dauphin, if he would match me in this set, we'll use such balls as will bring his painted court about his ears."

"Be not angry with me, my lord," Capon said in an injured voice. "It was at your own bidding that I gave this message. It is not customary for a King to inveigh against the person of an ambassador."

"Do you instruct us?" Henry asked in a shaking voice.

"I mean no harm," Capon said. "Your grace will not deny that your house is but newly come to King Richard's throne. It may be you teach us fresh styles in royalty. We have long wondered at your ways as prince—they seemed to us in France most strangely cast. I would not remark upon them, my lord, but it was to match them that the Dauphin sent his gift."

Dorset set his hand upon the King's knee. Henry strove to master his countenance, sitting as a stone. "We understand you," he said at last. "And we understand the Dauphin's message. He has our thanks. We had not heard the language of chivalry spoken thus until we heard it today as from his older royalty."

VI

When the Frenchmen had gone Henry walked alone in the garden, seeking to cool his rage. His mother's tomb rested in the castle chapel, newly fashioned this year at his bidding, and he cast himself down beside it against the cold stone. It was to him as though her effigy held a still semblance of her twenty-three-year-old beauty. He looked beyond the doors where lay the bailey garden hedged with the mulberry and lilac she had tended. There likewise was the terrace where he had looked his last on her, seeing her borne in his father's arms, her pointed shoes limp below her gown.

Presently Malbon came to him and stood in the doorway. "Your grace's pardon," he said, "the Welshman, Meredith Glendower, has kept faith. He rode in with Lord Talbot a few minutes past."

"Send him here," Henry said. "See that he comes alone."

"Your grace," Malbon said, "he bears his dagger on his hip. He was ever your enemy."

"I do not think so," Henry said.

Meredith came to him straightway, blinking as he stepped from the sun into the chapel's dimness. When he saw the King, he went on his knee that he might kiss his hand. He seemed as a sick man, spent and grief struck. "Welcome, friend," Henry said. "You bore your father's pardon to him?"

Meredith answered, "Oh, my lord, he would not take it."

Henry said, "I asked no conditions."

"That he understands. He returns you many thanks. He says that though the combat was fierce there was no hate betwixt you and him, yet he bids me tell you his outlawry has become precious to him. Rather would he lie fast-bound in his mountains than take what you offer and so lose the last thing left him. My lord, I urged him on my knees—an angel from heaven could not have moved him."

He shielded his face with his hand and began to weep. "Forgive me, my lord," he said, "that I am become before you as a woman. But I saw death in my father's face. Not again will I look on him." He went from the King that he might stand by the door and come again to control. Archbishop Bourges, savoring the afternoon sun, walked beyond them on the terrace. Meredith looked upon him and spoke bitterly. "It is his grace of Bourges," he said. "I remember him well when my father and I made our journey to Paris to seek aid from the King of France. High burned our star then."

"Tell me but this," Henry said. "If your father's arms had borne him to victory, what was agreed upon? What was de Valois's price?"

"The half of England," Meredith said. "To us, Wales."

After a space, Henry said, "What manner of man is the Dauphin?"

Meredith answered, "As his father was in youth—denying his body nothing, yet his wits sharp where the King's are dulled. My lord, sooner would I stir an adder from the grass than leave myself naked to the Dauphin."

The King said, "Does he bear such enmity toward us?"

"He bears much," Meredith said. "I recall once—my father, as our custom is when speaking of the English, had called them Saxon. The Dauphin would not have it so. He bade my father remember the field of Senlac, and how his Norman forebears had torn a kingdom from the Saxon's bellies. Then, turning to Orléans, he said that though the blood of the Plantagenets was kin to his, the fogs and rains of England has washed their Frenchness from them—they were no more than bastard Frenchmen now, their good, rich Anjou stock out-bred. Orléans said the days were ripe for a second Senlac. The Dauphin replied his father had long purposed it, and he did likewise. We rejoiced to hear them then, my lord. It seemed to us that when England lay at the foot of France, then would Wales be free."

The King sat with bowed head. Presently he spoke again of Glendower. "I would he had taken what I offered," he said. "Will nothing move him?"

"Nothing," Meredith said. "When the snows of winter give place, when another spring comes to the valleys, my father's eyes will not behold it." He turned back toward the King as with a high and touching dignity. "Here, then, my lord, am I. At your pleasure am I ready to take my journey back to London and the Tower."

"Get you back to Wales," Henry said. "Your father's pardon is yours, if you will have it. I would restore what I may to Glendower."

VII

Two days later, Archbishop Chichele rode from London to Leicester. As the pages brought him to the King's chamber, he saw that Tom paced beyond the half-open door, speaking with raised voice. "By all the saints," he was saying, "would you have him mock you as though you were a scullion kitchen boy? Thrust his tennis balls down his throat at the lance's point."

The King was seated under the canopy in the gilt chair of state. He had set the crown from him, hooking it about the fashioned knob of the chair's headrest, as a woman who had walked too far might kick off her shoes. Chichele went to him and spoke a blessing. It seemed to him the King's fingers set on the chair arms grew thin and that his state oppressed him.

"God with you, my liege," he said. "How do you fare?"

"Well in body," Henry said. "Less well in mind. You know of the Dauphin's message?"

"A vicious young man, I have heard," Chichele said. "This does not become him."

"I make no secret of it to you, Father," Henry said. "Each time I think of it, it is to me as a blow on a bruise. All Europe will make merry with the telling."

"Tell me, my son," Chichele said. "How did you receive this gift?"

The King twisted his mouth and said, "I did as they desired. I returned a blustering and empty answer. More would I have said if my uncle had not cooled me back to sense."

"What answer did he expect?" Chichele said. "Is this the tongue of chivalry?"

The King answered, "It may be I deserved such a gift and such a message, yet I think the Dauphin was not the one to send it."

"His own fame is not so fair," Chichele said. "Yet, my lord, howsoever hard this mock is to bear, let it not sway you in your policy."

"Thus did I tell myself," Henry said, "after I had cooled. But more has come about. Yesterday I summoned him of Bourges and

the others again to me. I told them that though the Dauphin's
message had given great offense to England, as it was meant it
should, it need not close our parley. We talked for three hours. In
all things they seemed most favorable, speaking of restoring
Aquitaine and Anjou and of granting me the Lady Katherine's
hand. I told them that on every count we could come to settle-
ment. His grace of Bourges at once said he had no power from his
master to pledge the terms he had spoken of. I asked him why then
he had so frittered time, saying that when again his master sent
ambassadors let them be of real sort and not mock ones. He answered me that his master would so send when it was no mock
King he had to deal with. Some of my lords stood about me—
Talbot, Huntingdon, Suffolk, and others. Turning to them he
called them the nobles of England and wondered that they had
bound themselves to Lancaster. He said their allegiance ought to
lie where his own business lay—with Richard's rightful heirs of the
blood and not with that son of a murderer."

Chichele exclaimed and said, "Son of a murderer? Were these
words so used?"

"They were—'fils d'un assassin.' Father, I could not speak. All
of us were silent."

"They came well barbed with insults," Chichele said. "It was a
strange embassage."

"What they intended I know not," Henry said. "They spoke,
when they first came, of renewing the truce. Yet it was an ill truce
that saw Glendower fed with guns; the Douglas fighting with
Frenchmen at Homildon Hill; Plymouth, Newport and Southampton burned; and my shipping so mangled in the Narrow Seas
that we almost spoke a Te Deum to see an English ship come safe
back to port in the Medway."

"Knowing all this, my son," Chichele said, "what do you purpose now?"

The King gave him a troubled look, not at once speaking. "I
have a great fear, Father," he said at last. "Of that you know. I do
not think my house is long for the throne and that when Lancaster

goes down it will be in blood. I purpose to regain Normandy or at least a strip of her coast, so that in the day civil strife comes to England she will have, in some sort, a buckler against the Dauphin."

"Can this be accomplished?" Chichele said. "France is a most mighty foe—populous, rich, of all Europe most skilled in battle. Are we not, even now, sore pressed to hold Guienne against Armagnac?"

"Each day she comes to greater strength," Henry said. "Watching her, I feel as my father must have felt watching Mowbray arm himself in the lists. I know well they may desire a few more years of truce. It would serve them until the Dauphin comes fully to power and manhood and Orléans and Armagnac bind up their quarrels."

"It is a hard decision," Chichele said. "Whether to lead men to their deaths now in the hope that fewer men may die in after-years."

"It has driven sleep from my bed these past nights," Henry said. "Yet I know no other answer. What safety have we known since Normandy was wrung from us?" He rose from the chair of state and went to the fire, his head bowed. "I shall write once more to Charles," he said. "In my own hand, after I have made some show of arming. I have done with embassages, but it may be a letter will move him."

"My son," Chichele said, "how speak your nobles in this?"

"They bid me go," Henry said. "But the yea or nay rests only upon the King. For this cause was I not crowned?" Presently he said, "It would greatly ease me to have your counsel in this. Yet I know not if I can ask it."

"Aye," Chichele said. "I would not counsel you before. Yet this time I do. Make an end, my lord. Spread your sails for France. It may be if you can deal them but one buffet, they will speak with you more readily and not with insults."

"Set your prayers upon me," Henry said. "To fail will mean the ruin of my house."

"Have I not told you before," Chichele said, "I never kneel to God without my tongue pleads for England and her Kings."

The King would no more receive the ambassadors. They went from him the next day, with much ceremony, their robes and hoods brilliant against the gray castle walls. The lords who set them on their way marked that Capon's smile was yet ever constant and the Archbishop of Bourges had time enough for pleasantries. It did not seem with them as though their mission had failed.

VIII

When June came, the King moved to Southampton that he might make ready to embark. His little fleet lay in Southampton Water, the lanthorns atop the clustered masts glinting like stars when dusk came. Many court retainers and the great lords thronged the town, their shields hung above the doors of the taverns and almshouses where they lodged. The court rested at the castle. Isabella Holland still waited upon her sister, Margaret, and they walked together in the sun upon the battlements of the keep. Margaret no longer strove to be youthful, and beside her young husband she often looked more than her years. Tom rarely had a glance to cast at her. Seeing him thus moved Isabella to fury.

There were some few nobles below them in the castle court. Isabella looked down upon them, seeing the King and his brothers as if they jested together. Presently Tom's bastard son, young Jack of Clarence, came running to his father, with an apple in his hand. He was a most goodly child, dark, so that no man might mistake his parentage that it was of Lancaster, eager and intelligent. His father swung him onto his shoulder, for he much loved him. The King joined their sport, the child seeming to delight in it and showing small shyness. When Margaret heard their laughter, she could bear it no more and went below, saying her head pained her. Isabella followed her, furious of face and in hatred of Lancaster.

That night she walked alone in the bailey garden. Cambridge,

Aumerle's younger brother, joined her, smiling as he marked the anger in her step. He had but newly married again, his second wife being Anne Mortimer, the sister of Edmund Mortimer and of Hotspur's widow. It was an alliance that had bound his fortunes strongly with three of Lancaster's great enemies—the Mortimers, the Percies, and the Hollands.

Presently Isabella said, "Cousin, when shall it be?"

Cambridge answered, "Tomorrow night. He goes to watch the victualling of the fleet, but he will be back by dusk. Only Scrope will be with him. He is to tell him he has a rondel for him to hear. When they are alone I and Thomas Grey will come to them bearing the petition." He laid a hand on his dagger and drew it. It was most splendidly fashioned, the quillons and pommel in silver, the blade double-edged and keen as quick frost. "It is well greased," he said. "It will come from its scabbard so smoothly he'll hear naught. When he bends his head to read, I or Scrope will thrust between the shoulders."

"In the back?" Isabella said. "Like a common cutthroat?"

Cambridge answered her on a laugh. He was in his mid-thirties now, as elegant and handsome-browed as when he had first quarreled with his boy cousin at Richard's court. "You grow squeamish, Cousin," he said. "Yet you love Harry Monmouth no more than do I. I grow weary of bending the knee to one who holds the kingship as by bastardy. Even as a boy I liked him but ill—he was as insolent and high-stomached as his father."

"Cousin," Isabella said, "I think he regards you in a like fashion. Take care, for he trusts you little."

"I well know it," Cambridge said, smiling. "But he trusts no man more than Scrope."

"Aye," Isabella said. "Save for his uncle and the archbishop, none lies closer to him. It will, in truth, be a mortal blow if Scrope's hand deals it."

"Mortal it must be," Cambridge said. "Sleep sweetly, Cousin. Tomorrow you'll kiss the hand of your well-loved Edmund Mortimer and call him King."

IX

On the morrow night the King sat late at his work, Hungerford with him. Presently there were hurrying footfalls on the stairs, and Dorset came in, at his back some of his men-at-arms in his own Beaufort livery. To the King he said, "Where's Lord Scrope?"

Henry answered that he was in the inner chamber. Dorset shut the doors between with his own hands, then set his back against them. "Praise God, Harry," he said. "I almost thought to find you dead."

The King laughed and said, "Is there yet another crazed Lollard behind the tapet?"

"Nay, do not jest," Dorset said. "Today Edmund Mortimer came to me. He has learned from his sister's mouth that some few of your nobles had intent to kill you this night here in Southampton and set the crown upon his head. He has known it for the past two weeks. Tonight his conscience would no more let him keep silence."

"He deals kindly with me, then," Henry said. "More kindly than Lancaster dealt with him." He asked whom Mortimer had named.

Dorset answered him in a troubled voice. "Sir Thomas Grey is of them," he said. "The knight of Northumberland that was kin to Hotspur. Another is your cousin—he of Cambridge."

The King looked upon him and said, "Not Aumerle?"

"No, no," Dorset said. "Nothing's named against him. His hands are clean in this."

"God be thanked for it," Henry said. "It would have dealt hard upon me if Aumerle were of them."

Dorset answered that he held these two secure. "Grey I caused to be apprehended at his lodging at the sign of the Crossed Keys," he said. "Cambridge was taken here a few moments gone. They are both below."

The King stood silent. Presently he said, "I would lief as not go down to them."

"Harry," Dorset said. "There's yet another."

"Who then?" the King said. "Name him, Uncle." When Dorset spoke Scrope's name, he said in a voice of fury, "If Mortimer says so, he lies."

"Harry, Harry," Dorset said. "Would I lie to you in this? Would Mortimer? I, too, could scarce believe it. I know well what favor he had at your hands—how he was as close to you as a brother. Yet it is so. There's Mortimer's deposition. Read for yourself."

The King looked upon the sheets, but set no hand to them. It seemed to Hungerford he could not well bear to scan them.

"Well," Dorset said, "have I your leave, Harry, to take him?"

"Aye, take him, if you must," Henry said. "Yet Mortimer is mistaken—I am assured."

Dorset called forward his men-at-arms and thrust open the inner door that led to the bedchamber. Inside a page moved, setting wine beside the lighted candles, and Scrope stood with his foot on a stool and his lute set against his knee. He plucked at it idly as if his fingers were an-itch for the strings. Of all men about the King he was the most skilled in music, and the idle notes fell sweet as blown blossom on the candle-lit room. When he saw Dorset, he smiled and said as pleasantly as he was ever wont, "How now, my lord of Dorset?"

Dorset set the doors to behind him and all was shut out. The King stood stiff and silent, but he spoke at last. "It cannot be," he said. "Scrope must deny it."

After a space the doors opened and Scrope came out between his guards. He looked whitely at the King and took a halting step toward him. "Oh, my lord," he said, "I was led to it. I beseech you, of your charity, to look on me with mercy."

Henry gave him no answer. Scope made as if to push past his guards toward him. "I freely acknowledge it, my lord," he said. "I will confess all. Only remember the many favors I have had at your hands, and, above them all, grant me pity."

"Have done," Dorset said gruffly. To Henry he said, "My lord, it is needful for you to come down."

The King answered he would come. When Dorset and the men-at-arms had gone from him, he sought to compose his face, then followed. Much people were in the great hall—the King's lords, the peering and frightened servants, and in the center the prisoners surrounded by the guards. Thomas Grey gave the King scarce a look. He was a thickset, aging man, by his aspect ill suited to treason, though his cousinship to Hotspur had long inclined him toward it. Cambridge stood at his side with folded arms. When he saw the King, he lifted his brows and smiled, his eyes as flints.

"God save your grace," Talbot said, as the King reached him. "It is a most excellent thing to us to see you safe."

"My lord," Dorset said, "if the charge of these men is to be mine, I beg you let us convene a court here in the castle tonight, hear their fault and pass judgment."

"Wait, my lords," Cambridge said. "My trial must be fully held before my peers."

"Given a fair wind, we embark tomorrow," Dorset said. "The King cannot delay."

Cambridge shrugged and answered, "Must I instruct my cousin of Lancaster in Magna Carta? I have my rights."

"Afore God," Talbot exclaimed, "would you endanger all our lives? Already the French are apprized of our purpose. Are the King's lords to sit trying you while the defenses grow daily at Harfleur?"

Almost there was an outcry at his words. Above it Dorset said grimly. "Do you seek to turn the verdict, my lord? On my word as a knight, I have enough evidence to hang you twenty times."

"Doubtless, my lord," Cambridge said. "Yet I do not forego my ancient and unalienable privileges so that my hot-blooded young cousin can rush off to his French sieges."

"Do you speak of hot blood?" Talbot said. "It was a cold-blooded blow you sought to strike this night."

The King bade them be silent, speaking in strained fashion. "These are his rights," he said. "Let him be tried here in Southampton before his peers."

When he would have gone, Scrope thrust out a hand to him.

"My lord," he said, "if I can seek no charity at your hands, these likewise are my rights." The lute yet dangled from his shoulder, but he set a trembling hand to it and cast it off. He stood close by the King, Hungerford seeing them as he had many times seen them together at Coldharbor when Scrope had ever seemed to him of all men the most likable—soft voiced, deprecating and easy. It was as if a changeling stood this night in his place.

The King could scarce look upon him. He went from them in silence. Cambridge watched him go, smiling yet but in hatred. "Well, my lord Scrope," he said in a loud voice, "I struck no blow this night, yet I doubt not that you struck one."

X

Aumerle came that same night, much distressed and kneeling to the King. "Oh, my lord," he said, using the phrase many times, "I am faithful."

The King sought to give him what comfort he could, though he himself was in like need. He slept not at all that night; and Hungerford, in the outer chamber, heard him pacing the floor until the cocks started to crow from the farmsteads. The next day came many of his nobles to him, all urging him to abandon for the present the French enterprise.

"It may be Scrope was lining his coffers with French gold," Dorset said. "I fear our plans are too well known at the Court of Paris."

Henry gave them no heed, for the high obstinacy of Lancaster was roused in him. He feared likewise that to draw back now would too much embolden the Dauphin and invite the greater danger. All the day that Cambridge, Scrope, and Grey came to their trial the wind blew strong and fair for France, the ships lying idle in Southampton Water. The King did not show himself, and Tom presided, relishing the judgment. Cambridge bore himself smilingly, with much high defiance. The King could not forbear to salute it. After sentence he restored to him his forfeited honors, thus ensuring that his estates might yet pertain to his heirs, and granted him death by the block. Scrope he allowed to be sentenced fiercely, to quartering and the drawer's knife that he might bear the full rigor of the law. Scrope wrote him a pitiable letter, entreating mercy, but it was less against the King than the King's love for him that he had struck. Henry seemed dead to pity. He was as a flint, moving hard-faced and silent among his troubled nobles.

Chichele came to him when the muffled and measured bells were sounding Cambridge to his death at the Bargate. He asked of Scrope, if he had already suffered. "His was a fierce death," he said, "if he died as the law required."

"He died by hanging only," Henry said. "I sent to him this morning that it would be as he wished."

Chichele answered that he was glad of it. Presently he said, "My son, can you not find it in your heart to give thanks to God that He chose to reveal this plot to you and spare your life?"

The King said, "Must it ever be my friends?" After a space he said, "Father, I cannot even now believe that if I had turned my back on Scrope that night he would have found my shoulders with his knife. When it is a foe I can be as gay as the next man and shrug it off. But when it is Hotspur or Oldcastle or Scrope, it leaves me a woman."

"Yet be thankful," Chichele said. "Seven times the shadow of assassination has fallen across you, and each time under the good hand of God you have had deliverance."

"Soon will it be the eighth," Henry said. "Richard spoke true when he said England bore naught but hate for her Norman Kings."

"You speak bitterly," Chichele said. "England has not dealt with you as she dealt with Richard."

"Not as yet, Father in God," Henry said and turned back to the papers on the table. Chichele watched him with a troubled face. "What are these?" he said. "What do you work at now?"

The King said, "My will."

"I am troubled for you," Chichele said. "You do not care whether your skull splits or no, and that is not healthful—it smells of the sickroom."

The King shrugged and went on writing. "Why should I not invite their blows?" he said. "I would liefer it were a Frenchman."

XI

For four days the wind remained contrary. The King sent his servants from him that he might ride alone over the downs. All was sunlit, the land so deep and richly green that it caught against the throat; and below the little ships rested in Southampton Water, their sides bright daubed with the charges of chivalry and the slender pennants idle about the mastheads. The King rode fiercely that he might ease his thoughts. There was a thicket atop the cliff face to the left, and presently a sparrow hawk, dark-plumed, belled and ringed, soared from it to come on stooped wing past where the King drew rein. Another horseman came round the curve of the downs, riding in pursuit, his falconer's lure outstretched. The sun glinted on his fair hair and pale, upturned face.

"Mortimer," Henry shouted. "Mortimer."

Mortimer had not seen him, but he wheeled as he heard the shout and rode toward him. "Your pardon, my liege," he said, "I was intent on the chase."

He spoke stammering and dropped his glance. Mortimer could rarely engage a man in speech and look him in the face. Thus had he often seemed no more than a golden shadow, his thoughts hidden from all men.

"I have long wanted speech with you, my lord," Henry said. "I have to thank you for my life."

Mortimer did not raise his eyes. "I could not stand by silent, my liege," he said. When the King was yet silent, he said, "Forgive me, my lord, that I intrude upon your riding. I left my servants yonder at the spur of the hill. I'll go back to them."

"Wait," Henry said. "I beg you remember your state and talk with me straightly." .

"My state, my lord?"

"You are the King of England."

A faint flush tinged Mortimer's pale cheeks. "You bear the crown, Cousin," he said briefly, his stammer for a space gone from him.

Henry looked back over the green and swelling uplands and the little ships straggling across the bay. "Cousin," he said, "this is your inheritance. Have you not often called me usurper and murderer in your heart?"

Mortimer at last looked upon him. After a space he said, "This I would know of you. How did Richard die?"

Henry answered, "I know not. That is the truth, yet will you not believe it."

"I think you speak true," Mortimer said. "And I, too, will speak truly. I grew from boyhood as the prisoner of your house, my inheritance the barred chambers of Windsor or the Tower. Cousin, many times could I have set my blade to your heart."

"It's easily done," Henry said. "We are alone here, and you have your dagger. I bear no arms."

They sat knee to knee on their restless horses, the lonely cliff shrouding them in its curtain of larch and sycamore. Mortimer looked at him, startled, not knowing whether he jested; then when the King returned his look, a small quiet smile of secret radiance lit his face. There was a thin jingling of silver bells, and the sparrow hawk beat down to settle on his glove. He fell to smoothing its plumage, absently yet smiling.

"Nay, Cousin," he said, "I savor my freedom after knowing none. I fill my days hunting and hawking, and at nights I lie easier since the crown rests not upon my pillow. You are the one to know prison now."

The King gave him no answer. Mortimer turned that he might look at the ships set in their painted lines across the bay. "Thus it contents me," he said. "I am not cast after a fashion to lead men, and I have seen too much of the perils that enround the King. Guard my inheritance, Cousin."

The King set his hand to the crucifix about his neck and said, "Thus have I sworn."

"Cousin," Mortimer said, "my sword is yours in earnest of my service. I'll follow you to France."

"No, my lord," Henry said. "Stay here. Tend your estates and ride to your hawking. Have I not claimed enough from you?" He bowed to him, low in the saddle, as in homage, and went from him.

When he rode back to the castle, Dorset came to him. They walked together beyond the outer bailey, where the tang of the sea blew sweet from the Solent and the gulls shone white as foam in the sun. Dorset spoke in grim voice of rumors that the French were reinforcing Harfleur.

"If the wind would but favor me, Uncle," Henry said.

"Naught else has," Dorset said gruffly. "We should have quartered Cambridge with hot knives and hung his flesh to the crows. He, a Plantagenet. It makes me thank the saints I was bastard-born."

Two waiting women sat on the grass among the buttercups by the curtain wall, and beyond them two noblemen's sons bearing small bows stalked sparrows. Henry paused in the shadow of the bailey that he might watch them.

"It's Cambridge's puppy," Dorset said.

"And Scrope's," Henry said. "Uncle, what am I to do with them?"

Dorset shrugged and said, "What care is it of yours?"

One of the arrows flew awry from the elder boy's bow and struck the ground at their feet. The younger ran to fetch it, coming upon them before the King could move back. He was a fair-haired lad, scarce yet seven, Scrope's only son and named after him. When he saw the King, he stopped short and looked fearful.

"How now, Harry," the King said. "I watched you—you draw bow like a yeoman."

The boy answered on a whisper, "Yes, my liege."

The King looked upon him with much compassion, seeing him as he himself had been when he had knelt to Richard in Dublin Castle, trembling and affrighted. Presently he said, "What if we found a place for you at Oxford, under the Bishop of Winchester? There you could hawk or hunt or study what you will. What say you to it?"

After a space the boy began to smile. "Oh, my liege," he said, "I should like it. I should like it very well."

Beyond the hillocks his companion shouted. "Have you not found it yet?" He came himself toward them over the rise of ground. He was Richard, Cambridge's son, a boy of eleven, already bearing much of his father in him. When he saw that it was the King who stood there, the hatred flamed into his face like a torch.

"Oh, Richard," Henry Scrope said, "I am to Oxford."

"What of you, Richard?" Henry said. "Will you not go with him?"

The boy said in a thin hard voice, "I am well enough here as I am, my lord."

"Think on it," the King said. "It may be you will change your mind."

"I do not change," the boy said. He lifted his head and looked upon the King, his face stiff with hate. Both stood silent, their shadows long upon the fair land's sunlit green.

"As you will," Henry said at last.

After he and Dorset came together to the barbican, he drew in his breath and sought to laugh. "Uncle," he said, "when that boy looked thus upon me, I could well have signed myself."

"He's like his father," Dorset said. "As eaten with hate as an apple with maggots."

As they walked the wind stirred the eel grass tufting the downs to deep ripples. One of the waiting women had risen to her feet, and with her, too, the wind played, stroking her long green sleeves outward. The King watched her with delight.

"It blows fair, Uncle," he said. "The wind blows fair."

XII

Foremost of the fleet was the *Royal Trinity*. She was the King's flagship, newly fitted at Greenwich, and she bore banners of leopards and ostrich feathers on poop and prow, her masthead decked with the five arms of the Plantagenets—the Trinity, Our Lady, St. Edward, St. George, and England. When the King boarded her, she hoisted her painted sails in signal to the rest of the fleet, and the little ships came clustering about her, dipping their pennants. Many were hung with Red Cross pavises, and their sails above their red-painted waists were richly embroidered with crimson antelopes and silver swans. Yet for all their holiday spendor ill fortune stalked them. Fire had swept one ship, leaping from her canvas to the two lying alongside. All three had burned out, the flames licking their chivalry into blackened hulks. Few believed it an accident, and even those named it ill-omened. The King had many voices about him now urging him to turn back, but he gave them small heed. Soon the land fell astern, fair as a dream, the little rose-red Domesday villages curtained in trees beyond the stern cliffs and swelling downs.

Hungerford spoke with Talbot on the prow of the *Royal Trinity*. "Well, my lord," he said, "we're bravely set."

"Bravely enough," Talbot said. He looked at the gilded top-castles and the tautened sails, and sighed. "It stirs my blood, too," he said. "Yet I well know that France has but to sneeze, and she can blow my young King Harry and all this fair show of our chivalry back into Southampton in tatters."

Many echoed him. France was the mistress Court of Europe, five times as populous England, and held by all men to be so skilled in battle that she had become the school for all knightly arms. Her provinces were rich and sun-kissed; and to three of them, Normandy, Anjou, and Aquitaine, England believed with a lover's passion that she had a most just and irrefutable claim. Aquitaine had been hers since Bretigny; Anjou had bred the Plantagenets, the mighty House of Anjou; and Normandy was her ruler's root stock. Yet to regain them had ever seemed beyond her. She was a weak land, "the most timid of the barbarians," and throughout her history she had been tossed as a tennis ball from conqueror to conqueror. Boadicea had withstood the Roman legions only to die among them at the last. Alfred had pitted himself against the Danes all his days. He who was half-myth and half-man, Arthur, strove against the Saxons until the Last Great Battle in the West had swept him away. And at Senlac Harold Godwinson had likewise uselessly given of his lifeblood against the Norman.

Since then England had lain under her French Kings and her high-stomached French nobles—Henry's great-grandfather, Edward, had been but the first Plantagenet to speak the English tongue, yet the courts of Europe reckoned them now as English. The vast tracts of France which had been their root soil were torn from them. Normandy, Anjou, Aquitaine, Maine, Brittany, Gascony, all of which had rested in the hands of the Plantagenets, fell one by one into the lap of the King of France, until of the once great empire of the Angevins only Guienne and the little conquest of England remained. Now, too, England found herself the heart of the empire, and that to her sorrow. Her past haunted her, and it seemed to her that only as part of a great lordship of her Kings could she rest secure from fresh conquest. So had her Saxon commons joined with her French nobles to fight under the banner of the Plantagenets against the lands that had first sired them and sent them out as conquerors.

This, then, was the quarrel whose beginnings slipped far back beyond the memory of man. A darker shadow lay across it now, the shadow of Isabella, She-wolf of France, Queen Consort of England, Queen Regnant, had there been no Salic Law, of France. The King preferred no claim here, but only to the Dukedom of

Normandy, which the Kings of England, since the Conquest, had ever held to be their true style.

No hostile sail showed the while the King's fleets beat down Channel. Many questioned this as strange, but Henry gave it no thought. On the first day of July the Lézarde estuary opened to them and the men crowded the ships' rails to look upon it. Presently she came to the sight—Harfleur, the proud pirate of the Narrow Seas, every turret, tower and keep of her boldly etched as though on a map. There were earthworks along the beaches, but they were not manned and nothing hindered the King's landing.

XIII

Men marked first the strange smell that hung about Harfleur. It blew over the mud flats on the east wind, sweet and cloying, as from overripe and crushed apples, to hang in the nostrils. None at first in the King's army greatly heeded it, but later it became to all more vile than the vilest stench from the London street kennels. Harfleur stood high above the mud flats on the land's spur. She was the strongest seaport in Normandy, and one of the strongest in France. Many questioned the King's choice of her as the point of attack, but Henry held long reckoning against her, for she above all ports had sheltered the Channel pirates, and from her Glendower had received his shiploads of guns and men. It was said in London that the King's guns had breached her, but they did not. After five weeks there was not in her walls crack enough for an English archer to put so much as his fist in. Henry, on his sailing, had sent word to his Council he would be in, in four weeks, but all men now knew he had spoken with overoptimism.

Many believed Charles would send to the garrison's relief, but never a Frenchman moved beyond the skyline over the mud flats. Yet Harfleur did not lack aid. The faint sweet smell clung about the English camp, the summer sun drawing up mists from the reeking earth to shroud it, and soon dysentery stalked among the bright tents and the sutlers' wagons. By the sixth week of the siege it had fallen upon the King's army more violently than any French. The Bishop of Norwich, the Earl of Suffolk, and the Earl of Arundel all died of it. Tom was greatly stricken. Presently it lay on every third man in the army, and the little ships which had beaten up the Lézarde in such proud and golden chivalry crept back one by one across the Channel, bearing the King's sick and wounded.

On the sixty-ninth day of the siege a lone ship came beating up the Lézarde toward the English camp. She was painted azure and scarlet and her sails were woven with the red dragon of Wales, which many held strange, for the dragon was the standard of the princes of Llewellyn and in men's minds stood for Welsh independence. She shipped so little water that she drove straight on to the sands, and the men on her waist leapt over and came wading ashore. First of them was a short, strutting, bustling figure. When he saw the King, he snatched off his hood and his hair flamed out like a kindled torch.

"Why, Davy Gam," Henry shouted. "Welcome, friend. What brings you here?"

"May God long preserve your grace," Gam roared back. "Good is it to see you again. Could I withhold the help of my right hand, look you, when it is need of it that you have."

He knelt to the King and kissed his hand, beaming. "It is from Cardiff that I come," he said, when Henry asked him of his passage. "Seven days out, with the winds contrary, look you, and never the sight nor the smell of a French sail did we get. Yet long have I purposed to join your grace and offer my sword to you, and though it was beforetimes bloody with the blood of Owen's enemies, yet now I think it has no dishonor if it be bloody with blood of yours."

"Davy Gam," Henry exclaimed, speaking as a Welshman, "good do you do my heart."

"Eh, but it is the echo of Wales that sits on your grace's tongue," Gam said delightedly. "And it is more Welshmen that I have brought you to swell your army. Raised them from the valleys have I, and it is my badge they wear on their sleeves, though I be commoner and no great lord." He looked as with disparagement toward the nobles who stood behind the King. Many had raised great levies; Talbot eighteen hundred men from the Shropshire hills, and Aumerle, from the great Yorkist holdings of the Plantagenets, nearly four thousand.

"Marshal them here, Davy," Henry said.

Gam clapped his hands, and three archers shuffled forward. They wore a badge of a fox running on their sleeves and though their bows were newly whittled they carried but three arrows apiece in their belts.

Henry said, "Are these all?"

"All," Gam repeated in a puzzled voice. "But they are good men. Each of them is a good man, now, and from Gwent as I am myself, and as you are, God send your grace safe. Does it please your grace to hear their names? Evan ap Williams is this, and next Griffiths ap Thomas of Brecon. He with the face so loutish and ill favored that it must, in faith, have soured his mother's milk, is Trefor ap Tudor—a better man than he looks, indeed now, and not to be put to shame whatever company he draws bow in. Would your grace have him show you of his skill?"

Henry answered with haste that he would see it later. "You have my thanks, friend," he said. "You are right welcome."

"What could I do less?" Gam said. "Did you not honor Owen and did he not honor you?"

He asked leave to withdraw and gestured his three archers to follow with a lordly wave of the hand. "For the honor of Wales," he was saying as he went. "Do you step trimly. Look valorous will you. No need to gaze at the sky, all soft and moony now as if you spoke love to a sea gull."

The King looked upon his nobles and smiled. "Well, lords," he said, "there's naught now can keep us from Harfleur."

The army now was much stricken, scabbling for food among the silbanks of the Lézarde or the scrawny fruit trees, edging the cliffs. The King knew himself to be in great straits. He put a cheerful face on it, strolling about the camp in a plain jerkin, all marks of royalty put aside. His only knightly accoutrement was his belt, worn, after the fashion of chivalry, about the hips. It was a rondel belt, each rondel a leopard's mask, in crimson enamel, and the clasp a lion passant, set with jewels. The gleam of it in the dusk of twilight or through the steamy vapors that hung about the Lézarde banks often broke on men's eyes cheeringly.

Each day, when the tide favored, came the long procession of men bearing the sick back to the ships. Tom was of them, though, since John remained in England as Regent, the King could ill spare him. He was borne from his tent on a litter, well wrapped in rugs and cursing feebly at the heat, the flies, the clumsiness of his servants and his own condition.

"I ought not to go," he said, when the King came to bid him farewell. "I ought not to leave you."

"What choice does your sickness give you?" Henry said. "The Kentish air will blow these vapors from you."

He took his brother's hand and wished him Godspeed. As the litter moved forward, Tom turned his yellowing face toward Harfleur. "Don't have it trouble you," he said. "You'll get in."

"Oh, for sure," Henry said. "Nurse yourself, Tom. I would have you quickly come to health."

When the ships slipped out with the tide, Hungerford spoke with Talbot of them. "My lord," he said, "another two weeks and we will all be creeping away back."

Talbot said in a gruff voice, "Does the King say it?"

"The lord Humphrey has said it. The King turned it to a jest. He said if we went back now, Southampton would shut her gates against us and we would find ourselves laying siege to her."

"He's not so wrong, by my faith," Talbot said. "If he goes back now, his army and his wealth wasted and naught gained, I think his throne can hardly sustain it. Certain he'll face a bankrupt realm, and that is poor defense against his gentle cousin, the Dauphin."

Hungerford looked toward Harfleur. "Tell me true, my lord," he said, "is it not beyond our strength, wasted as we are by sickness, to gain her?"

Talbot gave him no answer, but in that moment a distant hoarse voice broke in on them. Gam came running with much violent gesturing. "I pray you, good my lords," he was shouting, "will you not fetch the King? They are sounding for a parley."

XIV

Thus Henry gained Harfleur. Certain it was that his army could not have sustained another ten days of siege. Men saw the town fall to him as an overripe plum might fall to a man who had long sought to stretch his hand to it.

The garrison did not yet lack food. Also, since chivalry permitted it, Henry had allowed passage to their heralds that they might communicate with the French Court. All this was strange, yet such was the relief to be in that none thought on it. Men questioned what the King would do next. In a summer's hard fighting he had gained but one seaport, and the gaining of it had sapped his army to a skeleton thing—a shadowy mock of the array that so burnished Southampton Water with its gilt and heraldry. It was as though he could neither go forward nor back. He sent his heralds to offer challenge to the Dauphin as the Lionheart had once done to Philip of France, that on their combat might rest his claim. The Dauphin sent no reply though the King waited seven days for word, and those seven days were soon to become precious things.

Dorset he appointed Captain of Harfleur, and on the first day of October he gathered his nobles to him in Dorset's chamber in the castle. The Channel grew gray now, and from the slit windows men looked on the few ships that remained lying huddled for shelter in the roads, weather soiled and besmirched. Henry spoke of the Dauphin's silence, while his lords stood subdued and grim-faced about him. Talbot answered him first. "What now, my liege?" he said. "We cannot linger here."

Aumerle spoke up hesitantly. "The winter will be upon us soon," he said. "And there's dysentery inside the town now as well as out. If we are to go, we ought to go at once."

The King smiled and said, "We go tomorrow, Cousin." He looked upon them with humor as if he planned some outrageous jest. "I am mindful to see something of this coast," he said. "This is the Normandy that sired us, my lords, and it was here that our forefathers came to their great victories. Tomorrow we take some six thousand men—the bulk of the army—and march for Calais."

The nobles stirred and looked hard at each other. "It's rash, in faith," Cornwall muttered.

"Not so rash, my lords," Henry said. "The distance to Calais is no more than two hundred miles. I can be there in eight days. We may never see a Frenchman with a lance in his hand."

"I know not if we can get there in eight days," Aumerle said. "It seems too swift a reckoning. What of our supplies—our guns?"

"Our supplies we take with us," Henry said. "The guns I am shipping back to Southampton. They would be naught but a cumbrance to us." He looked round on them as they sat tensed and troubled and said in a mild voice, "Well, my lords? Have I so taken your breath?"

Dorset began to speak for the plan. "The French have not shown themselves all the while we have been at Harfleur," he said. "Is it too much to hope they will not show themselves for another eight days?"

"Yes, by the Mass, it is," Talbot said. He began to pace the room, his head bent. "The King and I have long been brothers-in-arms," he said. "And I'll use a brother's privilege and speak roundly. The King is a young man and the young men do not make the best commanders. They are too ready to believe they have only to shut fast their teeth in adversity and the tide will turn for them. I tell the King straightly he will not get fifty miles before he and his army are enrounded like sheep in the pens."

"Why, Talbot," Henry said, "I've had braver counsels from you. If I go back now, the Dauphin will say he has chased the King of England from the realm like a whipped cur."

Talbot answered him with grimness. "Aye," he said. "He will say it from the Paris rooftops. But should your grace accomplish such a march as this—with so small a force, two hundred miles through the heart of your enemies—it will be a blow in the face of the Dauphin that will rock the whole might and puissance of France. And that weighs too greatly with you. You are still too sore pricked from the mock of the tennis balls to think on it calmly. The Dauphin's name is a barb to you, to drive you, you know not where, as a horse is driven from overmuch spurring."

The lords looked upon one another in silence. Anger rushed into the King's face, but he had great love for Talbot and could bear much from him. He looked at him and half-smiled. "You speak true," he said. "I own the Dauphin touches me against the raw. All of you, my lords, know that. But I have weighed this matter well, and I say it can be done. Under the good Hand of God, we can reach Calais in safety." When they yet looked upon him, doubting, he said patiently, "What alternative, then, my lords? Let me hear it."

Dorset said, "What says the Duke of Aumerle?"

Aumerle sighed and ran a hand through his hair. "It is not for me to speak," he said. "Since it was my brother's crime that delayed us and so set us in these straits. I am content to follow wherever the King leads, if he can but trust me to do it with a loyal heart."

"Oh, Cousin," Henry said, "why do you speak so? No man about me is more trusted than you." He began to speak with the fire his great-grandfather, King Edward, had had in his youth. "In war there is no buckler like reputation," he said. "Our reputation lies in tatters now. Only a march such as I would accomplish to Calais can restore it to us again. What think you, my lords? Is it policy to go home—our banners torn and rent, our spirits sapped—in face of so emboldened and resolute an enemy? Let them see us as craven, and we'll invite the very blow we seek to avoid. Naught but the brave course is the safe one."

After a space Cornwall said, "There's much in what the King says."

"One word more, my lord," Talbot said. "To gain Calais our

road lies across the Somme, by way of the ford of Blanche-Taque. Were the French to dispatch a few hundred men they could with small toil bar our passage there."

"All that has been thought on," Henry said. "I have bidden the Captain of Calais send out a force to secure the ford for our coming." When Talbot's brows lifted he said, "Nonetheless, my lord, I earnestly desired your counsel."

"Your grace has put it to little use," Talbot said. "At what hour tomorrow do we march?"

XV

Dorset had been set in command of Harfleur. He bade the King farewell the next morning. "I would I was for the march with you," he said. "God with you, Harry. Are we still sane men or has this French air blown our wits from us?"

"Is it such arrant folly, Uncle?" Henry said.

"No, no," Dorset said. "I think you will get there, but you must be quick. If you're not there in eight days, I'll know no more sleep."

"Nor I," Henry said. He embraced his uncle and took his leave. Dorset stood at the window that he might watch his departure. All were assembled in the castle court, the archers and men-at-arms in their marching columns, and the pages standing at the heads of their lords' horses. They were but lads, gay in their bright hose, one stocking red and one yellow, or a violet and a green one. Each by custom would follow where his lord led, though he would do no fighting. The archers and men-at-arms likewise followed their own lords and wore their colors. It was thus never easy to command them, for their first allegiance lay with their lord and but their second with the King. The archers carried twelve arrows apiece in their belts, and their jerkins were of russet or Lincoln green.

Ned stood by the King's horse proudly, flaunting a jeweled cap with a crimson feather Henry had given him to mark the six years he had been of his household. When the King mounted, he clapped him on the shoulder and the boy looked up at him, beaming. Dorset watched as the columns moved from the court—the lean archers; the long line of horses; the standard bearers clasping the furled banners; the ten black-robed chaplains of the King's Chapel; the long-legged pages; the three heralds—Leicester, Guienne, and Ireland. When the King came to the portcullis he turned that he might wave, with no more care than if he rode on a morning's hawking. Talbot, too, turned and saluted, but his face was grim.

The first night the army pitched camp north of Montivilliers. It was but a mock of a camp, with neither tents nor pallets, braziers nor cooking utensils; no gun wagon or sutler's cart. At night nobles and commons alike lay in the open, wrapped about in their cloaks. The King's small force was near all Welsh and English, but he had with him likewise eight Hollanders, four Burgundian squires, and some few men of Guienne who ever counted themselves subjects of the King of England and who had ridden to Harfleur to join him. Among his nobles were many proven soldiers, Talbot and Aumerle, Sir John Cornwall, Gilbert de Umfraville, and Thomas Lord Camoys. Cornwall was wed to an aunt of the King's. His nickname, "Green" Cornwall, ill-suited him, for he was an unsmiling, bitter-tongued man, an inveterate grumbler, but a good soldier withal and careful of his men. De Umfraville was greatly younger. He was a northerner—his lordship being Redesdale in Northumberland, yet his attributes were of the south, and men marked him as gay and easy of temper. He well matched Lord Camoys, a man of chivalry likewise, deep-scarred from eyebrow to chin with an old wound that did not take off the pleasantry from his face.

Youngest of all was Michael de la Pole, the Earl of Suffolk, who was but nineteen. He had come to his title only five weeks past, on the death of his father at Harfleur. The King had a special care for him, for he had honored his father. Hungerford rode at his side throughout the next day's march. He was a contained boy, little given to speaking, but as the day wore on he began to complain

bitterly of the cold. He looked much pinched about the face, and
Hungerford began to fear he was sickening of the disease that
had killed his father. A few of the archers also had developed a
stooping and shuffling gait as of the London women who dredged
for fish in the Fleet. When the columns halted, these were the men
who sat down straightway, seeming not to care why they had
stopped.

De Umfraville himself rode back to speak with the King. There
were great trees, he said, felled and laid across the road. All the
afternoon the sweating archers toiled to shift them, and throughout the next day it was a like tale. It wasted much time for the
King, and by the time he reached Arques he was into the fifth day
of his march.

Many now believed themselves clear of danger. About the fires
they had kindled, the Welshmen sang in a tongue pleasant even to
ears that did not understand it. In the flickering dark the nobles
bunched themselves about the King and spoke cheerfully of the
morrow that would find them safely beyond Blanche-Taque. "Yet
those trees were felled to hinder us," de Umfraville said. "It almost
seems they knew of our coming."

"Why should they not?" Henry said. "You cannot march with
six thousand men and hide it."

"But they must have known our way, Brother," Humphrey of
Gloucester said. "And seemingly before we did. We are only five
days out from Harfleur." He had the King's coloring and had
grown much to resemble him, but he was stooped in the shoulders
where all his brothers were straight-backed, and his mouth was a
cynic's mouth—clever, sardonic and weak. Oftentimes he seemed
older than Henry, though not in the perplexities of command.

"I don't doubt they divined our purpose," Henry said. "We are
not the first Englishmen to walk this way." He spoke then of
Crécy, which lay beyond Blanche-Taque on the Calais road.
"There's a name to fire your blood," he said. "When I was a boy
it often held my dreams—the archers sitting in the rain thrusting
their bowstrings into their jerkins to keep them dry and the rooks

that flew from the trees. The day after tomorrow we shall see it."

"But none of that for us, my liege," Talbot said. "We seek no second Crécy."

"In faith, no," Henry said. "I seek no more than the Calais road. My numbers are too few and too lank from sickness to speak of a second Crécy."

By noon the next day the road dipped down to the valley of the Somme, and yet not a Frenchman showed to bar the King's path.

"I thought the King too bold," Hungerford said. "But he is going to be right. We are going to get through."

"There's the Lancaster luck for you," de Umfraville said and laughed.

"He is luckier than he deserves," Talbot said gruffly. Yet he, too, had ceased to look at every shrubbed thicket as if it concealed ten thousand Frenchmen.

XVI

Blanche-Taque, named in the English tongue the ford of the White Spot, lay across the Somme some miles from the river's mouth. Henry's great-grandfather, Edward III, and his great-uncle, the Black Prince, had forded the river here during their retreat from Picardy, and beyond had come upon the windmill, the spruce wood and the thorn thicket which men now named as Crécy. There was much to warm the heart here, and many friendly ghosts to walk alongside an English King; yet the way was hard, the approaches lying through marshland so treacherous that the mounted men had to dismount and lead their horses. There had been a causeway leading to the river, but it had been utterly destroyed. Nor was there yet a sign of the men the Calais garrison had dispatched to hold the ford, and that of all things was the most disquieting.

"Where are they?" de Umfraville said at last. "Where are their pickets? Have they not waited?"

"We are but a day late," Talbot said. "They would give us more grace than that."

"They had better," de Umfraville said. "If they've gone back, Harry will have their ears."

He led the vanward, while the King led the center column. Presently Henry signaled and all the columns came to a halt, the captains riding down the ranks that they might come about the King.

"The Calais men are not here, my lords," Henry said. "What's hindered them we know not. But certain it is that if they had command of the ford, we should have come upon them by this. Sir John Cornwall goes ahead with some two hundred archers to see what chances."

Cornwall returned after forty minutes, his archers strung out behind him. Henry asked him, "Well, sir knight?"

"Not a Frenchman, my lord," Cornwall said. "Neither is there an Englishman. Not a mortal soul."

Henry said, "No man bars our passage?"

"No man, my lord," Cornwall said. "But the river's staked. I misdoubt if we can pass. Does it please your grace to come and see for yourself?"

The river lay but a quarter mile distant. Tall rushes marked its margin and among them heron perched or flapped away. On the far bank cattle stood up to the fetlocks in muddy water. The river was deep and flowed powerfully on the ebb tide, breasting the ford in fierce turmoil. All its length it bristled with stout stakes. Between them the river sang and hissed like a maiden's hair parting to a comb.

Umfraville begged leave to essay a crossing. The trappings were taken from his horse and he urged him forward, but he could find no footing. He brought his horse back to the bank and dismounted, the water running from his legs and thighs.

"Well, my lord?" Henry said. "Have we but a chance?"

Umfraville looked at his feet. "No, my liege," he said. "It is not possible."

The silent columns of men stirred and shifted. "Well, no matter," Henry said cheerfully. "We can try higher upstream. There
must be a bridge this side of Abbeville."

When the order to go forward was given the men set off as briskly
as if they were fresh and had no day's march already behind them.
All went as though spur driven, fearing what they would find or fail
to find at Abbeville. Presently young Suffolk said in a small voice,
"My lord, it may be that the bridge at Abbeville is also destroyed."

He spoke as if wishing the King to contradict him, but Henry
said only that it was possible. On a sudden, without signaling, the
whole van came to a halt. Hungerford at the King's bidding
spurred forward to find what was amiss. He could see Umfraville
and Talbot sitting their horses, slack reined, and the archers about
them leaning on their bows, all men's eyes on the river. Where
they gazed had once been a bridge, but it was axed to pieces.
In the lengthening shadows its aspect was of a dead thing, its spars
and beams like hacked limbs thrusting stiffly skyward.

In that drear moment, when column after column dragged unbidden to a halt, Gam rode out from among his Welshmen, shouting and pointing, "The Calais men," he was saying. "Look you,
over the river yonder."

All round the men who had flopped down on to the grass came
to their feet again as with hope. Horsemen rode upon the far bank
of the river, emerging from the screening woods—both knights and
common lances. They rode in the deep pools of their own shadows
cast about them by the setting sun, the knights stiff in full steel.
Their chivalry was proud, but it was less that than their silent and
hostile approach that spoke for them.

"No, friend," Henry said, "they're Frenchmen."

"Battle formation, by my faith," Camoys muttered.

"What need have they for that," Cornwall said irritably. "The
bridge is down. We cannot cross."

"They give us fair warning not to try, Cousin," Henry said.

"What now, my lord?" Camoys said.

"We'll withdraw," Henry said. "Back into that spruce wood yonder. They can no more reach us than we can reach them, and the men are spent." He looked about at their anxious and haggard faces and smiled faintly. "We are all spent, my lords," he said. "Tomorrow, sleep will have cleared our wits. We can best consider then what we must do."

Once they had gained the spruces many of the nobles went to see for themselves where lay the outer fringes of the wood. After a space Camoys and Talbot came back to the camp, their archers with them. Two men walked in the midst of them. One was no more than nineteen, with a dull-witted face and the garb of a servant. The other was older, with a look at once bold and lethargic. He stared at Henry with a kind of languid hatred.

"Prisoners, my lord," Talbot said. "We came upon them yonder by the road between the woods."

"Do you know aught of them?" Henry asked.

"Little in all truth. He claims he is a gentleman of a good family —a Gascon from Bigorre. He will not give us his name. The other is his servant."

"You know me?" Henry said to the Gascon in French.

"I know you for the King of England," the Gascon said in an indifferent voice.

"Then you know I would have speech with you," Henry said. "I mean you no harm but I desire you to answer me."

"Oh, I can tell the King of England much," the Gascon said calmly. "Doubtless he wishes to know what became of the three hundred men that the Sire de Warwick dispatched a week ago from Calais. Most we buried some ten miles north of the ford of Blanche-Taque. A few we chased back. They did not pause to draw breath until the gates closed on them."

"Three hundred men," Cornwall said in disgust. "Has the Captain of Calais lost his wits to suppose he could secure Blanche-Taque with that?"

To the Gascon Henry said, "How many of your countrymen

hold the north bank of the Somme yonder and under which captain serve they?"

"Under the Marshal Boucicaut," the Gascon said. "His strength is not less than six thousand fighting men, the greater part mounted. He it was who disposed of the Calais force."

The King said, "Is there no bridge higher upstream that has not known your axes?"

The Gascon shrugged and studied his nails. "That is beyond my knowledge," he said. "The King of England desires passage of the Somme. It may be he will find means to attempt it. The Marshal Boucicaut awaits him."

"My lord," Talbot said, "tomorrow we must set back to Harfleur with all speed."

He spoke in English which the Gascon did not understand, but he heard the name Harfleur. "Is it that the King of England thinks to return to Harfleur?" he said. "I would not have him set high his hopes on it."

"What mean you?" Talbot said sharply.

The Gascon shrugged again and smiled. "I speak out of a grateful heart," he said in a silken voice. "The King of England has not yet strung me by the neck from one of yonder beeches, though doubtless he will do so before he leaves this wood. I would not have him think he can regain Harfleur in safety when the whole might and puissance of France stand in his way."

"Speak in plain fashion," Henry said.

"I shall, my lord, so please you," the Gascon said, still smiling. "The prince Dauphin and the High Constable left Rouen but two days after you left Harfleur. Their route I know not, but certain it is that they stand at your backs now, and with them the armies of France."

"Do they so?" Henry said. "I thought to see those armies before this, but they gave me no glimpse of them."

"Pah," the Gascon said. "The Dauphin but waited while the King of England battered himself and his chivalry to feebleness before Harfleur as a madman dashes his head against a wall. Yet even then he sent out muster calls to his princes. He has with him now the Dukes of Orléans, Brabant, Berri, Bar and Alençon and many lords. It was told us that when he left Rouen his army numbered forty-five thousand men."

Camoys exclaimed and said, "It cannot be."

"He's lying," Suffolk said in a voice of fear. "All Gascons are liars. My father used to say they were born with twisted tongues."

"No, under heaven he speaks true," Humphrey of Gloucester said. "It's the truth. It was always the truth, if we had had eyes enough to see it." He spoke with a twist of the mouth as if in humor, but the look he turned on his brother held a desperate sarcasm.

"Do you speak false?" Henry said to the Gascon.

"If the truth sounds darkly in the ears of the King of England, I cannot help it," the Gascon said. "Your enemies both face you and stand at your backs, and they are enough to swallow up these poor few and spew out the bones."

"They have yet to catch us," Henry said. He looked about at his captains in the thick dusk, the flicks of firelight starting against their steel and pale and weary faces. "We'll to our beds, my lords," he said. "Tomorrow, at prime, I would have you assemble here to me. We'll sleep and then decide what we must do."

XVII

With his captains assembled the next morning, Henry came to them. Hungerford did not know whether he had slept or what his dreams were if he had. He spoke straightway of the Gascon. "I do not think he lied," he said. "What say you, my lords? Do we press on or try to regain Harfleur?"

None answered him.

The King said, "This is our case—between us and Harfleur is the Dauphin with some forty-five thousand men. Between us and Calais is Marshal Boucicaut and six thousand and the river." He scratched a semicircle in the soil with his rowel spur, in shape like a letter C. "The river bends," he said. "Thus. And the bend is in our favor. Even should the bridges be destroyed and we must track the river to its source we can yet outdistance Boucicaut because he cannot short-cut the bend."

"You think he will follow us?" Aumerle said.

"Cousin, I am sure of it. His aim is to stop us crossing the river. He means to hold us here on this side until such time as the Dauphin can come upon us from the rear."

"But to track the river to its source, my lord . . ." Sir John Cornwall said and broke off. He went on more mildly, "We have no maps. We cannot tell how far it is."

"Some sixty miles," Henry said. "It cannot, in truth, be more."

"Our food is all but gone," Aumerle said in a troubled voice. "We have enough only for today and tomorrow."

"We must live off the land, Cousin," Henry said. "But we pay for all we take. It is to be as I told them at Harfleur. If there is a Frenchman pillaged or abused or a Frenchwoman raped, the man who so offends hangs."

"Then the King thinks we should keep on in spite of all?" Camoys said.

"I think so," Henry said. "Yet I well know, my lords, that my craft of battle measured against the French has been a poor thing. Small blame to you if you have no confidence in it. This time give me your frank thoughts and I'll abide by them."

Talbot answered that he purposed well. "If we go back and meet with the Dauphin," he said, "it will be the jaws of France that close about us. The hunted hare has more hope of life than the snared one."

"Now, by my faith," the King said, "this time I must be right. Not since we left Southampton has the lord Talbot agreed with me." They looked at each other with much affection, Talbot no longer pricked by the King's recklessness, nor the King by Talbot's caution. They were as close knit now as ever they had been in the Welsh Marches.

"It may be possible," Aumerle said at last, and one by one Cornwall, Erpyngham, Gam, and Suffolk made hesitant signs of assent.

"Then we press on," Henry said with joy. He clapped Erpyngham on the shoulder. "Gather the archers to me, old friend," he said. "I would speak with them."

"What of the Gascon?" Sir John Cornwall asked.

The King said, "He comes likewise."

XVIII

Erpyngham was Marshal of the Host, and it was he who summoned the archers to the King. Henry told them he still sought to bring them to Calais, buying bread for them in the villages they came to on the way, but he reiterated the threats he had made in Harfleur concerning any private hurt done to the French. Some of his nobles listened to him with expressions of gentle sarcasm. No King had yet succeeded in preventing Englishmen from looting in France nor sought to do so.

That day—the seventh out from Harfleur—was the twelfth day of October. As yet the weather held, and the woods that fell back from the marshy Somme stood out clear and brittle in raddled mock of their fresh summer greenery. The men made good speed, but Boucicaut moved too. When Henry pitched camp for the night, Boucicaut's fires glowed through the thinning trees across the river like the tormenting brands of hell fiends. That night saw Suffolk clawed by the disease that had killed his father before the walls of Harfleur. Throughout the day's march he had been alternately sweating and shaking. Twice Henry had come up to him and asked him how he fared, and he denied in a whisper that he was ill. But, at night, when Henry came to him again, he said in a frightened voice, "Oh, my lord, I have my father's sickness."

He lay on the ground rigid and shivering. The nobles piled their cloaks upon him, and the next morning he could scarce be borne into the saddle. All that day the route skirted the marshlands that fringed the river. Presently Nicholas Colnet came forward to speak with the King as he marched. Henry had five physicians and five surgeons with him, and Colnet was the chief. He was little changed from the day he had first come to dress the prince's wound in Shrewsbury Castle after Hayteley Field.

"My lord," he said, "does it please you to come to the Earl of Suffolk? He cannot go on."

Hungerford said, "Could we not prop him on his horse?"

"He has no heart for it," Colnet said. "He wants to be left, and I think if we bear him he'll lose the use of his legs. Already he broods on his father."

"He dies if he stays here," Henry said.

Talbot spoke in grave fashion. "If we could have found some knight or gentleman to deliver him to," he said. "But these about here are peasants. They would slit his throat for his boots and the ring on his finger."

"He must come," Henry said. He went back to where Suffolk lay in the tufted grass under a clump of alders and knelt beside him. "How now, Michael?" he said. "What is it?"

Suffolk made as though to paw at the ground with his hands— as feeble as a newborn calf seeking to rise. "I cannot go on, my lord," he said. "I beg you leave me. I'll yield myself to whoever next passes."

"I must bring you home," Henry said. "What would your mother say if I did not? Has she not known grief enough over your father?"

"She would pay my ransom," Suffolk said in a faint voice. "Whatever they asked she would find it."

"Why pour good de la Pole gold into their coffers?" Henry said. "Think what better use you can put it to when you get home. Your father oftentimes told me he wanted new granaries at Cottingham and a manor house in the Saffrons."

Suffolk's young face under its yellowing mask of skin crumpled as though he were about to weep. "I cannot do it, my lord," he said. "Calais is a great way, and I have no strength."

"Leave Calais from your thoughts," Henry said. "You have no more to do than to put one foot in front of the other, and thus Calais will come to you."

"No, my lord," Suffolk said. "No. My strength fails me."

"It was likewise with me at my anointing," the King said. "I thought I could not reach the High Altar. No man else knows it." He took Suffolk by the forearm. "Come," he said. "Rouse up that knightly de la Pole blood of yours. Calais is not so far as the High Altar was."

He put his shoulder behind Suffolk's and pushed. Suffolk came to his feet with an expression of astonishment on his face. He clung heavily to the King, but he did not fall. Henry supported him with one arm, while the marching columns went slowly past them, the men following their lords.

Ned came that he might stand by them. He but rarely lurked far from the King's heels, and it oftentimes seemed he doubted to trust Henry out of his sight. Henry looked down at him and smiled. "Ned," he said, "can you do me the service of a knight and help Lord Suffolk?"

It pleased Ned to be so called upon, and he set himself at Suffolk's side. Likewise one of the chaplains—Thomas Elmham, the King's confessor—came over to them and took Suffolk's other arm. Thus propped on either side, he went forward.

When they pitched camp the King took his brother and Hungerford and went with them down the ranks. About them the sprawling archers and men-at-arms opened their pouches and fell to chewing. All but a handful were eating the last of the food they had brought with them. As Hungerford watched, one by one folded his empty pouch flat and thrust it back into his belt. Almost he asked the King what hope there was of buying bread on the morrow, but he thought better of it. Henry had gone ahead through the wheat that dipped down to the river. On a sudden, as he trod through the wheat, clawed iron leaped from it and snatched fast at his foot.

Hungerford knelt to free him. He had been wearing leg armor —cuisses and greaves—and was not greatly hurt.

"A trap, my lord," Hungerford said, and flung it away.

"Aye," Henry said, "a trap." He spoke in bitter self-raillery. Humphrey marked him and broke into sour laughter.

"My lord," Hungerford said, "it cannot be. We gained Harfleur in the face of them."

"Oh, Walter, open your eyes," Henry said. "Harfleur yielded when the Dauphin bade her yield. Why else did he sit at Rouen with forty-five thousand men and not send to her relief?"

"The Dauphin would reckon thus, sir knight," Humphrey said sardonically. "Harfleur would be well lost for a few weeks if losing it would entrap the King and the armies of England."

The King looked back at the dim figures of the archers setting their pickets among the trees. "Poor fellows," he said. "If they know not now they'll know tomorrow when their bellies are empty that they follow a fool for a King."

"How could you know?" Hungerford said. "If from the first it was in sooth a trap, it was most cunningly sprung."

Presently they returned to the camp. The archers lay in slumbering groups, close together, their arrows beside them, their bows across their chests. Suffolk lay in taut sleep. His face was the color of yellow sandstone and sweat stood out on his forehead in glistening beads.

"You'll not bring him to Calais, Brother," Humphrey said softly.

"Yet I must," Henry said. "I'll bring them all to Calais. I owe them that."

XIX

Pont Remy, which the King reached the following day, had had two bridges across the Somme within a mile of each other. Both had been hatcheted to naught, so that the river swirled noisily among lumps of masonry and twisted starlings. Boucicaut's cavalry

yet stalked the King on the far bank. All men knew that if he
sought to cross here, lacking ford or bridge, he would be entrapped.

Thus the army took the Boves road, as with despair, all men well
knowing that each step brought them farther from Calais and
deeper into the land of their enemies. To the homesteads at Pont
Remy the King sent that he might buy bread. The villagers did
not withhold it, hearing the bilingual English nobles speaking
their Norman tongue as Frenchmen. They told them much, word
being about that a great army had left Rouen, though some held
it was in the command of Charles d'Albret, High Constable of
France, and not of the Dauphin. The Dauphin's tax gatherers had
been busy throughout Paris, Rouen and all the Île de France. They
were held in much hatred by the villagers, who called them rob-
bers, extortioners and murderers.

The hamlet yielded Henry's army bread scarce enough for every
man to have a mouthful, a few sacks of corn and some dried peas.
The army ate for the first time that day. When they came again to
the march the masklike yellow of Suffolk's face seemed to throw a
like cast across the faces of others of the archers. These began to
shuffle along, using their bows as staffs, and they dropped out
many times between the halts the King ordered along the way.
All had had dysentery at Harfleur and it had returned upon them
again, clawing at bowels and bellies and sucking all strength
from their limbs. They much slowed the pace of the whole, but
Henry ever waited for them. Men marked his vigilance that it was
ceaseless. He roamed back and forth along the lines, herding on
the stragglers as a watchdog might. He had said he would bring
them all to Calais, and his determination not to abandon a man
was to Hungerford as a fanatic's—dangerous and overzealous in
the hard case they found themselves in.

The King barely covered five miles in a day's march. Hungerford stood with him and Sir Thomas Erpyngham watching the last
archers drag themselves into the camp. Some made hard toil of
it, laboring over the hillocks and wind drifts of dead leaves. Almost the last came Suffolk, borne along between Ned and Thomas

Elmham. The three of them—the sick man, the boy, and the priest —against the sere background of autumn woods had the look of a saintly pilgrimage, such as the Church frescoes often depicted.

"Suffolk is going to throw off his sickness," Henry said. "I feel it in my bones."

"I feel more than that in my bones," Erpyngham said. "Mark it, my lord, it is going to rain. All my limbs pain me, and they are older limbs than the King's."

"They pain from the day's toil then," Henry said. "Have they not been good stout limbs in the service of Lancaster?" He walked back up the track and took Ned's place at Suffolk's side. "Michael," he said, "you do noble well. Don't speak to me again of ransom."

The rain which Erpyngham had foretold began that night, pattering on the shriveled leaves and the huddled forms of the sleepers about their embered fires. Of all things rain was the most to be dreaded by the Kings of England in hostile country, for, if the bowstring became sodden, the long bow, on which they much relied, was useless. Yet while France was commonly pictured as the most sun-blessed of countries and England as a dank and sodden bog, no King of England could set foot in France without his own realm's weather buffeting him at every step.

When at dawning the columns moved off, Colnet came to the King and Henry went back with him down the lines. One of the archers lay across the track where he had fallen as he marched. The King asked where he came from, and the man whispered he was from Bosworth in Leicestershire.

"I know the town," Henry said. "Good bowmen come from Bosworth. There must be others here from those parts."

He looked round at the archers about him. Three spoke up hesitantly, saying they too were from Bosworth. "We could mayhap bear him," one of the men said, "if we clasped hands chair-fashion and if he has the strength to sit."

"Better to fashion a litter," Henry said. "Cut two poles and sling a cloak between." He drew his cloak from his shoulders and tossed it to them. "We'll match our pace to yours," he said. "And

should it chance you have a same need, we'll do for you likewise."
He turned to the others peering at him through the slanting rain
and spoke in much earnest. "I would bring you all to Calais," he
said. "I know it is said among you that the commanders abandon
those that cannot keep up—all nations do it, and the English have
done it in these parts many times. But it is not so with us. We are
too few, and our fewness and the perils that enround us make us
brothers. I would have no man fear sickness or wounds—these
things do not lessen kinship. If the man beside you falls, prop him
up. He will do likewise with you. Thus will we come to Calais."

"You'll leave no man, sire?" one of the archers said incredu-
lously. "No man?"

"Not while he yet has breath, soldier," Henry said. To the sick
man at his feet he said. "When your strength returns, we'll find you
a horse. Until then your friends will bear you."

All day the rain hissed on to the dead leaves, and the Somme
landscape which before had been bright-defined in the autumn
sunshine hung about them blurred and sheeted. Soon there was
not a man but was soaked to his skin. In this new misery the toiling
columns took on a look of doom. The army was as a dying animal
dragging stiff limbs step by step up the course of the river, while
all about the land died likewise, the green of summer yellowing
into decay, the trees bloodless and shriveled. It was to them as a
hateful and hating country, snatching at feet with muddy claws
and whipping wet twigs across faces already stiff with rain. There
was but little provender, for Normandy lay behind, and this was
Picardy, sparse-populated and furbished with forest and swamp.
When the King was able to buy bread, it was always delivered
into the hands of the sergeant of the pantry for fair division. The
archers who sat in the rain with a shaving of pork or a handful of
dried peas had no more than the King and his nobles, and on the
fourteenth day of October when there was not a house in the day's
march, all had the same hunger.

The next day the Bosworth archer died from his dysentery. One
of the chaplains turned aside to pray for his soul's rest while the

columns marched past them. The King had faint hope some of the French might give him Christian burial before the wolves came upon him, but Hungerford doubted it. Now that death had at last penetrated the King's ranks, some of the archers seemed ready to drop. Those most stricken were strangely all men who had shown no sign of dysentery the previous day. They staggered along, gray-faced and twisted with pain, their pace becoming slower and slower. Henry halted again and sent for Colnet. "What's the matter?" he said. "What ails them?"

"They brought it on themselves," Colnet said. "This strikes at their bellies." He dropped into the King's hand a tiny green apple, hard as wood.

"They can't eat these," Henry exclaimed. To the archers he raised his voice. "They are not ripe," he said. "Would you poison yourself?"

"They are apples, my liege," one of the men said, and the look he gave the King seemed to Hungerford singularly defiant.

"Grise," Henry called, and the gray which bore the royal trappings ambled to his side. Henry caught his bridle and thrust the apple under his nose. The horse snuffed at it but would not eat.

"You see?" Henry said. "Even the horse has more wits than you." He tossed the apple from him. "Have patience," he said. "We cannot now be far from another hamlet. We have but to reach it to gain bread."

"What of the river's source where we can cross?" one of the men said timidly. "Is it far, think your grace?"

"Not far," Henry said. "If we find a bridge or a causeway un-mutilated we'll cross before that."

Talbot spoke quietly with the King. "Then will we march into Boucicaut's arms," he said. "Remember he is our equal in strength. He has six thousand men."

"I know it," Henry said. "But I have my bowmen and they are worth two of any other nation. Reckoning thus, we outnumber them."

"Ah, good my lord," Talbot said, smiling. "It takes Lancaster to

set six thousand against six thousand and find he has the greater."
With his beard and brows grizzled and his weather-beaten face,
he had the aspect of having been fashioned in bronze and stone
like a knight's effigy on a tomb. The old jousting jupon he wore
was ripped and the padding hung out in matted lumps. He looked
thus much dilapidated, but no more so than his fellows.

Yet they came to no bridge that day that remained whole. Soon
the men in their march looked anywhere but at the river, their
faces taking on a set and sullen look as though they reckoned themselves cheated by hope. The river had become to them as an accursed thing. There was now not a man in Henry's army who did
not see it rolling ever through his dreams and did not long for some
gentler river—the Wye, the Coquet, the Dee or the broad and
shining Thames.

xx

The next day Umfraville spoke with Hungerford of the King.
"Think you he will go back?" he said.

Hungerford answered him, "Not Lancaster."

"Indeed, no," Gam said. "I speak under reproof now, but I
know him better than any other man that marches here with him.
Did I not turn my sword's point against him for five years in the
hills of Wales? Always have I said it is best to fight both against
a man and for him. Thus does one know him in the round."

Presently the woods fell away to reveal a castle and a few homesteads. The castle was squat and four-turreted, with bake and brew
houses clustered against it, and fine granaries and wine presses
standing outside the walls alongside the vineyards. The drawbridge was up, and from the arrow-slits red rags for defiance spattered the walls like drops of blood.

Umfraville named it Boves Castle. He gave the signal to halt,
and the King and Talbot came spurring down the lines.

"Herald," Henry shouted, and Hugh Stafford, the Guienne Herald, came to his side. He looked a sorry replica of a herald, the once-gay colors of his tabard fading and creeping into each other and his chin thick coated in stubble.

"Who commands yonder?" Henry said. "Can you see his standard?"

Stafford shielded his eyes with his hands. The rain had ceased, but the land was misted and cloudy gray as in a dream. The heavy standard flapped wetly above the castle's foremost turret, its device not easily discernible. Most men could have told but little from it, but the heralds had to recognize the chivalry of Europe at a glance.

"Bar azure. Fetterlock," Stafford said. "It is Vaudémont. Le Comte de Vaudémont."

"I know naught of him," Henry said. "Is he high in the counsels of France?"

"Not France, my lord," Stafford said. "Vaudémont is fief to the Duke of Burgundy."

"You go to him, Umfraville," Henry said. "Take a herald and a trumpeter. Say it is the King of England and that I have treaty with his master of Burgundy. Say my soldiers are starving and I would buy bread. If he refuses, tell him I'll burn his barns."

Umfraville said, "I will, my lord."

"Give him a fair price," Henry shouted after him.

While Umfraville was gone, men and nobles alike sprawled wearily on the wet hillocks and the piles of dead leaves. They spoke little, but now and then one of them would pass his tongue over his cracked lips. Plainly they were ruminating on the food Boves Castle was going to yield them, in the hope it would be greater than any they had yet gained.

Umfraville rode back at length, and the King asked him of his faring. Umfraville answered him slowly. "Vaudémont says your grace may have believed yourself to have friendship with his master, but it is not so. Four days after we left Harfleur, Burgundy repudiated the treaty with his cousin England. Vaudémont says he rode to Rouen to offer his sword to the Dauphin."

"The damned weathercock," Cornwall said. "May the next fence he straddles split him from crutch to poll."

The King said, "Does Burgundy then ride with the Dauphin?"

"No, my lord," Umfraville said. "The Dauphin would not have him. He told Burgundy there were but few Englishmen to go round and that the share of honor among the French knights was already thinly spread. He said if Burgundy too coveted honor he should have declared himself from the first. Nonetheless, they are pledged to each other. Burgundy waits at Rouen."

It was the most ill news, for the Dauphin could now use every man under his command instead of setting aside a force to watch Burgundy, on whose menacing presence the English hopes had rested. Yet none seemed greatly disturbed. It was as though so many calamities had beset them since Harfleur that one more or less made little matter. Their case was beyond worsening.

"Yet Vaudémont hearkened to you?" Henry said.

"He hearkened," Umfraville said, "once I told him we would fire his barns else. I paid in nobles for the bread he gave me—two basketsful. He said he had no more."

"Two baskets," Henry exclaimed. "Was he lying?"

"I know not," Umfraville said. "He swore by every saint he could lay his tongue to, it was all he had. He says they grind on a Wednesday and today is Tuesday. Should I go back and ask another parley?"

"No," Henry said. "I dare say he speaks true, and if he does not we cannot lay our hands on it. Have them divide out the two baskets. It will be but a few crumbs each."

"I'd burn his barns for good measure," Sir John Cornwall said. "Maybe he lies; and if I could deal Burgundy a pinprick, by cock and pie, I'd do it."

"Let be," Henry said. "The men are weary and we must press on. Let them eat whatever they get on the march."

"We can look at those granaries," Cornwall said. "There's time enough for that."

He took a detachment of archers and searched through each, but all were as empty as if Vaudémont had swept them out with a broom. The winepresses, too, had no casks beside them. Henry and Talbot both supposed that the vats had been removed for safety within the castle walls, but in that they were wrong, and before Boves was half a league behind a sudden confused shouting broke in upon the captains. The King had gone ahead while the archers straggled after their lords, and it was from one of the groups that Aumerle came riding. "They've found the wine casks," he said. "Not a man but will be in his cups inside twenty minutes."

The vats of Boves stood a few yards off the road among the trees. About them a grunting press of archers pushed and fought, and from all sides others converged on them. Henry strode forward with upraised hand, but they took no heed of him. He shouted at them and again they ignored him, the smell of the wine in their nostrils.

"They've had scarce any food," Henry exclaimed. "They'll make themselves reeling drunk."

"Yet save your breath, Harry," Humphrey said. "It will take more than the King's majesty to make them listen now."

The tang of the wine lay in the air, sweet, heady, and invigorating. Even to smell it stirred the senses and fired the blood, and against its potency for bellies long soured with sodden bread and salt meat, Henry or any other king in Christendom could have shouted himself hoarse and been no more heeded than a tavern potboy. Soon the men who had drunk their fill began to stagger away, slack-lipped and witless-eyed. When darkness closed on them, half were mortal drunk.

The King set every watch himself as best he could, using squire or noble or even chaplain or page. The archers mostly lay in drunken stupors where they had fallen. Often in their russet jerkins they were hard to discern from the leaves they lay on. Hungerford tripped on one. He lay on his back, snoring in grunts like a frightened pig, his bow and his long-necked drinking bottle clutched to his chest. Each time he breathed wine from the bottle spilled on to his shirt. Hungerford stirred him with his foot, but he did not flicker an eyelid.

"As useless as a babe," Henry said. "May God strike with us if the Dauphin comes upon us now." He bent down and corked fast the drinking bottle thrusting it into the archer's belt. Then he dragged the man's head and shoulders clear of the pool of mud, spew, and wine in which he had been lying and set him against a tuft of moss.

"He'll draw bow again for you, my lord," Talbot said. "But not tonight."

"Tomorrow will see them no more in health," Henry said curtly. He was still angry, but when they reached the single fire the squires had kindled, he laughed. "Well," he said, "is there not a saving grace that guides the feet of fools and drunken men? And the King of England is of one sort and his bowmen of the other."

XXI

Talbot feared the King began to lose command. The next night at dusk when they halted, Henry went ahead to see if they might with safety pitch camp. While they waited, many of the archers went through the reeds to the river's edge to wash their drinking bottles and refill them. One of the Welshmen sat down on a felled tree near some few English archers. He had wine in his bottle, and he took a hunk of bread from his pouch and began to eat noisily. The Englishmen turned their heads to watch him. "They guzzle like pigs," one said.

"If you have eaten your own portion, it is no blame to me," the Welshman said in anger.

"How comes it you have bread?" another said. "We all ate our last this morning."

The Englishman who had first spoken laughed sourly. "Ask him whose pouch he filched while he slept," he said. "I know a Welshman."

"Know a Welshman, do you say?" the archer said in a voice of quivering rage. "Know a Welshman. Naught else do we hear from

Saxon tongues dripping their toad spittle. Not one of you but was begotten of a Norman dog out of his Saxon leman."

When he would have gone from them, the Englishman gained his feet and blocked his path. "Wait, my hinny," he said. "I kna' ye. You're of the traitor Glendower's men."

"What matter it?" the Welshman said loudly. "My bow is as loyally borne for the King now as it was once loyally borne for Owen."

"Hearken ti him," the other said. "He willna tell us, I reckon, how many honest skulls of Englishmen were split by him—the lousy Welshman."

"May God slit your scurvy Saxon's tongue," the Welshman said furiously. All about the archers came now to their feet, so that circles of Englishmen stood with two or three glowering Welshmen in their midst. On a sudden the Englishman hit the Welshman on the side of the jaw. By then another Welshman made to draw his knife, but Gam snatched the bow from his hand and hit him over the head with it with a crack as of an axe splintering wood. In the like moment the King came back toward them. The archers parted to let him come, but many went on fingering the weapons in their belts as in defiance.

"How now?" Henry said. "What's this?" He spoke mildly, in neither anger nor irritation.

Gam answered him in high choler. "We were awaiting your grace's commands," he said. "But a dispute has arisen—sorry to say. Why they should seek to break each other's pates, I know not, save that an Englishman would quarrel with his own guardian angel for lack of an enemy, look you, and a Welshman is no better. Yet though I be bold to say it, and prejudiced, too, it may be said, it was the Englishman who struck first."

"Yon fellow ought not ti strut alongside honest men," the archer said. "He fought against you, my lord. He's of Glendower's knaves. I've borne my bow wi' honor nigh on fifteen years, and I kna' his traitor kind."

His accent was harsh and long-voweled. Henry asked him where he was from, and he answered, "Wark," pronouncing it "Wa-ak," like an outdrawn croak of pain. "How comes it a Northumbrian knows so much of the Welsh?" Henry said.

"I served in Wales aal of five years," the archer said. "And at Grosmont. I saw yon traitor there among the prisoners."

The King said, "Were you likewise at the field of Shrewsbury?"

The man answered eagerly that he was, then fell on a sudden silent.

"Under which captain did you serve?" Henry said. The archer had no words, shuffling his feet as if the turf beneath them grew hot. When the King again asked him, he answered in a thick voice, "Under the lord Percy."

"Then all that day you drew bow against the King, my father, and against me," Henry said. He fingered the scar of Shrewsbury that lay under his hair. "See you this?" he said. "This I bore with me from the field that day, and for all I know it was a shaft from your hand that dealt me it." The man fell to mumbling. Henry said sharply, "Is it not possible?"

"Possible, aye, my lord," the archer said in a scared voice. "Yet it didna happen sae, I swear it."

"You cannot tell," Henry said. He spoke grim as a wolf, but suddenly he threw back his head and began to laugh. "By my faith," he said, "are you my champion?"

A thin tittering came from Glendower's Welshman. He was bent forward against his bow, his hand to his mouth; and as they saw the King laughing and the Welshman laughing, the others did likewise, even the Northumbrian grinning sheepishly. A Frenchman coming upon them now would have thought all crazed. Yet the laughter was almost as nourishment to the bones.

"Come," Henry said at last to the Welshman and the Northumbrian, "you two should be friends. You walk a common ground." He looked at the rest and spoke more hardly. "Do not seek quarrels," he said. "If the French come upon us, you'll lack none, I swear it. Neither will the Dauphin pause to ask whether you be Welshman or Englishman, Norman or Saxon, or if you drew bow for Harry Plantagenet or against him. Calais is no small distance, and we are much enrounded by perils. If it does not bind us one to another, then the march may prove, in truth, long and hard for us."

XXII

Suffolk seemed the next day to have come to a little strength. Henry set aside some of the wine of Boves for him, and at every halt he took a sip, before gaining his feet again, sometimes borne onward by Ned and Elmham, sometimes by Camoys and Hungerford. The archers trudged through the mud barefoot, their hose in tatters about their knees, their right sleeves torn away or hanging loose to keep the arm unhampered for drawing bow. All they and most of the nobles were bearded now, so that almost every man's face had the ragged and thin-cheeked look of the Apostles whose likeness crowded the frescoes of Westminster Palace. Hungerford looking upon his fellows saw them as strangers. Camoys's scar had sunk deep into his face, straining the flesh about it into a matted and ugly purple. Aumerle shuffled along, bone-weary and aging. Talbot halted on one leg, and the King too limped, his leg paining from the teeth of the trap. Sir Thomas Erpyngham, the oldest, did almost the best. Henry took much pleasure in his company. Often Erpyngham's white head glinted in the rain alongside the King's brown one.

Ever across the river was the gleam of Boucicaut's steel, masked now and then by the trees, then appearing again like a hungry Nemesis. "Damn them to hell," Humphrey of Gloucester said. "What are we going to do? Where is the bend you spoke of?" He glared at his brother. "We must have gone forty miles, but I can see none of it."

"It does bend," Henry said. "I'll go hazard with you. Pay me what you owe when we reach Calais."

That day—the seventeenth day of October—the rain never ceased. Until dusk the army stumbled through it in clothes so sod-

den that each step set the whole body chafing. There was not a
crust in the camp, but the hedges were clustered with ripening
walnuts, and at each halt the nobles and the archers alike grubbed
for them among the drenched thickets with fingers scarce able to
feel. But for the King their journey even now would have been
too great for them. Men marked that it was with him as if he knew
by instinct when a man was about to drop, and he was ever there
to hoist up or to set on foot again. For their cheer he fell to lying
to them, telling them the source of the river was not far and that
they would quickly come upon it. When he spoke thus, knowing
he lied, Hungerford saw his hand close about his Coronation ring
as though to blind it to any desecration of kingship. He had no
thought now but for his halting, staggering, bedraggled wreck
of scarecrows. He who at Harfleur had been no more heedful of his
men than any other of the kings of Europe had developed a lover's
care and tenderness for them. That night when the archers lay
burrowed for warmth beneath the piles of sodden leaves, Hungerford twice opened his eyes to see him gazing down at the groups
of prostrate figures, his brooding underlip thrust out, and knew
him to be ceaselessly scheming how he might yet bring them to
Calais and safety.

The next day brought them to Nesle, and the King was able to
buy bread for a day's journey. Nesle had its own church and some
fine orchards, pricking out the tawdry brown leaves with reddening
apples. The fruit made good eating after days of sodden bread,
but there was no time save for the men to snatch it off the trees
as they passed. The day following, when the King was about to
break camp, a French priest and two lay sisters in the habits of
Poor Clares came through the trees that screened the village. They
walked straightway to Aumerle, standing at the rear of the columns, his coat-of-arms bearing the griffin of the Plantagenets. It
was boldly done, for in the days of Edward, the armies of France
and England had not always dealt gently with such as they. The
men turned their heads to peer at them, and the King wheeled his
horse about. "What is it, Cousin?" he shouted.

Aumerle came slowly over the grass to him. "They are from Nesle, my lord," he said. "The priest says a soldier has looted his church."

"An Englishman," Henry said. He sounded as though he could scarce believe it.

"He holds it was an Englishman," Aumerle said reluctantly. "But one thing was stolen—the pyx. They say they will be content to take its value in silver."

"Let be, then," Humphrey said. "Pay them, Hal, and let's be off."

The King did not answer. He tossed his reins to Ned and dismounted.

"My lord," Aumerle said uneasily, "time is most precious to us. What can we do when he may be one of five thousand?"

"We'll find him, Cousin," Henry said. He shouted, and Umfraville came hurrying from among the baggage horses, half-shaved and wiping the water from his chin. "My lord," Henry said, "yesterday we lodged two hours in the town. Did not some of your men take their rest by the church?"

"Yes, my lord," Umfraville said. "Some of mine and some of the Shropshire men—Lord Talbot's."

"Have them out," Henry said. "Let them know the pyx is looted."

"Your grace means to search them?" Umfraville said. "All of them?"

"For the saints' sake, Harry," Humphrey exclaimed. "The Dauphin's at our back. There's no time."

The King said, "Tell them if needs be we'll look at the pouch of every man in the army."

The men were marshaled in long ragged lines of green and russet about the yellowing turf. Umfraville and John Bromley, the King's standard-bearer, with two squires and the sergeant of the pantry, moved among them that they might search each man's clothing and pouch and the quiver he carried. All was so still, one could hear their breathing.

Most stood quiet, but on a sudden Hungerford saw one man's

hand waver inch by inch toward his pouch. Umfraville saw it likewise and seized upon him. Something bright as light spun from his grasp to roll at the King's feet.

Henry picked it up and wiped it on the silken face of his jupon. It was a silver-gilt pyx, well wrought but not of great value. It was a most holy vessel, used to contain the Host. That a man should steal it, thereby committing sacrilege when he had but small hope of reaching England again, was a puzzling thing.

The King had Ned wrap it in a clean linen kerchief, and gave it into the priest's hands. "Your pardon, Father," he said in French. "This should not have been. I would have you take a purse of some twelve gold pieces—offer it for me, then use it as you will. For the rest, I am in truth sorry." To Camoys he said, "Mount them and bring them back to Nesle. Take twenty archers with you."

"God with you, my son," the priest said. When he had mounted beside Camoys, he turned in the saddle and signed the King.

"What of him that robbed them, my lord," Umfraville said. "What penalty?"

"You know what penalty," Henry said. "He hangs." He looked back to where the archer crouched between his guards like an entrapped animal, his eyes like slits. "He went in no ignorance," he said. "Thrice were they told, once before Harfleur, when we began the march and at Blanche-Taque. He knew I forbade pillage of all holy places on pain of death. He can expect naught else."

"My lord," Aumerle said hesitantly, "it may be you will need every man you have."

"Not him, Cousin," Henry said. "Better without such as he." He spoke then to the chaplains. "Let him be shriven," he said. "Then make an end. He's your man, Umfraville. Do as I bid you, but be quick."

Four of Umfraville's archers did the work, while the rest looked on.

"Three hours gone," Sir John Cornwall said. "And another Englishman less for the Dauphin."

"It is well done," Talbot said gruffly. "I had thought at Boves the King lost command, but he does not."

When the columns were formed, Henry rode out of the ranks and spoke to them. "Learn this," he said. "Think not because our numbers are few that all is safe and nothing will be exacted against any man. If there is robbery done or rape or pillage or any violence enacted unbidden against the French, the man who so offends will answer for it. The man who does these things is not fit to walk alongside you, nor will he. He still hangs, whether I have but fifty men left me and the Dauphin fifty thousand."

Above him the archer's body stirred in the wind. No man had cared to take possession of his bow, and it rested against the beech under his dangling feet. If the Dauphin passed that way next day or the day after, he would doubtless wonder who had been doing his work for him.

XXIII

That day the sun shone, setting asteam clothes still sodden from yesterday's rain. Walking or riding thus was to have every stitch cling to the body like wet seaweed. Yet it did portend something good, for in the afternoon Umfraville came spurring back to the King. "My lord," he said, "I think the river begins to curve."

He had already sent his archers up the trees to discern what they might. A begrimed and calloused foot dangled far above from one of the tall elms. "What see you, archer?" Umfraville shouted, "Does it bend?"

"Aye, my lord," a northern voice answered. "A canny bend, seemingly."

The King would see all for himself. He set hands and feet to the tree and went up it, the crimson of his rondel belt aglint in the foliage. When he dropped again to the ground, his face told them it was indeed the bend they had long looked to.

Thus they turned away from the river and into the woods. The King's pace was very slow. Boucicaut's pickets across the river would see an army crawling as though half-dead into the cover of the trees. Yet once they were hidden the nobles rode up and down the columns shouting hoarsely for speed.

Much hunger lay now on the marching columns. Presently this lack brought strange effects. The aching weariness went, and in its place men felt the sensation of floating alongside their bodies, apart from them. Yet there was no ease in this. Rather it was as in a nightmare, so that one struggled toward a far aspect and never attained it, thus knowing the despair of the eternal wanderings of the damned.

So feeble had become the column's strength that the King rested the following day, setting the army to cut staves out of tree branches. These the archers whittled to points at each end, and then thrust them into their belts to carry. The next day on the march the King summoned to his side the Welshman who had fought with the archer of Wark. "I, too, remember you from Grosmont," he said. "You gave Glendower faithful service."

"Aye, my lord," the man said, his face at the mention of Glendower becoming closed and wary.

Presently the King said, "I think you can give me knowledge of Glendower." When the man made no answer he went on, "Think you I seek to do him hurt?"

"Owen is beyond all hurt from you, my lord," the archer said at last. "Dead is he." He began to speak of it in slow fashion. "It was his own mountains which he loved, look you, that killed him. Thrice at the turn of the year the lady Gwenllian sought to lead men to his succor, and each time driven back was she under the snows and the blizzards. Only by his ring and his dagger did we know him when we came upon him. We brought him back to the valley and there buried him in Christian fashion."

He signed himself, and the King did likewise. After a while he said, "What is your name, soldier?"

"Thomas ap Parry, so please your grace."

When the archer had left him, the King walked silently. Presently he spoke with Hungerford as if in excuse. "You did not know him," he said. "You could not forbear to honor him."

Yet it seemed to Hungerford that he alone among the trudging group of nobles was moved by Parry's words. To the rest Glendower's slow and lonely death was a far-off thing, walled up into the past by their own hunger and weariness. And even thus the iron mountains of Wales seemed at that moment gentler than the erstwhile fair fields of France.

By noon they came upon a few homesteads, learning they were but a mile from the river again. Umfraville brought four of the villagers to the King. They seemed eager to answer all he asked, either for the gold Umfraville had promised them or because they feared the ragged, bearded, and hollow-eyed rabble that had crept upon them from the woods and wanted only to see their backs. There were two fords, they said, one at Bethancourt and the other at Voyennes, within a mile of each other. Whether they were intact they knew not, but a levy of the St. Quentin men, wearing the badge of the Sire de Rambures had been in the district four days back. Rambures had told them the King of England marched with but a poor and spent force, and already the path was hard to him. The King paid them, then set on to Bethancourt.

"Well, Brother," Humphrey said, "if fortune looks as sourly on you as she has up to now, we'll find no more than a broken ford." His beard clung blackly to his cheeks and his eyes glared scarce sanely, as with the look of a very sick man. It seemed to Hungerford that those who had bidden him farewell in London would but hardly have recognized him; yet it was with him as it was with all of them. If any of the tattered and dirt-encrusted nobles who stood about the King had been magically set down in his own castle or manor, he would have stood there a stranger.

Willows marked the way to the river in stark and ever dwindling clumps until the track lost itself in reedy pools and coarse grass tufts set about in slime. With the dark, Henry halted, but the next day, leaving the sick, the horses and the baggage, he set out in two columns through the swamp. One column sought the ford at Bethancourt and the other that at Voyennes. A causeway had breasted the swamp, but it was destroyed. All was ghostlike, the whole aspect of marsh and distant trees thin-lit as in sleep, and even the figures of the men floundering through the mud at one another's elbows were shadows drained of flesh and blood. It was not more than seven o'clock when Henry reached the ford of Bethancourt. The river flowed almost as broad and powerfully here as it had done at Blanche-Taque, and as at Blanche-Taque, too, the ford lay hacked and broken beneath it. Those that came first upon it did not trouble to call of it to the rest. Some did not even look at it, not choosing to see their dark expectations thus bleakly fulfilled.

Henry waited until Aumerle's party rejoined him from Voyennes. Humphrey hailed them in a voice cracked and savage. "See how right I was, Cousin," he said to Aumerle. "The ford here is broken. In truth, I knew not why we troubled to drag ourselves through that hell-spew of mud to see."

"Voyennes is likewise," Aumerle said. He cast himself down on the slanted trunk of a willow, and half-sat, half-lay there, heedless of the slime. In the distortion of the half-light he looked an old man, lost in weariness and dejection. "We came upon a peasant there," he said. "He told us the St. Quentin men had had the charge of both fords. They broke them up, then went back. They held it was not needful to mount a guard."

"Oh, they were right," Humphrey said. "Why mount a guard over a rabbit in a trap." He broke into sudden laughter, high and brittle.

The King waded out half a dozen paces and stood with the water awash about his thighs. There were walnuts in his pouch and he cracked two, tossing down the shells. They went bobbing on the current toward the sea and the English Channel in arrant mockery of the men who watched them. Presently he said, "My lords, they've made ill work of it. Straw and brushwood would serve to restore it."

"Good my lord," Sir John Cornwall said. "We would be long about this task and they'll come upon us as we labor. Boucicaut is yonder on the far bank."

"He cannot be," Henry said. "He had to hold to the river, while we came shortly through the woods. We must have outdistanced him."

"There's more than a day's work in this," Aumerle said uneasily. "I do not think we can have outdistanced Boucicaut by more than twenty-four hours, and it will be tomorrow before we cross."

"That we'll have to venture," Henry said. "My lords, this river has too long barred our path. Unless we can cross here my soldiers' hearts will altogether drop from them. Better to take what risk we must in the hope good will come of it, than to keep on losing all hope."

So early had they broken camp that it was still no more than eight o'clock. The King set about restoring both fords in order to accomplish his crossing more speedily. There were bales of straw and hay stacked in two old barns on the edge of the marsh and on these the archers fell like a swarm of tattered locusts. Others hacked brushwood from the scrub or sawed off branches. It was cruel labor, for all had to be dragged through the bog. The men working in the river were up to their waists and armpits in water. They worked no more than ten minutes at a time, but they came out shuddering, their hands blue and swollen as the hands of a drowned corpse. Oftentimes as they labored they made strangled sounds in their throats as though they began to whimper like dogs. The nobles worked alongside the common men. Thus in that bedraggled, swaying line a Plantagenet was cheek by jowl with a man from a London hovel, and a lord of Norman blood with his own fief lance. Even the chaplains kilted their robes and labored, sweating and silent.

As he toiled the King slipped and fell scabbling on hands and knees into the shallows. With a river awash about him, he began to sing the old air, beloved by Englishmen, "Summer is icumen in; loud sing cuckoo."

Seeing he could still fool, the others broke into wry laughter. Hungerford saw him gay as he had not been since the nights he had likewise fooled with the journeymen and apprentices in the London taverns and marveled that his peril was thus light to him.

"He is not like Richard," Hungerford said, "is he, Davy?"

"Indeed no," Gam said. "Richard much pitied himself. It may be Monmouth pities himself likewise but in secret is it—we see none of it."

XXIV

The work lasted from eight in the morning until darkness. Men in health could have labored quicker, but hunger had much sapped them. It took the strength of three English archers to bear a branch to the river's edge where once a single man would have counted it small toil.

For sleep the King led them back to the camp of the night before. All was loud with the croaking of frogs from the marsh and the howling of the Picardy wolves. The nobles wrapped themselves in their wet cloaks and lay with their swords unbuckled and placed hilt on chest. No man dared cover his sword arm nor wrap himself tightly for fear the French should come upon them.

Some of the knights sought small shelter from the rain under the thorn bushes. Talbot slept between the King and Humphrey of Gloucester, awaking at midnight to find the King gone. Presently he returned, stepping over the huddled figures of his knights. Talbot drew the sodden thicket aside and Henry crawled in.

"I feared for the watches," he said. "Poor fellows—they had toil enough in the day." He drew his cloak about him, and they lay down together but without sleep. After a space he said, "I know not why the English do not chain up their Kings as madmen."

"My lord," Talbot said, "you have their hearts. They follow you gladly."

"I know not why," the King said. He spoke then of all that had befallen him since his accession and of his great fears. "I thought

Richard spake true," he said. "I thought that the King could not walk in trust with Englishmen. All were to me as though they looked upon me with the face of Scrope. Yet my soldiers teach me a better lesson."

Talbot said, "You are not to us as Richard."

The King seemed as if he smiled in the dark and said, "Never was such a friend as you. The perils that enround us are as you spoke, yet you say no word of blame."

Humphrey stirred and spoke grumblingly. "Was the day not long enough for you to talk in?" he said. "Sweet heaven, will the rain never stop?" He shifted nearer his brother, cursing the drops showering from the bramble twigs above them. "All my bones ache," he said. "My faith, Harry, the lousiest, most flea-ridden pallet in London were a better bed than this."

All night it rained and in the dawn the marshy approaches to the Somme loomed ahead black as a quagmire, even the reedy tufts as though they drowned in it. At each step the men sank up to their knees and if they walked into the concealed defiles lining the broken causeway, they went up to their armpits. The horses had to be dragged through it up to their bellies. All went in sullen fury—fury at the entangling willow twigs, the hidden stones, the mud that bedeviled and fought them.

Henry was ever at hand to speed them. "Keep on," he was saying. "Help that boy yonder. Archer, pull up that man next to you." Thus he toiled back and forth along the columns, black as a crow with mud and ceaselessly wary.

He had sent the horses with each a rider higher up to Voyennes. The main body of men he kept with him at Bethancourt. Now when all were through the marsh, he asked of them two hundred archers who were strong swimmers to offer themselves to go first. At his words there was much scuffling among the Welsh and Gam's voice came loudly from them.

"For the honor of Wales," he was saying, "go forward will you. Swim as well, you can, as any of your like in England, and better if you are true-born Welsh. Do as I say now."

The three archers he had brought with him to Harfleur shuffled slowly forward in front of the King.

"Do you swim, soldier?" Henry asked Evan ap Williams.

"I know not, so please your grace," Williams said. "For never have I tried. Yet the captain holds that I can."

"He is a man of Gwent and he swims therefore," Gam said.

The King smiled and bade him wait. The archers set aside their bows and arrow quivers and took to the water, bearing only knives in their belts. They swam as in heaving jerks, until all the Somme seemed to be filled with black heads and rumps bobbing on the current.

The waiting columns shifted and stirred about their lords. They were pressing closer and closer to the water's edge as though they grew afraid. Presently Henry said, "What troubles them?"

"They fear the Dauphin, my lord," Talbot said. "They think he will come upon us before all are across."

"The French are more likely to come upon them on the other side," Henry said.

"Small use to tell them so," Umfraville said. "God with us if they panic."

The King said, "I'll take one of the posts. They will see we mean to get them all across."

He took Camoys and went through the slime to the brink of the river. They stood close so that there was room for but one man at a time to pass between them onto the ford. To the huddled mass of archers knee- and ankle-deep in mud he raised his voice. "All of you will be brought across in God's good time," he said. "The more calmly you go the quicker will it be accomplished."

"What if the Dauphin is at our backs?" one said urgently.

"No sign of him yet," Henry said. "He'll not greatly relish this weather for his march. It seems we've brought our own weather with us, and that must suit the Dauphin as ill as a bow in a Frenchman's hands."

The archers smeared the rain from their faces and chuckled in cracked fashion. They waited quietly while Henry sent across

Umfraville and Sir John Cornwall leading five hundred lances. These would fight with steel and the water would not harm them. If Boucicaut awaited them on the far bank, the King hoped thereby for some protection for his archers.

So began the sight which was to flicker in front of men's eyes all day—the unending, stumbling, snakelike chain of men creeping step by step through the river. Henry and Camoys fed the chain as they might have played out a rope. If a man hesitated they thrust him forward; if he seemed too eager they checked him.

On the far bank Umfraville left the river's margin and climbed the slope above him. The men about the King could not have told it were he save that his ragged blue surcoat with its six silver crosslets glinted and winked at them through the graying rain. On a sudden they saw him turn and wave his hand violently toward the men in the water, as though he waved a hound to ground. Instantly his own men flung themselves on their stomachs behind bush or slope or whatever offered. To the men in the water the King shouted, "Wait." At once the line halted. The archers stood still as stones, the river foaming about them waist and chest-high.

One of Umfraville's squires slid through the mud of the far bank and dropped noiselessly into the water. He swam strongly, gaining footground a few yards upstream from the ford, and came wading to the King. "The French, my lord," he said. "They came out of the woods behind the slope—a body of horsemen only. They rode straight across the clearing and back into the trees."

"Did they see us?" Henry asked.

"We know not, my lord. It did not seem so."

"God with us, Harry," Aumerle said. "What now?" That he called the King "Harry" well measured his agitation.

Henry bade them keep on. About them the river tugged and strained at its frail barriers. Hungerford saw much brushwood and straw working loose. "Talbot," he said, "I mislike the look of the ford."

"Already it rises near three inches," Talbot said. "I think the King will not get all across."

The King now checked the passage of the archers and said he was sending across the sick, the chaplains, and the boys. At his bidding Camoys left his post and went back to Suffolk. Camoys's scar showed a matted and empurpled weal, but he spoke cheerfully. "Come, Michael," he said, "we'll get you over."

Suffolk was sitting hunched in his cloak, his head in his hands. He looked like one who believed himself on the edge of death, but when Camoys hoisted him up he sought to stand. They went over the ford like two drunken men, swaying and staggering, yet keeping their feet. A dozen archers heaved pages on to their shoulders and followed. Ned would not go. He clung to Henry's side, a small and shivering shadow. The handful of sick were all borne across, but it was a slow matter. When it was done, the six hundred or so men who yet remained raced both the darkness and the cracking ford.

Of his knights only Talbot and Hungerford were left with the King. In the gathering dusk the foam marking the ford showed ghostly white and the men scrambled through it on one another's heels. One lost his footing and was swept out into the river. He spun downstream, threshing and giving gasping howls. Umfraville on the far bank snatched a lance from his squire's hand and thrust it outwards over the water. The man grabbed at it and held on, Umfraville and his squire landing him as they might a fish.

With his bow, swirling downstream, came much brushwood, straw, and twigs. All men knew the ford was disintegrating. Henry was left with some twenty archers about him, and these were of the King's bodyguard, the best men he had. He shouted at them to make their way over. Reeve, a Londoner, who had served with him at Shrewsbury and in the Marches, stood by him and to him he said, "Take the boy."

The archers threw themselves into the water. Talbot and Hungerford were already up to their waists, but they stayed to see what the King would do. "My liege," Talbot said, "look to yourself."

"Oh, my lord," Ned wailed, clinging to Reeve, "will you not hasten."

The King turned and looked up and down the bank. It lay to east and west, bleak and deserted, the yawning blackness of the marsh pricked out here and there with a gleam of water beneath the outline of the naked willows. No one remained. There was no man save himself.

The river roared in his ears, but above it was the roar of his own weariness. His limbs, stiffened by the nine hours he had stood in the slime, would scarce answer him. As the water clawed at him he would have gladly gone with it, borne in its cold embrace in sleep or death. "Dear Jesu," he prayed, "give me a little strength."

Talbot seized his hand. The Coronation ring slipped in his grasp, but the King's fingers fastened on it. Thus, slowly and yard by yard, they gained the bank. The nobles gathered about them, scarce able to speak in their relief. Umfraville laughed in strained fashion and said, "I never thought it could be done."

"Yet I thought it could," Erpyngham said. "I know the King. Have I not gone white in the service of Lancaster?"

"Ma foi," the Gascon said. "That would not take long."

XXV

After a space the archers grubbed for dry tinder, finding enough to set a few feeble fires kindling. In the thin glow of these some of the nobles stripped and strung their clothes on bushes in the hope they would dry. The Gascon, seeing them naked, exclaimed at them in feigned astonishment. "Are these Englishmen?" he said. "Always we most assuredly understood that the English have tails. Were they not cursed with them for the murder of the most sainted Thomas à Becket?"

The nobles grinned at him derisively. "Look well," Umfraville said. "It may be we grow horns likewise." They were content to treat it as a jest, but if he had so spoken the night before it would have been otherwise.

All things were good to them this night, men breaking into laughter at the feeblest jest. Presently the Welshmen drew together and began to sing. They had not sung since Blanche-Taque, and though the English mocked them good-humoredly, they listened in pleasure. "Well, my liege," Talbot said, "your Welsh have found voice again."

Ned stood by the King with a cup of water and a lump of sodden bread on a shield. "See what I've found you, my lord," he said. "It was in one of the saddlebags."

The King bade him have it, saying he himself had broken fast. He spoke heartily, but his hand closed about his Coronation ring in the gesture that told he was lying. Sir John Cornwall came to them from setting the pickets and asked if there was any food. Umfraville gave him a handful of walnuts and he tossed them into his mouth, cracking them with his teeth and spitting out the shells. Other of the knights shared soggy bread with their squires. They made more noise and gaiety over it than over a many-coursed banquet.

In the morning, all came to the march eagerly, knowing their steps no longer took them away from Calais but at last toward it.

"Not far from there we are now is it?" Gam said. "Never will I eat another walnut. The sainted David—he who is much reverenced in Wales—lived, it is said, a full two years on leeks and salt. Yet that is palatable food, look you. More would I reverence him had he fasted on walnuts and water."

"They serve good sturgeon in Calais, I'm told," Umfraville said. He broke into laughter. "We have got past both Boucicaut and the Dauphin," he said. "Did I not tell you none had Lancaster's luck?"

"Oh, peace," Hungerford said. "That sort of talk ill-fortunes a man."

All that day and the next morning the army pressed on through thinning drizzle. Hungerford could not remember them so cheerful. He rode with Aumerle and Umfraville leading the van. Once Umfraville bowed his head as though he hearkened, saying, "I thought I heard hoof beats."

Suddenly Hungerford heard him catch his breath as though he hissed. He looked up and saw ahead a group of seven horsemen riding calmly toward them from out of the scrub. The rain veiled the colors of their chivalry, but as they came, some trick of the light thinned it about them and the three silvered lilies of France smote like a blade in the watchers' eyes. Hungerford felt his heart lurch within him.

"Heralds," Umfraville whispered. "Afore God, they've found us."

There were three heralds, flanked by two trumpeters. The leader wore the tabard of the Court of France woven on chest and back with great fleur-de-lys and deeply fringed about his thighs. His legs beneath were mailed like a knight's. He had recognized Aumerle by his chivalry, for he gave him his title, calling him "your grace of York." "I bear my message to the King of England," he said. "My office you can see. I would be brought to him."

He spoke in English courteously and with a singular purity. None had looked to hear his tongue thus spoken in France, for English was held to be a barbarous language, the language of the conquered. It seemed Aumerle sought to answer him but could not. He set his horse's head about and led them down the lines.

"We should have sent to warn the King," Umfraville muttered. "I would not have him shamed before them all."

As the men saw the heralds, all stopped short. The archers crowded together in their wake, silent and peering. In all that ragged company the brilliant blue of the Frenchmen's tabards seemed as from another world.

The King had dismounted and was walking with Talbot and Sir Thomas Erpyngham. When he heard the horses he looked up. Hungerford saw him yet composed, his face unchanging, yet it seemed to him the sight of the Dauphin's heralds had struck chill upon him so that he mastered his countenance only hardly, knowing that if he showed aught they were lost indeed.

The heralds' spokesman looked upon him. He was a tall man, composed and grave of bearing, with a beard pointed and streaked with gray. For a space he hesitated as though disbelieving this tatterdemalion was the King he sought.

"Yonder the King," Aumerle said.

The herald bared his head and bowed in the saddle. About them the archers pressed closer, wordlessly, but trampling on each others' feet. Henry's calm was yet unchanged. "Who sends you, herald?" he said.

"The King of France and the prince Dauphin, so please your grace," the herald said. "My message is from them."

"Say on then," Henry said.

Aumerle exclaimed sharply, "Parlez en français. Le roi vous comprends."

"I am bidden to speak in your common tongue," the herald said. "My master, the Dauphin, would have his message understood by your soldiers of the lower sort."

"Speak in English, herald," Henry said. "I too want my soldiers to hear it."

"This, then, my lord," the herald said. "The Dauphin, prince of France, to his cousin, England. He bids you not to think your path leads you in safety to Calais. Much has he borne from you—the overtrampling of his realm, his father's city of Harfleur plucked from his hand, the mock of your challenge to his princely state. For all this he demands reckoning, and he demands it by the might of his arms. Herewith his gage of battle. He would have you know you have no third way but to fight or yield."

"I'll answer him when I meet with him," Henry said. "When will this be?"

"He assigns you neither time nor place, my lord," the herald said. "Only that you will be brought to battle before you reach Calais. Further he bids me say to those who march with you—doubtless you perceive where the folly of your King has brought you. His folly glares in the face of Europe. Knowing this, do you yet follow him?"

Reeve leaned upon his bow and spat on to the ground between his feet. Henry looked on him with delight. To the herald he said, "So brief a message from my cousin, the Dauphin? What is there more?"

"No more, my lord," the herald said. "Save only this. Hearing my master's message, do you seek terms? If so, I will convey it back. If not, the prince Dauphin desires to know by which road you go toward Calais, and bids you not to think you can escape him by turning aside."

"I seek no terms," Henry said. He looked about him at his peering archers and the nobles who breathed hoarsely at his elbow. "You see us as we are," he said. "There's not a man amongst us who does not lack for bread. The fields of France have so torn and mangled our chivalry that we are as paupers in arms and paupers, too, in numbers. None of this is hid from the Dauphin. Yet I do not think his terms will be fair enough to tempt me to yield. Tell him we press on to Calais and by the straightest road. If I can avoid him I will, but if not, I'll give him battle and at his jeopardy be it." He looked beyond the heralds at the yellowing grass and fading scrub. "Tell him," he said, "my archers still have it in them to sting. Ask him if he would have us dye his tawny fields with the red blood of his subjects?"

"I shall convey it, my lord," the herald said.

The King smiled and said, "I would know your name, herald."

"Jacques de Heilly, so please your grace."

The King said, "You speak our tongue excellent well."

"Four years was I prisoner in England seeking my ransom," the herald said. "I was taken in combat at Boulogne by your renowned knight—le Sire des Talons Chaud."

"Hot Heels?" Henry said. "Hotspur? The lord Percy?"

"Yes, sire," the herald said. "The lord Percy. He taught me much."

"He taught me much also, de Heilly," Henry said. They looked at each other with liking, speaking after the fashion of friends. "Tell me this," the King said, "did you know where to find us this day or was it that fortune failed us?"

"I know not whether my office permits me to speak of it," de Heilly said. "But we have sought you for a long time. We never thought to find you this side the Somme. The news that you had crossed was like a blow to the princes whom I serve."

"You've had much toil then," Henry said. "You've earned your herald's fee." He sent Ned among the sumpter horses. He came back bearing a purse, weighty and richly embossed. "By custom it should be a horse or apparel," Henry said. "I'll not shame you by giving you a horse—they are as sorry as their riders. As for my cloak, I think a beggar would not thank me for it. Take this, de Heilly. It is two hundred crowns. Say the English return your ransom to you again."

He tossed the purse and de Heilly caught it, smiling. "Indeed, I thank your grace," he said. "Farewell."

He bowed again and set his spurs to his horse, his fellow heralds and the wooden-faced trumpeters following. When he reached the fringe of trees, he turned and saluted the King with his herald's staff.

Aumerle swallowed and passed his tongue over his blue and scabbed lips. "We've had cruel fortune," he said. "We almost escaped them."

"Was it true, think you?" Suffolk said in a thin voice. "He assigned us no time or place for battle. May be the Dauphin seeks to trick us into turning aside and so gain time to come upon us."

Humphrey broke into loud laughter. "God's peace," he said. "Would you have us start hoping again? Not I. I've been fortune's fool long enough." To the King he said, "Did you speak true, Brother? Are we to try for Calais by the straightest road?"

"It is still the shortest," Henry said. "Whether the Dauphin be there or no. Should we not trust ourselves a little farther to God's mercy, my lord? For all the talk the Dauphin has not come upon us yet."

XXVI

The next day the road led them abreast of a large town. Crossbow-men rode from it, harrying the King's columns for close on two hours. Sir John Cornwall was eager to take a body of his archers and drive them back, but Henry would not have it. "Yonder town is Peronne," he said. "They have guns and they would draw us within range. Better to endure these gadflies."

Once clear of the town, the Frenchmen no longer followed. Henry bore with him now between thirty and forty wounded. The smell of blood lay about the marching columns as rancid as the odor of the unwashed bodies and ungroomed horses.

The road brought them past the village of Frévent and on to a watermill standing askew a thorn-covered bank. Below it, among slate-gray crags and sprawled willows frothed the Canche. It was half the breadth of the Somme, but it was bloated with the rains and most vicious. Some of the archers, when they saw it, drew in their breaths.

As with the Somme the King had to cross it. The archers formed two chains and passed their fellows through it, standing breast against the current, so that the men crossing bumped blunderingly from chest to chest. Twice the chain snapped and three archers and a squire went spinning downstream, turning over and over like tree trunks. The squire disappeared and the archers were all dead when they were brought out. Cornwall, whose men they were, had them laid side by side in the grass beneath the willows.

For half an hour after crossing the Canche Henry rested. Many of the wounded stripped off their dressings and wrung them out in the water. Others lay on their backs like so many bundles of sodden rags. Camoys, lying beside the King, spoke of the herald. "Strange he should have been prisoner to Hotspur," he said. "My mind has turned much on him of late."

"As has mine," Henry said. "He would have relished this."

"Aye, my lord," Camoys said. "It would have been meat and drink to him—the smell of danger and the harsh odds." He paused and fumbled for his words. "It is his widow I feel for," he said. "Poor lady, all things have gone ill against her—her husband slain in treason, her son prisoner in Scotland these past eleven years, her own blood that of Mortimer and therefore suspect."

The King said, "One of my father's knights called her the cornflower-eyed Mortimer."

"He spoke true," Camoys said. "Eyes as blue as heaven. No sweeter lady drew breath."

"I know not why you never spoke of this before, Camoys," Henry said. "If you loved her, why did you not ask for her?"

Camoys laughed shortly in embarrassment. "I expected to earn only your displeasure by it, my lord," he said. "She is in your wardship now as she was in your father's, and she is both Mortimer and Percy. The taint of so much hangs about those names. How could you be willing to see her wedded again to any man?"

"For the saints' sake, Camoys," Henry said, "you are my brother-in-arms, my loyal knight. Am I to trust you less because Elizabeth Percy has your heart?"

"Aye, I should have spoken," Camoys said. He raised himself on one elbow and drew his hand across his scarred cheek. "I know not why I trouble you thus at such a time, my lord," he said. "Yet it seems to me you are in a like case. I think you do not forget the Lady Katherine."

The King said. "She is ever under my eyelids—in the mud banks of the Lézarde, in the Somme marshes, in the rainy fields."

"It is hard that the full tide of battle flows between you," Camoys said. "I could wish—I could wish, my lord, you had more hope of gaining her."

Henry said, "I do not yet despair of her." He rose and gestured his nobles to do likewise. "We must march on," he said. "Camoys, when we come home to England, we'll gain the Lady Percy's hand for you."

Camoys smiled faintly, as if he doubted whether he would again come to England; yet the King spoke as he had ever done. With him Calais was always over the next river, beyond the next village, through the next swamp, and England no more than a pebble's throw from that. Hungerford knew not whether his cheerfulness was true or false; yet it seemed to him that it more than anything else had upborne them and brought them through the rivers, the bogs, and the hating land.

It was near twilight when Umfraville threw up his hand in the signal to halt. One of the squires came riding back down the lines. He was very young, his beard fluffy and sparse about his grimed cheeks, and in the half-light his face had a gray and ghostly tinge, as of the dead heads impaled on the spikes above London Bridge. "My liege," he said to the King, "does it please your grace to come forward? Lord Umfraville says it is of great moment."

Henry set spurs to his horse, Hungerford following. Umfraville, Aumerle, and Sir John Cornwall were all dismounted, Umfraville on one knee examining the ground. All about the grass had been churned to mud, with here and there the clear imprint of a horse's hoof or a steel-shod foot. Only a vast army could have so mangled the earth; an army far greater than the King's. Only the Dauphin's.

XXVII

The sight of the tracks across the Calais road was the death of hope. Henry rested that night and kept on the next day, but all men knew that beyond the leafless trees lurked another army— sleek-fed, with dry coats to their backs, their horses groomed and mail burnished. None voiced it, but ever was it a surprise when another hour passed and the road ahead was yet empty.

"Is Calais far, my lord?" Ned asked, when they were camped and he brought the King his day's bread.

"Not far," Henry said. "Only one more river away."

"We've come a long way round," Ned said. "But I did not find it so ill. It was good excitement. I'll have much to tell them in the Chepe when I get back."

Henry laughed and put an arm about his shoulder. "What do you think of my boy, Talbot?" he said. "Is he not true knight?"

"He is, in sooth, my lord," Talbot said. Ned blushed and mumbled, hanging his head in pleasure.

Sir John Cornwall came up, limping. After a space he flung himself down and nursed his foot, peering at his steel-shod shoe. "Worn through," he said. "Almost I go unshod."

"Make an offering to the shoemaker saints," Hungerford said. "It is their feast the day after tomorrow."

"Aye," Cornwall said. "Crispin and Crispinian. Theirs is too gentle a trade to serve us now." He took his last portion of bread and said, "How do we fare tomorrow?"

"We near Blangy," Henry said. "There we'll gain bread."

There was but little food to be had at Blangy, and the King dared not linger. Beyond the village a bridge spanned the Ternoise, of a single arch, so that the road seemed to take the river at a leap. As the columns approached figures came scurrying along the far bank, bearing axes. From the bridge itself came the sound of blows and splintering wood.

"Dear heaven," Humphrey exclaimed, "they're hewing it down."

Henry stood in the stirrups and shouted to Umfraville. "Go forward," he said. "Take your lances. Secure the bridge."

Both Umfraville and Cornwall plunged spurs to horse. After them went their knights riding as though the Fiend were at their heels. As each one approached the bridge he brought down his lance, sliding into the rest under his elbow.

By the time the main body came up the road was clear. Umfraville's knights were lolling against their horses, drawing their sleeves across their brows. "How many men did you lose, my lord?" Henry asked.

"Never a man," Umfraville said. "They showed but small fight. Yet there were soldiers amongst them."

The Ternoise was the last river. Ahead lay the Calais road, straight as a sword blade laid across the heart of the country, and Calais itself no more than fifty miles away. To be across was to feel as the Israelites when they dragged themselves over Jordan.

All afternoon the weary columns marched hard, as though the

men smelt Calais and strained toward her. When it neared dusk, Hungerford rode forward, at the King's bidding, to tell Umfraville to seek a place to halt. The road ran uphill for a space here. Umfraville had come upon the brow and checked his horse, gazing before him into the valley. As the leading columns came abreast of him they stopped likewise. Hungerford saw the archers sagging in weariness against their bows, their eyes fixed and staring.

He spurred that he might reach them and see what they looked upon. The Calais road ran down into the valley, and across it stood all the matchless chivalry of France. The thin sunlight gilded them, ripening to brilliance their silken heraldry and striking gloss from the flanks of their horses. It was a vast company that barred the King's passage—knights and foot soldiers, sutlers, crossbowmen and pikemen—and while the English yet watched, many more thronged out from among the trees. Between the trunks glinted the plumes—crimson, azure, or jet—bobbing from the helms the knights bore on head or crook of arm. Many laughed as they came, staring upward at the tattered scarecrows peering at them from the brow of the hill; and the archers, seeing their foes as a great cloud of locusts filling the valley, cast themselves down on the grass, heads and hands sagging. They dotted the ground scarce like men but like scrawny crows, ravening after a winter's leanness.

"That the Dauphin should come upon us now," Suffolk whispered. "When we've crossed the last river. When we had all but gained Calais. It could not be more cruel."

The King twisted in the saddle and shouted to the trumpeters. "Marshal the host," he said. "Sound for the battle array."

The trumpets shrilled, but the archers did not stir from the grass. "What use is it?" Cornwall said. His voice was thin and sullen. All heart had gone from them. It seemed to Hungerford that if the French chose to walk in amongst them at that moment, slitting the throat of every man they came to, not more than ten or twelve would raise a hand against them.

Henry seized his standard from the hand of John Bromley and

set spurs to his horse. "Get up," he shouted at the archers. "Get to your feet. Well have you done—thrice well. Have the rivers checked you or the swamps, or wounds or sickness or hunger? All this have we withstood. Can we not look proudly now on these?"

One by one, the archers took faint spark from him, crawling to their feet. They formed ragged lines about the standard, moving as in sleep, until the whole host stood in array.

Yet in the face of the Dauphin's numbers even the flame of Henry's courage flickered and dimmed. When the trumpets sounded again it was for parley, and the English heralds rode from their own lines toward the French.

XXVIII

Already, when the heralds came through the lines, the French sutlers had pitched many tents for their lords. The tents were rounded, fashioned in heavy silk, and topped gaily with pennons. After the manner of a joust, they bore the shields of their masters over the tent flaps.

Hugh Stafford, the Guienne herald, bore Henry's message. He was brought to the tent of Charles D'Albret, High Constable of France. With D'Albret sat the three dukes, Orléans, Bourbon and Berri; and Rambures, the Lord Admiral and Master of the Cross-bowmen. These were but a fraction of the chivalry that rode with him, and the Dauphin's muster-rolls were heavy with the greatest names in France.

D'Albret gave Stafford a courteous greeting. He was not yet forty, a raven-haired man, moustached and princely of bearing. Men named him chivalrous, but it was said his hands were light on the reins, and the richly garbed men about him seemed ill disposed to count his authority more than theirs. Bourbon was tall, saturnine of face and of humor. Rambures laughed where he thought his laughter would please, through closed lips, so that the sound was that of stifled tittering.

"How speaks your King, herald?" D'Albret said.

"He sues for terms, my lord," Stafford said. "His own I bear."

The nobles, excepting D'Albret, glanced at each other and laughed. Their laughter was echoed from outside, and as a servant drew aside the flap, Louis, Dauphin of France, stepped into the tent. He was a young man, his straw-colored hair round-cropped as by fashion, bearing much of the beauty of the House of de Valois, but in him all had run to thickness and he was thick of lips, of nose, of thigh, and of hands. About the blue of his immense sleeves swam the silver embroidered dolphins of his crest. So dazzlingly was he garbed that he could not move without striking color across the gloom of the tent. "What says my cousin of England?" he said. "Will he restore Harfleur?"

"He will, my lord," Stafford said. "Much English blood was spilled there, but if his soldiers are given passage into Calais, he will render it to you again. Further he will pay you whatsoever fine you demand, so far as his exchequer is able to bear it. In earnest of his good faith he will surrender to you hostages of whom he himself will be one. This he offers, not because he holds his cause the less just, but because the weal of his soldiers has come to mean much to him, and if he can he would purchase their lives and liberty."

"In faith," the Dauphin said, "this is much more humble." He beckoned and a servant brought him a goblet of wine on a tray. The Dauphin took it and sipped it. His fingers about the stem were so swollen with his rings that they looked bloated. Yet he bore his magnificence with an air at once arrogant and princely.

"Tell my cousin this," he said. "I reckon but little to his offers. Harfleur I can retake again when I will. As touching payment for the damage done—the exchequer of England is not great. Its gold will not suffice to render fair return for his folly. More do we ask from him."

"Your King cannot hope that we hearken to his terms, herald?" Bourbon asked.

"It is not for me to say, my lord," Stafford said. "But this he adds. If his terms are rejected, he asks two things of you. Firstly, that if he is to be brought to battle, it will be tomorrow."

"The times of battle are in our hands," D'Albret said. "What further?"

"He bids me say that if he fights his numbers are too small to permit the taking of prisoners. He will fight without quarter, and he asks you will do likewise."

Rambures broke at once into his hushed tittering. "Oh, we shall be kinder than that, herald," he said. "We shall, in sooth, be kind."

"Yes, we'll deal gently," the Dauphin said. He and Orléans met each other's eyes, and both laughed. "If any of the knights of England yield we shall take their gloves and open our purses to their ransoms. Let him do as he will. I do not think in this battle the English will find themselves greatly burdened with prisoners."

"What answer do I return then, my lords?" Stafford asked. "That all is rejected?"

"It is not for the King of England to make his own terms now, herald," D'Albret said. "Let him hear ours and bring us his answer."

He began to tabulate the French demands. The Dauphin walked to the flap of the tent and both Rambures and Bourbon followed him. When D'Albret and Stafford came out, they stood together drinking wine, the servants standing with flagons eager to replenish their goblets.

"You know our terms, herald?" Bourbon asked.

"I do, my lord."

"Your King is in a hard case," D'Albret said. "He is a young man, and I am sorry for it. What think you, herald? Would he take a gift at my hands?"

Stafford looked at him sharply, and the Dauphin broke into loud laughter. D'Albret flushed and said, "It will be no gift of discourtesy. I had in mind a cask of wine."

"He would give you thanks for it, my lord," Stafford said. "But

I do not think he will take it. He is as his soldiers are. He takes nothing that would favor him beyond them."

He bowed and asked leave to depart. D'Albret granted it. "Yonder my servants," he said. "They will give you your herald's fee."

The Dauphin watched Stafford go, smiling. "What is it that you give him, my lord High Constable?" he said. "Cousin England was generous to de Heilly even in his penury."

"One of the horses," D'Albret said curtly. "Full bridled."

"It will be the most handsome thing in the English camp," Bourbon said. "If he mounts, doubtless it will toss him and bolt back to us. The smell of those ungroomed jades will affront its nostrils."

The Dauphin yawned and said, "Almost would I call the herald back and send my cousin England a gift. The cushions he refused in London he might well thank me for now."

"Peace, my Prince," D'Albret said. "I would not mock this King too greatly. Already there has been a strength of anger in his march. None thought he would get thus far."

"Pah," the Dauphin said. "I could have checked him at the bridges had I sought to. I desired him to wind the noose about his own neck. Did I not tell him to stay at home and amuse himself with the tennis balls?" He set the goblet down violently on a tray one of the servants proffered and moved away. "He challenged me to single combat," he said. "He sought to turn the mock back on me. I wonder he found a man to follow him in the madness of this march, the English knowing what they had for a King—a usurper's son, a tavern crawler."

"He must most greatly wish himself back in his London taverns now," Orléans said.

"True," Rambures said eagerly. "Will he take our terms, think you?"

"My faith, I hope not," Bourbon said. He rubbed his hand on the pommel of his dagger. "The palm of my sword hand itches," he said. "It will bring me a good tally in this encounter, I trust."

"By the saints, D'Albret," the Dauphin said. "If he takes our terms, never look to me for favor again. The blame is to you if we are cheated from our sport."

"He will not take them," D'Albret said. "And I would have you play no part in this battle, my prince. You are the heir to France. You ought not to venture your person here against them."

"Against yon crawling scarecrows?" the Dauphin said. "Why, they are all but dead even now."

"They are desperate men," D'Albret said sharply. "And a desperate man fights as the fiend. Before we can ride them down, we shall be under the sting of their arrows. Their shafts have found the flower of French blood before this day."

The Dauphin rubbed his chin without speaking. Bourbon joined in urging him, but he cast a glance of much irony at Orléans. "Leave this to our swords," he said. "It is a very small task. There is little glory in it. You scorned to meet the tavern crawler blade to blade. Would you fall now to a meaner weapon in the hands of one of his bowmen?"

"Doubtless you speak true," the Dauphin said. "My father urged me not to ride against them. It may be I shall return to Rouen and await you there."

"Do that, my prince," Rambures said. "Join your most noble father. There at Rouen we will deliver your prisoners into your hands."

Orléans laughed and said, "King Harry bids us beware. He will take no prisoners."

"He seeks to make his common soldiers fight more cheerfully," Bourbon said. "There is no yielding for them. He would have them think the knights may not yield either."

"They'll yield," the Dauphin said. He shouted for his attendants and bade them unbuckle his leg armor. "Loose me from these greaves," he said. "I am returning to Rouen."

"We shall not be far behind, lord prince," Orléans said. "After what fashion shall we bring you the King of England?"

"As we planned," the Dauphin said. "In a painted cart with a halter about his neck. It will befit my challenger to come to me thus."

Rambures said, "It may be he will be slain."

"No, by the saints," the Dauphin said violently. "The man who strikes him down is banished France."

He went to prepare himself for his journey. Bourbon strolled back into the tent and picked up dice from the table. The others stood at his shoulder as he rolled them idly, marking how he cast. "My lord D'Albret," he said at last, "that was most neatly done. You have rid us of the Dauphin in this sport."

"Tush," Orléans said yawning. "He is a noble prince."

"Oh, for sure," Bourbon said. "Most noble and most valiant, as I doubt not. But there are too few of the enemy to suffice among us as it is."

Rambures drew up a rug-draped stool and sat facing Bourbon. "Tell me," he said. "What's their worth? What is their chivalry?"

"Not great," Bourbon said. "There are the King; the youngest of his brothers, he of Gloucester; and his cousin, the Duke of Aumerle and York. These three are princes of the blood, they are all Plantagenets. For the rest there are the Earl of Suffolk and the Earl of Salisbury, and some half-dozen barons. Then only knights."

"It is a feeble muster in all truth," Orléans said. He plucked the dice from out of Bourbon's palm and rattled them. "My lords," he said, "we'll go hazard on this scant chivalry. We here can set our prisoners in a common pool, the winner to claim as his own he who ranks highest."

"Well said," Rambures exclaimed. "The Dog throw claims either Duke. The Venus throw takes the King himself."

They began to play, the Duke of Berri and Boucicaut joining them. D'Albret watched them with a darkened face. "My lords," he said, "this is not seemly. If they refuse terms, we should prepare ourselves for the attack. There is still time before the dark to fall upon them and make an end."

"Not today, D'Albret," Berri said. "God's peace, not today. It begins to rain again outside. Let us eat in comfort and pass a night in good fellowship."

"Let them fast another night, my lord High Constable," Bourbon said. "It will not make our task the harder."

XXIX

One of Stafford's trumpeters led the horse D'Albret had given him back to the English lines. It was a fine roan, bridled in painted leather and glossy as burnished mail. The King and his nobles remarked on it enviously.

None seemed to care to hear D'Albret's message, but presently the King asked Stafford what had passed.

"They'll have none of it, my lord," Stafford said. "They state their own terms. Firstly, that you in respect of your great-grandsire renounce the Plantagenet claim to the throne of France."

"I laid no claim to it," Henry said. "That they know. What else?"

Stafford said, "That you likewise renounce the hand of the Lady Katherine."

The King looked at him through narrowed lids. Stafford went on, "Those two conditions fulfilled, they demand the person of the King and of every man who marches with him, all horses, all baggage, all weapons, the King's standards and his jewels. All are to be yielded into their hands as by right of conquest, to be dealt with as it pleases the King of France and his most dear son, the prince Dauphin."

"And how does it please them to use my soldiers?" Henry said. "With any clemency?"

"Oh, my lord," Stafford said. "With none. The Dauphin is as a wolf. He speaks of taking a third part of the archers and striking off their right hands. If we fight he threatens to strike off the hand of any archer taken alive and sell the fingers in the streets of Rouen for a blanc apiece."

The King exclaimed and said, "D'Albret is a man of honor. Would he exact this?"

"His hands are slack on the reins," Stafford said. "He would try to bridle the Dauphin, but I know not if he would succeed."

"Well, my lords," Henry said at last, "I think these terms were not meant for us to take." He doused the rain from his eyes and rose with fingers so thin that the Coronation ring slipped down to the knuckle. Hungerford saw the skin about it peeling grayly away. The nobles shifted in the mud and did not speak.

Presently Humphrey of Gloucester asked of the French strength.

"My lord," Stafford said, "they are not less than thirty-four thousand."

Humphrey twisted his mouth and said, "Then are they over five times greater than ourselves."

Suffolk said in a thin whisper, "Nor are they half-starved and spent by marching."

Much noise and laughter came from the French lines where the sutlers' wagons stood. Nobles moved there, most richly garbed, and the King pointed to them. "What are they about?" he said. "Yonder by the carts?"

"They make merry, my lord," Stafford said. "It is but their sport."

The King said, "Give me the truth."

"They paint a peasant's cart, my lord," Stafford said. "With their own hands."

Humphrey said, "God's peace, why?"

"That they may drag the King through the streets of Rouen in it," Stafford said. "This they told me. Through Rouen first and then Paris, with a halter about his neck. Thus must he make his submission on his knees to the Dauphin and King Charles."

The nobles stirred and murmured wordlessly. "For the saints' sake, my lord," Umfraville said, "let us fight. We be better dead."

"They mean to make us fight, my lords," Henry said. "We'll give them what they desire of us. We'll give battle."

"What of the prisoners?" Aumerle said. He stared over his shoulder to where the little group of French prisoners stood encircled by their guards. There were eight of them now, for as well as the three men of Arques and the Gascon three others had been taken outside Peronne and one at the bridge at Blangy. They stood in the rain, sodden and dejected. As they saw the heads of the nobles turn toward them, alarm swept into their faces. Only the Gascon stared boldly back, his lips drawn back against his teeth.

"Take them, my lord," Sir John Cornwall said. "Ask gentler terms of the Dauphin. If he will not listen strike off their right hands in lieu of it."

"I think it would not move the Dauphin," Henry said.

The Gascon raised his brows, still smiling. He did not understand the words but he comprehended the situation. "What now?" he said. "The King of England is trapped. Doubtless he will do with us as he did with his looter at Nesle."

One of the men of Arques broke into speech in his own tongue. He begged the King's charity and swore in a trembling voice not to turn his hand against his captors. When he had done, the Gascon spoke again. "It is not so with me," he said. "If the King turns his back on me in the battle, I would most joyfully use my dagger between his shoulders."

Henry looked at him with a masklike face. "Davy," he shouted, and Gam came hurrying through the mud to his side. "Davy, I am sending the prisoners across to their own lines. Go with the herald and conduct them thither."

"As it pleases your grace," Gam said. "They are a poor scurvy, lickspittle lot, and if they were strung up, look you, I think even their own mothers would not greatly mourn them, but your grace acts in charity." To the prisoners he made a lordly gesture. "Suivez moi, seigneurs," he said. "Je vous conduis à votre encampment. En avant and quickly now, I do beg and beseech you."

His French mystified the prisoners, but they understood his gestures. The Gascon went last as in astonishment. As he reached the thorn bushes marking the brow of the hill, he turned and bowed

to the King. "Adieu, sire," he said. "Almost you brought me prisoner into Calais."

"Farewell, Gascon," Henry said. "If the day is mine, render
yourself to me again."

"Ah, my lord," the Gascon said. "You have done wonders—I
acknowledge it. You cannot do miracles."

Stafford mounted and took his herald's staff from the hand of
his page. "Return my thanks to D'Albret," Henry said. "Tell him
his terms are too harsh for us. Say we will give him battle." As
Stafford set spurs to his horse he shouted after him, "Tell him I
hold to my right of claim to the Lady Katherine's hand. Say I do
not give her up."

xxx

Gam and Stafford were soon returned. As they rode back into the
camp there was much movement from the French lines, gray-
veiled by the rain and the increeping dusk. "They are breaking
ranks," Aumerle said. "It is not to be today."

"Oh, Cousin," Henry said, "I've been praying for that. My soldiers will get a night's rest. They are nigh spent."

The French were not content to camp where they were but
moved back into the woods. The King set his army to follow in
fear that he might be encircled by them. The archers staggered
through the rain, gray-faced with weariness, the darkness coming
swift upon them. In it they went too far, the forward columns
stumbling almost upon the French. The King had to retreat as
best he might, and in the rain and the clinging dark the army
groped its way back, no man knew whither.

The men were too wearied to go far. When the King halted, they
cast themselves down, hard by the French. The rain hissed on
French torches that licked a passage through the night from tent
to tent, pricking out in a red glow the devices of a shield hung
athwart the flaps or a scurrying servant in his master's livery. In the
silence of despair that lay upon the English all sounds struck

loudly—the laughter of the French nobles as they ate or diced; the shouts of their squires; the clink of armor, joint by joint under the testers' hammers, like the chiming of a hollow bell. Even the rain sang against the dead leaves with a witch's breathless laughter, on and on in endless fashion. Almost it was as if a living army camped alongside a dead one and that on the morrow the French would look out upon dead men and dead horses and so be cheated of their sport.

The track the English had followed had brought them near to the village of Maisoncelles, with another village, Tramecourt, beyond the woods on the left. Nearby stood a farmhouse, of one room only and poorly fashioned in mud and plaster after the manner of the London hovels. None remained in it. The King left his nobles there and went out to set his watchers, Hungerford with him. He went from post to post, enjoining the forward pickets to silence because of their nearness to the French. He spoke to them cheerfully as if the night were no different from the other nights they had lodged in the rain since Harfleur, and the knights in their thin cloaks and the ragged archers turned their heads to watch him pass as though eager for the gleam of his rondel belt in the dark. Most lay in silence, some sleeping, but more doubtless contemplating how many hours of life were left to them.

Presently voices came to them as they walked, and the King went toward them. "Aye, let him gie battle," a northern voice said. "He'll see the finish of it, likely. It's more than we will."

Reeve lay crouched in the rain behind the hawthorn bushes; with him was Parry, Glendower's Welshman, and the Northumbrian of Wark, Fowler, who had fought with Parry near Boves. They sat together amicably now as though they were bond brothers. When they saw the King standing by them, they looked startled, but into Fowler's face crept a thin defiance as though he reckoned himself beyond retribution. Henry asked him what troubled him and Reeve answered for him.

"He says your grace's life will be safe tomorrow," he said. "He says you and the nobles will pay your ransoms while our throats are cut."

"I told you no man would pay ransom for me," Henry said.

"Aye, you told us," Fowler said. "Your grace thought you spake true, likely, but it is one thing to say it when nae man threatens and another to say it wi' the French lances at your throat."

"We fight without quarter tomorrow," Henry said. "We take no prisoners nor do we yield any of ourselves."

Fowler laughed and drew his hand across his dirt encrusted face. "Yield?" he said. "That's not for us in any wise. Who of the common soldiers was ever taken alive in a battle? Quarter goes only to them that tender ransom."

"None will be tendered for me," Henry said. "God's peace, how many more times do I say it? Have I lied to you before?"

They did not answer him, and he drew his cloak about him and sat down with them among the bracken and the sodden leaves. "We've come a long road," he said. "The King does not think so lightly of your service to him that he would part from you at the end of it and yield himself whole if the manner of your yielding were harsher. He is too much beholden to you. He counts himself too closely bound to you." To Reeve he said, "Do you not believe this?"

"Aye, my lord," Reeve said. "I know the King's belly is as empty as the rest of ours. I think he'll not yield."

Parry, the Welshman, spoke up timidly. "Their numbers are very vast," he said. "How much greater than we ourselves does your grace reckon them?"

"They have a good strength," Henry said. "It is for you to strike down four men before you can fight equal-matched with the fifth."

"Then it's a fine, canny hope we hae," Fowler said. "We be dead men already."

"Why so?" Henry said sharply. "Our fathers were overmatched at Crécy and again at Poitiers."

"Not as greatly as we be," Fowler said. "Nor were they as us, half-starved, clarted wi' the mud and the rivers, our strength spent to the strength of a bairn. Reckoning that does the King still say we'll win the day?"

"I know not if I say we will win," Henry said. "Yet I say that we can. If God would bring us to Calais, D'Albret cannot stop us."

"Well, we'll claw some of them down in their blood," Reeve said. He uncorked his water bottle and drank, then handed the bottle to the King. "It's the last of the wine," he said. "Will your grace not take what's left?"

Henry thanked him and drank likewise, wiping his mouth with the back of his hand. Watching him, Hungerford was put in mind of the nights he had seen him drinking easefully in the taverns with the journeymen and the Chepe apprentices. Reeve took a lump of soggy bread from his pouch and offered the King half. When Henry refused, he urged him, and the King took it. "How will you break your fast tomorrow?" he said.

"There's enow left for that," Reeve said. "And I look no further. How does your grace reckon the hour?"

"What say you it is, Hungerford?" Henry said. "One of the clock? Two?"

"No more than one," Hungerford said, "I thought I heard a clock chime."

"I'm to my watch then," Reeve said. "God with your grace."

"God with you, friend," Henry said. "Shoot straightly tomorrow."

"None straighter," Reeve said. He rose and left them, Parry following. Fowler slept at the King's feet, his arms outflung across his bow, the rain coursing down his neck and bare feet.

Henry made as though to eat, then thrust the bread from him. When he tried to set the cork back into the water bottle, his hands would not answer him. Hungerford thought him spent near to swooning. "My lord," he said, "will you not come and take rest?"

"Aye, presently," Henry said. He put one knee to the ground and stayed himself on it. "One of the clock," he said. "Tomorrow at this time we will have made an end and all will be known. How will they speak of it—the Battle of Maisoncelles? Will they say that here Lancaster went to his atonement?"

The word struck chill against Hungerford's heart. "My lord," he said, "think not of Richard this night."

The King gave him a bitter smile and said, "He is ever under my eyes as he was the last time I saw him—dragged through the streets of London while the mob howled upon him. Would it not be a most just vengeance—that I should pass through the streets of Rouen with a halter about my neck to a like prison?" He looked down at Fowler sleeping where he knelt and said, "I have not prayed for victory since I came to France. I know not whether victory for my arms lies in the will of God, but for this have I greatly prayed—that my soldiers be brought in safety to Calais."

Hungerford answered him, "No man else could have thus nearly accomplished it."

The King answered as if he had not heard him. "It cannot be that God will lay the sins of Lancaster to their charge," he said. "It cannot. Already the odds are fearful against them. He will not set Richard's bloodguilt in the scales against them likewise?"

Hungerford strove to give him reply. The King said in a whisper, "If it must be that I atone for Richard's death, let it not be tomorrow—not with the blood of my soldiers."

Seeing him thus in weakness, Hungerford went from him. The King remained yet on his knees. The laughter of his enemies came loudly to him in the dark, and he felt a faintness, the chill of the sweat mingling with the rain against his face. He signed himself and spoke a prayer, "Ne Derelinquas Me Domine. Forsake me not utterly, oh Lord."

"My lord," Hungerford said, "your cousin comes—the Duke."

He went back to the King. Henry put a hand on his wrist and steadied himself as he rose. His weakness was masked again and he was calm. "It comes upon me thus sometimes," he said. "It did at my anointing, but Chichele was there to stiffen me. Give it no thought."

Aumerle came stiffly toward them through the mud and greeted them. "I was searching for you, my lord," he said. "Will you not to your bed? All's as well as we can make it."

"Is it quiet, Cousin?" Henry said. "I bound the watches to silence."

"Never a sound," Aumerle said. "Save from the enemy. They're loud enough." He fell in beside the King and laughed humorlessly. "The night passes well for them," he said. "Cousin, do you remember when I bore you off to the Lion Tower to see the King's beasts? Did I not tell you then it were always policy to choose an enemy smaller than yourself?"

The King laughed and said, "You did, in truth, Cousin."

"Yet I wonder on it," Aumerle said. "No man waded deeper in treason than I. I betrayed all men—Richard, your father, your father's enemies, you yourself, Cousin, as you know, but you had an affection for me and you winked at it. My ship star was the winning side. I should think it most strange if now I fought on the losing one. No, Cousin Harry, it'll not be." He spoke jestingly, the skin of his face puffed to a pasty grayness and his eyes sunken. It seemed he had suddenly come to grandeur. Henry looked at him with affection.

"Cousin," he said, "I trust no man more than I trust you. It's your Plantagenet blood that gives you this instinct. It tells you aright."

Thus joking they came to the farmhouse. The nobles lay together among the chicken droppings on the floor, befouled, bearded, and sodden. They lay in sleep as if they had fallen where they stood. One of the squires had striven to light a fire, but the wood was too wet for kindling and he lay on his face across it, his hands blackened in ash. There was garlic hung above the lintel of the door to banish witches, and the smell of it hung vilely upon air already tainted with sweat and unwashed bodies. Aumerle cast himself down, coming straightway to sleep, though he twitched where he lay. The King lay beside his brother. Humphrey stirred and flung an arm across him, so that the two brown heads of

Lancaster were close and it was hard to tell one from the other.

Hungerford slept but little. Presently it grew grayly light, and he heard the first crowing of the cocks. French cocks they were, and they shrilled of victory, tossing their high and triumphant calls back and forth, one to another, across the Maisoncelles slopes and the woods of Tramecourt. The nobles yet lay huddled about him. Looking at that tangle of heads and limbs, it was as if they were dead already, and it seemed a harsh thing that they would soon be roused to the day with all their dying yet to do.

XXXI

Before six the nobles began to arm, hiding their torn and filthy shirts first under fine shirts of link mail and then donning their plate armor and jupons. The squires had burnished the mail until it shone, and the commanders washed as best they might and hacked at their matted growths of beard. The razors were blunted and the water cold. Sir John Cornwall took the razor from the hand of his squire, groaning. "I know not why I do not leave this to the French," he said. "It's their work."

Shaven they had the look of strangers. The knights stared hard at one another's pinched and puffed faces as though searching for features they knew. Presently the King came to them. He gleamed in his mail most royally where previously he had gone as ragged as the most tattered archer, the arms on his jupon those of his great-grandfather, King Edward, the golden lilies of France charged on a blue ground, quartered with the golden leopards of England on a crimson. About his neck he wore the Lancaster collar of SS, fine-wrought in silver, and his rondel belt held his great sword. Only the spurs of knighthood were cast off and these he would not wear in case his archers thought him preparing for flight.

He gave the knights his battle order, setting each man in his place. "The command of the left wing is yours, Camoys," he said. "And you, good cousin Aumerle, I would have to lead the right.

The archers I am setting in wedges between. This was the forma-tion the Black Prince used at Poitiers and I know none better."

While he spoke, the armorers knelt behind him tightening the rivets of his cuisses. When he had done, Umfraville spoke up. "I am about the King's height," he said. "Will the King do me great honor this day and grant that I bear his coat-of-arms? Then if it pleases him he can bear mine."

"Why, Gilbert," Henry said, "here I am set. Would you have me start shedding my finery again so soon?"

"My lord," Talbot said, "it would have been a black day for Lancaster if your father at Shrewsbury had not masked his king-ship."

Aumerle too urged him. "We need your brain to direct the battle, Cousin," he said. "Did not our great-grandsire at Crécy watch from the windmill on the hill?"

"There's no windmill here," Henry said. "Cousin, we can spare no man from this battle, save the sick, the boys, and the priests. Them I'll send to the rear with the baggage." He began to speak of the Dauphin's terms, no longer with any lightness. "You know what has been promised to my archers," he said. "You, my lords, they'll take alive if they can, but the archers cannot yield. I doubt not there's no man among us so base as to ransom himself, know-ing this. The knight who yields, when he surrenders his right glove has set the severed hand of an archer inside it."

He dismissed them and went to the door of the farmstead. The armorers followed him, and Henry asked them if they knew what hour it was.

"Prime, my lord," one said. He took the King's right arm and moved it back and forth. "Does your grace move easefully?" he said. "I have not secured the pauldrons too tight?"

Humphrey came to them, yawning and chafing his arms as if he shivered. "Is it prime, Brother?" he said.

The King answered, "They'll be now setting open the gates of London."

"Aye," Humphrey said. "Often I've damned the first cart on the cobbles when it dragged me from sleep, but I would to God it were waking me now." He looked to where Nicholas Colnet and Thomas Morstrede, the surgeon, were tearing stained cloths into strips and said, "The rumble of the London carts were sweeter music than that."

The rain of the night had stopped. With the light the English found themselves lodged on the spurs of a gentle hill, with the enemy very close—not more than two bow shots away. On either hand were thick-tangled woods, and about the farmstead where they had slept were the wheatfields of Maisoncelles. There the army was shriven, the Host offered on the King's shield, if so be that God would look with mercy upon the arms of England. In the young damp wheat the King and his knights knelt in full mail, the banners unfurled and stirring above their heads; and the chaplains moved, thrusting the Holy Bread into the gnarled hands of the archers.

For the setting of his battle in array the King mounted. Before the English were fully marshaled the trumpets sounded and de Heilly and his attendant heralds rode across the lines. He came urging the King to yield. Henry greeted him with anger, for the fruitless journeying and the waiting in idleness tormented his soldiers.

De Heilly was grave, as though the King's plight moved him. "Hear me, sire," he said, when he had given D'Albret's message, "for I speak no more as herald. Our strength is full thirty-eight thousand, and the Duke of Brabant rides to us with a further two thousand men. What can there be for you and yon poor starved band save slaughter? Choose life, my lord. Chivalry will blame you not if you yield."

"The Dauphin's terms do not make life so pleasant for my soldiers or for me that we should greatly care to live," Henry said. "Bid them not to send you here again, de Heilly. God's peace, they have my answer. Tell D'Albret if he has some charity for us

in his bones, he'll ride upon us now and so make an end. Tell him
not to seek to bring me haltered into Rouen while I live."

"I shall tell the Lord High Constable," de Heilly said. "Farewell
to your grace. I would I might come to you again."

The King summoned the chaplains to him and delivered to
their care the sick and the boys. The horses, too, he purposed to
send with them out of the battle. His knights watched him grimly,
knowing that once that happened no man could fly.

The King dismounted and stood at the gray's head, fondling
him. He was not yet helmed and Ned clung to his side, bearing
his casque. To Suffolk Henry said, "Should you not go, Michael?
The day will be hard."

"Good my lord, no," Suffolk said. "I would rather stay here."

"Let me stay also, my lord," Ned said. "I can wield a sword. I
want to fight by you."

"You lack years, Ned," Henry said.

The boy looked at him in grief and said, "I dare swear I'm
fifteen. Your grace was no more than fifteen at Shrewsbury. Am I
to strike no blow for you?"

Henry said, "Lend me your prayers. They'll avail me much."

He would listen to no more. Ned tightened the rivets of his
helm, his hands trembling. The casque was embossed, and about
it in place of a crest rested a princely crown worked with gold
fleurons. In its center hung the great spinel ruby which Pedro the
Cruel of Aragon had given to the Black Prince after the Battle of
Najera; the ruby, in the language of stones, standing for valor. It
blazed above the King's brow like a huge drop of blood.

Ned took the gray's bridle and led him away. He did not turn
his head or look back at the King. The little procession wound its
way up the hill—the pages, all their finery wilted, their gay stock-
ings faded and begrimed; the handful of sick men; the priests; the
long line of the horses.

"I almost forget what day it is," Suffolk said. "It is Tuesday,
is it not?"

"Aye, Tuesday," Hungerford said. "England will be holidaying for St. Crispin. They'll be hauling the wooden pattens to the top of St. Bardolph's Tower. The shoemakers will be walking to the Guildhall in their livery."

"A holiday," Sir John Cornwall said bitterly. "God pity us."

The French were forming now into their battle lines. They moved leisurely, setting their guns and arblasts on either flank and their archers behind. Their main battle they set in three great lines as against the King's single one, the knights in each packed forty deep where the English mustered no more than four. The first line was mounted, but the other two formed on foot. Behind them the servants were tethering splendid horses, full-bridled and accoutred. The King asked Stafford their purpose, saying, "Why do they keep them back?"

"They are for the pursuit," Stafford said. "For when—for when we run."

"Oh, my lord," Hungerford said. "Many men in England this day must long to be with you. I would to God you had but ten thousand of them."

"God's peace, Hungerford," Henry said. "I want no man more." He went to the head of the archers and spoke to them gaily as if he took joy in the day's perils. "We few will suffice for this task," he said. "If we are to die, we are enough for England to mourn, and if we live and come to victory, we need of no man more to spread our honor thinner in our ranks. Yonder the enemy. Let not their numbers draw your courage from you. I would not willingly have a man more from England to share this day with us or trespass on our brotherhood. Archers—the yew fence which has before isled England here in France—stand as your fathers stood at Crécy and Poitiers. Remember England, your homes, your wives, your little ones, whose best hopes rest in you."

The men stirred like corn in the wind and hissed through their teeth. The King said, "Since Poitiers this has been the desire of France that a King of England should fall to them to avenge what befell their own King that day. They think the King of England already achieved, but it is not so. I have named you the yew fence of England—I name you more, the King's wall, his rampart, his deep and defensive moat, his countrymen and his brothers. I doubt not but that, God willing, we few can full match all the pride of France. All England prays for us. Let us to our work and God with you."

They answered him with much cheering, the French mocking it. The day wore on. The King's knights shifted from foot to foot in their heavy armor. The patient archers sat silent behind their implanted stakes, smoothing the gray goose feathers of their arrows.

"Oh, God," Suffolk said at last. "I would they would come." He yawned deeply, and then again, cracking yawns, as when a man feels the first clawings of seasickness. Humphrey of Gloucester drew off his gauntlets. The sweat coursed between his fingers and he wiped them against his jupon.

"In faith," Talbot said, "I have seen a cat deal kindlier with a mouse."

"Why should they come?" Sir John Cornwall said. "They have only to sit there long enough for hunger to do their work."

One of the archers rose and waved his fist toward the French lines. "The bastards," he said, "why do they not come?"

"Peace, soldier," Umfraville said, "we're not long for idleness."

The King looked toward the steely sea of the French below him in the valley and back at the five great banners, weighted with color, above his head. "Talbot," he said, "I am going to order an assault."

"My lord," Talbot said, "here what little advantage lies in the ground is ours."

"I must bring them to battle," Henry said. "They're proud men. I think they'll not sit and let such poor scarecrows as we be strike the offensive. Bid the archers take up their stakes and move to the attack, but let them come slowly. When I halt them they must stand straightway and hold their ground."

"Aye, my lord," Umfraville said. "Let us begin. They'll drive us crazed else."

Sir Thomas Erpyngham spoke to the archers. One by one they tightened their bowstrings, then laid hands on their stakes and drew them from the earth. Across the valley the mass of the French had fallen hushed and curious, only the rooks loud in their calls and all else still as an arid pool. The knights raised their swords to their lips. With his mailed hand the King signed himself, helm, breast, and pauldrons. As his standard-bearers moved about him, he said, "Forward, banners," and then, in prayer, in a low voice, "and God and St. George, thy mercy."

The archers about him heard his whisper of "St. George" and took it up with a loud shout. Some of them knelt and lifted a handful of earth to kiss in the old earth housel of the Saxons, which consecrated the ground they trod for England so that they would not fly. Slowly the banners moved toward the French, flowing downhill through the wheat and the plowed earth. The slender wave of the King's line looked that it would break uselessly against them as against a sea wall. But their chivalry was the proudest in Europe, and it could not suffer an attack from so paupered a foe. It was as if a shiver ran through their lines, the stirring of their steel in the breeze. No fear bred it, but the lowering of the lance points, one by one, while the trumpets shrilled, and from their ranks came the shouts of the battle cry of de Valois, "Mountjoie St. Denys."

The whole first battle line of the French began to move. The King swung round and flung up his hand. Instantly his army halted behind him, the archers ramming down their stakes deeply into the soft ground so that the sharpened tips bore outward. From the hill crest the priests and the boys watched their frantic thrustings, scarce able to watch, the boys whispering, "Quick, oh, quick."

The French bore onward, riding so close that their spurs locked and they seemed a great block of steel draped in the silks of heraldry. The mud snatched at the horses but scarce checked them.

When they saw that if they kept formation some would be driven onto the stakes, they converged on to the King's center, jostling for the foremost places.

The last stake was driven home. The priests looked down on the King's line, spun across the valley like a thin silver chain from covert to covert, the jupons of the knights strung upon it like clusters of jewels. On either side and in the center the archers stood in the wedges of Poitiers. Erpyngham shouted to them, "Kneel," and the foremost dropped on their right knees; "Stretch," and the bowstrings went back to the ear.

Erpyngham flung his Marshal's warder into the air. At once the whole valley was filled with the thin high singing of the arrows that had before sung their song over the fields of France. They fell among the French like rain falling among the leaves. But the knights, full-mailed, were vulnerable only between the eye slits of the visor and under the armpits. The archers drew bow again without pause, their movements flowing into each other swiftly and with beauty. Yet they could not halt the charge. The French massed onto the English center where the King stood. They smote against it, so that the clash of battle filled the ears of the priests—smote it and threw it back as if a giant's hand had picked up the whole English line and tossed it up the hill. The thin silver chain fluted over the brown earth, tautening and straining. It seemed as if it would most surely snap.

"They are through," one of the priests said. "All is lost." He put his hand to his crucifix. The sick men crossed themselves. Thomas Elmham, the King's confessor, who was mounted, spoke aloud in prayer, not knowing he did so. "Lord have mercy," he said. "Dear Jesu, look with mercy."

"They'll kill the King," Ned said. "They'll kill him as they did my father." He hid his face against Elmham's saddle trappings. But when he came to look again no Frenchman had yet pierced the silver line.

XXXII

The archers could no more use their bows for fear of harming their own. At the King's signal, they tossed them aside and drew their knives and gudgeons. They fought hand to hand as did the knights, but more nimbly. The center was most sorely pressed, for it was there that the full might of D'Albret's chivalry had struck. The King saw the Frenchmen lifting their lances as they rode by him that they might deal him no blow, and he fought in cold fury. There was much confusion, and the English scarce knew whether they lived or died.

Suffolk was struck down almost straightway. Talbot knelt by him and shouted to Hungerford for aid. "He's well stricken," he said. "Bear him out."

The mail above Suffolk's right breast showed battered and bloody. Hungerford seized his feet and helped to carry him out, not knowing if it was a dead man he lifted. They laid him in the grass beneath one of the elms. Aumerle lay there already. No discoloration of blood marked him, but he was dead. He lay unhelmed, his gray-spattered head propped on an old rolled surcoat, the griffin of the Plantagenets ablaze on his jupon. Beside him Suffolk's fair hair gleamed damply in the sun like wet silk. He yet breathed but faintly. Hungerford sought one of the surgeons, but when he came back, Suffolk's breathing had ceased. He and Aumerle lay calmly together in knightly company.

Talbot sent to the King, asking who was to take Aumerle's command, and Henry set Umfraville in his cousin's place. The whole line was still in much jeopardy, and there was time but for a few words. When a lull came in the fighting, Henry asked how his cousin had fallen. .

"We know not," Hungerford said. "There's not a mark. It was as though his heart stopped beating."

"All our hearts stopped beating," Humphrey of Gloucester said and laughed harshly.

Now the dismounted line of the French moved to the assault. They came ponderously through the mud, stiff in their steel, the blades of their great swords virgin in the sun. The earth grew mired, knee-deep. The knights reeled and floundered in it, their coats-of-arms blackened beyond all telling, and only by instinct could a man set friend from foe. It seemed to Hungerford less strange that he had escaped a Frenchman's sword than that he had not dropped dead from weariness alone. About him the archers and the King's knights peered at one another through their sweat in wonder that they were yet alive.

With his third attack D'Albret sent in his crossbowmen and another line of his knights. All these were fresh. They came into the assault behind Rambures's banner, trampling on their own dead and dying. Many of the French, if they fell in full mail, could not rise again and drowned in the mud, helpless as new-born calves. Against the fresh armor of Rambures's men the English stood a blackened and bloodied line, slime-caked to thighs and hips. It was as if the whole line creaked and groaned under the weight of the new assault. The fighting was as fierce as at the first. Yet now some of the French, when they believed themselves cut off from their own lines, began to seek quarter. Some surrendered ten times before they found an Englishman ready to take their gloves, but when they promised ransom there was ever one to set his back on the King's commands and take prisoners.

Rambures's banner drew back, floating over the helms of the French to the hill brow. There were yet many Frenchmen about, and it was hard to believe that this attack likewise was withdrawn. Humphrey of Gloucester pushed back his visor with a shaking hand. His breath came low as if he sobbed. "God with us," he said. "My heart's near bursting."

"That's thrice we've trimmed them," Umfraville said. "It can not be that——" He broke off as though not desiring to speak words which might seem he hoped.

"Our strength will not last," Humphrey said. "I can scarce lift my sword arm even now."

"Your strength will come again, Brother," Henry said, "when it must."

It was as if all the battle had in a moment lulled and died about them. The French were taking counsel, shifting their men on the hill brow, their third battle line still unused. As the King and his nobles rested gasping on their swords, Gam darted in among them. "The boys," he was shouting. "They have killed the boys."

XXXIII

The King had set his baggage on two of the sumpter horses. When he and his knights reached the hill crest, all had been plundered, the civic crown, the great seals, the jewels, and the purses. The ropes that had bound the chests dangled severed about the horses' girths. Some of the apparel and the wooden cups and bowls had been lain in a heap and fired. The embers smoldered in smoky grayness beside the withered broom bushes.

One of the sick men had tried to crawl for his life into the thorn thickets. His skull was split, and he lay half-hidden, his blood sliming the browned leaves. Beside him was a dead priest, his crucifix snatched from off his neck. Most of the boys had been struck down where they had tried to run. Some had had their throats slit, and some bore great wounds in thighs and chests. They lay in limbless fashion, their gay-stockinged legs twisted beneath them.

Gam went from one to another. He was weeping, and the spittle glistened on his beard. "I think not one of them is left," he said. "Not one."

"By all the saints," Hungerford said, "what knaves did this? Was it not enough for them that they had us at their swords' points?"

The King followed Gam among the dead as if he walked in his sleep. It was as if he sought for something. Presently Gam called to him from among the thorn bushes. "Here, my lord," he said. "Here. God with us—it was a foul thorough end they made here behind our backs."

Ned lay where he pointed. He had well fought, for the scrub

about was flat trampled and his boy's dagger lay beside him bloodied. Gam sought to raise him, but the King took him from him. He stood with him in his arms, much blood from the boy's chest and thighs staining his mail and muddy jupon. Ned yet struggled for breath. When he knew that it was the King who held him, he smiled. "Oh, my lord," he said, "you are safe. I said three Ave Marias for you."

Henry set him down among the moss and lichen grass. He said as if he choked, "Fetch me Colnet."

"Nay, my lord," Talbot said. "Let Colnet tend whomsoever he is tending. He can do no good here."

The King made no answer. There was a stirring among the scrub, and Thomas Elmham and two other of the priests rode out from the trees. They knelt to the King, shaking and pallid. They had ridden into the woods to view the battle closer. There they had heard the sounds of massacre, knowing themselves helpless and fearing to come forth.

Umfraville asked them who had done it. They did not know, saying they could not tell the chivalry, but there was a banner borne with stars upon it. Some peasants had likewise joined the mounted men, and it had been these who had robbed the sumpter horses. "The peasants came for plunder, my lord," Elmham said. "The rest for vengeance. In both were they pitiless."

The nobles shifted and looked at one another in helpless rage. The King remained on one knee beside Ned, scarce seeming to hear. From the valley, shrilling loud as the cock's crow, came the notes of the trumpets sounding the French banners again to the assault.

"They're coming again," Umfraville said. "God with us."

"Back, my lords," Talbot said, "each to his post."

It seemed to them, as they turned, that they looked on their ruin. The English line lay below them in the valley as it had done at the first, but everywhere was it broken. Umfraville saw first how it was, and exclaimed in horror. "Look yonder," he said. "They've taken prisoners. They have lost us all."

Many of the Englishmen had burdened themselves with prisoners from those of the French knights who had pledged ransoms. Hungerford looked down on them and saw many not yet unarmed. It seemed to him English greed had done what all the might of France's chivalry had failed to do, and the battle was now lost. When the wave of the new assault broke upon them, it would be that they drowned in that vast and lapping sea of Frenchmen.

Umfraville looked at them with a sick bitterness. "In faith," he said, "trust an Englishman—their gold is too much for us, even when their swords are not."

He looked back at the King, but he yet knelt heedless save for the boy. Talbot seized his arm as if to wake him from sleep. "My lord," he said, "arouse yourself. Your soldiers are in great danger."

Henry dragged himself to his feet and came to them. The trumpets shrilled nearer and nearer. Through the trees others answered them, distantly at first, then close at hand. From the ranks of the French rose a loud and triumphant shouting. "Brabant—Brabant."

"It's Brabant," Umfraville said. "God help. This is the finish."

He snatched his sword from the earth and ran toward his own men.

"My lord," Talbot said, "what of the prisoners?"

"I bade them take no prisoners," Henry said. "If any man has he must kill him."

One of the squires spoke up hesitantly. "They are worth much," he said. "We'll strike their ransoms down with them."

Gam fell to cursing him, asking him what purpose ransom would serve him when his throat was slit and he lay in the mud. "It is to this pass that such as you have brought us," he said.

"My lord," Hungerford said, "some of them are not armed."

The King turned his look back to the boys, the dead priests and the slaughtered sick. "Were these?" he said. His face was as hard as the Fiend's under the baleful ruby. All was with him now as wholly Plantagenet, and they saw him fired with his house's fierce and ruthless blood, with naught else in his mind save Calais. "I know not how else I can bring you to Calais," he said. "Do as I bid you. What bloodguilt there be, let it rest upon the King."

"The King is right," Talbot said. "What other way is there for us, now that Brabant rides upon us? They themselves did as much at Nicopolis."

Henry turned from them and spoke to the bodyguard of his archers. "This task is yours," he said. "Do it gently as you might."

The archers went slowly toward the groups of prisoners threading their arrows to their bows. Some divined their purpose and from them a thin cry went up. The swift fierce hiss of the arrows cut it short, as if a scythe had passed over them, the King watching, hard and still of face. All was so quickly done it was scarce to be realized, and now the new peril rode upon them. Through the trees glinted the jewel-like colors of the plumes and out of the woods on the right burst the banners of Brabant, rich and unspotted by any of the mud of battle. The King's knights stared at them without hope, staggering like drunken men as they sought to run to regain their places. The King stood where he was, and Talbot spoke to him with much urgency. "Look to your men, my lord," he said. "They are almost upon us."

"Let me be," Henry said. He shouted for Elmham and when he came to his side, said, "Is he dead, Father?"

"The boy?" Elmham said. "Aye, my lord. It was no grief to him once he had struck a blow for you."

The King looked toward the slaughtered French, the dead lying where the living had stood. His face was masked. Hungerford followed his eyes, taking no liking in what he saw. The King sighed and said, "If any live, look to them, Father." After a space he said, "It may be it was for my soldiers' sakes that the boy died. It was needful, yet I know not now how else I could have commanded it."

XXXIV

At last Brabant's attack also fell back, some of the French wavering. Bourbon rode amongst them, seeking to rally them. He was wounded in the face and the blood dripped between the eye slits of his visor onto the gilt stars of his armor. "Back at their throats," he said. "Would you be shamed by yon scrawny crows?"

Orléans rode at his side, gasping to draw breath. "No man knows what is commanded," he said. "Where is the Constable?"

"Fallen," Bourbon said. "Cousin, if you deem the command yours, take it, in God's name, and set this confusion to rights."

Rambures came upon them, weeping. "They do battle like the very fiends from hell," he said. "It is as if our own dead snatch themselves from the earth and fight for them. They have slaughtered twice their number."

Bourbon answered, "Then are we still three times their strength."

"It's wondrous to me," Orléans said, "that the tavern crawler can set us at such defiance."

"His blade is sober," Orléans said. "My lords, we've dealt too gently there. If we cannot bring him living to the Dauphin, better to bring his carcass than lose all honor."

"Aye," Orléans said. "If their King falls, I think we will yet bring them down in their blood. No men would stand, lacking such a captain."

Rambures answered that the matter had already been thought on. "See you those twenty knights," he said. "Gathered yonder under Vaudémont's banner. They have bound themselves by a most sacred oath they will not leave the field while the King of England lives."

The Duke of Alençon stood at his stirrup strap. He was one of the foremost fighters in France, expert in both lance and sword, strong made and tall. "Let me go first, lords," he said. "For the honor of France, it were better he should fall in single combat. Then if I fail the knights can do the work they are pledged to."

"Yes, yes," Rambures said eagerly. "Go strike him down, my lord. Hew off in blood the lilies he flaunts in our faces upon his surcoat."

Alençon smiled and took his sword from the hand of his squire.

"Can you mark him?" Orléans asked.

"I can mark the ruby," Alençon said. "Ride on them, my lords. The field is yet ours."

XXXV

Now the French untethered the horses they had held back for the pursuit and mounted. Their way lay among the heaps of their own slain lying in the narrow valley. The English watched them come in panting silence. "They are brave men," the King said. "They ride back on us again and again."

The fresh tide of Frenchmen swept upon the King's lines. The English found themselves struggling as though they drowned in a sea of their enemies. Their weariness lay on them like shackles of weighted iron on their limbs. They fought on speechless from it, feeling themselves choke in their own sweat. Humphrey of Gloucester was struck down beside his brother and lay in the mud, helpless and in his own blood. Henry bestrode him and fought hand to hand with the knights who pressed upon him. For a while both looked to be in much danger. The nobles could do no more than cast helpless glances at them, their own hands too full to aid. While the King strove, Humphrey crawled inch by inch from between his brother's mailed legs, his right arm dangling. Hungerford seized him and dragged him clear, laying him on the grass. The mail of his right forearm was cleaved, but the wound was not mortal. When Hungerford would have tended it, Humphrey struck at him, sobbing and panting. "The Fiend damn you," he said. "Look to Hal. He saved me."

The King was parted now from all his knights. Alençon came upon him, knowing him by the ruby in his helm. He had come to the charge on foot, his visor open, but when he drew near to the

King he lowered it and clasped up his two-handed sword. They closed together, gasping and slipping in the churned mud, like giants in their mail. It seemed to both they had not met the other's equal before.

Alençon had come to the charge fresh. The King's brain and arm grew laggard for very weariness. After a space he felt the mastery going from him. He went back step by step to the edge of the thorn thickets, where he could go no farther. Hungerford saw him brought to his knees among the brambles. He fought still but Alençon stood above him, his blade uplifted for the blow of grace. It seemed to Hungerford he would for a surety see the King's skull cleave under it. He cried out hoarsely, not knowing what he said.

Henry turned his head from the blow. It fell mightily, glancing from his helm and lopping a gold fleuron off the crown as if it had been wax. Henry swayed on his knees, stricken and much dazed. Alençon sought to draw back his arm to strike again, but the King groped toward him and set his arms about him, pinioning him.

Hungerford saw Reeve standing beside him, drawing at his bow. "For mercy, hold," he said. "You'll hit the King."

"Nay, sir," Reeve said, but he did not shoot.

The knights were closing about them. Alençon saw them and strove to loose himself. Henry plucked his enemy's dagger from his belt and struck at him across the fingers of his sword hand. As the blood spurted from them, Alençon drew back and fumbled with his glove. "I yield," he said. "I yield my sword to you."

The King shouted to his knights to spare him, but Reeve had straightway marked his opportunity and loosed. The arrow took Alençon below the armpit where the armor gaped. He fell forward upon the King, and they went down together among the thorn bushes.

Talbot reached them and thrust Alençon's body aside. Henry asked gasping of his brother. "Not greatly stricken," Talbot said. "God's peace, my lord, will you not guard yourself? They mean to kill you now."

Henry answered, "It's a good augury."

Now that Alençon had fallen, the twenty knights who had vowed to kill the King or die rode to make good their pledge. They made straight for the King, taking no heed of any other man. Reeve hurled himself at the first and clubbed him from his horse, snarling. The English knights divined their purpose and hacked despairingly at them, fearing they would in truth succeed. One by one they fell, their riderless horses charging on over the dead and writhing wounded, their painted reins flying.

The battle was now at its most desperate. Rambures again led his crossbowmen to the charge and fell at their head, his gallantry such as no man had imputed to him. Brabant died also, hacked from his horse as he rode on the English lines like a madman. Orléans, who had taken the command from D'Albret, yielded. Bourbon did likewise. Berri fled, riding into the Maisoncelles woods after one brief sip of battle. Yet for each who died or yielded or fled twenty remained to fight. It seemed to Hungerford the King's army was still no more than a mouse beneath the paw of a lion.

The English knew their strength to be failing. Many of the knights fought with open wounds, their blood and their sweat mingling. For all their labor, it was as if the reserves of their enemy were endless, and that though they hacked till they dropped they would still be outmatched. Some of them sobbed as they hewed for very weariness, even the King gasped, croaking at them as if his voice failed him. "Keep on, my few," he said. "A little more and it is done."

Thus they fought on, feeling the sight creeping from their eyes and the quickening from their limbs. It was as though the battle ebbed for a moment about them. On a sudden Hungerford heard the King sigh as in wonderment. He had dropped on one knee, and as Hungerford looked upon him he pushed up his visor with a shaking hand. Hungerford followed his eyes. Ahead lay the dark still woods and the white shaft of the Calais road striking between them, but where the matchless chivalry of France had stood were no more than the riderless horses, the tents and the quiet dead. No other Frenchmen stood between the King and Calais. As the archers and the nobles one by one lifted their heads to stare with him, there broke from the archers a thin and hollow cheering, as of so many ragged ghosts, a cheering that died on its own breath among the young damp wheat.

XXXVI

Orléans came out from among the prisoners. He went on one knee to the King, speaking in careful French, as if he were afraid Henry would not understand it. "All is yielded to you, sire," he said. "You hold the field."

"My lord, it cannot be," Henry said. "There are enough still of your countrymen when they re-form to strike all our lives into the hazard."

"Nonetheless, they are scattered," Orléans said. "My lord, the day is yours. We rest ourselves on your most knightly chivalry."

It might have been laughable to hear them arguing thus, the King against his victory and the Frenchman for it, but it was not so. The King set aside his helm. His face was sweat-drenched and blackening from Alençon's mighty blow. As the knights about him did likewise, they blinked at each other owlishly in the sun. It was to them as though they dreamed.

Henry asked for the lists of his dead, then turned to look at the field. Humphrey sat propped against an elm nearby, one of the priests binding his arm with strips of dirty cloth. When he saw the King, he rose and embraced him, finding no words but laughing whitely. From over the slimed and trodden field blackened figures came lurching, looking against the blaze of the autumnal woods like specters from the farthermost pit of hell.

"My men, Talbot," Henry said. "My archers."

"Aye," Talbot said. "It may well be it is a hard reckoning. Yet has God delivered us."

Hugh Stafford came plowing through the mud to kneel with

the lists of the slain. The King took it, his fingers shaking. Men saw that he shivered as if the sweat had cooled upon him. He read in wonder, then looked at Stafford.

"Sire," Stafford said, "it is complete. Save for your grace's cousin of Aumerle and Lord Suffolk, no man of title fell save Sir Richard Keighley. Seven squires were slain, and some thirty men-at-arms. I do not think you have lost upwards of two hundred men."

"Then all these?" Henry said. "Can they be French?"

"They are French, my lord," Stafford said. "I doubt not we have brought down more than twice our number. We have besides close on a thousand prisoners."

"Oh, God," Umfraville whispered, "it is not possible. It is a miracle."

The King said in a husky voice, "My lords, I think we have not wrought this ourselves. I think the Hand of God was upon us and to Him and not to ourselves be the praise."

Erpyngham said. "What field shall we tell them in England these things were done upon?"

Umfraville named it the field of Maisoncelles, but no man favored it. It rang with the echo of the night before, setting the mind back to hunger and despair and the chill of the rain. Henry pointed above the trees where a turret showed and asked Orléans in French what castle it was. Orléans answered that it was "Azzincourt," and the King, mishearing him, repeated it, "Agincourt." He said it in wonder as though he well liked it.

He bade them yet keep the field, for he feared the French would rally; then he went to where his cousin and Suffolk lay quietly side by side in the shadowed grass. Presently he stooped and drew off the cross Suffolk wore about his neck and his ring. All about them the knights began to drop to the ground, from weariness, where they stood. They lay or crouched, their bared heads lolling against their mailed arms. There were yet many wounded to be tended. The priests and the doctors toiled among them, the King with them. Colnet saw him and called sharply,

"My lord Talbot, will you desire the King to rest, or it will be with him as it was with his cousin of Aumerle."

Slowly the shadows crept grayly over the grass, longer and longer. Umfraville wiped the cold sweat from his face and spoke to the King. "They are not coming back," he said.

The King answered him in a still voice, "No," he said. "I think the day be ours."

He turned to the trumpeters and bade them sound the retreat. The notes hung long and golden on the shadowed air, falling richly on English ears that had not hoped to hear the sound again. The men gathered once more about the King, those who had found strength enough to rifle the French tents bearing their loot —cheeses and hams and prepared fowls. They carried them carefully, as though they were caskets of jewels, and they chewed as they came. In the dusk they were such a scant, ragged and foulsmelling band that the knights stared at them and at each other, marveling that somehow they had come to conquest.

Henry spoke with them haltingly, as if speech had all but gone from him. "The day's toil is done," he said. "And I would render my thanks to you. No King was served better. More would I have said to you, but the words cling hardly to my tongue."

They answered him with a ragged cheering. To Elmham he said, "Let Te Deum be sung, and Non nobis."

Some of the men had brought torches from the French tents, and these they kindled. They were resin scented and the savor of them hung sweet and cleanly in the evening air, the flames flickering jewellike against the dusk-touched woods. Slowly the archers began to leave the field, bearing their wounded in dark file. As they walked one of the ragged chaplains sang the two words, "Non nobis," in a thin voice, and the lines behind him began to sing likewise, "Non nobis, Domine, non nobis, sed nomine tuo da gloriam."

The tattered figures moved in the encroaching dark dimly as in a dream, and the ancient words, sung gruffly in English voices, as with reverence, tore at the King's heart beyond all he had yet known.

XXXVII

The King and his nobles stripped in the farmhouse where they had rested the previous night. Even those who lightly escaped were bruised from head to heel. It seemed to Hungerford he had never seen bodies so much a mass of bruises, strung together with old scars and new wounds.

Henry was afoot with the daylight. He alone of his army doubted his victory, and he was in fear that the French would reform and come upon him again. With morning some of the archers resought the field to fill their pouches with rings from the hands of the slain. Yet they were not the first, for the Maisoncelles peasants moved among the bodies of their own countrymen, stripping all raiment and all jewels from them. The King sent his heralds into Tramecourt pledging himself that the French could with safety come and bury their dead; but they could find no man in authority—all had scattered.

The few English dead were laid together and burned to save their bodies from the looters. The King watched their pyre with a stricken look, seeing his page, his cousin, and young Suffolk laid upon it. For all many had been spared him, in these three he had much grief.

The knights struggled groaning into their saddles, their stiff and bruised limbs scarce answering them. The first night they camped at dusk, and by daybreak the next morning they were afoot again. Calais was near now, but since Harfleur they had known so many cruel shocks, all believed they might well come upon a second French army blocking their path.

"In faith," Umfraville said suddenly, "I can smell the sea."

Ahead two men at work in the grainfields lifted their heads to look upon them. Umfraville hailed them, and they came slowly forward, staring. The nobles marked them that they were citizens of Calais and therefore of the King's realm.

"We thought you were dead, my lord," one said. "We thought you were all dead."

The King asked him of his realm.

"They are near crazed about you," the man said. "They pray daily in St. Paul's. Your grace's brother manned the ports, fearing the Dauphin's landing. It was told us the Dauphin had an army of forty-two thousand souls in the field. We thought for a surety you could not escape them."

The King answered they had given battle, saying, "God looked upon us with mercy."

Both stared upon him as if he were crazed, following when the horses went forward. On a sudden Calais rose in front of them, her gray walls sternly cast above the green and the red and white cross of St. George floating above each of her turrets. In the thin autumn sunshine she seemed of all things on earth the most beautiful. The King drew in his breath and said, "Yonder Calais."

One by one the mounted men set spur to horse until the whole plain was filled with running men and horses at full gallop. There were people on the walls, men and women, French and English, looking down upon the ragged and running men and the lean, ungroomed horses. For a space they did no more than stare, but on a sudden they broke into cheering, and beyond them the bells of Calais broke one after another into loud and triumphant song.

THE
LONG, LONG LOVE

Oh, where have you been, my long, long love,

These long seven years and more.

In England the days of dread, when men's minds had been filled with thoughts they dared not name, were likewise ended. At night had come the messengers pounding for admittance at the Stone Gate of London Bridge, and dawn had crept over the city to the pealing of bells, dragging the citizens to their doors to hear news they could scarce believe.

The King sent one of his own squires, John Bromley, to Lady Hereford at Pleshy. She had heard the ringing of the bells in the misty morning across the meadows, but had put hope from her, mistrusting it. When she heard Bromley's words, she sat silent, turning the tapestry she worked at about on her lap. Presently she asked of her grandsons.

"In health both," Bromley said. "The Lord Humphrey's wound mends. The King took many buffets, but none to open the flesh."

He went on to tell her all that had befallen. The King's fleets but now neared Dover. He had had hard passage from Calais, the Channel storms battering his ships, sinking two and driving many far off course. His men in the fierce reaction of their victory had come to believe themselves doomed, seeing the Hand of God so straitened upon them that after all their toil and perils they could look for naught but death within sight of their homeland. The King again had to summon up their spirits to drag them to a safety they had long believed themselves cheated of. This final toil had told more hardly upon him than all the rest.

When she had heard it all, Lady Hereford sighed and said, "How looks he?"

"His face bruised from Alençon's blow," Bromley said. "My lady, he's greatly wearied. He looks older."

"Older?" Lady Hereford said. "Aye, that I doubt not."

The King had sent from Calais that he desired no pageantry to greet his return. His subjects took small heed of him. The city bedecked herself and painted her face for him like a maid at her betrothed's homecoming. Conduits sprang up to run on the day of his coming with free wine, and the streets vied with each other in color and symbol—setting the royal purple, the roses of Lancaster, the crowns, and the stars, the greens, the gilts, and the scarlets spilling and rioting one upon another in the joy of victory. At the Stone Gate of London Bridge grew two giants of wickerwork to greet his eyes as he passed from Southwark, and flanking the Chepe were the great beasts of heraldry, the Lion of England, the Antelope of Lancaster, the Bull of Clarence, the Yale of the Beauforts, bearing their shields charged with the arms of the King's chivalry. Men had never marked the city so full. There was not an inn that was not filled to overflowing, and each day brought great flocks of provincial folk to sleep on the floors of churches or in the gutters.

Sleet had greeted the King on his landing, but the joy of his people in his triumph melted all coldness. To Eltham where he waited on the morning of Saturday rode Thomas Thetford, the new Abbot of Bermondsey, and Whittington to greet him. Whittington was no longer Lord Mayor, but men still reckoned him London's first citizen. With him rode his successor, "Witless Nick" Ballantire, a stout, overbusy, overanxious man, given to nervous chattering. Humphrey stood beside his brother. He bore his arm in a sling of woven silk and was loud and instant in his laughter, his spirits so high that the smallest jest found favor with him.

The King was much otherwise, stern of face and wearied. Whittington saw him cast low in the aftermath of victory, the ebb of spirit fierce upon him. Presently he asked if he might come without tumult into his capital, saying, "There are no crowds?"

"Oh, for the saints' sake, Harry," Humphrey said and laughed.

Whittington half-smiled and said, "They are packed cheek by jowl, my lord. If they swoon they'll not fall. I never saw London so full."

"I told them I wanted none of this," Henry said. "Why was it done?"

"My dear lord," Whittington said, "no man could stop them. Your people would show you their hearts."

The King said sharply, "Think you so? Would they not shout as loud for a dancing bear on a chain?"

"Nay, good my lord," Nicholas Ballantire said in a shocked voice.

"Your pardon, sirs," Henry said. "You will say victory turns me to a churl. But I am much spent. My brother of Gloucester will ride this day in my stead."

"Oh, they'll not like that," Humphrey said. "I can see their faces. Only the Duke of Gloucester, forsooth."

"As your grace wishes," Whittington said. "Yet they'll be sore disappointed. They were sleeping last night in the gutters and on the pavements to hold their places for all that it rained and was chill."

The King hesitated and set his hand across his eyes. Presently he said, "Let it be as you wish." He asked what route he must take.

Ballantire brought him a sketch of the streets and pointed a way through them, beaming. "Through Deptford and Southwark, my lord," he said. "Across the bridge and thence through the Chepe to St. Paul's. After which does it please your grace to proceed along the Strand to Westminster?"

The King half-smiled and said, "It seems it will have to." He took Ballantire's sketch and studied it. Ballantire darted from side to side behind his shoulders like an anxious bird, twisting hood and gown straight while he talked.

"Never have I seen the city so bedecked," he said. "I fear me we have done no work for three days, but then how often is it that we have such tidings? Is it permitted to bear your grace's sword and the helm, which was told us was battered by the Duke of Alençon's blow, before you in the procession?"

Henry answered curtly, "No."

Ballantire looked pained. "We have longed to feast our eyes on them, my lord," he said. "Your helm especially as witness of your valor."

"I tell you, no," Henry said. "Have I not bidden you give the glory to God? If His Hand had been against me, what could I have done?"

They mounted by the cloisters of the Abbey and set their horses' heads toward London. The King wore no finery save that his cloak was of the royal purple and held with a jeweled clasp. He rode bareheaded in the thin November sunshine; Ballantire and Whittington, in their aldermen's scarlet, on either hand.

Whittington talked quietly as they rode, his speech still the speech of Gloucestershire, where he had passed his youth. He spoke of the letters which the King had sent the city from France. "It seemed good to us that you wrote in English," he said. "And not, as by custom, in French. Now when the lords address themselves to us in the French tongue, we ask them if they do not know the King's English."

The people awaited the King, so tight packed they had scarce space to raise their arms. Sometimes at the street corners the tumblers would topple and spin for their amusement, but mostly these were keeping of their best until nightfall, when wine would have loosened the purse strings. Continually messengers rode down the route bringing news of the King's coming. He had met with the aldermen at Blackheath, and at the Stone Gate of the Bridge the keys of London had been delivered into his hand. There he had had his first sight of the city, and though he seemed sick and weary, as if the strength which had upborne him through rivers and marshlands and the swords of his enemies had gone, he had smiled, naming the city royal, and praying that God would forever keep her from all hurt.

Slowly the King came, moving inch by inch through the churning sea of his people. The whifflers who sought to keep clear his way, were quickly swamped, and the crowd pressed close upon him, setting hands against his feet, his mailed knees against his

horse's sides, his bridle, his stirrup leather, as though they feared
Harry had indeed left his bones at Agincourt and that this was no
more than his ghost that rode between them.

Apprentice boys, hidden in the niches about Queen Eleanor's
Cross, puffed gold dust upon him. Thus he rode under a golden
rain, his shoulders drooping and his brown head bowed. It was as
though he came not in victory but with the sorrow of defeat upon
him, as a captive and not as a conqueror. The people seeing him
silent and spent, with his bruised face and purple cloak yelled the
louder, reckoning him as Galahad with the vision of the Holy
Grail under his eyelids and all else shut out.

Above him, caged in a trellis of roses and fleur-de-lys, loomed
huge the silver figure of St. George, the dragon writhing greenly
at his lance's point, and ahead was the awning of the Chepe,
painted blue and set with stars. Here the pack was so great he
could move no farther. He waited, isled among the mob, his
whifflers scattered and his nobles, who rode with him, far to the
rear. His white horse, patient until now under the pawing hands
and the jostling bodies, began to prick and sweat, and the King
laid his hand upon its neck. Seeing him thus entrapped among his
subjects, his archers fought their way to him. Reeve put a hand to
the bridle and step by step the King went forward under the awning and into the Chepe.

At St. Paul's Gateway Joanna awaited him. The King entered
the great church to make his offering, and the people, hoarse from
cheering, took breath, resting their throats until he should come
again. He came at length to remount and, with Joanna riding at
his right hand and the Bishop of London at his left, turned toward the Strand, where lay the city's mansions and broad gardens.
Joanna was smiling now through the swirling shower of gold, her
blue skirts spread about her and her jeweled chaplet aglint in the
sunshine. Humphrey rode behind her, bearing the reins in the
hand of his injured arm that he might wave with the other, and, at
his back, the great citizens of London, the mayor, the aldermen,

and the merchants in the livery of their guilds. Slowly they came, half-blinded in gold dust, the King swaying in his high, painted saddle, as if he would drop from it from very weariness.

The great doors of the Abbey, through which the King had gone to his anointing, stood wide to him. He dismounted and for the first time saluted the people, as though with his hard passage done he no longer feared for his strength. Signing himself, he passed through the doors, the roar of his people's love at his heels.

II

His brothers greeted him in the Palace of Westminster, Tom with loud voice and high humor. "That I missed it, Hal," he exclaimed, striking his fist against his forehead. "That I missed it. Forty-two thousand Frenchmen and but six thousand half-starved English. God's peace, it sets my blood tingling." He followed the King to the stairway, talking the while. "How did you do it?" he said. "How did you set your archers?"

The King answered him shortly. "Ask Humphrey," he said. "He'll tell you all."

He went from them toward his chamber. Tom looked after him, scratching his head. "The saints with us," he grumbled. "Never was such a victory and Harry's sour as a priest. It was the same after Shrewsbury. I hope I never see him the day the battle goes ill for him."

"Peace, let him be," Humphrey said. "He's spent to swooning."

Henry went on into the Painted Chamber, where he had not slept for near on five months. It was all freshly spruced with new hangings on the great bed, crimson as blood, and new woven matting on the floor, while the brass ewers and jugs shone as gold. Malbon and two of his body squires awaited him there. They would have loosed the cloak from his shoulders, but he gestured them back. Suffolk's jeweled crucifix lay in his pouch, and he drew it out, weighing it in his palm. "John," he said, and John Bromley came out of the shadows to his side.

"My lord?"

The King said, "I would have you go to Cottingham to Lady Suffolk. Commend me to her, and give her this. Tell her that her son died at Agincourt as his father died at Harfleur—as a knight."

"I will, my lord," Bromley said.

The King sighed and said, "Tell her I will come to her myself when I am able. I would have her know Michael would not go out of the battle. He stayed the while by my standard."

When Bromley had gone, he went to the window and stood looking out. Already the bonfires were lit and the glow of them dotted the city, sending the shadows racing slantwise across cobbles and black-timbered walls. Below in the courtyard, one of the archers strolled, a girl at his side, her white-coifed head inclined toward his shoulder. Still Henry stood. Malbon began to fear he had forgotten he must feast this night with the mayor and aldermen, where he had feasted after his Coronation, at Westminster Hall.

"My lord," he said, "will you not make ready? You have but little time."

"Presently," the King said. "Is all set?"

"It is, my lord," Malbon said. "Shall I summon the boy Bryce? In truth, he should be here. He grows heedless, mayhap, with all this jollity."

"He is dead," Henry said. "He was slain at Agincourt."

"Oh, my lord," Malbon said. He began to dress the King himself, setting the Garter below his knee and helping him to don the cote-hardie. "It hangs loosely," he said. "Your grace has grown leaner in France."

Presently Lady Hereford sent asking audience. The King bade her enter, and she came in with her proud, high, youthful step, her chin firm-molded yet and raised like a queen's above her lawn coif. "God be praised," she said. "Oh, Harry, how you affrighted me. I never thought to look on you again."

When they were alone, he led her to the oaken chair by the window. He knelt and set his arms about her. There was much gold dust yet in his hair, and she put her fingers to it. Presently she said, "Where go you now?"

"I dine with the city fathers," he said. "Oh, grandmother, I am weary beyond all telling."

She answered him, "How could you not be?" Presently she spoke of Mary, on a sigh. "I would she had seen this day," she said. "Her sons were leopards to claw the very earth of Picardy."

"Oh, peace," he said. "The bells have clashed against my ears all day, yet I know not for what they ring. I was in France five months and I hold but one seaport. My cousin Edward fell. Suffolk—whom, for his mother's sake, I longed to bring safe to Calais —fell also. So did that boy who loved me."

"But many live," she said. "And it is a wondrous thing that they do. Is it so small a matter to rout a foe five times your strength—a handful of sick and spent men slaughtering a host? Is it too poor a victory to burnish the King's honor?"

"Honor!" he said. "After the boy died I fought with hatred. I slew the prisoners."

"Was it for hate of them?" she said. "Or for love of those that walked with you in the rain?"

He gave her no answer. "Harry, Harry," she said. "I know you to reckon little to your life, but I have often thought you overheedful of your soul. Was it not the atonement of Lancaster—to care but little for both the soul and body if so be your soldiers might live?"

The King said in a still voice, "If I could believe it."

"Nay," she said. "What more was there to give in the sight of God? The land joys in your victory. Can you not do likewise?"

"What do they know?" he said. "Nothing is solved in France. No great thing has been accomplished."

"Tush," she said. "It may be England is older and wiser than her King."

Malbon's voice came querulously through the door. "Your pardon, my lord," he said, "the aldermen are fully assembled."

"Go now," she said and kissed him. "Only a few more hours, then you can rest from all your labors. Your bed will be soft to you this night." He half-smiled and she spoke again. "Aye," she said. "I know it to be empty too. Perhaps the French princess dreams of you this night in her Paris bower. Have patience. Jacob labored in the field twice seven years to win Rachel."

"God's peace, sweetheart," he said. "Would you have that happen to me?"

"Nay," she said. "I would have you win her soon, Harry. Yet I would not have you desire her too greatly. There was a wise saying of the Saxons, 'Kingship and love but ill agree together.'"

While the King, his nobles and the aldermen feasted in Westminster Hall, the crowds boozed and sang and danced about the bonfires. After the lights were doused in the Hall and the city fathers dispersed, they grew louder still, tearing down the decorations in the Chepe and roaring out the songs the fiddlers scraped.

The light from the bonfires crept through the shutters of the Painted Chamber where the King was abed, licking in umbered shadow the high ceiling and the walls with their tapestries. The great bed of state, with its woven sheets and feather pillows, yielded oversoftly under him after the hard earth of France. He felt himself too spent for sleep. Till dawn he lay hearkening to the noise of the people.

III

Within the week Lady Percy rode to Westminster from the King's foundation at Syon House, where she had dwelt since Hotspur's death. She was forty-two now, sixteen years older than the King, and her griefs had marked her; but she was still blue-eyed as any other Mortimer.

"I would talk with you, lady," Henry said. "It is of Lord Camoys."

She looked at him on a sudden with dread. "Not slain?" she said. "It was told me he came safe."

"He is safe," the King said. "And he loves you. What say you, lady?"

She put her hands to her face as if she feared she would weep. "Oh, my lord," she said, "I was wife to Harry Percy."

"What of that?" Henry said. "Camoys has no care for it."

She said, "Yet you'll have care for it, my lord?"

The King answered, "I would trust Camoys with my life. Does it make him my enemy because he weds you?"

"Never," she said. "He is loyal; and all that was Percy and Mortimer in me died with Hotspur."

"Camoys walks yonder by the river," the King said. "If you will, go to him." When she would have gone, he said, "You must have loved Hotspur too. He was a great man."

"Aye, I loved him," she said. "Yet I never held him sleeping in my arms without I was in fear for him. His schemes prickspurred him as fiercely as he spurred his own mount, and now my youth's gone and I hunger for a gentler love. I hunger for Thomas Camoys's arms about me."

When they went to meat, Camoys sat with the King and his brothers at the high table, Lady Percy with him. She was flushed and straight-backed, the sorrows melting from her grave face. Already she wore her half-ring of betrothal on its silver chain about her neck. When later Hungerford came to the Painted Chamber to attend the King, Henry spoke of it. "They'll join the broken ring next week at the church porch," he said. "I am glad they'll tarry no longer."

He picked up his lute which lay among the cushions of the window seat and drew his fingers idly across the strings. It seemed to him he was much out of practice, and he set it from him.

"My lord," Hungerford said, "it's a long time since you gave us of your skill."

The King smiled and took up the lute once more. The notes fell clear so that even the pages lighting the sconces cocked their heads to listen. It was an old song, Petrarch's plaint of Laura.

Oh, ye lovers, that walk bathed in gladness,
If any drop of pity in you be.

When he had done, Humphrey applauded him lazily. "You're still skilled," he said. "But you could have given us something more jolly. What about the hymn of Agincourt?"

"That mock of a tune," Henry said. He walked to the window. Hungerford followed and spoke with him in a low voice. "My lord," he said, "do you go back?"

The King said, "Back, Walter?"

"To France, my lord."

He fell to twisting one of the rings on his hand. Hungerford saw it was the ring of the Queen of England, which at his anointing had been set on his little finger until such time as he took a wife. "I do not think so," the King said at last.

Hungerford said, "Is it gained then?"

"Harfleur is gained," Henry said. "And in the woods of Maisoncelles my knights and my bowmen mastered the whole chivalry of France. It may be the Narrow Seas will lie free to our ships, and Guienne will no more know siege nor the enemies of Lancaster find succor."

Hungerford said, "And the Lady Katherine?"

Henry gave him no answer. "My lord," Hungerford said, "Camoys's wooing goes aright. Must it be that yours does not prosper?"

"It's strange," the King said. "When we were seeking a passage of the Somme and all things went ill for us, I never lacked belief that I would win her. Now, in victory, I think she'll never be mine."

Hungerford answered him, "At one stride you've made England great—a long stride from Harfleur to Calais. Charles de Valois cannot gainsay you."

The King said in a low voice, "Would you have me go awooing with the blood of my soldiers?"

IV

The King from his own purse had ransomed Percy's son from
the Scots, and in April Lord Grey rode south with him from
Edinburgh. The Court was at Windsor, the King much occupied
with councils and petitions, closeted daylong with secretaries and
clerks. His nobles saw his high spirits leashed again to the task of
kingship, his gaiety gone. He rode and played but rarely, taking
small time for his pleasures; yet the land still joyed, the people
pressing upon him wherever they glimpsed him, the towns and
the cities thrusting their gifts into his hands—golden bowls filled
with crowns, golden caskets, jeweled loving cups, swords and spurs
fashioned with the silversmith's finest skill.

The King watched from the west turret while the men-at-arms
rode up from the river, then bade his servants send Percy to him.
It seemed to him that it was Hotspur who came again to him,
mounting through the trapdoor onto the roof. All Hotspur's likeness sat youthfully upon the son—the great shoulders and the
high color—but the hugeness of spirit was gone. Percy knelt stiffly
to the King with coldness.

After a space the King said, "You are free. Your ransom is full
paid."

"That they told me," Percy said. "But from the King's lips I
looked for the truth."

The King answered, "Have you not heard it?"

Percy grinned at him in angry fashion. "You count me as a
fool," he said. "Lancaster ne'er offered his hand tae Percy yet wi'out
there was a dagger in the cuff."

The few lords about the King shifted and glared upon him, but
the King signed them to silence. "I count you as a fool in truth,"
he said. "Your mother walks yonder—she who is now Lady
Camoys. Go and talk with her."

Presently when the King walked in the park lands with Archbishop Chichele, Percy returned to him. He thanked the King

stammering. "My lord," he said, "canna my sword render you thanks?"

"I need it in the north," Henry said. "I would have you stand sentinel over the Border's peace."

"Gladly will I go," Percy said. "My lord, hear me but this once. My father's bones and skull still blacken on London Bridge. Of your mercy grant that I may bear them wi' me back tae Alnwick for Christian burial in the place my father, of aal others, loved right well."

The King looked at him, remembering Hotspur in the Castle of Shrewsbury, and what he had said of his homecoming in triumph to Alnwick. "The lions on the stone bridge across the Aln will mayhap remember they are Percy and roar for me." Without intention he spoke the words aloud. Percy looked at him startled. "My lord," he said, "you knew of the bridge and its lions?"

"Your father spoke of them," Henry said. "Give him knightly burial, my lord. May God rest him and grant England of his spirit."

After Percy had gone, the King and Chichele walked on toward the river. The first bluebells bruised the grass beneath the trees, and drifts of willows screened the castle walls gray-lit among the early green. Presently Chichele spoke of Hotspur.

The King said, "He was the fashioner of my youth."

"Aye," Chichele said. "He and Richard and Glendower. Richard you brought to lie in Westminster as he had ever desired, and Glendower you would have pardoned. Thus are all debts paid."

"It was a poor and sorry payment," Henry said. "The men you spoke of—all are dead. To see their heirs fed and their bones lain honorably to rest is cold charity."

"Will you not turn your mind to the heirs of England," Chichele said. "They, too, should claim your thoughts."

He looked at Henry, but the King's face was set. "Father," he said, "who sent you to me?"

"Your brother John," Chichele said. "It troubles him that the land has no heir save Thomas. He would have you matched with your cousin of Portugal."

Henry made no answer. Beyond the paddock set in its yew hedge stood the butts, gaudy-striped among the green, and round them grouped the archers and a few of the townspeople. When they saw the King walking beyond the yew, they broke into eager cheering and crowded forward. Henry saluted them and walked back the way he had come.

"Your brother is of careful mind," Chichele said. "Yet there is much in what he says. It is to those yonder, who shout their love for you, that your duty lies."

"I cannot do it," Henry said. "Give me a year, Father—but twelve months more. Then if all hope of Kate is dead, it will be as you wish. But I cannot now set her behind me. It would kill me."

V

That winter the Dauphin Louis died in Paris. His brother, Charles, stood now in his stead—an enigmatic, closed-faced young man none could read. It was as if all things turned against Henry's enemies, but in the second week in April one of the King's ships beat into the Thames, bringing ill news from Dorset in Harfleur. Count Bernard of Armagnac had moved against the port, and Dorset lay now under siege, his castle windows looking at all points upon tents and siege guns and the standards of Armagnac and Gascony. The Count had ever been a lusty hater of England. He was free again from the sickness which had held him from Agincourt and swearing himself the avenger of his countrymen. Dorset sent he was able to hold as long as the King could victual him from the sea, but he feared that the fleets of France should likewise ring him about, bringing him to starvation and ruin.

The King awaited the state visit of Sigismund of Bohemia and was much tied. Both sides greatly courted this man, who was Emperor of the Holy Roman Empire and President of the Council of Constance and to whom much of Europe bowed. France had already had his ear, for he had wintered three months in Paris at the Court of the French King. Many Englishmen feared that he came to them already won to the cause of their enemies and that if he made peace between them it would be the peace of Charles de Valois.

Sigismund landed at Dover on the first day of May and came straightway to London, where the King awaited him at Black-heath. He came in much splendor, with five hundred men-at-arms wearing the badge of an ash-gray cross on the breasts and himself dressed in royal crimson—a man of large stature, inclining now to heaviness, bluff-mannered and smiling, but with eyes keen and swift as a lance's point. He embraced Henry and kissed him, calling him "cousin," but he did so in wariness. Throughout their journey into London by way of the river, they tried to weigh each other.

They talked in French, for Henry had no German and Sigismund only a few words of English, though he was versed in many languages. What he knew he tried hard to use, striking his forehead when the word escaped him. When he saw the throng of people lining the banks, greedy to glimpse the King, he spoke in surprise. "Is it always thus when you go abroad, cousin?" he said. "I do not walk in Prague to such cheering, yet I ever heard the English had but small love for their Kings." He looked upon the bargemen bending at their oars and the few escort, and said, "Do you never fear the assassin's knife or the poisoner's cup?"

The King smiled and said, "God has kept me from both."

"I, too, have long acquaintance with such," Sigismund said. "Seven times a murderer's sword was near my flesh. Four times was I poisoned—so thorough was it last done that my servants had to hang me three days by the heels that the poison might drain from me. 'Tis a good remedy, cousin. You yourself should use it when next you have need."

That spring—the first of Agincourt—was favored in all things, the land so deeply green that it clawed against the heart; the

great castles, gray as thunderclaps, above their curtaining trees,
turreted and merlined; the meadows that crept up to caress their
barbican walls gilded with buttercup and strewn with byronny and
thyme; the slow rivers, flowing between willow and weeping ash,
the drowsing cattle on their banks acloud in flies; the almshouses
and cloistered cathedrals; the timbered inns and trim manors,
checkered in black and white as in a picture; fair London set in
her walls, her busy river upbearing the painted sails of the King's
ships and the stately swans. Everywhere life quickened the land as
the people felt themselves grown to greatness. Seeing his realm
thus, so green and so fair, it seemed to Henry almost that his
taking of her was no longer adultery, with the putting away of
Richard between them, but a holy thing, as though their love each
for the other had hallowed his kingship.

Sigismund was eager for the sights and saw all he could. All
that he saw he praised. Yet of the great issues that hung about
France and England he would not speak. The King did not know
whether he found favor or not.

When they rode together Sigismund spoke of his meeting with
Henry's father, twenty-five years ago in Vienna. "I dwell much
on it, cousin," he said. "Your father was the Duke of Derby then
—noble-born but no more. Two years later he was an exile, and a
year thence he was King of England." He talked also of his sister,
Anne, who had been Richard's first wife, asking to see her tomb
in Westminster. It seemed the King could in no case escape
Richard's shadow. He went with Sigismund to Anne's tomb,
troubled that it was Richard's brother-in-law to whom he stood as
host. Sigismund read him shrewdly, yet talked without concern.

"Poor Anne," he said. "She was a learned little mouse and
would as lief have made a book her bedfellow as any man. Yet
they say Richard had love for her. Had she lived, cousin, she would
be fifty. Ah, but the years grant us no quarter."

"I never saw her," the King said.

"No, no," Sigismund said. "You would be but a boy. Yet no
ill came from that alliance, Bohemia and England. I have a

daughter, a fair one. What say you to a princess of Bohemia as a queen for England?"

Henry did not know if he joked. He smiled and did not answer.

"Is it still the little French fleur-de-lys?" Sigismund said. "Well, I blame you not. Thrice we pledged each other at her father's board. She smiled at me with her eyes—and they were pretty eyes, too, the prettiest in France. Yet yours is like to be a mighty long wooing, cousin."

"You talked with her, my lord," Henry said. "Is she—is she fair?"

Sigismund looked at him and laughed. "Fair enough," he said. "She has the de Valois nose." When he saw Henry's face change, he laughed even more hugely and wiped his eyes. "Nay," he said. "That was a jest, and a good one too. Her nose is the nose of an angel. She is most fair. Yet her hand is not for the enemy of her father."

Three days later, when Sigismund rode to hunt in the forests of Windsor, the King learned that what he and Dorset had feared was accomplished. Harfleur was beleaguered now from both land and sea, and the great Genoese carracks lay to, ringed across the mouth of the Lézarde. No English ship could pierce the cordon. Dorset found himself in great straits, his rations dwindling, and his men again smitten with dysentery, so that men feared he would be brought to yield.

Henry would have gone at once to his aid, but Sigismund's presence tied his hands. He could not tell which way Sigismund leaned. The English ambassadors even now sat about the council tables in Paris; but Charles felt himself stronger than at any time since Agincourt and ill disposed to talk. Many men believed he and Sigismund were already bonded together in secret treaty. The King misdoubted it yet knew that if he moved falsely he would bring upon him the full weight of Sigismund's empire. He longed for Sigismund to go, but Sigismund never spoke of it. He was a bluff, easy-mannered man, delighting in wine and hunting and fair women and speaking in praise of all the King showed him.

Henry, in spite of himself, found that he grew in liking toward him.

That night when they sat at meat, Sigismund marked his mood. Few things escaped him. He spoke to Henry in a chiding voice. "You are silent tonight, cousin," he said. "Give me of your thoughts."

"They are of Harfleur, my lord," Henry said. "I would turn to her succor."

"Be patient, cousin," Sigismund said. "I would not have you act in violence now, when we talk of treaty. You are a young man and patience is penance to the young, but take hold of it."

"I have patience, my lord," Henry said, "but my men starve."

Sigismund smiled and shrugged. "They will eat the cats and the rats," he said. "Neither is ill meat. A cat is better tasting than a rabbit; and naught to give you a queasy belly, believe me. They'll do well enough. Wait a little."

"I cannot wait," the King said. "My ambassadors and the French may yet talk for weeks around their council tables, but the men of Harfleur are hungering to death."

"Patience, patience," Sigismund said soothingly. "You're too hot upon this scent. Let us see what answer our cousin of France renders you." When he thought the King would speak again, he went on more insistently, "I am your guest, good my friend. I would take it amiss if you set aside my counsel."

The King said no more. He sat on with Humphrey and Hungerford after Sigismund had gone, fingering his wine but not drinking.

Humphrey asked, "Can they long hold at Harfleur?"

Henry answered, "Scarce more than three weeks."

"What can we do?" Hungerford said. "Sigismund's shrewd as a fox. If we make open preparation, he'll see it."

"And noise it all word by word into the ears of France, as like as not," Humphrey said. "I'd give much to see his letters that he sends his Council. Walk yarely, Harry. He'll trip you if he can."

The King looked down the long table at what was left of the

great shoulders of mutton, the sauces, the fruits, and the jellies. Hungerford knew his mind to be all of Harfleur. Presently he spoke of it. "I cannot wait," he said. "Starvation gives no quarter."

VI

On the last night of May a great storm lashed the city, hissing upon the Thames and sending the Londoners scurrying from the streets. The King had given over Westminster to Sigismund, and himself lodged at Lambeth Palace with Chichele. The Archbishop sat at work while the storm buffeted the shutters and stirred the latch of the door. After a space Henry came to him, cloaked and sodden with the rain. When Chichele bade him dry himself, he answered he must go out again. "Where, my son?" Chichele asked.

"Upon the tower with your watchmen," Henry said. "Father, when you kneel this night pray for God's blessing upon the King's arms."

"What enterprise is this?" Chichele said. "What's afoot?"

"My ships sail to the relief of Harfleur," Henry said. "They slipped their moorings but fifteen minutes ago in the Thames. John commands."

"They go on such a night?" Chichele said. "Is it wisdom?"

"The storm is their cover," the King said. "We awaited it. The Genoese and the French will not look for their coming now." He began to tell Chichele how it had been accomplished. "For twelve days we victualed the fleet in secret," he said. "Sigismund was hunting at Waltham and Canterbury. I think he suspected nothing."

"Yet it must be that he will find out," Chichele said.

The King looked at him with grimness. "Aye," he said. "I think this night's storm is as nothing to the one that comes." He moved across the floor in restlessness, his wet cloak clinging about his thighs. "I find it hard to see them go and not go with them," he said. "But for Sigismund I should be there. May heaven damn him—your pardon, Father."

While he spoke a servant came to them, round-eyed and apprehensive. "Your grace," he said. "The Emperor is here."

Sigismund stalked at his heels. He, too, was drenched for he had been rowed by wherry from Westminster Stairs, and the water dripped from the skirt of his embroidered houppelande. Three of his men-at-arms came with him, but he snarled at them in his own tongue and they fell back from the door.

Sigismund looked from the King to the Archbishop in anger. He started to speak in German, then remembering Henry did not understand it, changed to harsh French. "Cousin," he said, "I think you deal somewhat strangely with me this night. Yonder ships that beat downstream with the tide—where go they?"

"They are bound for the Narrow Seas, my lord," Henry said. "To Harfleur."

"So!" Sigismund said. "Cousin, this was dealt behind my back, and I do not like it. Did I not bid you wait? Did I not say I would take it amiss were you to move now against the French?" To Chichele he said, "And you, my lord—a holy man, a hooded head —could you not have revealed these things to me?"

Chichele half-smiled and drew his papers together. "My lord," he said, "I am sworn liege man to my King and to no other."

He bowed and left them. As he would have closed the door one of the watchmen came into the room, rubbing his hands across the wet sleeves of his jerkin. When he saw Sigismund he hesitated and checked his speech.

"Speak what you have to tell me," Henry said.

"The ships are past Greenwich, your grace," the man said. "The beacon is alight on Westminster Wharf."

He spoke in English, but Sigismund understood the words. "Cousin," he said, when the man had gone, "I am much angered. Did I think you had even small hope of success, I should be angrier."

"They have a fair, good hope of success, my lord," Henry said.

"Pah," Sigismund said. "After Agincourt I knew you for a madman. First must they do battle with the storm and then with the great fleets of France. They'll never get through." He wiped the rain from his brow with a silken kerchief and added, speaking his thoughts, "But they might."

The idea pricked him anew, and he broke out in fresh anger. "I am Emperor of the Most Holy Roman Empire, cousin, or had you forgot it? My realm could swallow the realm of England six times. I am King of Hungary and President of the Council of Constance. Even the Turk bows to me. Yet you use me thus. I take it ill. I take it very ill."

"I, too, could complain, my lord," Henry said. "Your presence has shackled me here. But for you I would be with my brother on the *Trinity's* prow."

"Take thought what you say," Sigismund said. "Do not drive me into enmity. I can range all Europe against you."

The King made no reply. Sigismund said sharply, "Speak up, cousin. Were that to happen you would not keep on?"

"My lord," Henry said, "I would have gladly clasped hands with you in friendship, but to change policy for lack of it—no, by my faith."

"Then are you more crazed than I thought," Sigismund said. "Good night to you, cousin. Bear me word how many of your ships were smitten by the storm and how many by the French, and what few crept home to you again."

VII

After a six-hour battle with the storm the English neared the Lézarde in calm. They flew no colors from their mastheads but the Frenchmen knew them, and the great carracks with their painted sides bore down upon them. With dusk the mastery went to the English, and the King's ships, bearing their grain sacks and their salted meat, ran on into Harfleur.

Henry was at Windsor when this news was brought him. Below in the bailey garden Sigismund stood at the butts, a longbow in his hands. He had never before used one, and the arrows he had unloosed prickled like quills from the trunks of the trees, only the target virgin and untouched. Behind him the pages cowered against the buttresses as for cover.

The King sent John Bromley to him with word of his ships' success. He feared he had lost all hope of Sigismund's friendship and saw both Sigismund and France leagued against him. When Bromley came back, he asked him what the Emperor had said. "He laughed, your grace," Bromley said. "He said he had not thought it possible. He sends you his felicitations."

The King said to Humphrey in bewildered fashion, "What do you make of him?"

"I know not," Humphrey said. "I thought all was lost after what he said to you that night at Lambeth."

Sigismund spent three weeks at Windsor, hunting by day and eating and drinking heartily with the King each night. All his pleasantry had returned, and he was ever eager for sport, for travel or for reveling. Each day Henry accompanied him when he rode or saw the sights, but on the Thursday, after the Feast of the Trinity, he did not come. Sigismund banqueted alone, and when he went to his chamber he did so without having spoken with the King. His windows looked out upon the royal apartments across the court, and he saw Henry working at the open casement, a quill in his hand and the Great Seal set beside him on the table. About him moved the secretaries and the grim-faced lords, all bright lit in the candlelight.

Sigismund woke at four when the sky was lightening and the first cocks were beginning to crow in the Berkshire meadows. He roused his servant and sent him to the window, asking if the King were still there. "He is still at work, most redoubted lord," the man said. "The secretaries are with him."

"So," Sigismund said. "They have gutted some few candles this night."

With the morning he rode in the park lands unattended until Walter Hungerford came to him on foot. Sigismund beamed on him, bidding him good day and inquiring after the King. "How is he?" he said. "I think he slept ill last night. Come, now, my friend, tell me the truth. What goes amiss?"

"My lord," Hungerford said, "the King sends you his greeting and renders up excuse. Yesterday the French landed at Southampton and burned it. The day previously they used Portland likewise."

"God defend us," Sigismund said. "Are you then invaded?"

"No, no," Hungerford said. "They withdrew, but their ships lie to off the Solent. We fear for all our southern coast. We know not where they will fall next."

"Aye," Sigismund said. "That method pays them best. Were many slain?"

"Not as many as we first feared," Hungerford said. "At Southampton the townsfolk recognized the carracks when they saw them in Southampton Water. Most of them fled, but the French fired the grain fields for seven miles and drove the cattle into the sea. At Portland they ravaged all the isle. The King seeks now to find food for the people, otherwise it may be they'll starve."

"This was shrewdly planned," Sigismund said. He sat musing, smoothing the folds of his saddle trappings. It seemed to Hungerford that his admiration lay now with the French. Presently he said, "Yet have you not many times suffered in like manner?"

"Aye, my lord," Hungerford said. "We have suffered thus for nigh on a hundred years."

Sigismund looked from him to the castle, gray above the trees, and to the river flowing between its rushes. "Tell me but this," he said. "You are the King's knight, Sir Walter. I think you have his heart. Will he now seek to make an end? Will he go back to France?"

"Yes," Hungerford said, "he will go back."

"Were I to oppose him?" Sigismund said. "Were I likewise to send my armies against him?"

"My lord," Hungerford said, "he will go back."

VIII

After their landing at Portland the French and Genoese fell upon the Isle of Wight. The island's strength was feeble, with only few fortifications, and they could not be withstood. No man knew where next they would strike. They lay off the Needles, the watchmen on the towers of Hurst Castle seeing them with their great sails as goshawks stooping on stiff wings above a prey.

The King now set his face on returning to France. He made preparation openly, not caring if Sigismund knew it or no. In July he went to Hythe and from thence to Southampton, where many of his ships had been burned as they lay at their moorings. The town was much stricken, the houses blackened shells, and the Bargate, where Cambridge and Scrope had met their deaths, charred and defaced. It clawed at the King's heart to see the town as though plague walked the streets where a year gone it had thrived. Yet even now the carpenters hewed at their wood among the gutted roofs and the people were returning from the abbeys and priories which had tried to give them subsistence in their flight. Their loss seemed no strange thing to them. When the King went among them, they told him how it had often been so. "Five times have I run from them," an old man said. "The first was I snatched from my cradle. It was in your grace's great-grand-da's time and all thought the town would be laid in rubble. That day the Bishop of Winchester rallied even the lads to him to drive them back, with a sword, they say, in one hand and his crucifix in the other. It goes beyond memory when the seas were quiet."

His great-grandson stood at his elbow, with a boy's eagerness to talk of his own flight. "We watched from Netley Hill," he said. "There were fires everywhere. I never saw the like with smoke and flames. I wish your grace had been there."

Henry returned to Windsor where Sigismund still lodged, escaping the summer heat which lay on London. They dined together for the first time in three weeks, the King silent and eating little. Sigismund spoke of Southampton, then asked him of his plans. "Cousin," he said, "do you return to France?"

"Aye, my lord," Henry said. "I am sorry that your journey has been fruitless and that we must part in enmity."

"Enmity?" Sigismund said. "No, no, my friend." He clapped his hands and one of his servants came in bearing a tray set with inkwells and stiff parchments and Sigismund's own seal with its great wrought handle. "This is Bruno, my good secretary," Sigismund said. "Cousin, I would have you read this when the time is convenient. It is a draft of treaty betwixt us both, that we may clasp hands and swear our friendship one to another." He looked at the King and broke into loud laughter. "Nay," he said. "Be not so surprised. We spoke hotly to each other, in truth, but you are a very stubborn young man, cousin, and I am a quarrelsome one and grown imperious. It was not possible we should walk the same ground for near on five months and not speak in anger."

The King said, "I ever thought you did not favor me."

"My mind was open when I set foot in your realm," Sigismund said. "But I have bent it much to your quarrel with France. I have studied and seen its root soil, and now it seems to me that your claims are just and your quarrel honorable."

"My lord," Henry said, "I never desired a friendship as I desired yours."

Sigismund drew his brows together and said, "Yet one thing I would know. Your great-grandsire laid claim to the throne of de Valois. We held then it was not possible the Kings of England could enforce it, but with you, cousin, I think it is no longer impossible. Should all things promise fair, would you too claim, not only your realm's lost possessions, but the throne?"

"No, my lord," Henry said. "My claim is to Normandy and Aquitaine, not to the crown."

"You'll think of the crown before you are finished, believe me," Sigismund said. "Could you hold Normandy against de Valois on your doorstep? Never. You'll be fighting till the trump of the last judgment. Yet unless you hold Normandy your ports burn and your ships sink and the land languishes."

The King said, "I'll not die King of France though I were crowned it."

Sigismund looked upon him with lowered brows as if he strove to read him. "Cousin," he said, "shall I tell you what I thought to find in you—a lordly young man, swollen fat with success and blown with his own fame; but it is not so. I think you know a dream. Be frank with me. If England were so secure in her strength that she feared none, and France were in quietness so that you might turn your back on her, where would your steps lead?" Henry did not at once answer, and Sigismund spoke for him. "To Palestine, my friend? Is it not so?"

"You read me well, my lord," Henry said.

"A fourth crusade?" Sigismund said. "The old dream of the Kings of England, yet it broke in pieces before against the walls of Jerusalem."

"Was it not a dream worth the dying for?" Henry said. "Since I was a boy, my lord, these things have stirred me. It has often seemed to me that to see the Holy Cross flying again from the walls of Jerusalem would heal the great breach of Christendom and unite all Europe."

"It may be so," Sigismund said. "These things are near to my heart also, cousin; but the world was young then, and now it grows old and the paladins are passed. Soon only the Kings of England will still dream of Jerusalem." He smiled and said, "Were you in my country I could show you the Castle of Durnstein, a day's journey from Vienna. There a Plantagenet King lay imprisoned four years after he withdrew his steps from the Holy Land."

"The Lionheart," Henry said.

"Aye," Sigismund said. "Richard of Anjou. Yet are not the Kings of England bred—each one—with the heart of a lion in battle?" The King flushed and could find no answer. Sigismund broke into loud laughter and began to mock him. "What, cousin," he said, "I praise you and you blush like a country wench. I have known many Kings, but none your like."

Henry answered him in a troubled voice. "My lord," he said, "you're kin to Richard by marriage, and I'll make no pretense with you. You know it was no straight road that led me to this throne."

"I know it," Sigismund said. He leaned toward the King, speaking with earnestness. "Take counsel from me," he said. "I am a King likewise. They bind great vows upon us at our hallowings. Yet we are men still for all the Holy Oil of consecration; and our flesh remains flesh and subject to this world's ills—to death, to woundings, to hunger and weariness and running sores, to cold and sickness. Bend a little, cousin. Take hold on pleasure. I have twice your years. I am old enough to have sired you, yet I think that I shall still be wearing my crown when you lie in your tomb." When Henry made no answer, he looked at him somberly. "I counsel you for your good," he said. "No King who set his kingship thus high ever made old bones."

IX

A year later, when it was chill October, the King lay encamped with his army against Rouen. The Normandy coast was his, and for the time he stood master of the Narrow Seas, but the French would neither parley nor fight with him, but stored and garrisoned the two great towns of Caen and Rouen against him and fed the castles of Normandy, so that his campaign was to him as the long sick toil of Harfleur and not the swift glory of Agincourt. He knew the nobles of the French King to have learned wisdom and the task he had set himself to be harsh and long.

On the fourteenth day of the siege Walter Hungerford saw men running together on the outskirts of the camp. Talbot and the King had ridden out to view the displacements, and Hungerford called to Talbot's squire, fearing for them.

The boy bore his master's shield and looked white and harassed.

"It is Lord Talbot," he said. "He's smitten in the arm. The King cast his own shield over him and crouched with him until the knights went to his aid. They were hurling all manner of missiles upon us from the walls."

The knights rode slowly into the camp, bearing Talbot in their midst. He had gone out unhelmed, and for all he clasped his shoulder and was blood drenched, his great grizzled head was still uplifted. The King rode behind, dust spattered and likewise bloodied. He watched with set face as the knights put Talbot to the ground. Talbot would not have them bear him into his tent. He walked without aid, though stiffly as if his shoulder were braced in staves. Hungerford did not like his look. To the King he said, "My lord, how did it come about?"

"It was a sally from the north gate," Henry said. "They led us back too close beneath the crossbowmen."

Talbot seemed at first to mend, but on the fourth day his strength was less and the flesh of the wound was still unknit and odorous. The King greatly feared for him. He who previously had appeared to all men, in the face of the blackest calamity, to keep a cheerful countenance now went about the camp grim and troubled. There was ill news also from London, though the messengers believed that they carried good and spoke heartily. "My lord," the spokesman said, "we have good tidings from your lord brother. Oldcastle is taken."

Oldcastle was he whom the King, in the first few weeks of his reign, had contrived to let escape from the Tower after sentence for heresy. He had long believed Oldcastle to be beyond the law's vengeance, safe as Glendower had known safety in the bastion of the Welsh mountains. He well knew of the many Lollard plots Oldcastle had set afoot for his life, yet his flesh crawled at the thought of Oldcastle going to the sentence Arundel had passed upon him seven years gone. It seemed to him that the messengers' words blew into his nostrils the stench of burning flesh.

As by custom, he went to Talbot's tent after he had heard vespers. The page and the squire who sat there scrambled to their feet and withdrew. Talbot was propped on the raised pallet, his face beneath his grizzled brows yellowing and cracked as a mummer's mask. There was no strength in the hand that lay above the bed coverings. The King talked with him cheerfully, but Talbot lay watching him and presently asked him what troubled him.

"Troubles me?" Henry said. "Nothing—save I would have you in health again."

"Is it that there's ill news from home?" Talbot said. "My lord, I have been with you a long time. I should take it kindly were you to tell me."

The King said, "Oldcastle is taken."

"After these many years," Talbot said. "How, my lord?"

"He ventured into Shrewsbury," Henry said. "A friar recognized him in the streets and led the officers to his lodging house."

Talbot said, "Do these men go rewarded?"

"We'll pay them what we promised," Henry said. "I would we could thrust it down their throats and choke them with it." He rose from the stool and began to move about the tent. "I've racked my wits all day," he said. "If I could bid John make the charge treason and not heresy, I would do it; yet he is already convicted and I know not if I can."

"You'll be too late, my lord," Talbot said. "And you should thank God for it. That man is thrice your enemy—your body's foe, your land's foe, and your faith's. Did you not vow you would no more shield him if he were taken?"

"The man I vowed it to is dead," Henry said. "He was dying then, and I vowed it to ease him."

"I do not think it less to keep faith with the dead than with the living," Talbot said. "My lord, what can you do? He knew his road would lead him to the stake."

Within a week Dorset reached the camp from Calais, bringing news of Oldcastle's death. Henry knew now he had been dead before the tidings of his capture had reached France. He asked how Oldcastle had met his end.

"With much courage," Dorset said. He spoke grudgingly, for he had long hated Oldcastle, laying at his door all the Lollard threats to the King's life. "There was no repentance in him. To the end he spoke of his brave new faith, saying it stirred the dust which lay upon men's souls, freeing them from popes and cardinals and the hand of Rome; and setting to each man salvation by the light of his own conscience and not by papal edicts. I never heard the like, Harry. His tongue dripped heresy."

"He was always a brave man," Henry said.

"Brave as a madman," Dorset said. "And with murder in his heart to you. God's peace, waste no pity on him. If he had taken you at St. Giles's Field he would have dealt with you as we have dealt with him. While he lived, I went in fear for you."

The King folded his brother's letter in his hand and went to the tent flap. It was November now and growing chill, with the morning frost rimming the bare trees and iron turf. "He asked no pity," he said. "It's well, for he got none. What came upon us that I could use him more hardly than any other man?"

He spoke no more of it, but all that week went about his task of reducing Rouen. The town was in great straits and seeking terms, but the King demanded their total yielding and would not talk with their heralds as long as they spoke of conditions. He had small pity for the town. It was Rouen that had cast the guns which had long fed Glendower in his mountains, and it had been here, in the streets of Rouen, that the Dauphin had sworn to sell the living fingers of the English bowmen at a blanc apiece. Many of the English, kinder than their King, wondered at it. Men marked him now as a stranger, hard faced, and with his chivalry stale about him.

Talbot likewise urged him to receive the heralds and grant the city terms.

"I cannot do it," Henry said. "If I invite further siege, I pay for it in the blood of my soldiers."

"Aye, my lord," Talbot said. "You are right. I have thanked God I am not a man who is right thus often as you are."

The King said in a low voice, "Yet am I not a man. I am the King of England and the one bastion of my soldiers. If you should come upon me, here or hereafter, when I am no more than a man, I pray you use me with charity."

"My dear lord," Talbot said, "will you not use charity upon yourself? Will you rend the French for what has come upon Oldcastle and for what is about to come upon me?"

Henry looked at him in dread. Talbot met his look with such stillness of face that he felt his heart chill. "What do you talk of?" he said. "I hold you dearer to me than ever I held Oldcastle."

"I know what comes upon me, my lord," Talbot said. "This wound does not heal."

"It does heal," Henry said. "Let it have time." He began to talk in forced fashion of his plans of sending Talbot back to England. "I would have you go as soon as you have strength," he said. "The Welsh air has healing in it. Why did you follow me this time, Gilbert? Was the long hard road I took you from Harfleur to Calais not enough?"

"My lord, I would have followed you whithersoever you led," Talbot said. "And I never sought death but by battle. When I think by what means men die, by the plague or starvation in the streets, by the stake or leprosy or rotting diseases, it seems to me there are many worse ends than a clean sword thrust in God's air. So did I welcome it."

Henry said fiercely, "God's peace, why must you talk after this manner? It's not so. You mend."

He sat on with Talbot while the daylight darkened, and the pages came bearing tapers. It seemed to him the stench of death lay in the tent, no longer to be gainsaid. When he summoned the physicians, both said the pulse had not changed. Talbot urged him to his own bed, and he left him unwillingly. Colnet followed him, and the King asked him what should happen.

"I know not," Colnet said. "I do not like his look."

Henry said, "Rouse me, if he should worsen."

He went to his own tent. His three squires of the body waited there to unclothe him. He sent them from him and cast himself down on the bed, lying without sleep until one of the pages came to rouse him.

Talbot lay racked with harsh breathing, the two physicians and Thomas Elmham by his bed and Dorset and Hungerford standing by the tent flap. When the King bent over him, he seemed to rally a little and his yellowing lids flickered. "My lord," he said, "is it you?"

"Yes," Henry said. "Yes, Gilbert."

"I have this to ask of you, my lord," Talbot said. "For your own sake, grant Rouen terms."

"Yes," Henry said again. "It shall be as you desire. I so promise."

"I know you for a keeper of your word," Talbot said. Presently he stirred in the bed and spoke again. "We quit your service together," he said. "Oldcastle and I. Let it not grieve you, my lord."

Henry could not find words to answer him. He sat for two hours beside Talbot's bed until he and the others who kept vigil with him knew him to be dead. The King closed Talbot's eyes himself, men reckoning this much honor. When he had done, he went from them and gained the lonely shelter of his own tent.

x

The King spoke with the heralds next day and four days later Rouen yielded to him. Though he gave the city its terms, granting the garrison the full honors of war, it seemed to men it was Talbot's charity and not Harry's that did so. They saw him since Talbot's death as grown hard, given to cold rages that blew up suddenly upon him. It seemed now that all the fury of the Plantagenets was his and that it lay loosely leashed beneath the surface.

Rouen was the second city of France, and its yielding was a great buffet in the face of the French King. Henry could now in truth style himself Duke of Normandy, a title more ancient to his line than that of King of England. He brought all his skill of governance to the city, setting open markets where the towns-folk and those from the surrounding countryside could freely trade. The poor had justice above any they had yet known; yet the wear of Rouen's winning had been great and, after Agincourt, the King found the taste of his victory cold in his mouth.

Talbot's loss was sharper to him than any he had suffered since his crowning. It seemed to him he could not set his love upon any man without losing him. Percy, Scrope, and Oldcastle had gone from him in treason; Aumerle and Talbot in loyal service. To think of them was like fingering separate scars. He felt their hurt as other men felt old wounds, sorest in stress or weariness.

All was very ordered now. The King would suffer none of his army to thieve or plunder or force a woman and fell in fury upon the only man who did. No other dared disobey him, the bowmen reckoning his watchfulness as a hawk's. Men marveled at the grip he kept upon his soldiers, recalling that even the Black Prince had failed to bridle them before. Umfraville spoke of it in the castle keep to Dorset, saying presently, "Does he yet sit at his papers?"

"When does he ever leave them?" Dorset said. "It frets me to see him as he is." He spoke gloomily of Talbot's death and how it had struck at the King. "More than any man Harry grieves for him," he said. "I would to God I could see him weep over it. Richard raged often. Many times I saw him hurl at his lords whatever came to his hand, inkwells or books or purses. Once he snatched Aumerle's hat from his head and kicked it across the room. Yet I think now his raging kept him in his wits. It is with Harry as though he binds himself with iron."

"It is because he finds himself anointed and crowned," Hunger-ford said, "yet believing himself no King. I know how it is with him. He must be twice the King other men are."

"He cannot keep on," Dorset said. "It's madness."

He left them and went to the small circular stone room in the west turret in which the King worked. Richard Holme, the King's secretary, met with him on the threshold, his arms filled with papers and annotations set with their seals. Dorset sent him away, saying he had business with the King. When Henry saw his uncle, he greeted him shortly and asked where Holme was.

"Let him be," Dorset said. "The day's fine, Harry. Come, we'll take falcons and ride."

"How can I?" Henry said. "Is there not work enough here?"

"Your father often spoke those words," Dorset said. "You had his look there when you said it."

The King glanced at him sharply. Dorset began to urge him again to set aside his work and take some pleasure. "You'll kill yourself," he said. "What is there to spoil here if it were left for tomorrow?"

"Oh, let me be," Henry said. "I did not come into France to play games."

"Afore God, Harry," Dorset said, "I wish there were a Chepe tavern round the corner and you were sat there at your ale."

The King half-smiled and said, "You never wished it, Uncle, when I were."

"I wish it now," Dorset said. "I'd gladly see you in your cups this night. Must it be that you shut up all things within you?"

The King answered him with a look of impatience and turned back to his work. "Nay, but listen to me," Dorset said. "It would grieve me less if you were wedded and had your lady to set her hand in yours. I'd liefer have you matched with the dullest-faced troll in Europe than as you are now—monk, for a woman you never saw, and never will see unless there's a miracle for us."

Henry lifted his head and Dorset saw he was angered. He hoped he would unleash his rage, but the King read his purpose. He went to the window, then turned back smiling. "Uncle," he said, "you are more to me than any man. I know not how to repay the long debt I owe you."

On a sudden something caught his eye from the casement and he beckoned Dorset to him. A little group of horsemen rode toward the town, their azure tabards aglint in the pale sun and each leader flanked with two trumpeters in black and gold.

"Heralds," Dorset said. "In faith, Harry, it cannot be."

"It is," Henry said. "From Burgundy, Uncle, I swear it. He would never send to me but to hear my terms."

He waited with impatience until the heralds were brought to him. They knelt, each holding his silver-tipped staff athwart his knee. "My lord," the spokesman said. "The King of England?"

"The King of England," Henry said. "Who sends you, herald?"

"The Duke of Burgundy, so please your grace," the man said. "And in his name the Queen of France sends also. They give you greeting and would meet with you fairly to hear your terms and fairly to give you answer on them."

That Burgundy should thus desire a meeting between them was beyond all that the King had hoped. Never had the heralds of France come to him with such deference in their mouths. He talked with them for a long time, sending greetings to Burgundy and the Queen and binding himself to meet with them as soon as it should please them. As the heralds were about to go, the spokesman gave into Dorset's hands a flat leather casket fastened with gold clasps. "As touching one of the King's demands," he said, "the Duke bids me give him this."

The King thanked him, waiting until they had gone. Dorset stood with the casket in his hands and spoke exultantly. "Last time when their heralds spoke with you by the Somme, it was with rougher tongues. Now they bow and bring gifts."

"Open it, Uncle," Henry said. When Dorset was long in speaking, he laughed and asked, "Is it more tennis balls?"

"No, no," Dorset said. "It is something you'll like better. See, my lord."

He showed Henry what he had taken from the casket. It was a portrait set on vellum and bound upon strips of wood, so freshly done that the paint seemed almost to glisten wet upon it. Henry saw Katherine's face looking out upon him. He had carried her image with him since he had first looked upon her likeness six years ago in the Tower. Then she had been a child, barely fifteen, grave, with her laughter masked. Now he saw her as she had become, twenty-one, full grown and most fair, with all her laughter gay upon her like a bright cloak. He knew himself to have been right and that he could love no other. The six years' toil that lay between his first sight of her painted likeness and this was as a lifetime, and he felt himself ache for her as a wretch imprisoned in a dungeon might ache for the feel of the sun upon his shackled limbs.

XI

Burgundy professed himself eager to speed the meeting between himself and the King. The place of meeting was midway between Meulan and Mézy, near the Île de Seine, a place of meadows and woods only, bordered by the river on the south and on the north by marshlands, where at night the frogs croaked and the waterfowl cried thinly. Tall chestnuts stood about it, stiff in blossom, for it was now late May. It seemed to the King greatly suited for a lovers' trysting as in the old tales of forests and green glades, wherein the knights had ridden with their ladies.

Both French and English came with great pomp, each side striving to outdo the other in splendor. The French lodged at Meulan, but Burgundy pitched tents for himself and his lords on the eastern half of the place of meeting, with a vast pavilion of cloth-of-gold set in the center. Henry pitched to the west, with his army farther back in an area fenced off with stakes, beyond which the soldiers had not to come. This was at Burgundy's desire, for the French feared to be within range of the bowmen. Many of the English were offended that their trust was reckoned at so little, but the King would take no umbrage. He came in his robes at the head of his lords to await the Queen before the great golden pavilion. His heralds stood about him in their scarlet and azure tabards, and behind them the three pursuivants, Blue Mantle, Rouge Croix, and Portcullis, in their crimson cloaks and bearing their white wands. The French approached from the east in a great company, Queen Isabeau borne in a litter hung with blue damask, her ladies round her. She alighted by the tents, and with Burgundy came over the grass. The English saw her stoop-shouldered in her splendid gown of cloth-of-gold, little, black-browed, black Italian-eyed, foul-mouthed and sensual. When she saw the tall King, her face quickened for an instant as a brach might quicken to a hound or a Cock Lane harlot to a young lord. Yet she bore herself in manner as a queen, bowing to Henry and kissing him on both cheeks. All the world named Burgundy her lover. He followed close upon her heels, a man of large stature, florid, smiling and still stamped with a bold high countenance which in his handsome youth had led men to call him "Jean sans Peur." Yet he was not a bold man, and many now questioned it. He too kissed the King on both cheeks, slightly inclining the knee, and Henry, remembering the many times he had nearly become Burgundy's son-in-law, gave him his hand.

"Cousin, we greet you well," Isabeau said. "I stand here for my husband, the King. His sickness is upon him. He cannot come."

"It makes no matter, cousin," Burgundy said. He set his hand on the King's shoulder in friendly fashion and smiled upon him. "We are here as his tongue and his ears. All will be conveyed back to him when his mind is cleared. I pledge it."

"It is always thus with him in the summer," Isabeau said. "When the leaves fall it will pass."

She stood talking for some little time, but she would not yet go into the pavilion. More and more French were coming to gather about Burgundy's tent, lords on fine horses and a few ladies on their palfreys. Isabeau looked toward them and smiled at the King. "I did not come here alone of my house, cousin," she said. "There is one other with me. I pray you wait."

She went back a short way to where the bedecked ladies had dismounted. One in bright green stood in their midst, her great skirts spread about her. Isabeau took her wrist to bring her forward on a jerk, then angrily twitched at her kirtle to set it into place.

The girl waited as one much used to such dealings until all was set to rights. Henry knew her to be Katherine. He saw her as he had long seen her in the mists of the Welsh mountains or in the mud of Agincourt. She came forward with her mother leading her by the hand, her skirts atrail behind her over the sunlit grass. There were silver bells stitched about the neck of her gown, with two each at the wrists where the undersleeves of her violet kirtle showed, and her small head was swathed in a jeweled silken coif, fold on fold, like the petals of a flower.

Never shall I forget the green gown, and the arm full of violets.
That love was armed withall when first she conquered me.

Burgundy surveyed her in satisfaction. "A pretty gown, is it not?" he said. "It should be, in truth. It cost us a hundred florins." He checked himself, but the King scarcely heard. Isabeau came to him, smiling again. All her black look of anger when she had twitched straight the kirtle was gone. She was smaller than her daughter, and her thin fingers, stiff in their rings, looked like claws about Katherine's hand.

"This is the youngest of my nestlings, cousin," she said. "This is Katherine. She is as yet a silly girl withal but she has some beauty. Nor does she lack instruction, cousin, in all things needful to a King's court."

Katherine made to bow, but the King raised her. He served her as Isabeau and Burgundy had served him, kissing her first on one cheek and then on the other. "Welcome, cousin," he said. "I would greet you in French fashion."

Presently Burgundy brought both sides into the pavilion to talk. His own son, Philip of Charolois, stood with him, a young man, cold-voiced and as chill of manner as Burgundy was hearty. Also nearby stood the Count St. Pol, Burgundy's nephew, who had escorted Katherine from Paris. It had been his father who had led the French upon Devon and died there when Henry had been seventeen and Lancaster greatly buffeted on the throne. Both he and the King remembered it and looked hard at each other. He was of Henry's age, of much elegance and seeming to lack all the soldierly gifts which had brought his father's landing in England close to success. The King judged him an enemy but of small consequence.

The French princess sat still as a mouse on her velvet chair, but she could not keep her eyes from the King. When their glances met, she flushed in confusion, the color creeping up from her throat out of the silken barbette she wore under her chin. She was grave now as in her portraits, but under it he marked her light of heart and merry as a spring day. He knew himself lost to her, seeing her even beyond his dreams. It seemed strange to him now that he had found patience to wait six years with no more than the dream of her to hold in his arms.

Isabeau began to speak of the issues between them, oftentimes setting her thin fingers upon the King's arm. Many who watched judged her willing to play harlot to the King, but Henry's mind was full of Kate and he took no note of it. "Your great-grandsire claimed the throne of France, cousin," Isabeau said. "To the great hurt of our house. Is it to be so with you?"

"I do not seek it, lady," Henry said. He spoke of Aquitaine, long promised to England but never restored, and of Normandy, out of which had grown all the English realm. Isabeau listened with seeming favor, promising to convey all back to Paris.

"I shall come again, cousin," she said, "and render you our answer." She took her leave of him graciously and of his lords. Kate rose too and bowed to him without speech, for it was not seemly that they should talk with each other yet except in greeting. When she went back to her palfrey, she turned her head that she might yet look upon him and his eyes clung to her.

Burgundy came to walk with the King by the river's margin. "Then you do not look to the throne, cousin?" he said. "Were we to render Normandy and Aquitaine into your hands, you would rest content?"

"Aye, my lord duke," Henry said. "They are the full sum of our demands."

"The full sum," Burgundy said and laughed. "The full sum. Come, cousin, what of that which holds your eyes—the fair little Paris flower yonder. What of her?"

The King smiled and said, "You speak just, my lord. If it pleases her, I would ask her likewise."

"It does not please her ill," Burgundy said. He winked and spread wide his hands. "Cousin, I should be grieved at this. Have you not turned your back these many times on my poor Anne? I would have gladly seen you bedded with her or her sister—they are good girls both and good breeders of heirs, I'll warrant, yet yonder's the green gown you would have. Well, I blame you not." He set his hand on the King's arm and walked with him, pace for pace, along the cool grass. "All will be as you desire, I am sure," he said. "Charles will gladly abide by these terms."

"Will the Dauphin Charles, my lord?" Henry asked.

"Pah," Burgundy said. "A sullen, heavy youth. Take no heed of him, cousin. Will you come to this place again to hear our final answer?"

"Willingly," Henry said. "When would you have me here?"

"In a month's time," Burgundy said carelessly. "Let us say July —the third of July, another Wednesday."

"It's six weeks," Henry said. "My lord, I would have it sooner."

"We cannot do it," Burgundy said. "The King's wits are scattered and we can but hasten slowly." When Henry would have spoken again, he clapped him on the shoulder, laughing. "Have patience," he said. "You are eager for sight of your green gown and all time's a laggard to you. Yet six weeks is not long. Deal patiently with us now, and she'll be yours before August is upon us."

The King answered it would be as he wished. Burgundy again bent the knee to him in leave-taking. "Till then farewell, cousin," he said. He gave the King a sidelong glance, sly and smiling, though his manner was broad and open as the wind. "We are at truce till then?"

"Aye," the King said. "Would you have me pledge it?"

"No, no," Burgundy said. "Your word suffices." Isabeau's litter was leaving the clearing, Kate riding beside her, and he watched them go with satisfaction. "I wonder that yon witless dotard in Paris could have sired her," he said. "There's none so pretty in the realm. Nonetheless, cousin, I'll warrant you'll find a jade in Mézy comely enough to make shift with until all's signed and sealed on the treaty and I bring the princess hither for your bed."

It seemed to Henry useless to seek to explain. He went from Burgundy back to his waiting lords without an answer. All the way Burgundy's eyes followed him. The King might have recalled the eyes of Hotspur and Northumberland following him in Shrewsbury Castle in like manner fifteen years ago, but his mind was full of Kate and he did not mark it.

XII

The King kept strictly to the truce and did nothing to renew his campaign. He believed his task in France almost accomplished and saw his great dreams realized, with his land at peace and unmenaced and for his Queen the lady of his heart. Not since his hallowing had he known such hopes. He rode in July to keep his tryst with Burgundy in blinding sunshine, as though all things matched his expectations. Dorset rode at his side and spoke of Burgundy. "I did not like him," he said. "Sigismund told me of him in London. A smiling, all-hailing fellow, he said, ever ready to clap you on the back, yet forgetting to take the knife from his hand when he did so."

The King said, "Yet it was he who sent to treat with us. For that I'll count him my life's friend."

"Better to count him that than your father-in-law," Dorset said. "What say you, Harry?"

The King laughed, flinging back his head. The sun was on his face and the horses moved easefully over turf, sweet smelling and yielding. "In faith, Uncle," he said, "it is with me as the words of the psalm—'all my bones rejoice.'"

By noon of the second of the month they had reached the place of their former meeting. The river ran lower now than it had done in May, for the summer drought lay on the land and the reeds stood tall in their shallows. There was yet no sign of Burgundy nor of any Frenchman, and all was quiet, the trees hanging still and breathless above the river.

Once the bowmen were camped Henry went among them as was his custom to see they had all things needful to them. Many of the men of Agincourt still followed him, and he spoke with Reeve, who had never quit his service. Reeve asked if they must remain behind the barriers as previously.

"Suffer it this once," the King said. "We are making an end. You'll be home by Christmas."

"It'll come strangely to me," Reeve said. "I'll know not how to fill my days."

The King said, "Does it not please you?"

"Either way it contents me," Reeve said. "If it is peace—well; and if not—then well again, for we'll keep on with the task."

The next day was the third, the day arranged for the meeting. Till dusk the sentries kept watch on the Meulan road, but Burgundy did not come. Henry waited one more day, then sent Gilbert de Umfraville with heralds to glean news from the surrounding hamlets.

The lords awaited his return in small groups, speaking little. The hot air seemed to them now full of foreboding as before a storm, and the pleasant riverside meadow, where the tents of Burgundy and France and the great cloth-of-gold pavilion had stood, lay empty and arid about them. The cry of the bittern above the marshes came to them in their silence as a mock.

The King walked alone by the river's edge. He knew himself now to have been tricked, but his mind still closed against it. He paced as if in thought so that his lords saw only his straight back and bent head. Umfraville rode back at last into the camp, the dust of his journey whitely upon him. Henry said, "Well, friend?"

Umfraville answered him slowly. "Burgundy does not come," he said. "Today he was proclaimed Regent of France."

"Burgundy?" Dorset said. "Without the connivance of de Valois?"

"Oh, he has that," Umfraville said. "He and the Dauphin Charles are pledged friends. Burgundy sent to him seven weeks ago—five days before he sent to us."

The lords shifted and stared upon each other. "He came to us pledged to the Dauphin?" Camoys said. "He pretended to seek treaty with us after he had kissed the Dauphin's hand?"

"He proclaims that by next spring he will hold all Normandy and have us into the sea," Umfraville said. "He boasts openly of his treachery. When the Dauphin Charles asked him how he had dealt with us, Burgundy laughed and said he had made the King of England look a——" He fumbled in his speech and used the French phrase, "Un beau nient."

"A fine fool," Henry said bitterly. "Right. He says true." He struck the trunk of the tree he stood by a single blow with his hand, then rested upon it. His lords saw that he shook with anger, but he kept it from his face. They looked at each other, not daring to speak.

"And the six weeks of truce I kept for him?" Henry said at last. "He's used them well, I'll warrant."

"He used them to strengthen all defenses," Umfraville said reluctantly. "Paris is strong fortified now, so is Pontoise. They say Meulan's granaries are near bursting with grain, sufficient to withstand a siege of eighteen months."

The King twisted his mouth and said, "What of Katherine?" When Umfraville hesitated he said, "Let me hear it."

"She is in Paris," Umfraville said. "Burgundy greatly desires to marry her to his nephew, St. Pol, but I do not think the Dauphin Charles favors it. He fears the match will place too much power in Burgundy's hands. For the moment he withstands it."

"Aye, for the moment," the King said. He paced toward the

river, then came back toward them with decision. "Paris is no great way," he said. "From Rouen I could be there in eight days."

"My lord, hear me," Dorset said. "Burgundy has so strengthened the land that he goes in no fear of you. Such a move is what he hopes for."

"Let him have what he hopes," the King said. "He'll rue it at the finish."

"Afore God, Harry," Dorset said, "you spoke once before of leading yon poor fellows to another place hence in eight days—do you not remember?"

The King checked and looked at him. "Aye, you are right," he said at last. "It is not to be thought of." To Umfraville he said, "Thanks to you, Gil. This news was not easily come by."

"I could wish it made better hearing," Umfraville said. "It's as though my tongue were traitor."

XIII

The King withdrew his men and for the night lodged hard by Mézy. The little town was stocked with summer plenty, and the villagers, when they saw the tents, came to the outskirts of the camp to sell to the English soldiers. One of the peasant girls called to the King, setting her basket against her hips. "See, lord," she said, "these cheeses would well grace your table."

One of the soldiers would have set her from their path, but she saw the King's eyes upon her and thrust him off. "Let me be," she said, "all here is meet for a King."

She gave the King a harlot's glance, sidelong and knowing. He saw her as a tawdry imitation of Kate, French likewise and of Katherine's height and fair fresh skin. It seemed to him he would come no nearer Kate than her. He said, "Let her stay."

He went into his own tent and cast off his cloak. Dorset and Hungerford stood with him, seeing him as if he had been a stranger. His calm was more troubling to them than if he had raged.

Dorset said at last, "Would you have that French brach outside?"

"She's willing," Henry said. "Does it fret you?"

"I fear for you," Dorset said. "I scarce know you this night. Never have I seen you so smitten."

"Get you to your bed, Uncle," Henry said. "You, too, Walter. You're weary."

When they had gone Thomas Elmham, his confessor, came to him. Henry was dearly fond of him, for he had been brought up in the priesthood by Chichele and seemed to the King possessed of the Archbishop's spirit. Yet he greeted him irritably, asking who had sent him. "Your lord uncle," Elmham said. "My son, have you forgot the Lady Katherine? Was it not in some measure for her that you kept yourself clean these many years?"

"To what end, Father?" Henry said. "I had hoped for her this night—and not for her only, but for peace. In both was I their dupe. She will never be mine. I know it now."

"She is not yet another man's," Elmham said.

"Not yet," Henry said. "She will be. Leave it so, Father. I am sick of this day's work. I seek some ease."

"Your flesh is not your own," Elmham said. "Were you not thus in the Abbey hallowed King?"

The King broke into hard laughter. "It means naught," he said. "Let me be."

Elmham went from him and he stood alone in the tent. His mind was of St. Pol in Burgundy's great pavilion, a perfumed gallant, primped and bejeweled, with his hand about Kate's. Of all thoughts this was the most tormenting. He felt the day's disappointment upon him like a sickness, long festered by the six years of his waiting.

Bromley came into the tent to unclothe him. He had but lately married a young wife, and he was downcast, knowing himself now to be still far from her. "May Burgundy rot in hell," he said. "It's full twelve months now since I left Alys. It is long to lack sight or touch of her."

"Long in truth," the King said. "Is there no woman else for your pleasure?"

Bromley looked surprised. "Nay, my lord," he said. "I'll lie cold until I lie again with her. I love her dearly. We are pledged."

The King turned from him as in self-contempt. Bromley lit the tapers and set them about the bed. "I talk of myself," he said. "Yet your grace's case is worse. It has fallen out so ill for you. Of a truth, my lord, I am sorry." When the King made no answer, he feared he had said too much and stood hesitantly at the door. "Is there naught else?" he said. "All's quiet save there's a woman yonder by the sutlers' wagons. I know not who she is."

The King spoke an oath and said, "Give her five silver crowns and send her away."

When Bromley was returned, he went to the King's bed. Bromley's young puckered face was lit by the candles, and the King felt his own troubles less. "God keep you, John," he said. "I would have you back with Alys soon."

XIV

With morning Henry prepared to make his journey back to Rouen. He spoke with Hungerford in bitterness, naming himself the "beau nient" Burgundy had styled him.

"How could you know?" Hungerford said. "It would stick in my throat less if they had not met us with such smiles and fair blandishments." He sought to speak cheerfully to ease the King. "We'll keep on, nonetheless," he said. "Next time they send to you it will be to grant what you ask—Normandy and Aquitaine."

The King stood silent, his head tilted back against the upright of the tent. Hungerford saw his face set and hardened. Without knowing why, he felt chilled. Presently the King said, "More do I ask now. I ask the throne."

Hungerford said, "My lord?"

The King said in a low voice, "Afore God, Walter, I have borne all I can bear from the house of de Valois."

"Aye," Hungerford said. "They've greatly buffeted you."

"Sigismund told me there would be no way but this," Henry said, "I know now he spoke true. What if I come to treaty with one of them—with Burgundy or King or Dauphin or Armagnac's heirs? They will each say they speak for France, yet in two months another will snatch power and all will be repudiated. We'll never have done with the fight, and our strength is small against theirs and will grow wan. If we want peace, we must bind it upon them."

Hungerford said, "Can this be yours?"

"It will not fall to me," Henry said. "But to my son—the son my French Kate shall bear me. If I never vowed aught before, I have vowed this—she'll yet be mine and our son shall inherit Plantagenet and de Valois."

"This was your great-grandsire's dream," Hungerford said. "He found France vast."

"I'll set no foot south of the Seine," Henry said. "Let the Dauphin rule there if he will, but north of it I'll make him a bastard in his father's house. I've been fool to de Valois long enough. God's peace, Walter, is there a man among them who would not cheat us of all things before the wax lay cold on the treaty." He went to the door of the tent and looked out across the yellowing cornfields and the wooded slopes. "I have thought on it before," he said. "If it could be that a Frenchman was likewise a citizen of England and Englishmen plied their trade here as men of France. We have a common stock and common laws. Could not a King, bred from both Plantagenet and de Valois, so knit together these realms that all would be bound together in unity and strength?" He spoke eagerly now, as if the dream warmed him. "Thus would all our labor come to great ends," he said. "England and France so enjoined could set their peace on Europe for a hundred years."

"They could in truth," Hungerford said. "But will they? Our toil here has been long—through four reigns, from your great-grandfather's time to yours. Will this not make it longer—too long for our strength?"

"There is no way else," the King said again. "They will honor no treaty they pen. I dare not trust them more."

Hungerford saw him resolved. Only he doubted the King's wisdom in this. Dorset and his lords, after Henry had spoken with them in the same fashion, urged him to go the way he planned, remembering the previous times he had spoken of impossible ends and rendered them achieved. Yet Burgundy sat strong in Paris and in face of that all their talk seemed airy as the September mists.

xv

In November Henry sent his heralds into Paris with jewelry for Kate worth three thousand crowns that his gold- and silversmiths had fashioned. The English were skilled in this craft, and the rings and combs and collars, the ouches and crosses and worked pouches were in all ways most beautiful. None reached Kate, the French robbing the heralds at the gates of Paris and murdering the carriers. The King knew his gifts to be scattered among the city harlots or sent to purchase cannons and crossbows against himself.

He showed anger no more, but was calm and as tender of his men as he had ever been. Yet Hungerford knew him to have all but despaired of Katherine, waking each morning to thoughts that this day would surely see her betrothed to St. Pol and thus, in the eyes of the Church, bound to him as by marriage. With spring the King moved against Pontoise, swift taking it. Burgundy had left the castle strong fortified and believed it to be impregnable. All men held Pontoise the key to Paris, and Burgundy moved now in fear, ill suiting his nickname "Jean sans Peur." When Henry was at Gisors thirty miles from Paris, he sent ambassadors to him, unbeknown to the Dauphin Charles, and offered his hand by treaty. The King would not see them and sent them back without audience.

On the last day of May, when the King sat at meat in Gisors Castle, a servant came to him in haste from the courtyard. "My lord," he said, "it is the Duke of Burgundy. He casts himself on your most knightly chivalry."

"What!" Dorset said. "God's peace, Harry, he has good impudence."

There were men and horses in the courtyard, and from among them came Philip of Charleroi, stiff and halting from his ride. When he saw the King he cast himself on his knee before him. He was much disheveled, his hair bound together with sweat and his hose above his spurs bloody and foamed.

"It is you then, my lord," Henry said. "The servant gave you your father's title. He named you Duke of Burgundy."

"He named me right, my lord," Philip said. "For a day and a night have I borne that style." He swayed as he knelt. Henry gave him a jug of wine from the table, and he drank deeply, like a man far gone in thirst. "That will give me tongue enough, I trust," he said when he had finished. "My lord, five days ago the Dauphin sent to my father desiring to meet with him. I think my father even then feared—though they were bound to each other—for he asked of the Dauphin his sworn word no harm would come to him. This the Dauphin gave, and so they met on the bridge of Montereau, spanning the Seine. My lord—my father trusted to the Dauphin's oath. He went with but a poor and feeble guard about him; the Dauphin was strongly attended. When my father dismounted, the Dauphin's creature, du Tanguy, came on him from behind and split his skull with his battle sword. All his escort was served likewise. As it was done the Dauphin stood by smiling, his hands in his belt."

The King drew in his breath but did not speak. His lords stood cold-faced about him, and Duke Philip, seeing them so, spoke louder, his voice shaking. "I know your thoughts," he said. "You cannot weep for my father—so be it; yet, my lord, I have come to offer you my hand in friendship. Help me avenge myself upon my father's murderers."

"I, my lord?" Henry said. "How can I reach them?"

"The Dauphin has fled Paris," Duke Philip said. "He has fled northern France and crossed the Seine. He goes beyond vengeance, but the men who struck the blows are yet near. My lord, I would bind myself with you against them, for I think you will not serve me as they served my father."

"My lord," Dorset said, "your father—God assoil him—dealt ill with us at Mézy. Why should we desire to avenge him?"

"The saints witness for me," Duke Philip said. "I seek the King of England's good. Let him but help me smoke these adders from their nests and I will bind myself to him in true alliance. I, too, have a great reckoning against de Valois."

He and the King talked far into the night. When Duke Philip had gone to his bed, Henry stood with Dorset in the same room, speaking of Duke John. "God keep me from such an end," Henry said. "A battle sword in the back of the skull, and that from his pledged friend."

"He went by treachery as he lived by it," Dorset said. "I can find no tears for him." He turned to the gifts Philip had brought the King from Nevers—wine and two rolls of linen damask, very richly woven. The King felt the cloth and said, "I know not how I can use this. It's not soldiers' garb."

Dorset smiled and said, "It will serve for your wedding." The King turned to him startled. Dorset looked on him with affection and laid a hand on his arm. "She's yours now, Harry," he said. "This was a mighty rough wooing."

XVI

The King reached Paris within the week and the city set wide her gates to him. Civil strife had boiled in her, Burgundy's adherents and such as were left of the Dauphin's creatures robbing, murdering and lusting in copy of what was done when the Armagnac lords had perished in her streets. It seemed to the people that only Henry could bring them government. When he rode through the streets, they crowded upon him, shouting, "Noël," in welcome, as once the men and women of Calais had done.

King Charles, too, gave him greeting and came to ride beside him. For a space his wits were with him, yet even so his glance fell vacantly from face to face and object to object with no heed to what he saw. He was much befouled, for in his madness he feared water and would not wash. Henry in all things gave him honor and could have pitied him. Yet the French King, in his fierce and terrible youth, had dreamed only of the conquest of England, swearing by the holy relics to strike off the right hand of every English soldier he took, of burning London to the ground and selling both men and women into slavery. Many men, seeing him riding with the King of England on his left hand, wondered if his cloudy mind held thoughts still of it, or if he knew who rode with him. Paris had long since turned from him, though she had had strange affection for Burgundy, who had tricked and cheated all men. The English had found his body thrown behind a pew in the church of Montereau. The skull was split almost in twain and he bore upon him forty-two stab wounds. It seemed that many of the people thereabout had been eager to deal death upon him.

In all things the King found his demands met. He knew now that Katherine was his, yet she was still kept from his sight, dwelling at Troyes, hard by the capital. It seemed to him that only she could sweeten the Paris Court for him. He was thirty-two now. It was seven years since he had first desired her and a year since he had met with her in Burgundy's great pavilion at Mézy, and he thirsted for sight of her as the land about the city was thirsting for rain. It fretted him that he could not know her mind. He knew not whether or no she loved him; and many times he recalled the words of the Northumbrian love tale he had heard on Hotspur's lips.

> *Oh, where have you been, my long, long love,*
> *These long seven years or more?*
> *For I have come to claim those vows,*
> *You promised me before.*

Then the lady had answered—

Oh, speak not of my former vows,
For they have caused much strife.

The name of the song was "The Demon Lover." It seemed to
him so he must be to Kate, coming upon her in the smoke and
tumult of war to bear her to his island stronghold, and at such
times he could do no more than picture her in hatred of him.

Presently Dorset brought him word of her. "She lodges hard by
the cathedral at Troyes," he said. "It is said she walks every morning in the cloister garden."

Henry took Hungerford and Umfraville and rode the sixteen
miles to Troyes. He would not summon the porters to admit him,
but went to the cloister wall which barred him from the screened
garden. "My lord," Umfraville said, "there's no way here. The porters will not hinder us when they know you."

"They'll bring the lay brothers and the abbot," Henry said.
"God's peace, Gil, I cannot talk with her with all the chapter about
us. This is our way."

He set a foot against the wall and began to scale it. Umfraville
and Hungerford looked at each other and followed him. It put
Hungerford much in mind of the nights in London when he
had first entered Henry's service and gone scrambling after him
into the taverns and city streets. There was none at hand to witness the King's coming. The garden lay quiet in its sheltering
walls, curtained in peaches and swelling apricots. Katherine sat
with her maidens and an older woman, their French chatter as
light and laughing as the summer babbling of a rill. There were
roses on her lap, but when she saw the King coming upon her
through the trees she sprang up, shedding them on the grass.
Around her the girls scattered with gasps. The older woman took
a trembling step forward.

"Good day, cousin," Henry said. "Good day, cousin Katherine."

He spoke in the stiff French of Normandy, graver and slower

than her Parisian tongue. She smiled at it and bowed low to him, skirts and sleeves and jeweled girdle dipping to earth, fold on fold, like the blown petals of a flower. "My lord," she said. "My lord."

"My lord," the older woman said uncertainly. "No one told us of your coming. You see us all unprepared."

"I put by all ceremony, lady," Henry said. "I wanted to talk with my cousin."

"Oh, my lord," the woman said in a faint voice. "I know not if it is seemly. We are but poorly attended."

"This way it pleases me," Henry said. To Katherine he said, "Come, cousin, will you walk with me?"

The older woman spread out her hands and looked at Umfraville. He came to her side and walked with her, praising the gardens and the vines and herself in such a manner that she could not take offense but found his courtliness pleasing. In this way they dropped a little behind while the King and Katherine went on together toward the south porch of the cathedral.

Now that he was with her, the King could find no words. He spoke both tongues equally, but he longed to be able to talk with her in English, which seemed to him better to speak love than French, which was the language of Parliament, the law, and the embassies. He looked at the great gray pile of the cathedral above them and began to praise it. "It seems very fine," he said. "I should like to see it."

She had walked demurely, but now she glanced at him sideways from under her long lashes and smiled. "The abbot will show you it, my lord," she said. "I will send to summon him."

"Oh, Kate," Henry said, "you would make a fair, sweet torturer."

"Kate?" she said. "Kate, my lord?"

"I have always called you so."

She looked upon him in puzzlement and said, "But my lord has never spoken with me until today."

"I have spoken with you many times," the King said. "If I could but ride alone, I spoke with you, or in my bed at nights, and it was always 'Kate.' Does it not please you?"

She smiled again and said, "I like it well, my lord."

The King drew in his breath and said, "Now you have seen me and spoken with me, how is it with you? Tell me true, cousin, would you say 'aye' to our betrothal?"

"What need has your grace to ask?" she said. "Are you not my father's choice for me?"

"Sweetheart," Henry said. "I would know this. Am I yours?"

She answered him in puzzled fashion. "I am a princess of the blood. My marriage is as my father's policy."

"This I vow to you," Henry said. "If you do not wish it, it will not be."

It seemed to him her small face hardened and his heart chilled. She said at length, "Unless we wed you'll not set your seal to this treaty. Can I thus injure France?"

"Have they told you that?" Henry said. "God's peace, Kate, it is not so. Say 'no' if you will, and I'll lay my hand on yonder holy relics and swear no hurt will come to France because of it. Some other plan will be thought on. I pledge it. Only tell me of your own lips if you cannot love me so that I may know in truth."

He had drawn her into the cathedral and they stood at the top of the great nave under the span of the pillars, their bright clothes trailing brilliance against the cool gray stone at their backs. Katherine set her head against it and looked toward the distant High Altar, dim lit like a jewel. It seemed to the King she was long in replying and his hopes lay coldly on him. "My lord," she said at last, "is it that I do not please you?"

"Oh, Kate," Henry said. "It is that you please me too well. I cannot have you bound to me coldly by wax on a treaty. It may be there's naught in me you can love. Then say it roundly, and I'll not trouble you again."

"My lord," she said, "when you were entrapped at Agincourt it was told me you would not renounce me. I was but a child then. I was fifteen, yet it seemed to me most wondrous that in such straits you would not give me up. I sat alone all that night in my bower at Rouen. At daybreak my brother rode to us—he who is dead now, may God assoil him. He said mocking that if I so greatly desired the King of England his French knights would bring him to me in a painted cart with a halter about his neck. My lord, I wept for you. I never wanted you to be brought to me so. And how you have come to me now, it contents me well, for when I saw you at Mézy you were as I had many times pictured you, and I have wanted no other."

"Oh, my Kate," Henry said. "There was never another save you. Believe this if you have believed naught else." He drew the Queen of England's ring from off his little finger and set it on her wedding finger. It fitted well, for they were both slender of hand. She looked at it in wonder and twisted it, so that the cross of rubies and diamonds winked in the gray light. "I have no ring of betrothal fashioned on a chain to set about your neck," he said. "This is the ring of the Queen of England—none other may wear it. If the King goes to his hallowing alone, it is set on his hand until such time as he binds himself to a wife. Will you not take it, for it gives you England, and—for what little worth he is, save that he truly loves you—it gives you the King of England."

"I should not wear it yet," she said. "Not till it pleases your grace to have me crowned your Queen."

"Were you not always so?" he said. "Take it, sweet. It was hallowed at my anointing, and it has hallowed all my love for you."

"Oh, my lord," she said, "I'll wear it gladly."

The King said, "Not 'my lord,' Kate."

She glanced at him, sidelong and smilingly. "I have but little of the English tongue," she said. "I know not how to say it—'Arri."

He knew himself enchanted by her. He set his arms fiercely about her, but they were princes of the blood and it was not seemly they should kiss before marriage except in greeting, and not even that they should talk alone together. She sought to free herself, and he let her go, standing tranquilly away until of herself she came to him. He took her and kissed her lips.

"It is not right," she said on a whisper. "We are not wed."

"When, Kate?" he said. "When, my sweet? Next Holy Day—Trinity Sunday?"

"No, no," she said. "It is too soon. It is not the custom of a daughter of a King to wed within a month of betrothal."

"It's been seven years," he said. "Full seven years. Sweetheart, I can set no more days and weeks between us now. In truth, I've waited for you long enough."

She sighed and set her hand gently against his cheek. "Yes," she said. "I, too, have waited long enough."

It was August before the messengers from France rode to Chichele at Lambeth Palace. The Archbishop saw John Bromley among them and went out to him through the cloister gate. "The King," Chichele said, "how does he?"

Bromley smiled and said, "He does very well. He asks your grace's blessing. He and the Lady Katherine of France were wed on Trinity Sunday in the cathedral at Troyes."

XVII

The King's pact with Philip of Burgundy had bound him to seek out the murderers of Duke John for the son's vengeance. The Burgundians were ever insistent of it, and Henry was given but two days to set aside for his honeymoon. Philip was already encamped against Meulan. The town was strongly held against him by Arnaud Guillaume, the Sire de Barbazan. This man was of the Dauphin's followers, a resourceful, clever captain, and a most lusty fighter, whose craft of battle had almost overborne the Burgundians. Philip believed him to have been among those who had struck down his father on the Bridge of Montereau and would not rest while he walked at liberty. It was to this siege that Henry came—riding each morning from Corbeil where Kate lodged, and each evening, with the dust and sweat of battle upon him, riding back to her arms and herb-scented bed. Their marriage was not yet a week old, and his men thought it hard he should venture himself thus early. "Do you fear to leave it to us?" Reeve said to him. "We are all honest fellows, and we fight lustily. You should be back with your lady."

The Burgundians urged the opposite upon him, for his battle craft was necessary to them. The siege was as hard as anything the English had known. They dug mines, tunneling deep toward the walls of Meulan, but Barbazan met them there, body to body, from his own shafts. The mines were stifling and stench ridden, and there a man fought single-handed and in the dark, often fearing himself lost. The strain of combat was great, and in it even the lords fell to quarreling over little matters. On the eve of one of the sallies Umfraville and John Bromley both demanded the right to enter the mine first, falling to high words. That he might compose the quarrel, the King himself took the right and went in at the head of all. After a while in the winding darkness he found himself alone. His dagger had dropped from his belt, and he laid aside his right gauntlet to grope for it. As he searched a voice called softly, "Jacques," and mailed feet came toward him in the mud.

Only an airhole in the earth, no bigger than a man's fist, gave ghostly light. The King faintly discerned a figure, dim clad in armor, beyond him in the tunnel. He had no wish to be caught thus, unhelmed and without dagger or gauntlet, and he answered as gruffly as he might, "Oui, seigneur."

"Écoutez," the other said sharply, "Ils sont ici, n'est-ce pas?"

"Je n'entends rien," Henry answered.

It seemed the other was about to pass on satisfied, but he stooped and picked up the King's dagger from the ground at his feet, then tossed it away. "Come out, Englishman," he said, and himself drew both sword and dagger.

The King gripped his sword and closed with him. They fought hand to hand, striving for breath in the airless dark, their feet traitors to them in the mud. The King found himself engaged with a mighty fighter. Not since Alençon had he been so hard pressed.

When both were close on choking for breath, they drew away. The King asked, gasping, "Who are you?"

"The Sire de Barbazan," the other said. "And you?"

"It's of no matter," Henry said.

"Come," Barbazan said, "did I not freely give you my name?"

"It is the King of England that you fight with," Henry said.

"So," Barbazan said, and laughed. "I am sorry to make the Lady Katherine a widow after five days." He drew back his sword as he spoke. The King took the blow on his mailed left forearm. It struck all life from it, and he fought on with it hanging. For a space his love for Katherine bred fear in him, but the stifling air snatched all their strength from them, so that they thrust feebly at each other like drunkards. It seemed to the King he heard faint sounds behind him in the tunnel. He said, "I think my soldiers are not far."

"Nor yet are mine," Barbazan said. "Shall we cry quittance?"

The King held his useless arm and said, "Not since I came into France this second time have I known such a fight."

Barbazan smiled and wiped his brow. "I bear as many bruises on my body as the King does on his," he said. "Farewell, my lord, until our next encounter."

Henry let him go without check from his soldiers. He held Barbazan now in more honor than he held any other man in France, and it troubled him that Duke Philip had marked him for the hanging when the city should yield.

XVIII

Meulan yielded on the eighteenth of November. Barbazan himself bore the keys of the city to the King. He believed himself doomed and had little courtesy to spare on his vanquisher. The King praised his courage and that of his garrison but in a chill voice. "You fought me well," he said. "I would have your soldiers take the full honors of war. I ask only of each man that he will take an oath not to bear arms against me for three years, then he can return straightway to his home."

"Is that all you would ask?" Barbazan said.

"It contents me," Henry said. After a little time he said, "You do not enquire about yourself?"

Barbazan laughed with hardness. "By God's very truth," he said, "what need have I to ask? Summon your friends of Burgundy and deliver me to them."

"The Duke demands you of my hands," Henry said. "He holds you one of the several guilty of his father's blood at Montereau."

"He may say so," Barbazan said. "He is my enemy and I am his. Yet I was not there. Since May have I been here at Meulan preparing against the King of England."

"Burgundy is assured you were there," Henry said.

"I was not," Barbazan said. "Yet it makes small matter. Had I been there I would gladly have kissed the axe that split the traitor skull of Jean sans Peur. That the son knows."

Henry said, "You have little love for Duke Philip."

"He is as cold of heart as he is of face," Barbazan said. "He has all his father's venom. So long as the English prosper he will be their good and constant friend, but let the wind begin to blow in their faces and they had best not lean on Burgundy."

Dorset came in and stood at the King's side. Henry drew him away the length of the chamber where they could talk with no man hearing their words. "Uncle," he said, "I mislike this business. Barbazan was not at Montereau."

"Does he say so?" Dorset said. "Well, it may be he would. His life hangs by it."

"This man is not a liar," Henry said. "He fought with me like a lion in the mines. I'd gladly not render him to the Duke."

"Barbazan is the Dauphin's creature," Dorset said. "He is that, whether or no he struck down Jean sans Peur. It would be policy to give him up."

Barbazan knew that they talked of him. When Henry turned back, he gave him a hard smile of mockery and spoke loudly.

"Why waste breath on it?" he said. "The King of England knows what he will do. Let him not make a pretense of justice."

"Guard your tongue," Henry said. "It rests in my hands what shall come upon you."

"My lord, I know your judgment," Barbazan said. "You'll not offend your ally, Burgundy. He would prize nothing so much as my body in chains."

"I am not answerable to Burgundy," Henry said.

"No?" Barbazan said. "Yet I do not think that the King of England will of himself grant me my life. He knows too well that if he did I would use it to the uttermost to drive him and his army step by step out of Normandy."

Henry looked at him with narrowed eyes and said in a still voice, "Of a truth, my lord, you are a brave man."

Barbazan shrugged and made no answer. For a long while the King stood looking at him, then he dismissed him back to his lodging in the castle of Meulan under guard. When after three days Philip came to him desiring Barbazan, he would not give him up. Philip was much angered and there were high words between them. Many men feared that Philip would withdraw the armies of Burgundy from Henry's command, but though he threatened it, he did not do so.

Barbazan came again into the King's presence the next day. The siege still marked him but less deeply, and he wore hose and surcoat which Henry had sent him. It seemed to the King that he bore upon him the full fair chivalry of France, which had many times looked to be a sickly and dying thing. It lifted his heart to see it.

Barbazan spoke with him gravely. "My lord," he said, "I hear you withstand Burgundy on my behalf. I am grateful, yet, my lord, I would have you know this. I am liege man to my master, the Dauphin, and my sword and my fealty are his. I can take no oath to you."

"Have I asked it?" Henry said. "Do I not read you too well to ask it?"

"Am I your life's prisoner then?" Barbazan asked. "Stone walls are harsh punishment. It may be the day will come when I'll think Burgundy's hangman's rope kinder."

"My lord, I ask nothing of you," Henry said. "I would set the Seine between us, but from thence you may go where you will."

"It would be to the Dauphin's side," Barbazan said. "I speak straightly with you. If I ride from here, I go your enemy."

The King smiled and said, "So be it, then."

Barbazan looked long at him, then smiled also. "It may be we are enemies," he said. "But we do not spit upon each other. I thank your grace. I think since we fought together in the mines we be brothers-in-arms." He asked then why the King sought to free him.

"Not since I came into France have I met your like," Henry said. "You put me much in mind of another—one called Owen Glendower."

He did not again speak with Barbazan, but the next day sent him from him across the Seine which marked the limit of the English claims. Barbazan rode with an escort of the King's bowmen, passing beneath the castle barbican. A group of Burgundians stood there, and at sight of him broke out in angry words. Louis Bournel, one of Burgundy's lords, laid a hand on his bridle. "Take heed," he said. "Before the New Year we'll have you hanging by your neck."

Barbazan smiled and shook his head.

"Mark it," Bournel said. "You be a dead man already."

"I do not think so," Barbazan said. "Is it not the King of England who stands before me like a rock?"

XIX

In northern France only Meulan had withstood the Treaty of Troyes, and with its fall quiet came upon the land. It was now February and the letters from England spoke of the land growing to early greenness. Not for three and a half years had the King seen his own realm. He but rarely spoke his own tongue, and he longed now to go back and bring his bride with him. Dorset knew his thoughts and spoke with him. "All's quiet here," he said. "And your people would see their Queen and hallow her. Take her to England."

"There's still much toil to my hands here in France," Henry said.

"In God's good time, Harry," Dorset said. "Meanwhile give England taste and sight of you again."

Tom had lately joined his brother from Calais, bringing news of London. He, too, had been away from the King eighteen months, and he came thicker of form with no leanness left to him and seemingly older than his thirty-one years. He who had longed to prove his puissance and to find glory in battle had always been cheated of it. Even his marriage, which had seemed no more than sport to him at seventeen, was a bitter thing now. Yet, for all his troubles, he was yet lusty and confident.

"Yours is the devil's luck, Harry," he said. "Not only is she fair as a flower, but she's given you a realm, and, I doubt not, she'll give you a prince. Margaret has given me naught."

He asked the King that, when he left for England, he would leave him in command. "It is but my right, Harry," he said. "I know that when your Kate is brought to bed of a son, my nose will be twisted from its joint; but now I am still your heir, and this task is mine."

"You'll walk carefully?" Henry said. "You'll do naught that's rash?"

"Tush," Tom said. "Never did I know such a man for fretting. You think no other can shoulder your tasks. You'll not believe it, Harry, but I am as skilled in government as you."

Henry felt his heart sink a little. He began to reason patiently. "It's not that I doubt you," he said. "But all we do here must be done most delicately. I'll leave Gil Umfraville and Thomas Salisbury with you. Both are good counsellors and good soldiers. Lean to them, Tom, in all things."

"Oh, for the saints' sake," Tom said. "They are no older than I—neither of them. I trust myself more."

The King said more sharply, "Mark what I say."

"Oh, for sure," Tom said, grinning. "Normandy will still be here when you come back. Peace now and ease your mind. London is all bedecked for you again."

Henry journeyed slowly to the coast, lodging each night in one of his fief castles. All the towns of Normandy gave him good greeting, flocking to look upon his queen. The King could not blame them, himself deep in love with her. Yet, now that she was at last his, he found himself anxious for their homecoming, fearing that his strange people might turn from her, as they had so often turned from their foreign queens, or that she might set her face against them and desire only warm France.

Dover welcomed him as on his return from Agincourt, the barons in their silken hose and rich surcoats, wading through the chill sea to bear him and the Queen on their shoulders to shore. Yet still he mistrusted his welcome. He left Kate in Canterbury and went on into London to prepare all things for her coming. On the first day of March he brought her into the city. Again the people thronged the narrow streets avid to glimpse them—the fair French princess, eager to smile, her white palfrey caparisoned with silver bells and her chaplet bright with jewels; and the tall King, gay as he had been before his stern hallowing and still bearing all the dark grace of the de Bohuns. In the thunder of their welcome Henry could doubt their love no longer. He and Katherine rode together under clashing bells while the crowds pressed and heaved about them, seeing them as lovers and themselves wild to show their own love.

Almost straightway the King bore Katherine off to Pleshy, where his grandmother kept her household. The past three and a half years had brought the Countess at last to old age, and she was much enfeebled, resting day long in her chair. Only her mind was still as bright and cool as in her early widowhood. She kissed

Katherine and greeted her lovingly, speaking in rusted French, for unlike many of the land's great ladies she rarely spoke it. "How fair she is, Hal," she said. "Prettier, in truth, than her portrait." She touched Kate's cheek and smiled upon her. "It is a little head for a crown," she said. "Tell me what color your hair is."

"Rich and brown," Henry said. He drew off the coif which bound Kate's head so that her chestnut hair fell thick about her shoulders. "For shame," she said. "I'm wed, and it is not for me to show my hair."

The King took the coif from her hands and tried to set it in place, with but small success. "I cannot do it, sweet," he said at last. "It's as if I have ten thumbs."

When they turned to the mirror and saw how he had dressed it, over one ear and one eye, they both broke into laughter. "Fie on you," Kate said. "I've wed a sorry-handed craftsman."

When she had gone with her ladies, the King sat on alone with his grandmother. She began to speak warmly of Katherine, praising her gracious ways and her beauty. "She has a merry heart," she said. "And that pleases me most. Life will not trouble her greatly, nor kingship, nor blood, nor battle. It may be she will give you your laughter again, and I have desired no more than that for you."

The King said in a low voice, "Have I become so hard, then?"

"Nay, now," she said, "why do you ask?"

"But it is true, is it not?" he said. "You'll have heard tell of me in France. When the hard choices came there, I made such my flesh would have crawled from ten years ago."

"War is a hard thing," she said. "And power corrodes. How could you not be marked?"

"So much?" he said. "So greatly?"

After a space she said, "I remembered your grandfather's brother, Edward; him they called the Black Prince. There was no more knightly man in his youth, yet his years of battle in France hardened him to flint. I feared for you, Harry. I thought you went this same way; but it is not so. You are still as you always were, and I doubt not but that your love for Kate will keep you so."

The King said, "If I could but think it."

"It will be so," she said. "You've gained her in time, Harry. Only heed an old woman's words and reach not for too much in France."

Archbishop Chichele had ridden with the Court from London, and he came now and sat with them. Henry began to speak with him of his plans for founding a new college at Oxford in memory of the men who had fallen at Agincourt. After a little he said, "What think you of the foundation for scholars old William of Wykeham established at Winchester?"

"A good thing, I am persuaded," Chichele said.

"I am told Thomas Langley plans to found another such place at Durham," Henry said. "It seems to me hard that the south and the north should lead in this matter and London lag. I, too, would well like to make my own foundation—some fifty boys to be housed and schooled within the city." When he saw that Chichele welcomed his words, he went on, speaking eagerly, "I would set it at Smithfield," he said. "The fields are broad and pleasant there and meet for boys, and the Carthusian monastery stands hard by. From that we could name it Charterhouse."

When the King made ready to go, Lady Hereford would have kept him longer. "I have scarcely spoken with you," she said. "When do you come again?"

The King answered, "As soon as Kate and I are returned from the north."

She said, "Do you go there?"

"They desire to see us," he said. "We'll be gone all the summer months."

"Harry," she said, "take some rest. It is needful."

He smiled and shook his head. "You are more spent than you know," she said. "Believe me when I say it is needful—yet, I know you for a silly boy, and you'll not do it."

"Do you say it, my lady?" Chichele said, smiling. "Others among us would be in the Tower for less. But grandmothers are favored."

Henry said, "Aye, they are greatly privileged." When Lady Hereford began stiffly to get to her feet, he pressed her down into the chair and set a cushion at her back. "Nay, now," he said, "do not rise."

"Yet I must," she said. "You are the King."

"I am no more than a silly boy to you," he said. "Did you not say it?"

XX

All the realm clamored for sight of the King and his bride, and the progress planned for them in the north was heavy. Henry brought Kate first to Gaunt's old castle of Leicester, where he had many times dwelt since he was a boy, and whose gardens he had set out himself with mulberry, pear trees, roses, and sweet herbs in the year he had first sailed to France. From there he desired to take the Queen to quiet and distant Monmouth, but the time was not to be spared. They could go no farther than Warwick, journeying through the forest of Arden, where the wild boar drank in the gentle Avon and fledgling ducklings chased among the reeds. There was a tennis court at Warwick, and on the evening of their arrival the King and Camoys matched themselves against Hungerford and John Bromley. Hungerford and Bromley won with ease, carrying their own chases where the King could not strike a length. No man had ever seen him play so badly.

"Your grace is out of practice," Bromley said. "Or else I grow better." He had never beaten the King before, and he was delighted, swinging his racket with eagerness. Humphrey had sat watching throughout in the gallery, and he called to the King, "Marriage agrees ill with your game, Harry."

"God's peace, my lord," old Thomas Erpyngham said. "Had I known you meant to play thus I would have matched you myself —aye, and won too, I'll warrant, could I have summoned breath enough to my lungs."

They had previously held him able to outplay all men, and they were loud in their chafing. Henry bore with it gaily. "Let me be," he said. "I know it was bad without words from you."

Hungerford stood by, silently. When the rest had gone, he waited beside the gallery of the penthouse. The King tarried also, leaning against the rail in his silken shirt. The pages had brought in ewers and towels, and he wiped the sweat from his hands and face.

"My lord," Hungerford said, "will you not tell me in truth what is wrong?"

"It's very little," Henry said. "I seem to lack the strength I had before. I got weary and I could not sight the ball. It was as though I were in my cups. I saw it double."

"My lord," Hungerford said, "summon Colnet."

"What can he do?" Henry said. "It's only that I am wearied."

At first he was not to be moved, but when Hungerford began to urge him, naming the Queen and his love for her, he said presently he would do as it was desired of him.

XXI

From Warwick the Court went to Shrewsbury, and it was in the cold castle there, where Colnet had first tended the King as a boy, that he came to him again. Henry welcomed him but would not readily submit to him. "I know not why we summoned you," he said. "I am not ill."

Colnet was fifty-seven now, graying and grave of manner, but both direct and of a ready tenderness. The King held him the finest physician in Europe and at Agincourt had gladly consigned his soldiers into his care. He bore with Colnet where he would have borne with no other.

Colnet did not force himself upon him but talked with him intermittently, questioning him in gradual fashion. He would have had the King cast all his cares of state onto his nobles and go with his Queen to his own Castle of Monmouth. "I would have you lie abed each day until ten," he said, "and if you went abroad, it would be no farther than to the Monnow bridge to watch the salmon leap."

The King smiled and shook his head. "I am to Chester next week," he said. "And afterward to York and Pontefract, Beverley, Barnard Castle, and Durham."

"It is a heavy progress," Colnet said. "Must it be undertaken at this time?"

"They all await me," Henry said. "I know they will have lain out their plate and fine linen, bedecked their streets and fashioned the loving cups they would give me. I am bounden to go." He began to speak besides of the work he had to do at each place where he lodged. "I have been away a long time," he said. "I would hear their petitions and know all is justly administered. These places are distant, and it is a good thing when they can reach the King's ear."

Colnet gnawed his lip and asked him of France. "When do you return?" he said. "Is all this to be repeated there, since you are pledged to divide your time between both realms?"

"I'll go in November," Henry said.

"My lord," Colnet said, "have you at some time watched a meteor? They are very bright; while they last they light the whole land, yet they are swift burnt-out."

"In truth, Colnet," Henry said, "what would you have me think? I am not greatly sick."

"You are not yet greatly sick," Colnet said. "It is that I fear you will become so. Have I not tended you from a boy, here in this place, where Hotspur all but had your blood? You were never strong, my lord, yet you yourself know what tax is laid upon you."

"I will do what you wish of me," the King said at last, "if it lies within reason. But I cannot yet withdraw to Monmouth."

"Well, do as you have planned in this undertaking," Colnet said. "But let it be done gently. I have watched your grace ride in these parts. Not Hotspur himself could have set so fierce a pace. Next time you would gallop check your horse to a trot, and if the Queen would dance all night let it be with the lord Humphrey or Walter

Hungerford. Nor would I have you so much as set your hand to a tennis racket."

"God's peace, Colnet," Henry said. "What can I do?"

"Is it so hard to sit and rest?" Colnet said. "If it must be otherwise, have Erpyngham teach you bowls."

"Bowls!" Henry said. "For the saints' sake."

"It's a good game," Colnet said. "Your grace will find it'll test your skill. I would have you test no more than that for a summer's space."

Later Hungerford saw Colnet walking alone in the bailey garden and went to him. The Court was moving to Chester on the morrow, and the stewards stood under the arch of the courtyard ordering the sumpter horses. Hungerford watched them for a while, then asked Colnet if he returned to London. Colnet answered, "I think my way is with the King."

"Sir," Hungerford said, "give me the truth. How is it with him?"

"We need not yet fear," Colnet said. "But this he must do. He must husband his strength."

"You think he will do it?" Hungerford said.

Colnet half-smiled. "Aye," he said. "We have a dagger now to hold against his throat. He has much love for the Queen. He will guard himself now, where before he had no care."

XXII

The King stayed in Chester a week, then journeyed across the land to Beverley, halting at many places on the way to hold council and hear the petitions brought him. He took more heed of himself and was better, though often the days when he sat in council, dubbing new knights and receiving the gifts of the townsfolk, were long and toilsome. Colnet was constant at his side. He kept a still tongue, and none beyond those closest to the King knew how it had been with him.

Beverley had been called in the old tongue Beaverlac or the lake of Beavers. The King had long wanted to visit it, for its great

minster, cast in Purbeck stone, was of a splendor only matched in
the north by York and Durham. The land about, too, was rich in
religious houses and fair abbeys; save for Canterbury, no other
part of England had come so early to the Christian faith.

The Court lodged in Baynard Castle, hard by the little town to
the south. The air was fresh here, tanged with sea salt from the
great basin of the Humber and moor scented. The King felt his
strength returning to him almost daily. His life was sweet to him
now as it had been at no time since his childhood at Monmouth,
his way made warm in his love for the Queen and in his people's
love for him. He went to the Minster to give thanks for the deliverance of his soldiers at Agincourt, kneeling beneath the banner
of John of Beverley—that which had been borne to victory in the
Battle of the Standard, so rent with age that it floated cobweblike,
gray and rotting, from the roof. There was much here to recall
Westminster, and he remembered his words to Chichele before
his anointing that he was not long for the throne. Then had it
seemed that Lancaster must swiftly go to his atonement for the
blood of Richard—that he or his son would die as Richard had
died, friendless in a prison, no man knowing by what means, save
that an Englishman's hand had struck the blow. The memory of
his words came back cold and darkly. He went to the south door
of the Minster where the sun of the April morning flooded his
path and the growing town, bustling and gay with flags that
marked his coming, lay under his eyes. He said aloud, speaking
his thoughts, "I'll not believe it."

It seemed to him his own heart whispered in reply, "Do you
not?"

XXIII

At Baynard the lords went hawking. The King was no falconer and
took little pleasure in the sport, but because the Queen rode, he
rode also. Humphrey had brought with him a newly trained merlin, very swift but not yet used to his calls. When the bird was

loosed and beat away, he set his spurs to his horse, the others following. Henry laid his hand on Kate's bridle and drew her horse back among the hawthorn. It grew tall and thick-tangled there and they sat silent in their saddles as the hoof beats echoed past them to the pursuit. "They are intent on the chase," she said. "They'll lose us."

The King laughed and said, "So much I hoped for."

She looked at him smilingly from under her long lashes and pretended to chide. "Oh fie, Harry," she said. "Fie on you."

"Sweetheart," he said, "I am so little alone with you."

Their reins had become entangled together, and he dismounted to unloose them. She sat still in the tall saddle, bright-painted with the arms of England at front and back, her skirts spread about her, for she rode astride. She was clad in green, which she much favored and a kirtle of primrose yellow so full that only the toes of her pointed shoes showed beneath the stirrups. It seemed to him none had her like in beauty or laughter.

"Kate," he said, "tell me this. Is it that you are happy?"

She said, "Why do you ask it?"

"It must all be strange to you," he said. "England has little of France. Men reckon her a cold, rough, unbiddable land when they do not know her. Has she seemed so to you?"

She set her hands upon his shoulders and smiled down on him. "Mon cher Anglais," she said, "I am happy. I am content."

He lifted her from the saddle and set her down, his arms still about her. "It's a poor life for you," he said. "Wed at twenty-one to an old man of thirty-three who can scarce dance with you of nights or wear your favors and outride all others for love of you in the morning."

"It doesn't fret me," she said. After a space she said, "Is there none other save me?"

"None," he said. "None, Greensleeves. I swear it."

She smiled and said, "I know not why I should believe you."

"Shame on you if you should not," he said. "It's a King's word."

The hawthorn parted and a laborer came through the midst, in dirty russet homespun, his plowshare athwart his shoulder. When he saw the King and Katherine in his arms he grinned at them and winked. "Pardon, master," he said. "I never knew you were here with your lass. Let pass, and I'll not long trouble you." As Henry stood aside, he clapped him on the shoulder. "A pretty one, too," he said. "There now, master, I'm to the field yonder, and no man else comes by this path. You'll not be troubled."   .

The King smiled and said, "We are on our way." He asked the other where lay the road to Cottingham, giving him a groat.

"I reckoned you were not of these parts," the man said. "Yonder runs the road, past the larch coppice. Not ten minutes gone was I asked the same by another—he and his horse lathered in sweat and spew. He had less time to waste on a man than you, master. He gave me poor thanks for my pains."

He led the horses for the King and set them as far as the road. Katherine could not follow his words, for he spoke broadly and she herself had only little English. She asked Henry in French what it was they spoke of.

When they reached the road, the man gave back the reins into the King's hands. Katherine's speech had puzzled him, and he looked curiously upon her. "Your lady's Welsh, then, master," he said. "I heard the tongue once from a soldier who lodged in an almshouse with me, far side of York, and I ne'er forgot it. 'Tis a heathen speech and all. I know not how a Christian man understands aught of it." He bade the King safe journey and stood back pointing the way. "Yonder's your road," he said. "There's been many comings and goings upon it of late, but Harry lodges at Baynard and there'll be men riding upon his business. You'll not miss it. Fare you safely."

Henry sat Katherine once more in her saddle and rode beside her. They went slowly, joying that they rode alone and in the spring's sweetness. It was near evening when they came upon the castle. Some of the King's gentlemen stood in the meadows outside the moat, scanning the lanes and distant hedgerows. When the King rode to the drawbridge, Dorset came over it to meet him.

"My lord," he said, "where have you been? We've had men as far as Cottingham and Hull sent in search of you."

Henry said, "I've been out of your sight but three hours."

"There was need of you here," Dorset said. "I have a messenger to speak with you." When he saw the Queen's eyes upon him, he became silent. Henry looked at him and asked no questions. They rode on together, Dorset walking beside the horses until they came to the inner courtyard. Henry lifted Katherine to the ground before the pages could reach them. "Are you weary?" he said. "It's been a long day, this."

"I had joy in it all," she said. "Are you not happy too?"

"Yes," he said. "Yes, in truth."

After she had gone, Dorset walked with him to the room he often used in the west tower. The King stood for a space before the narrow window, drawing off his gloves. All about the castle walls the broom grew golden as far as the eye could see, and from the wild cherry the blackbird sang for spring. It seemed to him he could hear Kate's laughter below him. Dorset saw that he found it hard to set aside the day's joy.

"Well, Uncle," the King said at length, "give me your ill news."

"It is ill, Harry," Dorset said. "After your sailing the Dauphin brought his army up across the Seine. Tom took a small force and met with him at Beaugé by the fork of the river. He was overmatched and put to rout."

"Was the loss great?" Henry said.

"Some half the force," Dorset said. "Less than it well might have been. The rest escaped."

The King sighed and said, "I would it need not have been, yet have we looked at defeat before this."

"Tom is dead," Dorset said.

He began to praise his nephew's valor, speaking in a thick voice. "When he saw how it must end, he fought as a lion," he said. "He and de Umfraville never left each other's side and gave never a step. They were struck down together."

"Gil too?" Henry said. He turned from his uncle to the window.

"Harry," Dorset said, "I thought to give you this at my own lips. The messenger waits in yonder room. Will you now talk with him?"

Thomas of Salisbury had sent one of Tom's own body squires with the news for the King. He came in now with Walter Hungerford, his hose caked ugly yellow in his horse's foam, and his limbs stiff from riding. The King bade him tell all he knew.

"We heard the Dauphin's French had reached the river hard by Beaugé," the other said. He was a young man and he spoke at first haltingly, then with greater ease. "Your grace's brother was encamped at La Lande Chasles with but a small force. It was a dark night, very chill, and wild with wind and rain. When word was brought of the French advance, your lord brother determined to ride upon them straightway before the main body of our force under the lord Salisbury had come up. The lord de Umfraville pleaded with him not to go, for the French were some three times stronger, having with them pikemen and crossbows. Your brother would not heed, saying one Englishman was master of any three French, and the rain was good augury, since it had also rained before Agincourt. When the lord de Umfraville urged him more strongly to return he named him for a coward, telling him to go back if he feared for his life. Umfraville answered he would in no case forsake him."

Hungerford exclaimed in a low voice. "How could he say it?" he said. "To Gil of all men?"

"He said as much to me," Henry said. "He never meant these words."

"My lord, they died as knights," the messenger said. "When your brother found all his force at the mercy of the crossbows, surrounded and overmatched by three to one, he drove his horse at the very center of the French, Umfraville with him. They fought as fiends. It was the Sire de Lacy who finally took your brother in the breast with his lance. Umfraville died trying to bring de Lacy to the ground. It was said that in death he and the Duke lay side by side under the very fetlocks of the French."

The King drew in his breath. Dorset saw that for a space he

found it hard to speak and began to question the messenger. "It were a miracle half our force got away," he said. "It seems to me they well might all have died."

"The lord Salisbury came up and rallied them," the other said. "The Dauphin gave chase, but Salisbury used the confusion and the thick dark and got away by way of La Flèche. It was God's mercy that he did. Had the Dauphin swallowed up him and his army likewise, our case in France would be black."

Hungerford said, "I do not envy Salisbury that march in the rain and dark with thrice his strength of French crossbows about him."

"He's a good soldier," Henry said. "I know none better." He asked the messenger what effect the battle had had upon the land.

"It has much heartened the Dauphin's people," the man said. "They say now the English run as sheep as fast as other men. The Dauphin boasts he has shown that even the English bowmen can yet know defeat."

The King talked with him for some little time, then sent him from him. "Get you some rest," he said. As the man turned to the door he called him back and spoke in a low voice. "My brother's body?" he said. "Was it left to the French?"

"Nay, my lord," the other said. "His own son, the Bastard of Clarence, desired Salisbury he might go back into the battle to find his father's body. Some twelve men-at-arms and three of his squires went with him. How we do not know, but he found his father's body and the lord de Umfraville's and brought them back to us."

"That lad?" Henry said. "He went back with no more than a dozen men?"

"He shapes well," the man said. "In truth, my lord, I think he had died rather than leave his father's body to the Dauphin's hands." He undid the belted pouch which hung at his waist and fumbled in it. "I bear your lord brother's tokens with me," he said. "The collar of SS which we took from off his armor, his ring of estate, and his wedding ring. I knew not whether to give them to your grace or to the Lady Margaret."

"Give them to me," Henry said. "I'll deliver them to the Lady Margaret's hands."

When the messenger had gone, he stood with the great Lancastrian collar of SS in his hands, folding the silver-gilt links each on each. All was hard to him, but hardest was that Tom should have ridden to his death taunting Umfraville with dark words; and that Umfraville should likewise have died with them in his ears. It seemed to the King no man had served him as gaily and chivalrously as Umfraville. Yet Tom had likewise served him. He who as a boy had so greatly desired to become Duke of Lancaster had desired no less to be King of England. Henry knew himself to be the brother whose birth had cheated Tom of all power and all title; yet, since his accession, Tom had been stanch at his side. From him he had had a knight's constancy. He felt his loss deep upon him.

XXIV

The Queen had been told of Beaugé by her ladies while Henry was yet in council with his lords. As the night grew older she could not rest in her bed, but wrapped herself in her bedgown and sat by the oriel window which looked upon the inner court. It seemed to her it grew near morning when the latch stirred on the door of the outer room. John Bromley had lit the King to his bedchamber. He would have stayed to attend him, but the King bade him go in a quiet voice and took the candle from him. They talked a little in low tones before Henry entered the inner chamber. He saw Katherine in her furred bedgown, her feet bare upon the matting of the floor, and spoke in astonishment. "Are you not abed?" he said. "It's after two of the clock."

She answered, "I thought you would not come to me tonight."

"Why not, Kate?" he said. "Why not, my sweet?"

She said, "My brother has killed your brother—whom you loved —and all you have wrought in France lies menaced. I thought you could have no love toward me in your heart this night."

"How could you think it?" he said. "Is it so weak and pale a thing —my love for you? Sweet, you talk nonsense."

When he saw that she shivered, he set the candle against the overshelf and lifted her upon the bed. She clung to him and spoke as if she all but wept. "I am afraid for us," she said. "I know not what will come upon us."

"What can come upon us?" he said. "There is nothing to fear."

"The flood of war beats between us," she said. "You love me now, but what if defeat begins to come upon you, and your brothers and your friends go to their deaths at my brother's hands? Will you not come to hate me and all things French?"

"Hate you?" he said. "It was you that I thought must hate, yet you suffered me at Troyes. Kate, I have loved none as I love you."

The cloud of her hair fell about them, richly, like a veil, and he drew his hand over it, savoring its softness. "Hear me now, sweet," he said. "It is not an easy thing that I try to do in France, yet by God's grace when it's achieved, peace and weal will follow. I would love you, whatsoever you be, but in that you are French, I love you doubly. I need you, Kate. Be to me as the voice of all your realm. When it comes that you see me deal ill, when it seems to you justice is for English blood and not for French—speak for France, Kate, speak for France."

She sighed and pressed upon him closer. "Mine was foolish talk," she said. "Forgive me. It is that I love you, Harry."

"And I love you," he said. "So much—so much."

He set her back upon the pillows and piled the sheets about her. She lay in seeming quiet, but when he came beside her, she clung to him again and began to speak fearfully. "What do you do?" she said. "Do you go back to France?"

"I know not," he said. "I'll set aside all plans until I talk with Salisbury."

"Nay, do not go," she said. "As you love me, do not go."

"You're weary," he said. "Try to sleep."

"My brother will kill you," she said. "You do not know him as I do—he is a cold, clinging, tenacious man—he will never cease from your heels."

The King answered her as he might a child. "You ride your nightmare," he said. "All will seem less ill tomorrow." Presently he knew that she slept.

XXV

The King left his northern progress on the morrow and journeyed for London. There was little news for him there, save that young Jack of Clarence had already crossed from France bearing his father's body with him. He had borne it tenderly to Canterbury to the great tomb that stood hard by Henry of Derby's. At the King's bidding, Jack came to him at Westminster. He was fifteen now, tall and straight limbed, with all the comeliness of Lancaster, brown haired and brown eyed. No man seeing him could mistake his birth. It seemed to the King he looked upon the heir of all his house. He kept the boy by him at Court, setting him at his own table as though his bastardy had no meaning and he were, in truth, a prince of the blood.

Margaret kept her household still at the Savoy, and Henry went to her there. She talked with him in calm fashion, seated in her bower, but without her women so that they might talk unheard. Her lonely love had marked her, and she looked older. It seemed to all men that this, her second widowhood, lay more harshly on her than her first, yet only in the early marriage had she come to happiness.

She spoke steadily of Tom and asked the King of the battle. He told her as he might, speaking much of his brother's valor. "Yet it was folly," she said, when he had done. "It was madness to seek such a battle."

Henry said, "He could not rest for that he was not there with me on Crispin's Day. It may be I killed him as much as did de Lacy's lance."

"He was young," she said. "He always seemed to me no more

than a boy—as does your grace. It was for that I loved him, yet he should have kept to naming me 'aunt' not 'wife!' "

"Margaret," Henry said, "in truth, he loved you."

"No," she said. "I gave him naught—neither heir, nor wealth, nor youth, nor beauty. I wonder now how I once thought I could give happiness to him."

"Dear sister," Henry said again, "he loved you more than he knew."

They sat in talk until the summer evening began to darken and the pages brought in the waxen candles. When the King was about to go, he paused and looked at her. "Margaret," he said at last, "I have Jack with me. Will you not see him?"

"Jack?" she said, and twisted her kerchief together in her fingers. "How many years has he now?"

"He is fifteen," Henry said.

She exclaimed and said, "Is he as old as that? Yet he will be. Tom was but eighteen when he sired him."

"Let me bring him to you," the King said. "He loved Tom likewise."

After the boy came to him, he put an arm about his shoulders and brought him into the bower. When Margaret turned and saw them standing together and their great likeness, she drew in her breath in astonishment. "He is all Lancaster," she said. "Never saw I so bold a birthmark."

"Jack," Henry said, "yonder the Lady Margaret. When next you ride to Canterbury will you take her with you?"

"Gladly, my lord," the boy said. He went to Margaret, bowed and gave her the kiss of courtesy on the right cheek. For a little space they stood apart, then embraced each other so warmly that they might have been mother and son.

Margaret stood back at length and took his hands, smiling upon him. "Your father walks in you," she said. "Dear Jack—I would know you better."

"I'll come again, lady," he said. "As soon as you can bear with me, send and I'll come."

"Take care what you speak," she said, still smiling. "It may be very soon."

XXVI

Colnet had not left the King's side since his return from the north. He came to him on the same night as he returned to Westminster from the Savoy to speak to the Queen. "I think your grace yourself has suspected it," he said. "That she was with child."

"I wondered at it," Henry said. "You are sure?"

"Now we are sure," Colnet said. "We would not speak before."

"Colnet," Henry said, "is all well with her?"

Colnet smiled and said, "Excellently well, my lord."

"I would have her know all care," the King said. "It is hard for her that it should be now, when we are like to be separated."

Colnet gave him a grave look and did not speak. After a little he said, "How does it come that you are like to be separated, my lord?"

The King said, "It may be that I must return to France."

"My lord," Colnet said, "I speak plain with you. You must not go."

"Oh, God's peace, Colnet," Henry said. "Was it not of the Queen that you came to talk with me?"

"The Queen is in health," Colnet said. "She is with child, but she is still in health. I would you were."

"Well, let it rest," Henry said. "I know not yet whether I go or no."

Salisbury rode into the city the next day, sooner than the King had expected him, but he had had fair winds from Calais. He was a tall young man, fair, with a stern, strong face, untidily garbed as if he had slept in his surcoat and hose for many nights, never stripping. Men thought it likely he had done so, knowing what great need he had had for vigilance since Beaugé. Of all Henry's younger commanders he promised most as a soldier. The King much valued his allegiance, for his father had died because of his loyalty to Richard, he alone of the nobles of England keeping faith with the fallen King.

Salisbury came to the King's presence in the great Painted Chamber of Westminster. Katherine sat with her husband, and some few of the nobles. Salisbury knew of her pregnancy and of the rumors of the King's sickness, and though he spoke bluntly of Beaugé he kept cheerful face, painting the scene neither too black nor too golden. "This defeat was needful to us," he said. "We were growing too fat with confidence. Every time we met them lance to lance we looked for another Agincourt."

"Well," Dorset said, "the lesson's learned. Is it not quickly put to rights?"

Salisbury met his eyes and after a little inclined his head. The nobles about the King began to speak as if the Dauphin's victory was of little consequence. "He's gained naught," Camoys said. "The Normandy defenses are soon strengthened. I and the Duke of Dorset can take ship tomorrow and look to them."

Henry said, "It may be the task is mine to go."

"What need?" Dorset said. He gave Salisbury a fierce look and said, "Is there any cause for the King to go again into France?"

"None, my lord Duke," Salisbury said slowly.

"Tell me this of yourself, Salisbury," Henry said. "Would you have me return to France?"

"My lord——" Salisbury began and hesitated.

"I charge you to give me the truth," Henry said. "Is it necessary for me to come?"

Katherine leaned forward a little in her chair and set her eyes on Salisbury's face. He looked from her to his boots and then to the King, but he spoke at last steadily. "It is necessary, my lord," he said. "This victory has so heartened the Dauphin that unless you come I think there's not an English soldier in Normandy whose life is not endangered."

Katherine said sharply, "Can all this rest on the King's presence?"

"Lady," Salisbury said, "since Agincourt the King's name has ever been a strong shield to his soldiers. Let it be known that he walks again on French soil and much heart will go from his enemies."

Henry rose from his chair and walked to the great overmantel hung with tapestry woven to picture the Wars of the Maccabees. "I come," he said. "Bid them in Paris I'll be with them by the Feast of St. John."

Katherine bowed her small head. The ladies about her saw that she wept, and Salisbury looked at her in much distress. "Oh, my lord," he said to the King, "I would I could have told you otherwise."

Henry looked at him and half-smiled. "God with you, Salisbury," he said. "You're an honest man. You did not lie."

XXVII

The King at once began to make preparation for his return to France, working in the Painted Chamber late into the night. It was there that Nicholas Colnet came to him. He gave him a grim look and did not set aside his papers. "I know what brings you," he said. "Let me be. It is useless."

"My lord," Colnet said, "if this journey must be undertaken, at least let it not be until the New Year."

The King laughed shortly and said, "The Dauphin has no mind to wait upon my health."

"My lord," Colnet said, "hearken to my words."

"I cannot," the King said. "Colnet, if it were possible I should gladly bide here, but I have talked with Salisbury. There's naught else to be done."

"It is your father's crown that you bear," Colnet said. "Would you have it be with you as it was with him?"

The King's face changed, and Colnet saw that he feared. This was the room where Derby had often lain in the long years of his sickness. It was as if the odor of his foulness hung again upon the air, strong of scabs and running sores.

Colnet said, "When you were but a boy and your father was first stricken, you named his sickness rightly. You put your hand to the crown and said it was his murderer."

Henry said in a still voice, "You know well how to affright me." He rose and went to the stone recess of the window, out of the brightness of the candles, and stood there in the shadows.

"It need not be," Colnet said. "Your strength will come again if you do as I bid you. Take rest."

"I cannot," Henry said. He came back to the table and took up his quill. When Colnet saw he was not to be moved, he no longer tried to urge him. After a while Henry asked him of the Queen. "She weeps for this parting," Colnet said. "It was she who sent me to you."

"Colnet," Henry said, "what have you told her?"

"Nothing, my lord," Colnet said. "I have spoken of your case to no one save Sir Walter Hungerford, and he will keep his counsel."

"It is well," Henry said. "I would not have the Queen troubled at this time." He began to speak of when the child should come. "I know for a surety I'll still be in France," he said. "It will ease me to know you'll be there when the child is delivered."

"Sire," Colnet said, "I will set the best midwives in the land to tend the Queen. It is not needful for a physician to be there."

The King gave him an angry look and said, "I've heard such talk before; yet it was thus that my mother died."

"The Lady Mary's case was much different," Colnet said. "She was brought to bed of her seventh child in as many years. My way lies with you."

The King half-smiled and shook his head. "Good my friend," he said, "I charge you with the Queen. Be at her side at all times. When I come again, have her safe delivered of the child and the child lusty to greet me."

After a little Colnet said, "It shall be as you say. When your grace comes again we shall set the heir of England in your arms. Only take what ease you may in France, and rest yourself when it is possible."

"That I promise you," Henry said.

When he went to his bed that night Katherine pretended sleep, her head turned from him. The King knew that she wept. He had not before known woman's tears, and he could find no words to comfort her.

"If you loved me, you would not go," she said when he had spoken. "I need you, Harry. Should it be with you as it was with Tom, I would leave my wits."

He said, "I never yet bore more than a bruise on my body out of France."

She said in a hard voice, "It is that you want to go. You've known the glory of battle and you thirst for it. I was your fool to reckon you content to bide with me."

"Want to?" he said. "Want to, Kate?"

She cast her arms about him and clung to him. "Stay, then," she said. "What need is there for you to go? Stay at least until Christmas when the child will be born."

"I dare not wait," he said. "You heard what Salisbury said. There's not a man in Normandy who's not endangered."

"Can they not fend but a little for themselves?" she said. "They are your liege men. Let them stand to their arms in this without you."

He said, "I led them to it."

She lay quiet and still for a little, then spoke again. "I believed you," she said. "You said you had no love save me, and I believed it. If it were some pretty maid I could match her, tear her cheeks and her hair and win you back again, but I know not how to fight your soldiers. They have your love, and I am but French and I cannot match the English bowmen."

"Sweetheart," Henry said, "if I have not shown you yet that I love you, I know not how. Bear with this parting. I'll be back to your arms before you know it."

She saw that all her words were useless and clung to him silently but with a fierce passion. The King came to her on the morning of the fifth day to take his farewell. They stood alone in their chamber, Kate's hair loose about her shoulders, for she had just left her bed, and her bedrobe cast round her. She no longer wept but held him as if she feared she would hold him no more.

"Let me bring you to Southampton," she said when he would have set her from him.

"No," he said. "Rest you here, Kate. It is better so." He began to speak of the child. "Nicholas Colnet will be with you," he said. "His skill is great. He'll tend you as his own."

She asked what she should name the babe.

"Let her bear your name if it is a girl," he said. "I know none sweeter."

She said, "It is your son I carry. Your heir."

After a little both fell silent. "Kate," he said presently, "if it should be God's will that I come no more back here, turn to my uncle and Chichele in all things."

She said in a sharp voice, "Yet you'll come back."

"Yes," he said. "But if—if I do not, you are as free as hand and heart can make you. I have told them you are to go back to France and the home of your parents if you wish it."

"I would not go back again," she said. "More happiness have I had here than ever my childhood gave me."

Her words touched him. He kissed her again with hunger, as if the taste of her lips might never be his again. "Never doubt I love you," he said. "I'll keep all faith with you—I swear it."

After he had gone, the Queen sat before her mirror with a stony face while her ladies robed her. Isabella Holland, Margaret's sister, came to tire her hair. Much of her former hatred of Lancaster was dead in her now, and she had consented to wait upon the Queen, serving her with loyalty. When she saw that Katherine sat in tears she spoke to cheer her. "He'll come again, madam," she said. "He always does."

"I did not think he would forsake me," Katherine said. "After so little time."

Isabella said in a gentle voice, "Madam, he loves you."

The Queen bowed her head and nodded. "It affrights me," she

said. "His love for me. I am de Valois, not Plantagenet, and this fierce Plantagenet love that outburns the stars was never taught me in my father's court. Were I to die with the child, I think there would never be another in my place. But if he should die, going from me thus, I know not if I could keep a like constancy. Yet God witness for me that I love him. I desire only that he come back to me."

"He will come," Isabella said. "The whole land has trembled for him before now, and always has it been well."

The Queen said in a whisper, "God grant it so again."

XXVIII

Twice had the King embarked from Southampton with only ill omen and the land's dread to speed him, and both times had he returned in triumph. Men no longer feared for him. The town, thriving now where once it had known desolation, gave him good greeting, and the little ships hoisted sail to bear him into the Solent. Again the warm air, sharp and salt with the tang of the sea, lay in the nostrils, and men heard as before the straining rigging and the thin-voiced gulls crying above the masts.

The King stood in the stern, close wrapped in his cloak, watching as the land fell behind him. It was June again and the cliffs lay mantled in leaf, green and bright as an emerald, the rolling downlands cleft by the gray castle. His eyes clung to his realm as his lips had clung to Kate's mouth, with a parched thirst. Hungerford and John Bromley, who stood with him, saw that he found this parting a hard one. After a while Bromley asked if he would come below.

"Presently," Henry said. "The land looks so fair."

"She will look as fair when your grace returns," Bromley said. "I'll warrant it'll not be long before we carry you back to her again."

The King turned and looked whitely at him. "Carry me?" he said. "Carry me back?"

"Why, my lord," Bromley said bewildered, "I meant only that

the barons will bear you in triumph on their shoulders as they've twice done before."

After a little he left them and went below.

"My lord," Hungerford said, "what is it?"

The King sought to laugh and could not. "In faith, Walter," he said, "it was as though he walked alongside my tomb."

XXIX

On his return to France Henry sought to tempt the Dauphin to battle, riding through the country with a force so small it could scarce be called an escort. He hoped to fight and come to terms, thereby sparing the land long sieges, but the name of Agincourt hung about him as a coat of magic, and at the news of his coming the Dauphin and all his army withdrew back across the Seine.

The King moved against Meaux which lay close to Paris on the upper reaches of the river. This place was held for the Dauphin by the Bastard of Vaurus, a man of much ill repute, lustful and of a violence so fierce the English had never met his like. Salisbury came to the King with many tales of him. "He's well named 'Bastard,'" he said. "The word 'chivalry' lies about this place as a stench."

Henry found that he spoke true. Every Englishman that was taken was hanged, his gallows the great tree which stood just outside the walls of the town by the west gate. Men came to call this "Englishman's Elm," but Burgundians also suffered upon it, and even the French peasants whom the defenders carried off from the fields during their sallies. Of these Vaurus demanded ransom, and when they could not pay sent them to their deaths. That the peasants of France should suffer at the hands of their own countrymen much troubled the King. When word was brought him that more had been seized he sent his heralds to the city, pledging himself that the men taken were in truth Frenchmen—as Vaurus must know—and in no wise allied to him. Vaurus sent back that if they were not Englishmen they were Burgundians, allies of the

English, and fit only to hang. The King knew him to be determined on their deaths and himself powerless. He set himself to the siege with a cold hatred.

Vaurus's best hope lay in an early attack by the English while his own strength was great. He was a skilled captain, cunning in all the arts of defense, and he strove to provoke the King, hanging his English captives one by one within sight of the attackers. Sometimes the hanging was a slow one and the Bastard's captains called to the dying, "Patience. It may be your King will come and save you." When no more were left him, Vaurus set his men to beat an ass beneath the walls until it brayed, and the beaters shouted in mockery to the English that their King was crying for help. This was done in the King's hearing and in the hearing of the Burgundians, Vaurus timing it for when Henry rode to view the displacements. The English listened in sullen wrath, straining for command to storm the walls. Even Salisbury urged it, setting his horse alongside the King's.

"Afore God, my liege," he said, "let us go in. I think we have strength enough. This place offends my nostrils."

"Aye, do what the Bastard hopes," Henry said. "To go in now would cost us a great price in blood." He would listen to no argument. Many men, recalling how the Dauphin's gift of tennis balls had pricked him to folly, wondered at his calm. Dorset spoke of it as they rode back to the camp.

"It was a pretty insult," he said. "Did it not move you, Harry?"

The King smiled grimly and said, "I grow used to it."

"Let the Bastard have his mock," Salisbury said. He was still raging and his hands shook upon the reins. "Your grace will yet teach him more courtly manners."

"For sure, I hope to," Henry said. He rode for a while in silence, then his eyes turned toward the great elm, with a glint in them. "This was a little thing," he said. "But what he did yonder—I'll have his head for it. He had done better to have shown some pity to my soldiers if he desires it for himself."

Vaurus knew his acts to have put him outside the King's mercy, and he fought stubbornly without sign of surrender. The siege was long and hard, and the winter closed about the land in snow and biting frosts, rimming the siege guns in white and bringing much hardship to the soldiers. The King knew Kate's time to be near. He was daily in anxiety for her, the memory of his mother darkening his mind. He wrote to her as often as he might. At first he strove for formality, naming her "the most gracious lady, Katherine, Queen of England," but soon the "sweet Kates," "fair Kates," lay thick about the pages in mockery of all that was held regarding the marriages of princes.

On the eighth day of December Philip of Burgundy rode to the camp to greet the King. They met with some coldness, for since their quarrel over Barbazan there had been other matters of discord between them. Philip did not intend to abide long in the camp. He greeted Henry with a chill kiss of courtesy and looked hard upon him. "Why, cousin," he said, "are you ailing? You look poorer in health than you did."

"I am well enough," Henry said. "It's a harsh December. It breeds many ills."

"It never troubled you before," Philip said. He went on talking of it in a bored voice. "Is it because your lady is with child? Often have I heard it said by the women that when a wife breeds the husband will come out in all manner of boils and running sores. It is the mark of true love, they say."

The King smiled and made no answer. Philip rode with him that afternoon to view the siege. He was eager for an assault and urged it upon the King, but Henry feared great loss among his soldiers and set his face against it. While they talked the Bastard's men upon the walls drew their crossbows upon them, marking their chivalry. Philip rode in full armor, but the King wore no mail and was struck across the wrist.

The hurt was slight, but Philip out of courtesy sent his own physician to dress it. He was a stoop-shouldered Frenchman, quick and skillful in his fingers as a woman at her spindle. When he had done, the King thanked him, and they fell to talk, standing alone in the tent.

After a little the King said slowly, "I have something I would ask of you. There is one here among the English lords, who seems to ail, yet no man can name his sickness. He himself scarce knows whether he is sick or not. Has such come your way before?"

"It is not easy to know," the Frenchman said. "My lord, in what manner does he complain?"

"He lacks all strength," the King said. "Before he could march or hunt or ride beyond what others could do, yet now it has left him. All he does now he must drive himself to."

"He is a noble, you say?" the Frenchman said. "Is he but young?"

The King said, "He is four and thirty."

The Frenchman gave him a sharp look. It seemed he had guessed at the truth, but the King could not be sure. "Your grace will understand," he said at length. "It is hard for me to tell without I see the man. Yet he is a young man. He should not so greatly want for strength. Send him home where he can rest."

"He cannot go," Henry said. "He believes his presence here is needful."

"That may he do," the Frenchman said. "Yet if he came to me I would bid him use himself gently, or the time may come when the choice will not be his. Beyond that I can say no more."

The King looked at him straightly. "I thank you," he said. "I will convey all you speak to him."

After the other had gone, he stood for a little in the dim-lit tent. He had dined in state with Philip, wearing the crown, and he lifted it now from its leather casket, looking upon it. He saw it as the killer of his father and of Richard, and as his own most mortal foe. It seemed to him—he who had ever known victory—that against this he could not prevail. The chill of it struck upon his hands, as a knight in the lists might feel the chill of his enemy's steel against his own flesh, to fight on, gasping and stricken.

After a while he laid the crown back in its place and went to the door of the tent. The night air blew coldly upon him as his own thoughts had blown cold, but he lifted his head and sought to put them behind him. About him the camp lay still under the sharp snow, frosted upon the tents, but there were horses new ridden into it, and presently Dorset came toward him, walking with quickened strides. When he saw the King standing at the tent flap, his face lightened and he called to him.

"God with you, Harry," he said. "We have news from London. All's well. You have a son."

xxx

In the New Year Hungerford crossed to England upon the King's business, riding to Windsor, where the Queen had lodged since the birth of her child. The baby was some five weeks now, but the land still joyed in his coming, the bells pealing every time the Queen went abroad. The people reckoned it an excellent thing that Harry should have a son and that there was now a prince to Lancaster.

Isabella Holland brought Hungerford into the great chamber where the baby lay. The cradle stood back against the arras of the far wall, and she pointed to it. "We have another Prince Hal," she said. "Yonder."

She took the baby from the cradle and set him in Hungerford's arms. The baby opened vacant blue eyes and stared upon him, lying quiet and listless in his swathing bands against Hungerford's velvet sleeves. He had no look of the King.

Isabella spoke as with her old antipathy to Lancaster. "Is he a Prince Hal, in truth?" she said. "Will he have all London by the ears and roister his nights away in some Chepeside tavern?"

"He has small likeness to the King," Hungerford said in a curt voice.

John Bromley, who had ridden with him, came to his side and

looked upon the babe. He said, "He has his grandfather's likeness."

Isabella answered, "I see naught of Henry of Derby in him."

"I mean his French strain," Bromley said. "Charles of Valois."

Isabella took the child from Hungerford and set her arms about him as a shield. She said in a still voice, "You are mistaken."

"For sure," Bromley said hastily. "It was but a trick of the light."

At length Katherine herself came into the chamber. She was in no wise altered, her beauty as unchanged and as youthful as when Hungerford had first seen her by the side of St. Pol. She looked proudly upon the babe and began to speak of the King. "I have given him a son," she said. "What does he say?"

"Lady, he had great joy in the news," Hungerford said. "He renders you his thanks and his blessing and bids me say he loves you."

The Queen smiled and was slow in answering. "I would he could see the babe," she said at last. "Or that I might join him."

"He thinks it is not yet safe," Hungerford said. "As soon as the land is quiet he will send."

Katherine asked if the King still lay at Meaux with the army.

"He has gone to Thierry," Hungerford said. "It is but a few miles away. He has given over the command into the Duke of Dorset's hands."

The Queen said sharply, "Does he ail?"

"No, no," Hungerford said. "Some half the army fell sick of dysentery, and the King likewise took it. But that was in mid-December and he mends. It is only that the physicians would have him take rest for a while."

"I hope he will not venture himself," Katherine said. "Bid him think of me and of the child."

"Lady," Hungerford said, "his thoughts are always toward you."

Some of the townspeople stood below with their wares in the castle courtyard, for it was market day. Isabella bore the baby to the open casement and held him there in the winter sunshine so that they might glimpse their prince. At sight of him they broke into eager cheering.

The baby lay quiet for a little, then broke into a wailing cry. The nurse, who had stood back the while behind where the cradle rested, came and took him from her. "He hungers, poor poppet," she said. "There, my sweet lamb, my little princeling. Hush you."

"Tell the King I have a high-stomached son, Sir Walter," Katherine said. "Tell him he'll most proudly bear the crown of both our realms."

Hungerford went from her that same night and made ready to return to France. While he awaited the saddling of the horses, Nicholas Colnet came to him by the archway of the keep and stood against the buttress in his black physician's gown. "I hear the King has rendered up the command into his uncle's hands," he said. "It is not like him."

"He was sick," Hungerford said. "But he seems recovered. He has much joy in the Queen's deliverance."

Colnet made no answer. Hungerford looked at him, and saw his face hard and troubled. "The child is healthy," he said. "Does it not please you?"

"He seems healthy," Colnet said. "Yet for my part I would not have grieved if this union had gone unblessed."

"In faith, Colnet!" Hungerford said.

"Aye, I speak treason," Colnet said. "But the Queen is de Valois. Is there a sicklier stock in all Europe than de Valois—a more debauched or weaker stock? And the Plantagenets please me little better."

"The Plantagenets were ever fine figures of men," Hungerford said. "Fine men and great Kings."

"Great Kings they may have been," Colnet said. "But walk by their tombs in Westminster and look upon their effigies. Think what they were. Men like Richard, given to a woman's hysteria, or like Edward Longshanks, to rages so black none dare approach him. Or the Lionheart, so nerve ridden that he could not rest even in church, but had to walk about the aisle while his bishops preached to him. Or John, whom in his vengeance men could scarce call sane, or the others, the second Edward, mayhap, and the Counts of Anjou, whom it was said the love of women could not suffice. This is the King's stock—as wrapped in greatness as other men wrap them in their cloaks, but plagued with a dark strain in nerves and mind to set their souls in torment."

"But the King," Hungerford said. "The King is not so."

"The King is Plantagenet," Colnet said. "He is as racked with fret nerves as ever Richard was and with the same black fury. But he grinds it down. He will not show it. Yet for that I think he pays and will pay a good price." He stood brooding for a while then spoke again. "It is these two black strains together—Plantagenet and de Valois—this troubles me. I would he had not loved her."

"Sir," Hungerford said, "what do you fear?"

"It may be I start at a shadow," Colnet said. "Yet I pray God the babe inherits no more from Charles de Valois than the crown of France."

XXXI

Meaux had not withstood the King four months. It was a place of much natural strength, bounded on three sides by the river and on the fourth by craggy marshes, ill smelling and moisture laden. As at Harfleur some half the English force were stricken with dysentery, but this time the King was of them. Men blamed the tainted water as the cause of the attackers' sickness, and this could not be remedied.

In February, when the snows had given, Philip came again into the camp. The length of the siege greatly irked him, and he was determined on an assault by the armies of Burgundy. This Henry could not prevent, but he would not send a single Englishman to the attack. The Burgundians were beaten back easily by Vaurus and with much loss.

The King judged his own assault ready by the end of April. Before commanding it, he sent his heralds into the town, bidding it yield and exempting all but four persons from vengeance. This Vaurus answered with insult. He set his forces strongly, and the English were given such fighting as they had not tasted since Agincourt. By noon the next day they had carried all but the market place. The Bastard himself fought with a furious courage, defending himself with a spit from his own kitchen and then seeking to take horse. The English had kept especial watch for him, and Salisbury himself rode on his heels and brought him down by the castle donjon. He and his men-at-arms at once took him to the King.

Henry had no words to say to him. Vaurus knew his doom assured and glared back upon him, silent likewise and with a fury's hate. The King could not help but mark his ruffian's valor. He sent him to his death on the morrow by the axe, as with honor, but the body and the severed head he had set upon the elm which had long borne the bones of the Bastard's captives.

With the fall of Meaux the land was quiet, the Dauphin no more venturing beyond the boundary of the Seine. Men saw the King master of all northern France, the old empire of Normandy and Anjou welded together once more as in the most proud days of the Angevins. That this was done by so small a realm—the little hare among nations—against a realm of five times her strength and in the face of so mighty a house of princes as the de Valois was wonderful to the Courts of Europe. For the first time since his boyhood the King's way seemed to lie fair and broad ahead of him. He seemed to have still the same careless and fierce vigor, but sometimes at nights Hungerford marked that his mask dropped from him and he could do no more than lie back in his chair, listless and spent.

"The land grows quiet," Henry said one night when they talked together. "Soon it'll be fit for Kate to take her journey." Presently he said in a quiet voice, "I feared I would not see her again. My going this time seemed much ill omened."

"I feared likewise," Hungerford said. "Yet it is well."

After a space the King spoke of his son, saying, "He'll be five months now. I wonder if he thrives."

"I don't doubt it," Hungerford said. "He was weaned as his father came to victory here at Meaux."

"Poor little mite," Henry said. "I've begat him to a long sorrow."

Hungerford knew he spoke of the kingship. He lifted his head and saw the King's face wearied, with something of Derby's look in it. "He does well, my lord," he said. "Remember your heritage—a sickly land, a land despoiled and enfeebled, of all Europe the most poor in its purse and in its soul. But it will fall a mighty realm to him. Have you not brought the whole land to greatness?"

"He has a hard task," Henry said. "I found one crown heavy. He will bear two—the crowns of England and France." He looked from the casement upon the broken curtain walls of the castle where the Bastard had long defied him. "It is for him to heal these scars," he said. "If they will but accept a prince of the line of the Plantagenets. Yet he is de Valois too. He had all his mother's lineage, and there is much French blood in me. Between us we will have bred a son more French than English." His mind stayed still with his son. When he was about to go to his bed, he spoke of him again. "At least he is born prince," he said. "It will not be thrust upon him suddenly as it was with me."

By the middle of May the King was returned to Paris. The people gave him warm welcome, but after the toil of battle the toil of governance was now his. He found much work to his hands, laboring with his secretaries throughout the days and into the nights. The city had order and justice such as she had long desired, and the poor a tenderness beyond any they had known. The King saw much accomplished here, but in other parts of France he knew his task to be no more than beginning.

On the last day of the month John Bromley came to the room where he worked. Dorset stood with the King and Bromley spoke to him in a quiet voice. "There is a lady here, my lord," he said. "She begs audience with the King."

Henry bade his uncle see to it. When Dorset went into the outer chamber, Katherine stood there with Isabella Holland and three more of her ladies. The King had not yet summoned her from England. When she saw Dorset, she smiled and held a finger to her lips.

The King sat bent over his papers and did not turn his head. He heard them whispering and called, "What is it, Uncle?"

"A French lady is yonder, Hal," Dorset said. "A lady of some consequence."

"A French lady?" Henry said. "What does she want?"

"In faith, I know not," Dorset said. "Unless it be your arms about her."

The King looked at him with delight and turned to the door. When she came to him, he swept her from her feet so that she clung to him in laughter. "My head turns," she said. "Harry, put me down."

He set her gently on her feet and took her face in his hands, the better to look upon her. "Oh, my fair Kate," he said. "As fair and as sweet."

"I had to come," she said. "It has been a year—a full year."

He said in a still voice, "Never knew I a longer." He asked her how she had fared when the child was born.

"They tended me well," she said. "I have not brought the babe, Harry. He is but little yet and precious to both of us. I feared the journey for him."

"You did well to leave him," he said. "Where is he now?"

"He lies at Windsor," she said. "Colnet is there and his great-granddam, Lady Hereford, and many nurses and worthy women. They all cosset and wait upon him. He lacks no care."

"Colnet will see he does well," the King said.

"Yes," she said. "All the land cares for him, Harry. Never saw I such joy before at the birth of a prince. It was as if he was born to them of their own flesh—another Prince Hal." She set her arms round his neck and pressed closer to him. "He is not yet greatly like you," she said. "But I think he will grow so."

They were alone now in the chamber, for Dorset had left them.

When Katherine drew off her cloak the King led her to the great settle, piled with scarlet cushions, that stood before the hearth. Only a low fire burned, for the days grew warmer. They sat before it in talk, heedless of the time, until the room was dark about them.

Katherine spoke gaily now of the year that had gone. "You will never know how I trembled for you," she said. "When we were just wed and you rode from me each day to fight in the mines at Meulan, I feared for you. But the day you set sail from Southampton, I thought my heart would burst. Yet I know not why I feared. They told me that always you came back."

Her hand lay idle in her lap, and he took it, cradling it in his, and pressed the palm to his lips. She looked smilingly upon him, her small head in its jeweled chaplet bent toward the dying glow of the coals. "You love me?" she said. "You love me, Harry?"

"God knows I do," he said. "Sweet, since I went from you, all has been winter and rough weather. It was as spring to see you standing yonder."

Presently Dorset came to them and stood on the threshold, looking upon them with affection. "Do you sit in the dark all night?" he said. "Harry, take some sup here with your lady, if you will, but let it be in the light and with a kindled fire."

He summoned the pages, and they brought in candles already lit. The Queen lifted her eyes to Henry, seeing him for the first time in the full flood of the light. She stopped in the midst of speech, then said, "Harry, do you ail?"

He spoke teasingly, touching her cheek. "It is because of you," he said. "When your time was near, Burgundy told me I should suffer boils and all manner of running sores. It's a test of true love, he said. You see now how hard it went with me."

She laughed and shook her head at him. "In faith," she said, "they'll ask next which of us twain has had the babe." After a little she said, "You have not been greatly sick?"

He answered, "It was but slight."

"Now I am here all will be well again," she said. "Oh, Harry,

I've wept in my bed for you these many nights. I thought I would not hold you again."

The King scarce knew how to answer her. It almost seemed to him, in the joy of her voice and her touch, that he had dreamed this her coming and that the morrow's awakening would see the Narrow Seas still between them, with himself in Paris and her in her Windsor bower.

XXXII

With June the blaze of summer came harshly upon the land. The King could remember no summer as hot since that which he had spent in Ireland as a boy, the year his father returned from exile to claim Richard's throne. He who had always known drenching rains and chill winds now had only sun and cloudless skies. Men made a jest of it, saying the King's weather had become a turncoat.

With the Queen's coming the Court had taken on a greater gaiety. She and the King dined each night in state at their raised table in the great hall, and when the meal was ended and the servants had pushed aside the trestle tables, the musicians in the gallery would play for the dance. Katherine was light of foot and ever eager to lead the dancers. She and the King danced hand in hand, their eyes ever seeking each other's faces, like new-wed lovers. Henry took much delight in her, but he found it hard to match her strength.

On the eighth evening of her coming they sat as usual in the great hall. The casements stood wide to entrap what cool there was, but the night lay on the city no less stifling than the day. Henry was tardy in dancing and Katherine spoke to him pleadingly. "Will you not dance with me, Harry?" she said. "It is lavolta —my favorite."

He took her by the hand and led her down onto the floor. The dancers parted so that they might take their places at the head of the lines, and the music hushed until they were set ready. When they danced the King swung Katherine off her feet in the leaps of the lavolta with as much seeming ease as if she had been a feather's weight. Yet after a little he set her down by one of the pillars and checked in the steps. "Walter Hungerford will finish the dance for you," he said. "He or Lord Robsart. They both make good partners."

"Nay, Harry," she said. "They do not dance like you. Finish it with me. We have danced so little together."

He smiled and let her draw him back among the dancers. When it was done and they had moved from the floor, she turned to him, seeing him on a sudden so white that she caught his hands in fear. "Harry," she said, "what ails you? What is it?"

One of the casements stood open near by, and he went to it, standing bowed against the lintel, his face to the night air. A stone alcove jutted here, narrowing toward the hall, and no man observed them. After a little she saw he was revived. "Shall I not fetch your gentlemen?" she said. "Or your uncle of Dorset?"

He said, "It has passed."

"Oh, my love," she said. "It was the heat, was it not?"

"Aye," he said. "The heat."

"I should have taken thought," she said. "My father was ever stricken in the Paris heat. Until you are stronger, will you not do as he and remove to Senlis? The air blows cooler there from the hills, and it is a healthful place. We could go tomorrow."

She urged it on him, Dorset doing likewise. Henry hearkened to them and at the end of the week set out from Paris. Senlis lay to the north of the city, not too far distanced. It was a pleasant town, rich in merchandise and set high on a hill above its vineyards. The King seemed almost at once to be better, and his nobles were jubilant, seeing him as of old. Now also was much hope of a signed peace; yet, though the Dauphin professed himself willing to talk, word came that he and his armies were meantime moving against Cosne.

This town was fief to Burgundy and its men-at-arms were all

Burgundians. Philip feared its loss, for it was thinly garrisoned. He sent his messengers at once to Henry, urging the treaty which lay between them and begging the King to come to the aid of the besieged.

The messengers talked with Henry in the castle of Senlis, stressing the town's plight. "Their case is very hard, my lord," the spokesman said. "They are near starving. The governor sends us word he can endure no longer than a week. Unless help reaches him within these seven days, he must perforce yield himself and all the souls in his charge into the Dauphin's hands."

Dorset spoke with the King. "We can spare some thousand men," he said. "My lord, I beg you let me lead them."

"My lord," the messenger said, "my master, the Duke, desires that the King himself will come. His skill is needful to us in the raising of this siege."

"The King is not in full health," Dorset said.

"My master urges it strongly," the man said. "He begs the King remember the pact between them. He says he has aided the King, let the King now come to his aid."

Henry said, "Tell your master, the Duke, that I come."

He worked late into the night to prepare for his going, then at length went to his bed. Katherine already slept, her hair thick upon the pillow, rich and sweet smelling, and her arms bare above the spun sheets. He saw her in the thin light of the candle as he had first seen her in her portrait, merry hearted and of a Queen's grace, so that he had ever loved her and none other.

When he came beside her, she woke and asked what had kept him.

"I go from you again, my sweet," he said and told her all Burgundy's messengers had spoken.

"It will be quickly done, will it not?" she said. "It is but a small siege."

He said, "By God's grace we'll do it quickly and with small loss."

It seemed to her now that his life was charmed and she had no more fear for him. "It will not be as Meulan and Meaux," she said. "You'll not tarry, Hal, when it is done? You'll come straightway back to me?"

"Straightway," he said. "I vow it."

"It is not that I would have you ever tied to my girdle," she said. "A man's not a man who sits daylong by the fire. But we have been so little time together. We have been wed two years, and for a year were we parted." She pressed closer to him and spoke gaily. "Yet we have a full lifetime," she said. "Have we not, my love?"

He answered her as she wished.

"And after the siege at Cosne is raised?" she said. "Harry, your son lies in England. Do you not long to see him?"

He said in a low voice, "God knows how much."

"I hope he smiles when you first take him in your arms," she said. "He is solemn sometimes. Archbishop Chichele and your brother Humphrey both strove hard to make him laugh and could not."

The King said, "I'll be but a stranger to him."

"He will know you by instinct," she said. "Can we not go to him soon? By Hallowe'en? By Christmas?"

He said, "By Christmas if God wills it."

"Let us spend it at Windsor," she said. "You will scarce know it now. We have planted seven pear trees along the east bailey, and where all was tangle and thick undergrowth we have cleared and made meadow. There you can ride, and the babe, too, when he is grown. They have already set aside your gray mare to foal for him, and Lord Surrey promises he will breed him a hound, and his uncle John a falcon."

Henry said, "They treat him kindly."

"He lacks for nothing," she said. "Yet you yourself must teach him to ride, for I would he'll grow to have your horsemanship." After a little she spoke again. "It will be good to have Christmas at Windsor," she said. "And later, when the spring comes and the snows have given, will you not show me of the land? I would go to Monmouth and the fair places of your realm. Did you not say yourself you have much to show me?"

"Yes," he said. "Yes, my Kate, I have much to show you."

Her words brought to him all the fragrance of the land, as of salt spray above the fierce cliffs, of the herb gardens and trodden pine and of the London mists. When she slept he lay wakeful long into the night, but when the sounds of morning roused her he had already risen and gone from her. He came to her bower to take his leave of her, cloaked already against the journey, greaved and spurred, and with his crimson rondel belt set above the mail.

She kissed him and smiled. "You'll not be gone long from me," she said. "Harry, you have health enough for this journey?"

"Yes," he said. "Enough, God willing." He set his arms about her and kissed her once more with a passion so fierce it was to her as if she drowned in it. It awoke her de Valois blood, and she clung to him with a like intensity, not comprehending but slow to leave him. "Farewell, Kate," he said. "Adieu, Greensleeves. You have made it all so sweet."

"Nay, now," she said, laughing. "What have I made sweet?"

"This my way," he said, "the King's path."

When the mounted men rode out from the castle courtyard, the Queen and her ladies stood on the battlements to watch them go. The sun was climbing, and the great horses, hooded to the fetlocks in their rich trappings, moved in floated color atop the arid grass. The King rode at their head, his own mount trapped in scarlet, blue and gold, in the arms of England and France. He found it hard to take his eyes from the Queen. She had leaned forward the better to look, and he saw her with her long sleeves astir in the wind, her small chin lifted by its silken barbette. It seemed to him a goodly picture to carry into eternity under his eyelids. He kept his eyes upon her until his way took him behind the curtain of the trees.

XXXIII

The King spoke but little on the day's journey, and it seemed to all men he had pain and found the rough and sun-steeled roads of summer France harsh toil to ride over. By nightfall they had reached Corbeil. That night when Dorset and Hungerford walked in the herb garden one of the bowmen came hard running. Dorset asked him what ailed him, and he spoke in a youth's voice, halting and affrighted. "I am sent for aid," he said. "One of the gentlemen is very sick." He pointed to the river. "I was at my watch yonder," he said, "when he came and talked with me, speaking friendly. On a sudden he fell forward as if he swooned. I called to the next watch which was John Reeve of Deptford. Sir, it was he who bid me run and seek the Duke of Dorset."

"I am he," Dorset said. "What would you have with me?"

"Oh, my lord," the boy said in a frightened voice. "I am only lately come from England. I did not know him, but Reeve says it is the King."

Even the King acknowledged now he could go no farther. He sent on all his force with Dorset at their head to Cosne, but himself remained at Corbeil with some few of his household to tend him. At first he spoke cheerfully of joining his army again the day following, but all knew he could not. At last he was prevailed upon to go back to Paris. Never in all the hard paths he had gone had he once turned his face back, and his lords, seeing him do so, felt themselves chilled as by foreboding.

The King was brought by barge, for greater ease, as far as Charenton. The great trees hung, sick with heat, about the river, and, by the rowlocks, the paint grew cracked and blistered as the watermen toiled. They were wont to sing as they rowed, but today they had no voice. The King lay quietly on his cushions as if he slept. Hungerford found himself put in mind of Arthur, rowed in his black-draped barge to Avalon—as men said—and had no liking for his thoughts.

It was planned to bring the King to the Bois de Vincennes that he might take rest. The castle stood a mile's distance from the river, and the horses and the squires waited at the river stairs with a horse litter to bear him in. It pricked him that he had been brought down the Seine lain on cushions like a woman, and when he saw the litter he turned aside and called for his own horse. All knew him to be beyond riding, and his gentlemen—Hungerford and Bromley—and even the master of the bowmen sought to turn him from his purpose, arguing and pleading, but uselessly, while the horses fretted in the heat and the French waited in much astonishment. The King himself gained the saddle. Men marveled that he could sit in it, knowing he could scarce stir on his cushions on the barge. It seemed to Hungerford he was as stubborn of will as he had ever been. When they went forward, he saw the King's face close as a mask against his pain, as a knight striving in combat might close his visor against the foe.

It was beyond what even he could bear, and after but a few paces he near fell from the saddle, as if he swooned. Hungerford caught him, and with Bromley laid him on the grass. He said, in a whisper, "Good my friend, you were right. I could not do it."

They laid him on the litter as gently as they might, and so began the journey. The road was rough, strewn with great stones and potholed, and the horses uncertain in the heat. The King lay quiet, not speaking, nor did he make any plaint. Each time the horses stumbled, it was to Hungerford that the King's pain jarred like a barb into his own flesh. Bromley was likewise. After a little he fell to cursing the groom and himself took the reins from his hands.

Thus they came to the castle of the Bois de Vincennes—that fair and pleasant place set on the hill slope, its gardens herb scented and hung with the scarlet roses of Lancaster. There was a chamber prepared for the King and two French physicians to tend him. They seemed to Hungerford skilled and wise men, but they could not surely name his sickness.

On the fifth day, as the King kept his bed, Dorset rode back to him. He came straightway to the King's chamber, clad as he was, spurred and yellowed in the dust of travel. Henry greeted him warmly and in pleasure, asking if Cosne was relieved.

"Two days ago," Dorset said. "I've left some half of our force in the town with the Burgundians. All's well there."

The King said, "This was swiftly done. You did not miss me, seemingly."

"There was naught to do," Dorset said. "The Dauphin ran from us like a hare from the dogs. Only the tents and the siege guns were left us." He looked closely upon the King and said, "How fare you, Harry? Do you mend?"

Henry answered he was much better. He spoke heartily, but his hand closed about his Coronation ring as when he knew himself to be lying. Presently the physicians came to bleed him. He suffered them patiently, himself baring his arm for them. "Indeed, my lord," one said, "we are sorry to give you pain."

The King answered in a quiet voice, "Let it not trouble you. Remember the prisoners at Agincourt."

When they left him, bearing the basin, the surgeon's knife and the bloody cloths into the outer chamber, Dorset went with them. He cast his cloak from him and turned to the casement. Hungerford saw him gray of head and aging.

"It tears me," he said. "I have no son. I know not whether it be treason to say the sooth, but Harry—but the King has ever been to me as my son. I cannot rest to see him so."

Bromley spoke in a frightened voice, saying, "We cannot move him now."

"For the saints' sake," Dorset said, "Fetch Colnet."

Dorset dispatched his messengers that night, but without the King's knowledge. It seemed to Hungerford that all came to look for Colnet's coming as besieged and starving men might look for the banners of those who marched to their relief, ever at the casements or upon the battlements. All their thoughts plagued them, dwelling on contrary winds, lamed horses, the storms that beat the Narrow Seas, the Dauphin's lances. Yet in a week the men-at-arms rode into the courtyard and with them Colnet, tall and lean and of all men the most welcome to the sight.

He spoke with Dorset first, asking of the King's winter fighting and of his living.

Dorset answered, "He lived as his soldiers."

"Aye, I'll warrant it," Colnet said. "Drinking the tainted waters of Meaux."

One of the French physicians spoke, naming the King's symptoms. "He has dysentery," he said. "But I do not think that is all. There is something other. It may be that he suffers some internal ulceration which we cannot stanch."

"It may be," Colnet said. "We must see."

"Yet, under God," Dorset said, "surely it is not beyond your wit to cure it. The King is a young man. He is but thirty-four."

"The King is young," Colnet said, "but his way has ever been hard to him."

"Oh, tell me not that," Dorset said fiercely. "Tell me not that the crown is his sickness."

Colnet said, "I can tell nothing until I see him."

After he had talked with the physicians, he went into the King's chamber. Henry turned his head and greeted him in astonishment. "Nicholas Colnet," he said, "what brings you?"

"Sire," Colnet said, "I heard you were sick. I thought my place was here."

"Did they send for you, then?" Henry said. "They must think me sick in truth." After a little he said, "You've come swiftly. The winds were surely fair."

"Almost I failed to reach your grace," Colnet said. "I took my way from Harfleur through the Dauphin's country, thinking to reach you quicker, but we fell into ambush. He who commanded against us was the Sire de Barbazan. When he knew my mission, he bade me ride on. He likewise bids me say he is sorry his brother-at-arms, the King of England, lies sick."

The King smiled and said, "He is a man of much honor."

When they had talked, Colnet set aside the sheets and began

to probe the King's body. He worked slowly and ever gently, but after a little he asked if he had much pain. Henry answered lightly, as he was wont to do, saying it was not great.

"Then is it strange," Colnet said dryly. He set his hands on the King's stomach and pressed more fiercely, so that the King writhed.

Colnet said in an angry voice, "You do not lie to me." It was round speech for the King's ears, but Henry took it meekly. When Colnet was done, he set the sheets back in place. For a space he stood silent, then he smiled. "Your grace's sickness has not been light," he said. "We will see whether we cannot ease it."

Men knew by his words that he still had hope of the King's life. It was to Hungerford that where before the room had hung still and quiet, all took breath again as in unspeakable relief.

XXXIV

Colnet set well about his task, so that in the succeeding days it was as if he fought death across the King's body or that they twain fought him, the stricken and the whole, and found him a mighty foe. Colnet was ever at the King's bed. It was as though he took small time either to eat or sleep, and he had no heed for the stench of sickness which lay strong in the room.

The sick heat added much to the King's toil, and for this the French physicians would have bled him. Colnet withstood them, fearing his great weakness, though Hungerford, when he saw him much fevered and unable to sweat, while all about dripped, their very surcoats sodden in the stifling air, questioned who was right. Beyond the Bois de Vincennes his illness was not known, but, as by instinct, his friends came to him: old Erpyngham; Ludovic Robsart, the Frenchman who had ever served him; Camoys from England; and Gilbert de Lannoy from the Holy Land, where he had journeyed on the King's mission. Henry and he spoke long together and alone—their talk the old dream of the Kings of England, to win again the Holy Places for Christendom.

When de Lannoy had gone, Bromley went to the King and raised him, shaking up his pillows. Henry spoke jestingly to him, naming him a good nurse. There had been no village women brought to look to him at the Bois de Vincennes, but it seemed to Hungerford that his friends tended him as gently as any women. Yet he misdoubted that the King mended. His pain was ever on him. Often it was great, and when he believed himself alone and beyond the ears of others he sometimes groaned. After a space his fingers grew so thin his Coronation ring had to be bound upon him with scarlet thread. Yet in all he was gay and seemingly as full of hope as ever men remembered him before Agincourt. This grace was strong in him, and, seeing it, his lords recalled how often in the dark places of his path he had come as by a miracle to victory, and themselves took hope from him.

There were Welshmen with the English encamped about the castle, and these were wont to sing at nights, the King taking much pleasure in it. Yet by day the soldiers were beginning to go about their tasks silently as if they were in dread for him. Reeve found many excuses to come to the inner keep to ask news. Henry heard of it and sent for him to his chamber.

When Reeve came into the room, the King asked him how he was faring in the camp. Reeve answered gruffly that he did well. He stood in awkward fashion in the center of the great chamber, running his fingers along his bowshaft, as if the King's look gave him distress. After a little Henry took a ring from off his hand and would have given it to him. "You served me well," he said. "It is but a small return."

"I want none of it," Reeve said fiercely. "I did but my duty, as your grace well knows."

The King smiled and said, "Come, take it. It will help to buy you a stall in Chepeside when you come home. I led you some hard paths and you trod them all."

"I minded them not," Reeve said. "I would have followed had your grace led me to hell."

"Then you're a fool," Henry said. He pressed the ring upon him, and at length Reeve put out his hand for it. "I'll take it, my lord," he said, "since it is yours." He went on his knee by the bed and kissed the King's hand, roughly and in no courtly fashion but yet in manner to kindle the King's heart. "Thanks to your grace," he said. "God with you. May He send you health and long time to reign."

Bromley said on a whisper that the King could not hear, "Amen to that."

That night was the worst the King had yet suffered. The next day, when Colnet urged him, he tried to take a little broth, lying propped in Hungerford's arms, while Bromley fed him spoonful by spoonful as one might a babe. He bore it cheerfully, finding it in him to jest at his plight.

Dorset came to him that day, desiring him to send for the Queen. "We are all clumsy oafs," he said. "You need a woman's touch, Hal. Can we not bring your lady to you?"

Katherine had remained at Senlis since he had parted from her. The King had sent naught but cheerful words to her, and she was in ignorance of all that had befallen him. Hungerford wondered how she would bear to come and find him thus, but the King would not send. Bois de Vincennes was near the Dauphin's lines and he feared for her; nor did he desire her to find him so greatly stricken and in his weakness. He spoke of this at last. "I would not have her see me now," he said. "So weak that a pewling kitten would have the greater strength—not even able to feed myself."

"Yet for this were you wed," Dorset said. "She's bounden to you, Hal, in sickness as in health."

The King answered, "We have said all there was need to say. She knows I love her."

That night he sent all from him save Hungerford. He had read much before and there had always been books scattered about the coverlet, but now he could not. Hungerford talked with him of idle matters, striving neither to weary him nor to seem too downcast. Presently the King turned to the table by his bed. "Yonder is a codicil to my will," he said. "I had the secretaries set it down this noon."

Hungerford said, "My lord, what need is there for that?"

"No, let us speak of it," Henry said. "I cannot talk with my uncle—it too greatly frets him—but were I to die before the babe is grown the land would fall to a regency. I would have my uncle the sole regent."

Hungerford asked of France and the de Valois inheritance. He answered, "Let this be Burgundy's until the babe is of age. It had better go to a man of French blood." He looked at Hungerford and spoke in a low voice. "I likewise desired to give you voice in the counsels of England, but my proud Norman brothers and their peers would not bear with your yeoman stock. Yet there is another charge. In my will I have delivered my son into your hands."

Hungerford scarce knew how to answer him. The King spoke again in a voice more troubled. "You will care for him?" he said. "He is but a babe, and if he lacks a father I would not have him lack counselors and friends. Instruct him in all the ways of his path."

"Yes," Hungerford said. "Yes—as God will give me grace."

The King strove to smile and said, "Let him not be the fool his father was in his youth. Tell him how oftentimes you carried me home drunk from the Thames-side taverns." Even as he jested he turned away his head and groaned. "I know not what evil I've begotten him to," he said. "His may be the atonement for Richard's blood."

"Afore God, no," Hungerford said. "It is paid. Lancaster has paid."

He answered, "It cannot be till the crown is rendered back. I beg you stand with him. Many may forsake him."

Hungerford saw him now in distress. He went on his knee beside him, and drew his dagger, setting his hand upon the cross of the quillions and pommel. "I swear it," he said. "By the Cross of Our Saviour. If all England turns from him, yet will not I nor my house." Without intent he spoke the words of the homage at the King's anointing. "I, Walter of Hungerford, do become your liege man of life and limb, and of earthly worship; and faith and truth I will bear unto you, to live and die, against all manner of folks. So help me God and All Hallows."

Henry said in a whisper, "Good my friend, he will do well if he has you." Presently he stirred in the bed and said as though he spoke his thoughts, "It may be, growing thus in his kingship, he'll not fear. Tell him he has no need—he has the prayers of the living and of the dead and the Hand of God." After a space he said in a still voice, "And I never saw him. Walter, when you ride to Windsor, take him in your arms for me."

It seemed to Hungerford that the feel of death was hard to him, now that Katherine was his and all his dreams lay in his lap as for the plucking. He saw in the King's face his great desire to live and strove to speak lightly. "That you should talk so," he said, "you of all men."

The King began to speak cheerfully again, saying the next week would see him back on his feet. As darkness fell and Hungerford would have gone from him, he said, "Set the casement open. I would hear my Welshmen singing."

Hungerford went from him, walking with John Bromley and Camoys in the bailey garden. The night air lay cloyingly about them, hot and damp to the face like a fiend's breath. They saw that Colnet walked there also and marked him with surprise, for he seemed never to go beyond the outer chamber where the King lay.

Bromley asked him how the King did. Colnet sighed and drew a hand across his brow. "You know what it is to strive to the uttermost and come to victory," he said. "But to strive until one can strive no more and come only to defeat—it is a hard thing."

Hungerford said in a thin voice, "Then he is dying?"

"Aye," Colnet said, "he is dying."

Bromley broke out into a fierce laugh. "I'll not believe it," he said. "You do not know him as I do. I've seen him before sore pressed, beaten to his knees, but the tide of battle always turns, the miracle always happens."

"Yes," Colnet said. "But there is an end to miracles." The

words seemed to fall gently as a pebble might into a deep pool, and no man gave him answer.

Bromley would have spoken with the King. "Should we not tell him?" he said. "Then can he compose his soul."

"Afore God, no," Camoys said. "Have pity. He has great love toward Katherine and he tastes victory. He wants to live."

It was now the last day of August, and neither Colnet nor the French physicians thought the King would outlive the day. The heat was as sore as it had ever been, and though the King lay quiet in the bed, it added much to all he bore. Colnet gave him what ease he might. After a space, when he had wiped the King's face, Henry spoke his name.

"My lord?" Colnet said.

The King said in a whisper, "How long have I to live?"

"Why, my lord," Colnet said, "if it be God's will, you'll have many years yet."

Hungerford saw the King's eyes narrow and knew he would gain the truth. He said in the tone Colnet had beforetimes used to him, as if he gently mocked him, "You do not lie to me."

Colnet went from him and spoke a little with the two Frenchmen. When he turned back his face was working, and he cast himself on his knee by the bed, as if he did the King homage. "Oh, my lord," he said, "we do not think you can live above two hours."

The King's face did not change. He said in a voice of wonder, "Have I so little time?"

Colnet made him no answer. He stirred then a little in the bed and bade send for his priests. They came—the two Thomases—Thomas Elmham, who had ever been with him and who dearly loved him, and Thomas Netter, his gentle confessor. His lords stood apart while they shrove him, not hearkening to what was said. He had yet to sign the new depositions of his will, and Colnet raised him while Hungerford steadied his hand against the parchment. It cost him great labor, and for a space he was spent beyond speech; then, when he could, he opened his eyes and half-smiled. "I thank you all," he said. "My very dear uncle, and you, Walter; Camoys and John and my lord Robsart; and you, my good old knight of Erpyngham. No man had better friends."

None could answer him.

He said, as if speaking his thoughts, "All that was laid upon me at my hallowing have I tried to keep. I tried to be as a King to you, though I were no King."

"Sir," Erpyngham said, "you have been the lodestar of England. We never had a King until your time."

"Yes, good my friend," Henry said. "You've long served Lancaster. You would say it." He spoke then of the war with France and his hopes for peace. "Tighten your bowstrings a little longer," he said. "We have almost made an end. It may be, when we have done, we will come to a just peace."

Dorset said, "It will be done."

The King sighed and said, "It may be I have led you too far along this road. Yet there is no way but this now, and I think never was. We could not ever live under sick truces, fearing their might."

"Aye, my lord," Erpyngham said, "this was our way."

The King drew in his breath and said, "Can a man fail and yet gain his ends, coming to them by thorny paths and by defeat? Yet if all these toils have fashioned our land to greatness it is well done."

They saw then that he began to fret for all he must leave, for Katherine and his son and for the land which he had ever loved and which loved him. "I know not what will come upon the realm," he said. "With a babe for a King and so great a foe across the Narrow Seas."

"It will be well, my lord," Erpyngham said.

The King said in a tortured voice, "Yet if it is not—God knows if my dying could but set her secure, I could better bear with it."

"My lord," Colnet said, "before I came here I spoke with Archbishop Chichele. He bade me, if your sickness was great, to tell you this. Much as you love her, your England lies safer in the Hands of God than ever she lay in yours."

Thereafter he lay quiet. The priests began softly to speak the Seven Penitential Psalms as he had bidden them. The King lay propped in the arms of Thomas Elmham, his lips moving soundlessly as with the words. When they came to the line, "Benigne fac ex benevolentia tua Sioni, aedifica muros Hierusalem," he whispered, "God knows my intent was, if I had lived, to build again the walls of Jerusalem."

His lords saw him in death whispering of Jerusalem, as so many of England's Kings had whispered. Their vigil was hard to them. After a space Dorset broke down so utterly that, for fear his grief would bear upon the King, he went from them. The rest sat on, stifling their grief as they might. The night crept haltingly past. September came, and the midnight clocks tolled its hour into the heat and the sickly air. The two hours Colnet had given him became four, and yet he struggled against Death and warded him away. Men heard his breathing turn to racked gasps, until he gained each breath tortuously and by aching effort. Of all that had been Harry, it seemed to them only these rending gasps remained.

After a little he seemed to drift from them. He whispered of Monmouth and his mother, saying, "I am glad you did not become a nun." Once he said strongly, "On to Calais." Yet the black shadow which had darkened all his path still clawed against him, rending his peace. As death seemed to prevail upon him, he gave one fierce cry, as of horror, and called out, "You lie. My part is in Christ."

It was to Hungerford that a fair, frail man stood before him in the shadows, and that he looked again on Richard of Bordeaux. He took the King's hand, seeking to ease him, for Richard would come to him not in vengeance but as a friend. He felt the hand chill as if the King wore mail and the wild flickering of the pulse against his grip, like the beating of an insect's wings.

The serenity crept back into the King's face. As Elmham raised the cross to his lips, he said calmly and in a strong voice, "Into Thine Hands, O Lord." Then did he gesture away his life quietly as he might have set it aside and on a sigh. He had sighed so once before, when the French ranks broke at Agincourt.

Colnet bent above him and sought his pulse. After a space he set the King's hands gently on his breast and turned away. Men saw that he wept. "God rest him," he said. "It is over."

"It cannot be," Bromley said. "He spoke so strongly. My lords, it cannot be." He went on, arguing thus, in a high, petulant child's voice none cared to answer.

No man else had words in the grief-filled room. When Hungerford again raised his head, he saw Elmham had broken the scarlet thread and was drawing off the ring of anointing. It came with much ease from Henry's finger. Thus he parted with it, being no more King of England.

E P I L O G U E

(As set down by Walter Hungerford, Knight, of the county of Berkshire, one-time Steward of the King's Household.)

So did I lose him who was both my liege lord and my friend—Harry of England. When morning came—since I had been steward of his household—John Bromley brought me his great casket. I found, along with much else, his cross, which he had ever kept by him, and the ring, set in enamel and bearing the chained swan of the de Bohuns, and the cross of St. George, which he had worn as a prince. There were sheets of scored music likewise, and Bromley drew them out and began to hum the notes softly. They fell on the morning air light and charming as a May Day's wooing.

Camoys said sharply, "Sir, have pity on us."

"Aye," Bromley said. After a little he said, "He must have written it."

Presently Reeve came to us from his watch, asking of the King. When he heard, he set his hands to his eyes and I saw between the calluses the bowstring had wrought on his fingers that he wept. As we stood silent and in grief, he turned from us.

I went at prime to the bedchamber to look my last on Harry. Elmham knelt there in the new-perfumed room, his face as waxen as the candles that burned about the bed, and Dorset stood by the window. Even seeing him thus, with his back to the room, he looked so broken that I did not think he would long survive Harry's going.

They had dressed the King in his armor, his gauntleted hands folded on his breast as in prayer. Beneath the open visor his face was calm browed and humored, the harsh marks of his kingship gone from it. What they would do to him on the morrow, when his flesh would be burned from his bones, I well knew. Yet now he looked no more than that he lay on his bed of a night—the King at his rest, the Lion of England sleeping.

I did not lightly part from him, riding that same night to Calais. My way took me past the crossroads that led to Agincourt. It might be that the King's spirit walked there that night, yet it seemed to me the heart went homeward in death; and if he lingered, it would be by the river at Monmouth, where the salmon leap silver under the moon, or through the London streets which he loved. Thus the Narrow Seas bore me back. The fog lay gray over the coast and pall-like too about my own heart, and the villages and fair towns were silent and shuttered as though the whole land mourned. I could do no more than think of the words of Ecclesiastes, "Woe unto thee, O land, when thy King is a child." The babe lay now in his cradle at Windsor. Thence would I go to take him in my arms for Harry; and I wondered of the days to come, how he, who had never seen his father, would see him all his life only through our eyes, and if he would yawn over our words and find them tedious.

I rode first to Westminster, to Chichele, sitting with him in the abbot's chamber that we might talk. I knew not if Lady Hereford had received our tidings and asked of her. "We bore it all to her," Chichele said. "Age does not quail at death like youth. She spoke of him calmly. She said no more than 'Is he dead, then—my knightly Harry?'"

I told him then of all the King had spoken to me before his dying. The Council had met that day to speak of the regency and the babe's governors, and when I had done he was long in answering. At last he spoke, saying, "My son, I think this charge will never be yours. They cannot stomach that you should have the babe nor that the Duke of Dorset becomes regent. To them he is no more than Gaunt's bastard son, and you the son of Gaunt's steward. They hold these tasks are only for princes."

"It was the King's will," I said. "His express desire."

"They say he was close on death," Chichele said. "They misdoubt if he knew of what he spoke."

"Afore God, my lord Archbishop," I said. "His mind was as clear as is the crystal. He knew in all things what he did."

"What would you, my son?" Chichele said. "The dead cannot answer the living."

I bowed my head and went from him to the casement. Presently he asked of all the King's great intent in France, saying, "Will this come to fruit?"

I answered him, "It was with him as it was with Glendower—a dream worth the dying for. I think without him we will come to naught but ruin."

He said, "Yet not as we did in former years. You are Saxon as I am. You know the land's wounds and her old scars and her conquests. But when again our hands begin to tremble on the bow, we will think on Agincourt." After a little he said, "When is he brought home?"

I answered it would be in November, saying, "The men of Paris greatly desired us to set him in his tomb at St. Denis."

"Let him be brought home," he said. "Let him be set here in the Abbey, where the London mists lie about the river and the city grows without the walls. So will the feet of the Kings of England go past him to their crownings and the feet of those who bear them thence to their buryings."

When I had left him I went up the great nave toward the High Altar. The Abbey was dark, soft lit by candle and lanthorn, and I saw the great pillars stretch high above me, pearl-gray as the vaults of heaven. In my ears came again—ghostly as an echo—the shout of acclamation as I had heard it at his hallowing, "Long live the King, God save the King, May the King live forever."

I cast myself on my knees to beseech God for the land's weal and for his rest, yet I could say no more than, "Oh God, have him always in Thy care." Thus I prayed for him, and as for him so for the babe at Windsor and for the land. All the future hung darkly about me, and I feared as I knelt there, as he had feared, that Lancaster would come to ruin. Yet whatever befell—when the dust lay upon our chivalry and the earth on the graves of the men who had fought at Agincourt, it seemed to me some part of his spirit must ever lie in the realm, as sunlight lies imprisoned on an Abbey floor or in a forest, in shafts and slants of brightness. And the name Agincourt was a goodly thing to string like a jewel about the neck of the land's history.

When I had done I rose from my knees and went to the West Door. All the close was silent, the wind creaking the shutters and whipping the wall cressets to a scurrying madness. I know not if I dreamed, but it seemed to me, as I stood there, that I saw him walking beyond me in the shadow of the abbot's garden, his crimson rondel belt about his hips. I called his name as we had always called him, "Harry." It was as if he half-turned and looked upon me, gaily, as I had oftentimes seen him do. I tried to gain his side, yet when I came to the wall of the cloister, nothing stirred under the stars. I was alone there with the tossing trees and the great walls and the blaze of memory.

DATE DUE

DEC 2 1970			
Not Pd			
DEC 29 '92			
DEC 7 94			
GAYLORD			PRINTED IN U.S.A.